FRED NICHOLLS was born near Canterbury, Kent, and edu-cated at Blean School, Simon Langton Boys' School and St Ed-mund Hall, Oxford. He worked as a cub reporter and farm-hand, before settling down in his profession as a teacher of Eng-lish in Haverfordwest, Pembrokeshire. During World War Two he served for three years in the Royal Navy, ending up as a watch-keeping officer in a fleet mine-sweeper. He has written extensively for Yachts & Yachting and The Countryman, reflect-ing his love of the countryside and the sea. He has been for many years a small boat sailor. He was for several years half of the Welsh team in the Radio Four series 'Round Britain Quiz'. He now lives with his wife Ann in Newport, on the North Pem-brokeshire coast.

Also by Fred Nicholls

Published by Wm Heinemann Ltd:

THE LOG OF THE 'SARDIS'
THE FREE TRADERS
HONEST THIEVES (non-fiction)

Published by Tynron Press:

THE LOBSTER PIRATES
INTO THE FIRE

Fred Nicholls

–

MASTER UNDER GOD

Starborn
SPRINTER

MASTER UNDER GOD

Fred Nicholls

First published in 2004
by Starborn Books
(Sprinter Series)

The publisher wishes to thank Andrew Mann Ltd and The Art Archive
for permission to use Cornelis de Vries' painting *The Passat* for the
cover of this book.

ISBN   1 899530 20 7

WEBSITE
www.starbornsprinter.co.uk
E-MAIL
starbornsprinter@starbornbooks.co.uk

To Ann and Sonnie and other members of my family,
without whose help and support this book
would have remained a dream

Foreword

As a Royal Navy Officer and Warfare Officer with some 35 years' service, mostly spent at sea at operational theatres, I am well qualified to recognize a really fine sea story, and *Master under God* is such a book.

The story is set against a background of a most realistic tapestry of life at sea in late Victorian times. It dwells on hardship and vivid personal relationships, and is hard to put down. Mr Nicholls knows his stuff: He understands the sea, ships, and the vocation of the whole crew, from the most junior deckhand to the master.

This book grips by its breadth of vision and the precision of its touch. It includes examples of horror, black amusement and droll humour, and is packed with splendid cameos. I am a book collector who, due to over-collecting, is now sadly having to discard rather than to garner fresh volumes, but this book will be one of the survivors.

Strongly recommended!

Commodore A.J.G. Miller, CBE, RN,
Former Commander of Amphibious
Forces in the present Iraq Conflict,
and himself a survivor of two
sinkings in the Falklands War

AUTHOR'S NOTE

During the fifty or so years before the First World War, many Welsh ships were involved in the trade in Chile nitrate, a mineral found in the rainless desert of northern Chile, and exported in huge quantities to Europe by British, French, and, notably, German sailing-ships for use as fertilizer, or as an ingredient for high-explosives.

These large barques were the bulk-carriers of their day, designed to carry heavy cargoes, not to go fast, and hence rather derisively christened 'windjammers' by contemporary sailors.

The Chile nitrate trade was a hard trade, involving a return passage round Cape Horn, crews often suffering fatalities and terrible hardships in the stormy seas of the Roaring Forties of southerly latitude. Another danger lay in the fact that the 'ports' where they unloaded and loaded were often simply small notches in the Chilean coastline, offering no safe mooring or anchorage in bad weather.

Welsh ships tended to be crewed largely by men from the farms, villages and small ports of the west coast of the principality, who were often neighbours ashore, and therefore more likely to form a stable community aboard than the miscellaneous international collections of seafarers in ships of other nations. There would often be much use of the Welsh language in the running of the ship. This, as my story shows, could itself be a source of tension aboard, as was the common practice (found among my own distant forebears) of captains taking their wives and families to sea with them.

MASTER UNDER GOD seeks to be a truthful, candid and admiring portrait of the men and women who led these very hard, hazardous and isolated lives – for wireless was yet to be found in sailing-ships. Their way of life has gone for ever; we shall not see their like again.

Newport, 2004

MASTER UNDER GOD

PROLOGUE:
THE SHIP

The Pacific Ocean; an endless desert of water; the eye aches at the blue perfection of the sea and the tropic sky. All day the sun and the sky have steeped and charged the water with heat and blue light. Now, as evening approaches, the colour and warmth are beginning to steal away. In an hour the sea will be a glassy grey, the sky white and the sun a distant glowing disc among the few orange-red clouds of the trade winds. Yet the scene is not totally lifeless: above you, the trade-wind clouds drift to the north-west, never absent, yet never interrupting the fierce reign of the sun; the south-east trade is here a gentle giant, stitching and frilling the flanks of its great swells, darkening the whole plain of the sea with densely-blue ruffles, except for the strange long fingers and rivers of glossy calm that run through the hemisphere of water. The swells too bring life of a sort to the scene, for endlessly, monotonously, they alter the sea's surface, never permitting a moment's stillness or rest.

But as the sun sinks and colour drains from sea and sky, your eye catches a new colour, a new shape, no more than a speck, which was not there when you last looked. Due south, a long way off, something on the sea's rim catches and holds the warm gold of the sun's glow - something too solid for cloud. Seen through a good glass, it is a small rectangle of golden light, turned towards the sun and seen in perspective. Moments later, a new perspective opens: to the right of the first patch of gold, two others appear, and soon, below the first shape, another golden patch. Now you can be sure it is a ship approaching; the first shapes were her royals - her topmost sails - which you have seen, as it were, over the rim of the world; you've seen these sails, set and spread a hundred and eighty feet above her deck, long before the ship herself comes into view. She herself is hull-down, and will be for some time, for the wind, though favourable, is moderate. But under her keel the cool thrust of the Peruvian Current urges her on, and sail after sail comes climbing above the crinkled edge of the sea, until three graceful leaning towers of sunlit canvas are in sight. Every stitch of sail is set, and every stitch is firm and fleshed out plumply by the south-east trade on her starboard quarter. A smaller, fourth mast, with a thin spike of fore-and-aft sail appears, and shows her to be a ship with the latest in rigs – a four-masted barque. She seems a newish ship too, for her sails show no patches. She is close enough now, if you look carefully, for you to see the smart yellow paint of her masts. Her headsails show up now as thin slices of red-gold (for the sun has changed colour richly as it falls towards the sea); then appear the angled, forward-pointing bow-sprit, and at last the hull, a solid shapely bulk painted black. She is no swift, yacht-like clipper, slicing the seas with a sharp bow and fine entry; she is one of the latest generation of ships – a windjammer - a heavy, full-bodied carrier of vast bulks of cargo. Her bow is bluntly rounded, and she blunders heavily into the moving hills of water, dipping and wallowing, rolling over a ream of water under her bow, sometimes dropping clumsily into a trough; but she is spreading forty thousand square feet of canvas to the wind, and under her hatches are three thousand tons of Welsh coal, so her huge momentum carries her down and up again over the smooth, whale-backed swells.

Close up, the ship now shows as a long, low, massive shape of steel, sliding silently through the calm sea; her masts and sails like four distinct spires of grey (for now the sun's colour has quite gone) – the fore, main and mizzen masts, and a small slender one, the jigger mast. Air and space are, as it were, trapped inside the huge cage of wood, steel, wire, canvas and rope – a cage three hundred feet long, and a hundred and eighty high, eighty feet wide at the bottom, tapering to forty at the top. Each spire is supported, each sail is trimmed, and each yard is held up by a beautiful and complex web of wire and hemp.

No-one moves aloft among the sails, for it is the second dog-watch, and work is over for the day. Small knots of men in shirt-sleeves and dungaree trousers loll and sprawl in the warm evening air on the foc'sle head and main deck; right for'ard, in the eyes of the ship, the lookout – who is nominally at work – rests his back against the capstan-barrel and stares sleepily between his raised knees at a horizon which has been empty for a fortnight. The small whiffs of smoke from his (illicit) clay pipe scarcely move in the gentle following breeze, but drift slowly forward and upward. On the for'ard hatch three men are absorbed in cards, while two others chat as they darn socks. From the port side, where a group lounges on a spare spar, their backs to the steel bulwark, comes the thin reedy wheezing of a concertina making the best it can of the old song 'Clementine', the group growling cheerfully through the choruses as a man with a fine tenor voice ends each improbable verse.

On the midship hatch two older men sit yarning and smoking. One, in grubby white coat and duck trousers, is the cook, stout and black, with tightly-curled grey hair. His galley fire, made up for the night, emits thin wisps of smoke, black now against the sky.

Between the galley and the raised poop deck in the stern, the home of the ship's officers, several young men – some hardly more than boys – sit and read, or skylark aimlessly outside the half-deck – the deckhouse where they live. Two experiment, coughing loudly, with clay pipes, sending up clouds of smoke from cheap strong shag tobacco. A small, neat, genteel, white-coated steward hurries self-importantly aft from the galley, his form keeping pace with the flecked water that slides by. A moment after he disappears into the passage under the poop, you hear the faint sound of a discreet gong; the officers' supper is ready on the mess-room table. The day's shipboard routine has drawn to its inevitable, unalterable, mildly tedious end, and, as if to mark this, the mate sends a hand for'ard to light the navigation lights, each in its metal tower on the foc'sle; here on the port beam, the red light shines out clear on an unheeding sea; from the far side, you see the faint green glow of the starboard side-light on the clustering darkness. Lights come on here and there, for'ard and aft; the ship is now a darker blur on the sea, her sails black shapes against the pale eastern sky. You hear hollow footsteps, the sharp drum-sound of a dropped coil of rope, voices, the doleful concertina, the brook-like, steady water-sound of her passing

As the stern slides by, the binnacle light catches the face of the helmsman, who stands by the great double wheel, but scarcely needs to shift a spoke, so easily does she steer. An apprentice rings one bell – half-past-six; the sound is startlingly clear. The ship passes, and it is now only just possible to read, picked out in bright gold letters on her over-hanging black counter, the words: FIGARO - CARDIFF.

1

When the mutiny broke out on the Cardiff barque 'Figaro', it was, of course, Billy John Ffynnongroes who started it; any of the crowd could have told you it would be. On the heaving foc'sle in the grey dawn off Caleta Buena, Chile, he stood, his handsome ruddy face set in a sullen scowl, thick black hair and whiskers tousled, dark eyes thunderous, threatening. He held the heavy ash capstan bar like a menacing club and glared with blazing eyes at the mate David Evans - tall and old, with the gauntness of a grey skeleton. A moment of silence passed, then Billy spat and growled: 'Do what? You're bloody mad, mun.'

'You heard what I said, John. Ship that bar - all of you now - and put your damned backs into it. We're weighing anchor. Captain's orders.'

'Well then, he's bloody mad too. Bloody mad they are, all them aft, isn't it, boys?'

The old mate's heart sank as he saw the nods, heard the growls of agreement from the seven men who stood round the capstan. *Iesu Mawr*, this was going to be ugly. Any minute now, by the look of it, this hoodlum might take a swing at him and that'd be mutiny. Nobody knew how a mutiny would end, once it got hold - knives, pistols, bloodshed - who knew? Nip it in the bud, then: 'Right, John, I'll see you logged and fined for insolence and refusal to obey orders. Now, the rest of you, take no notice of the stupid idiot. You know better, isn't it? Ship the bars and walk her round quick sharp.'

Nobody moved. Silence again. Then Jimmy Protheroe, Billy's hanger-on and sea-lawyer, spat on the deck and said: 'That be fucked for a yarn, you old dodderer. Only got here last night, for Christ's sake, after ninety days at sea. Too few hands, too much work, no pay, no booze, no shore leave, no fanny neither. Hoist the bastard yourself,' and he threw his bar clattering to the deck. Three others did the same, the rest standing hesitant, torn between fear and defiance.

'Very well, then. You've all had your chance. Now you'll get real trouble.' He half-turned to an apprentice at his elbow: 'Raven, ask the captain to come for'ard.'

Billy yelled furiously: 'Hey, brass bounder, you'd better bloody well stop where you are!' but the young man was gone, ignoring him, clattering down the ladder to the main deck. He was saved most of his journey, for he met his captain, Jacob Roberts, striding urgently for'ard, his square tanned face set in lines of fury: 'Raven, what in God's name is happening up there? I've had men standing by for ten minutes to set the tops'ls.'

'Trouble, sir. It's the crowd - they won't turn to at the capstan.'

'Oh, indeed? By Christ, we'll soon see about that.' Unlike the mate, he felt wrath and frustration, not fear. He'd been too long at sea, been through too much for that.

He burst with the ponderous bulk and energy of a bull into the stalemate, the ring of still figures on the foc'sle head, and his fury was indiscriminate. He turned first to the mate: 'Mister, what's the meaning of this? Why are these men standing round like useless sojers? That hook should be aweigh by now.'

'The men are refusing duty, sir. William John was the –'

'John Ffynnongroes! I thought as much. You - John - come by here! Stand up straight, you useless ullage!' The man drew himself up from his slouch, cowed by the sheer strident ferocity of his captain, but stubborn still. 'Well, what have you got to say for yourself, eh? Spit it out, mun!'

'It's not fair, capten. All of us says so, eh, boys? Not bloody fair. I mean, we only dropped the anchor last night. We've had a hard ninety days at sea out from Penarth: no pay, no shore leave. Then he comes and rousts us all out and says get the hook up. Well, we ain't bloody doing it - right, boys?'

There were shifty, half-muttered growls of agreement from the rest of the foc'sle party; the captain's arrival had partly doused their will and spirit. Baiting Evans was one thing, but defying old Jake was quite another. They knew he'd come from a hard school and feared nobody. Roberts scented their wavering, and kept his shrewdness, despite his passion. No point in making them all his enemies. Billy John was clearly the driving force of this rabble, so go for him first, and go hard too. Get him away from them, if that could be done. Then demolish the young bastard.

'I might have known you'd be at the bottom of this, you snivelling whiner!' With a sudden lunge he took two great handfuls of

John's jersey; using surprise and his immense strength, he took him off his feet and thrust him into the solid trunk of the capstan, bending him agonizingly backwards over it, leaning forward, his purple face practically touching the sailor's: 'By Christ, mun, I only signed you on to please your uncle. I promised to try and make a man and a sailor out of you, but be damned if I'll try any longer - why should I? D'you think you know better than I do how to run this ship? Eh? Eh?' With each exclaimed question he shook the man like a rat, grinding his spine cruelly against the steel pillar. Choked by the pain in his back, John could only gasp and shake his head slowly.

'Right then. I want a word with you aft. Get your useless carcass onto the poop and quick about it.' He hauled Billy clear of the capstan and gave him a shove that sent him stumbling towards the ladder, to miss his footing on the top rung and half-run, half-fall down, landing in a heap on the steel main deck. Roberts turned to the mate and his irresolute men: 'Now mind, that's the end of it! No more bloody nonsense and shenanigans! I may as well tell you why we're weighing anchor. I believe – I'm certain – there's a bad storm coming - a norther. Look at that sky! If you were any sort of sailors you'd know that in a gale of wind, no ship should stay anchored off a lee shore with no shelter. Stay here, and by tomorrow we may all be dead mutton and the ship a heap of scrap on the rocks. Is that what you want? Now then, mister, let me have a report on this business later and tell me whether anyone else deserves to be punished' - he raked them all with his glare – 'for by Christ above I'm having no more of this on my ship. Look sharp now, mister. I'll send a proper man for'ard to replace that miserable *crwt*.'

In five hectic minutes the captain, with his huge certainty, his aura of power and his blend of physical brutality and political cunning, had transformed the situation: the foc'sle party was silently shipping the capstan bars in their slots, then tramping round, still in sullen silence, bringing the shining wet chain cable up through the hawsepipe with a slow grinding rattle, while the pawl - the ratchet that stopped the capstan from reversing - began to click, click, click. He had, he hoped, now bolstered the mate's authority, given the men a reason for his decision to weigh anchor, and, above all, isolated and humiliated John in front of them. He'd also sent him aft where he could keep a good eye on him. But he had by no means finished with him yet.

He walked back aft, with dignity this time, not haste, calling to his second mate Leyshon: 'Set tops'ls on port tack, mister, as soon as she's aweigh.' Billy John was standing waiting at the top of the poop ladder. He was bent forward by the fierce pain in his back and ribs, but he was desperately attempting to recover some of his assurance and reputation as a hard nut by grinning at the men standing by the mizzen braces. He got little response, for they had heard, and respected, Jake's fury. No point, they thought, in getting sacked and put ashore in this Chilean hell-hole and having to ship out, maybe on some Yankee hooker with a big-booted hulk of a bucko mate. Better stick to a berth on a tidy Welsh barque, even if the food was lousy. They heard indistinctly the long angry diatribe on the poop, old Jake's voice rising and falling, the brusque questions, the muffled sullen grunts from Billy. They exchanged private grins and winks; like many subversives, Billy was by no means as popular as he thought with the crowd he'd hoped to lead.

The second mate's rasping voice cut in: 'Never mind grinning like bloody monkeys. Stand by to sheet home when she's aweigh.' Privately, under that official severity, the saturnine Leyshon could see the makings of a gloomy comedy in it all: the crowd too damned childish and stupid to think, to try to understand what the Old Man was at. Did they think he was weighing anchor and going back out just to spite them? Yes, probably - some of them were dull enough to think that - Billy John for one, Protheroe for another. But then, look at the Old Man: wasn't he nearly as daft? All this playing God, the way he had down in the mess-room last night. 'I am master under God,' he liked to say when he had a few rums under his belt...Must have read it somewhere...Master under God! Not very far under God either, sometimes! Old Jacob liked the sound of that. So because God never explained anything, neither would he. Wouldn't come down off his bloody poop and say to the crowd: 'Listen now, *bois bach*, it's going to blow like a bastard, so we better ride it out at sea, isn't it? So come on then, grab a capstan bar and let's hear the good old *"Mochyn Du."*' That was the song Welsh boys liked best for breaking out an anchor; a good chantey - that was better than six more men on the bars.

But just look at them all today: the Old Man in his temper - black as pitch he looked, up on the poop; the hands dead silent and just about moving that capstan round, the gears just about turning the massive cable-holder windlass on the deck below, the cable coming in inch by inch, link by link, and himself and Dai Evans, two poor skinny old buggers, standing there shouting at the silly idiots! The only ones with any life in them were the young brassbounders up there on the mizzen-mast, loosening the rope gaskets that held the topsails furled. Those daft boys didn't seem to care about anything much, as long as their bellies were filled. Limbs of Satan! *Duw!* what it'd be to be that age again! Look at them! If their posh mothers could see them now: togged up like tramps, not a penny in their pockets, eighty feet up off the deck with only a bobbing, swinging wire to stand on, and they still jabbered and clowned like a pack of monkeys up there. Young and dull - that was the way to be, only it didn't last!

Up on the poop, Jacob Roberts had one ear cocked for the cry 'Anchor's aweigh!' to tell him that the ship was now free, loosed from the ground, but he had by no means finished his demolition of the hapless mutineer: 'Right then, before you get back to work you just listen to me, because this is the last warning I will ever give you. I'm logging you and fining you five pounds, so that's nearly two months' pay gone. What sort of discharge you get from me at the end of the trip will depend on how you behave from now on. But I don't think you realize how dangerous things were for you, you stupid young cub. I suppose you had your capstan-bar, and you were shaping up to the mate with it. Now then, just listen and *think,* for once in your useless life: if you'd cut loose and hit him with it - and you'd half a mind to do that, so don't deny it – I'd have had no choice but to send you ashore to the calaboose for mutiny. They'd have taken my word for everything - you wouldn't have had a leg to stand on. Right, well, have you any idea what life is like in a Chilean jail? Eh? Just sheer hell, that's what. They'd have had you out in the Atacama Desert, in all that sand and rock and heat, working in a chain-gang. I've seen the poor bastards myself, when I've been on the train to Iquique. Scarecrows! Wrecks! Scorched by the sun, dressed in rags. Chileno guards with clubs and rifles! And God alone knows when they'd let you out. D'you think they'd give a fish's tit whether you lived or died? By Christ, you'd suffer, mun, you'd suffer... And you'd risk all that so that you can look big in front of your mates! God-damned stupid blow-hard, full of piss and wind! Now, one more caper like that, and you'll be in jail ashore, or in irons aboard for the rest of the trip. Now get down that ladder and report to Mr Leyshon.'

*   *   *

Jacob walked to the poop rail and looked for'ard. Through the dense web of masts, ropes and stays he could see the men still trudging slowly round the capstan. He'd have a while to wait; the water was deep and they'd paid out a lot of cable last night; that'd take a long time to come in at the best of times. His hands trembled slightly on the polished mahogany rail with the aftermath of his anger. He was tortured too by the treacherous fear that maybe, maybe, the grudging, unwilling crowd were right after all. Odder things had happened at sea. Perhaps what was coming was no more than a bluster they could ride out.... But he'd had to decide about leaving first thing today; once the norther started to blow it'd be too late. *Annwyl Duw!* Who'd be a poor bloody skipper?

He grunted with self-derision: how pleased, how cocky he'd been with himself yesterday, when they'd sighted land! Things had seemed so good yesterday. He went over it again in his mind. There he was, master of a brand-new Cardiff four-master, the latest thing off the Clyde slipways. He'd raised his telescope, steadied it against the shrouds of the jigger mast and focused it on the shoreline. Yes, this must be it - Caleta Buena, Chile, after three months of empty seas. Room for a bit of pride there in his navigation: not a sight of land since a last look at Lundy Island in the Bristol Channel, before a rain-squall blotted it out and buried the barque's rail deep as she heeled to it. Then, apart from a glimpse of the storm-battered island of Diego Ramirez (Digger Ramrods, the crowd for'ard called it) off the Horn, nothing but eight thousand miles of sea between that grey-brown Bristol Channel and this tropic sea, with its glassy swells, its dark catspaws of wind. And now to the east, the first sight of the last resort of the ocean-going sailing ship, the WCSA - the west coast of South America - a thousand miles of Peru and Chile, of yellow-brown rocky desert, without a tree or a bush on it, and every fifty miles or so some little, hot, dusty, pox-ridden, drink-sodden port where you came to unload coal and load nitrate.

The latitude was right, down to the minute; the mountains behind looked just right too when compared with the chart and the pilot. After three months, here it was - Caleta Buena, a cluster of white, run-down buildings huddled on a narrow coastal strip; a small pier, some black lighters moored off it - that was all, yet the little bay was full of shipping - some local steamers, but mostly big barques from Europe, waiting for their cargoes of the precious *nitrado de Chile*, with which the buyers could enrich their fields or blow their enemies to bits, as the fancy took them.

Roberts gauged carefully the gap between his ship, gliding slowly under lower topsails only, and the high bow of an anchored English barque. Close enough now. He said aside to the helmsman nearby: 'Hard down the helm,' and then, as the ship swung slowly up into the wind, so that the topsails fluttered and then backed, he called with an easy bellow to the mate right for'ard on the foc'sle head: 'Let go!' There was a deep booming splash as the anchor plunged down; with a light orange cloud of rust, the chain cable followed, shaking to and fro as it ran out, and making a hollow, metallic rattling music that was magical to all who went to sea for a living. That music said: Anchored! Harbour at last! No more night watches at the wheel or lookout, no more struggling and hauling on a steep wet deck up to the waist in icy water. No more of all that, for a time at least, and in a slow, one-horse port like this, for quite a long time.

The mate left the bosun to clear up on the foc'sle and walked the hundred or so yards aft to consult his captain. The hook down, well held by the sand, the sails furled, a little peace at last before the unloading started tomorrow...Odd, old Jake would usually be below by now, entering up the log in his cabin, but there he was in his sacred place by the weather end of the poop rail, looking about him - to the sky, the light clouds, the heaving swells passing under the ship - as if he were worried, in doubt, unsure of something important. Something must be wrong.

He climbed the ladder to the raised poop deck and reported: 'Ship's got her anchor, capten. Forty fathoms on deck.' He spoke in Welsh, for he, the captain, and most of the crew came from the southwestern seaboard of Wales. Still abstracted, his captain mumbled a curt acknowledgement and went on staring into vacancy ahead to the north. What could be the matter with the old devil? He was a tidy enough skipper, take him all round, most of the time.

Roberts was stocky, even tubby, of only middling height, his red-brown face lined about the eyes, his hair dark, but turning fast now to iron-grey. His figure had no glamour, grace, dash or elegance; he was not a 'gentleman' and made no pretence of being one. Most of the young officers nowadays were doctors', lawyers', parsons' sons, who had been to public school, then been college-trained at Conway or Worcester, and had risen from being indentured apprentices to a third mate's ticket, and then steadily climbed the scales of rank. He'd had to start as a half-starved peggy - a ship's boy - and had struggled and fought his way up with bitter effort: ordinary seaman, able seaman, bosun, third mate and so on. It had taken half a lifetime, and the bitterness of the struggle had never quite gone from his soul. He could never quite forget that it had cost him years of suffering and strife to get what rich men's sons were handed on a plate.

He wore no uniform except on special occasions in port, or for one of the innumerable studio photographs so beloved by captains of the day; he didn't hide his head in a gold-braided cap, but sported, on hot days like this, a panama hat of indeterminate shape and ragged brim; on cold days an elderly billycock - a kind of square-profiled bowler, green with age, dully whitened by dried-on sea-spray. Only for a ceremonial visit to his owner, to a British consul or a wealthy foreign charterer did he dress awkwardly in full fig - navy-blue serge suit with brass buttons, high starched wing collar, frock coat and gold-braided cap. Even then he used to look at his image in the looking-glass and grunt scornfully: 'Huh! Look at you! Jake Roberts Ty Coch. All got up like a pox-doctor's clerk!'

Evans cleared his throat, waiting respectfully for the captain's attention; at last Roberts swivelled round, apparently surprised and irritated to see him there: 'Yes, mister? What is it now?'

'About tomorrow, sir, when the hands turn to: after they've washed down decks: I take it you'd like a proper harbour stow on the sails - get them squared-off and tidy-like? The apprentices can do that. I daresay you'll be going ashore to arrange about lighters and so on? I thought I'd drop the port anchor ahead while Mr Leyshon and the other watch get the hatches off the for'ard hold. Is there anything else you wish?'

'Too early to say about all that, mister. As for lighters, you can see the swell's already too heavy for them to come alongside. As for the ship, she may not be here. From what I can see, we may be weighing anchor and making sail again tomorrow.'

A harsh sneering voice close by said: 'Making *what*, in God's name?' The second mate was standing right below them on the main deck, staring up, his sallow face dark with anger. 'When we've just got here? What's this god-damned nonsense about?'

Two hands coiling and stowing ropes nearby looked up, caught by the raised voices, and grinned at each other. The afterguard having a scrap! That'd be worth listening to - make a good yarn to tell in the foc'sle later. Roberts glanced at them and came out of his reverie in a mood of intense irritation. 'That'll do, mister,' he said to Leyshon. 'My cabin, if you please, both of you.' Then, in a furious aside: 'D'you want every Tom, Dick and Harry to hear you making a fool of yourself, Leyshon?' Scowling and muttering, Leyshon disappeared into the passage that led aft under the poop-deck to the cabin. Silent and embarrassed by the outburst, Evans followed his captain dog-like into the chartroom and down the spiral ladder to the captain's quarters. The air in the cabin was as hot and oppressive as the anger simmering between them. Roberts shouted 'Peggy!' and when Davey Jones the young peggy appeared, sleepy and flustered from his nap in the steward's pantry, Roberts' irritation flashed into irrational fury: 'What's the meaning of this, boy? Cabin's like a bloody oven! Get the sky-light and ports open, and quick about it.'

'Aye aye, sir, but I thought you said...'

'Get on with it, halfwit! You never had a thought in your life, nor any of your Ty-croes lot neither.'

The three men stood in a heavy silence while the frightened boy bustled about, every moment dreading a stunning cuff from the skipper's hand; the silence stretched unbearably, the stocky captain behind his solid mahogany table, as if behind a barricade, the two mates, twin-like, both tall, grey and cadaverous, their faces burnt red by sun and wind, grey whiskers framing their sunken cheeks. At last the boy had finished and gone, and the tension relaxed a little. At last they could speak their minds. Evans cleared his throat nervously and said: 'Capten, I don't think ...'

Roberts cut in, his voice troubled but firm, restraining himself with an effort: 'Gentlemen, let's all take a seat. Good... Now then, Mr Leyshon, let's be clear about one thing: I'm not, I hope, a tyrant or an unreasonable man, but I am, under God, master of this ship, and it's for me to decide how she is managed. Me, and *only* me. If I ask for your advice, that's another matter. On this occasion I haven't asked because I cannot, for I believe it to be a matter of life and death, so I must bear the responsibility alone - and I am not enjoying that, believe me.'

Leyshon was more restrained, but still seething inside: 'That's all very well,' he said morosely, 'but I still don't see...'

'Wait! If you don't believe me, just look at this.' Roberts strode to the round brass barometer on the bulkhead and tapped it with his knuckle: 'Look at that, will you, and tell me everything's all right! It's dropped another half-inch – that's one and a half inches in twenty-four hours. We are in for a really bad norther, I'm certain.' Even saying the word 'norther' aloud sent a cold shudder through Roberts, and the far-off winter of 1870 came back to him with its attendant horror.

For ninety-nine weeks out of a hundred, the ships at Chilean ports rolled in smooth swells, in feather-light breezes and grilling heat, securely anchored bow and stern in little benighted bays along a thousand miles of coast from Pisagua to Talcahuano. A thousand miles, and hardly a decent safe anchorage all the way; yet hundreds of ships lay loading and unloading, each ship usually stuck there for weeks on end. Sometimes, though, the gods of the huge Pacific struck out, and the cold norther, a furious on-shore gale, lashed at the moored ships, lashed at them so hard that not all of them stayed moored.

Leyshon broke in upon his thoughts with his curt, truculent tone: 'What of it? We've all seen northers and we've all ridden them out safely. Two good anchors out ahead, one astern. Nothing'll shift that.'

'You think not, mister? Listen, you've seen northers, but not the way I've seen them - not the kind I think we're going to get soon. Eighteen-seventy it was, midwinter, twenty-five years ago this June, at Valparaiso. I'd just been made up to third mate of a Swansea copper-ore barque, the "Fanciulla". She had two anchors down, same as you say. And they might have held, I daresay.... only we had a big Italian barque anchored ahead of us - in ballast she was, up out of the water like a bloody haystack. Well, in a bad squall she dragged down on top of us, and that did it: our cables parted, and up we went on the shore - no time to do anything. The Italian lost every man jack on the stones; we were lucky - they got us all off with a breeches buoy before she went to pieces. But that was the only time I ever saw a ship's captain cry.'

'Cry?'

'Yes, cry. He'd got his wife and six-months-old baby aboard, you see... Thought they were goners. I thought we all were. I was young then, young and strong and nimble. Skipper got me to take the kiddie ashore tied to my chest, sliding along a rope between the main-top and the shore - like a bead on a string. Only, what with the height of the sea and the mast swaying, we kept getting ducked right under, then hove up again as the rope tightened. And *cold!* I can still hear that poor little dab crying fit to kill. She was nearly gone, they said. And I remember there was a big strong young woman in the crowd watching on the *malecon* - you know, the promenade arrangement they have there. She looked as if she might have been a whore - I don't know. Anyway, she just pulled all her coat, blouse, stays, everything, open - right down to the skin, and shoved that poor wet little scrap in - to warm it up, like. Saved its life. And d'you remember old Charlie Preece from Dinas - a sail-maker, terrible man for the women? Well, he was standing there too, wet to the skin and frozen: "O *Iesu Mawr*, missis" he says, "my turn in there next, is it?" Dirty old devil! Well, you don't forget that sort of thing. There was six ships went ashore that night - scores of hands lost.'

Leyshon started to say belligerently: 'I don't see that...' but Evans cut in diplomatically: 'So what do you intend, capten?'

'Well, I think we can risk it here till dawn.'

'Risk it?' said the second. 'Risk what? It's bloody flat calm out there. And what the devil are you proposing to do at dawn?'

'Weigh anchor, make sail. Get fifty miles offshore; get some sea-room and ride it out there. Much safer, though it'll be no picnic, I'm sure. Good God, mun, you're supposed to be a seaman. Don't you see? This ship is designed to come through storms at sea, where there's room under her lee - room for her to drift, if necessary. Here, she's stuck like a rat in a trap, just at the mercy of whatever wind chances to blow. D'you think I like the idea of going back to sea after such a long trip here? I'm doing it because I'm the one responsible, and I hope to God you'd do the same if you were captain. Believe me, there'll be terrible trouble in this anchorage tomorrow, if the glass means anything. And once the norther starts it'll be too late to get her under way. It has to be done before the storm.'

Leyshon pushed back his chair in a fury and jumped up: 'Weigh anchor? Just because of a barometer? After ninety days dawdling about at sea? And all because of what you say happened in 1870?'

Roberts leapt up too, his short hair and whiskers bristling, his eyes snapping, his voice a snarling roar: 'No mister! Not because of 1870! Because I am capten of this ship, and that is my decision.'

'Well then, by Christ, I shan't lift a finger ...'

The captain's huge hand came down on the table in a hammer-blow that sent the inkstand dancing: 'One moment, Mister Leyshon! Unless you want your career with this company to end here and now, you'd better think before you say one more word.' There was a pause, both men dully flushed with rage and breathing heavily. 'That's better,' Roberts said at last. 'Now go from here - go back to your cabin and think, mun, about who you are and who I am. D'you think I'm going to stand by here and let you yap at me like a damned jackal? Go from here before I log you for insubordination!'

Leyshon stood still and glowered for a second or two, then strode out, slamming the cabin door. Evans lifted his arms, gesturing anxiously, helplessly. There was another long silence: 'Listen – he'll be all right, sir. He'll do his job. Just give him time to cool down, isn't it?'

Roberts grunted: 'I know him - not a bad man, but a proper blow-hard. His uncle was the same. By Christ, when I was a third mate, and got spoken to like that by one of the crowd for'ard, I used to give the bastards such a poke in the guts they couldn't even stand for half-an-hour... Well now, what do *you* say, mister?'

Evans had been afraid of that question. He knew it would come, and that he was being tested, rather than consulted. If Jacob had made up his mind, and had that scene with Leyshon, he wasn't going to change his plan for anyone: 'Well, sir,' he said reluctantly, the words dragged out of him, 'no doubt what you've decided is prudent enough, but I think there'll be trouble - with the hands, I mean. After this long trip, they'll be looking forward to a run ashore.' He licked his dry lips. 'I mean, it's only natural, isn't it? And we being short-handed, they've had to work hard all the way, fair play to them.'

'They'll go ashore all right, only not tomorrow or the next day. And they'll go ashore alive, in a boat - not washed up as corpses. That time I was telling you about, there was poor devils washed up with no heads, no arms and no legs...Cut to bits by the surf on the rocks. Is that how they want to go ashore?'

'Aye, sir, I know. But - look at it their way: begging your pardon, you can't be certain the storm will be that bad - not absolutely certain, can you? And suppose it didn't come to anything much? You know what they're like - like big children. You can't reason with them, once they get an idea in their stupid heads. That's why there'll be trouble.'

'Look here, mister: you've got a goodish crowd for'ard there - mostly tidy Welsh boys we've known for years. Not the usual windjammer collection of drunks, bummers, loafers and scum out of some jail. And what I say to you is this: you're chief mate, and it's your job to see that the men obey all reasonable orders from me. Well, isn't my decision reasonable?'

'O yes, yes, sir; to me it's reasonable. But it's what they will think...I mean, I was handy enough with my fists twenty years ago - so was Leyshon for that matter - but we can't beat and kick like buckos any more, can we?'

'You've done six voyages with me, David Evans, and you know I've no time for bucko mates, all boots and belaying-pins. Leave that sort of thing to the damn Yankees. You've got decent boys, as I say. You worry too much, mister; if I've made the wrong decision, it's me they'll curse at. You just damn well make them do their job, isn't it? I'll be on the poop, and God help any mother's son who won't turn to. Very well, then.' His tone signified that the discussion was ended. 'I want an anchor-watch tonight.' He handed the mate a scrap of paper. 'These are the anchor bearings, to be checked every half-hour. I am to be informed if the wind freshens.' Then he cast off his professional air and looked sympathetically at the deep lines of tiredness and worry on Evans' face. He laid a hand on his sleeve. 'Remember what the Book says: "Be not therefore anxious for the morrow, for the morrow will be anxious for itself". Sufficient, David, sufficient unto the day is the evil thereof.'

Evans, embarrassed at this unusual intimacy, could only cough loudly and say, 'Yes, just so. Thank you, capten.'

Roberts spoke again, more as a captain, but still with an edge of pity: 'That senior apprentice Raven - he seems a half-way decent seaman.'

Evans' eyes flashed angrily: 'He is a graceless and godless young English scoundrel, sir, as I know to my cost...'

'Yes, yes, I know all that, mun. He's as big a thief as any of the brassbounders, and I've dosed him for the clap twice - no doubt he thought he needed it. But he's a smart fellow about the deck, I've noticed; he's got some backbone, and his sun-sights are as good as yours or mine. I'll get him to keep your anchor-watches for you. Get some sleep, mister; you'll have a busy day tomorrow, I dare say.'

Evans flushed and bridled: 'My watches? Raven? Thank you capten, but that will not be necessary. Of course, if you're not satisfied with my work or capability - if you think, in short, that I'm unfit for my duties...'

'All right, mister, all right. Don't fly off in a pother like that. You know what I think of your work.'

Evans was still unreasonably nettled; his age was a raw, tender topic with him: 'Very well, sir, in that case I shall stand my watch, and pass your instructions on to the second in due course. I will wish you goodnight, sir.' With a slight, stiff, coldly-formal bow, he made his way to the door with great dignity.

As he opened it, however, and raised his leg to step over the coaming, Roberts said casually: 'You know, I believe I may have a drop of rum left in my locker here. Would you care for a tot, mister?'

Evans' surprise and pleasure at the offer robbed him at once of his dignity; he had a three-months' thirst on him. He paused, his leg still tentatively raised: 'Rum? Well, that's ... that's.... ah... most kind, I'm sure, sir. Most kind. Just a small tot, yes, that would be most welcome.'

Roberts allowed his bitter self a little reflection: look at the fellow! Just pull a cork out and he's forgotten all his precious dignity and all his worries about tomorrow. What it is not to be captain! If this storm never turns up, or isn't too severe, they'll all curse me and mock at me for the rest of their lives as a stupid chicken-hearted old woman; and if I'm right, they'll just forget all about it. Nobody spends time or breath praising the Old Man – that's a story not worth telling.

When the mate had gone, wiping his mouth appreciatively, Captain Roberts lowered himself into the heavy horsehair-stuffed, leather-seated chair and drew it up to the table. He reached out for the open log-book and slid it towards him over the polished mahogany. The movement turned itself into a long, passionate stretch and yawn, for he was dog-tired. He'd had a long day on deck at the end of a long passage, not to mention having tiresome rows with John and that fellow Leyshon. He felt the bliss of sitting, felt the back, arms and seat of the chair supporting him, pressing on his flesh and then yielding as the barque pitched and rolled in the swell; felt the blessed ease seeping into his tired feet and legs. It had been a long day, and now, when it should be all over, with the hook down in the ground and all secured - now this other business. 'Getting too old for this game, mun,' he whispered to himself. 'Too bloody old. Fifty-five in June.' But he had half-an-hour before the mates joined him for supper; better to do the ship's log while it was all fresh in his head.

He dipped his steel pen, its handle looking like a straw in his great brown fist. He wrote carefully in the copper-plate hand that had been beaten into him in the little grey-stone school in Newport, Pembrokeshire, nearly fifty years ago. His tongue showing a tiny pink tip in his concentration, he ceremoniously began a new page:

Log of the Barque Figaro, Penarth to Caleta Buena., Chile. January 17th, 1895...

Miles away to the west, over the heaving face of the Pacific, the sun was going down, glaring red and angry, shooting a. narrow livid ray through a cleft in the cloud. The horrible orange glare was reflected off the water, up through the cabin ports, to flicker on the white deckhead of his cabin. The ship's bones of wood and metal creaked as she wallowed in the steep swells. Quite unconsciously, he glanced up at the tell-tale compass mounted in the deckhead; she was pointing north, taking the great smooth rolling slabs of water on the nose. He felt everything was wrong; he felt uneasy, like a trapped animal. With a deep rumbling sigh he blotted the title carefully. No smudges in his log... neat... shipshape. But who'd ever read it? The owner - old John Powell in his dusty office looking out over Bute Street, Cardiff? No, he wanted to see accounts, invoices, bills of lading, charter-parties, or, best of all, drafts of freight money coming in from Melbourne, Callao, Noumea, San Francisco, Iquique, Valparaiso - wherever he sent his great ships. Anywhere, any currency, so long as it could be turned into sovereigns.

With an effort he got himself back to the task of the moment. The last of the eighty-six days of the voyage from Penarth began to appear in cryptic, spidery characters on the page - latitude, longitude, courses steered, bearings, wind directions, the tasks imposed by the mate, by the captain, by necessity or by the sea: 'Hands employed in hawling up and shackling on anchor cables, and preparing anchors for letting go. 4 p.m. Mt Cerro Toroni bore ENE. Altered course to E by N. Wind southerly, light airs. Long northerly swell.' He pondered for a moment, then turned his last full-stop into a comma and added: 'which I do not think it is a good sign at this place, and at this time of the year. All signs of a bad norther.'

He sat back, feeling a little better at having written his worry down on the paper before him, having published his anxiety, so that it no longer lurked at the back of his mind. But *Duw!* how little the log told! Nothing about feelings, worries, relief, hope, despair and petty quarrels. Shipowners didn't want to read about those. He shut the book wearily and sat back, thinking: Is there any poor bastard on earth lonelier than a ship's captain?

2

Dawn over Caleta Buena. Simon Grant, first mate of the Liverpool barque 'Birkdale', came out of the chart-room, looked at the grey bow of cloud to the north-west, at the sickly, pale-misted rising sun, and groaned in despair, mentally cursing his captain, the ship's crew and the Chilean lancheros for their sins of omission and commission. That god-damned McMasters above all for his absence; for such a critical, demanding man, the captain had the devil's luck (or was it luck?) in never being on hand when things were bad. The old sod was always there when you didn't want him, never there when you did, and, above all, never satisfied with what you had decided to do in his absence.

For instance, this present moment: that dispute about the charter-party. God knows he'd done enough fussing and muttering and fuming about it; so anxious not to lose a damned peso over the deal that he forgot about his ship. And what a greaser! What an unsurpassed arse-licker! The Owners this, the Owners that, I must protect the Owners' interests in foreign ports, and so on, and so on, and so on. Maybe he did have to go off on the train down the coast to the agents in Iquique; but did he have to pick a day when a norther was brewing? If he could read the lawyers' mumbo-jumbo in a charter agreement, couldn't he read a barometer too, especially when the bottom was dropping out of it? Always off ashore as soon as the hook was down, and always a complaint, a hazing for somebody when he came back aboard, smelling of brandy and good Havana cigars - free ones, by courtesy of some wily ship's chandler, no doubt. Self-important, selfish old fool....

Grant stood at the break of the poop, gripping the teak rail, looking for'ard at the long perspective of the main deck below. He was bronzed, fair, well-built, an ex-athlete beginning to thicken slightly amidships, just as his fair hair was beginning to grizzle at the temples; he was clean-shaven but for a neat moustache, and you could see his jaw muscles tighten and bulge as he raged at his fate. And even if he wasn't by nature the most cheerful or optimistic of men, he certainly had plenty of worries now, the worst of them being the sheer quiet and emptiness of the decks in front of him: no decent crowd of hands with a bosun touching his cap and saying: 'Port watch aft, sir.'

They'd had a good enough crowd when they came into Valparaiso - a mixed lot as usual these days, but fair play – they'd put up with a long trip under a pernickety captain, with grub even more shocking than usual, but two hours after the ship had anchored there hadn't been one of them left; they'd all sheered off in shore-boats with boarding-house runners. Stupid fools - they never learned anything. All their miserable pay forfeited - three months of it - half of them going off in the clothes they stood up in. Gormless shiftless idiots...All going off as happy as Larry with a tot or two of liquor in their bellies as bait, to be fleeced of anything they did have, poxed by some cantina whore, and shanghaied back to sea again. And all for a swig or two of pisco and a bit of drunken, fumbling jig-a-jig on a dirty mattress... Sailors!

So who now was left? He noticed an acrid whiff of coal-smoke from the galley funnel; the cook, he was still there, and the steward, the carpenter, and the aged sailmaker. No good ordering any of those aloft! That left the bosun, the other two mates, himself, and five brass-bounders, two of them only sixteen, on their first trip. Say seven men really, on a barque of two thousand tons burthen - hopeless, hopeless, bloody hopeless.... only, as senior officer, he could never admit that it was.

Of course, in the normal run of things, the captain and his precious Owners (he always spoke of them with a capital O) would be glad enough to see the last of the foc'sle crowd; all their back pay - two pounds fifteen a month each! - would be saved, as well as the cost of the so-called food they would have eaten during the two or three months in harbour. There'd be plenty of long-shore bums and drifters and other feckless halfwits when the ship needed a new crew. But now - it was a disaster, being left like this. The 'Birkdale' was a great unhandy scow at the best of times, but they'd not long arrived from Valparaiso in ballast to pick up nitrate. It had been - for Grant at least - a worrying trip. They'd had only a scratch crew, and at Valparaiso they'd taken on some rock ballast to keep her stiff and upright, but only a couple of hundred tons, not enough, in his judgement. So now she lay, virtually unmanned and sticking up out the water like a cliff-face, about as seaworthy as a barn or a haystack.

He crossed to the port rail and peered over; by God, it looked half a mile down to the greasy calm water that sullenly rose and fell as the glassy humps and lumps of swell slid under her. The air was still.

Every swinish roll made her webbed forest of masts and spars groan and creak with the strain; the hinged metal covers of the main-deck wash-ports opened and closed with dismal barren clangs, a cacophonous tolling at the passing of the swells. The sound brought to his mind a memory from twenty or more years back, and brought too the image of his father at the tiller of his beautiful cutter, sailing it so close to a huge clanging bell-buoy outside Harwich that Simon, sitting beside him, felt his heart clutched by terror, and by guilt at feeling that terror in his father's presence. The buoy was a giant cylindrical tank, green and grey with weed and shell at the waterline, its top a great red iron basket; it leant and turned slowly in the pull of the tide and its bell gave out the bleakest, most desolate, heart-chilling noise he had ever heard. And among all the streaks of rust and white gull-shit, the words 'Long Sand Head' came sluggishly spinning into view and then as slowly spun away. He could hear the rush of the tide against the huge slab of steel. He looked quickly up at his father, and saw at once that he was shaving the buoy close so as to frighten him; or, as Father would have put it, to 'make a man of him'.

That lonely, ceaseless tolling, the hiss and rip of the tide, the bowel-churning sensation of fear, the carelessly cruel smile on his father's whiskered lips...Old Will Wordsworth was right - the Child was Father of the Man. When you had a father as rich, handsome, confident and consistently successful as his pater had been, it was hard, even years later, to feel full confidence in yourself. You felt you were still a puny, weedy little failure and that you always had to try that much harder than everyone else. It was hard today not to feel some of that old, almost-but-not-quite-conquered fear, as he looked aloft at the tall yellow masts - nearly two hundred feet high, and at the steel yards, ninety feet across. He noted while looking how the grey rags of high cloud were hurrying through the steel and wire tracery. However much weight up there? Must be sixty tons or so, put it all together; a hell of a lot to be swaying and lurching to and fro. And how the gale when it came shrieking in would pluck and tear savagely at every square inch of windage aloft, doing its damnedest to topple her over! What with that and the hull sticking up like a haystack - how could two bits of chain hope to hold her? Just two bits of chain cable and two hooks in the sea-bed? And yet what else was there to do? He remembered his father's handsome mouth saying: 'Don't worry so much, Simon, old fellow. Don't be such a wet-leg. She'll be all right, you clown. Do grow up, old chap.'

He came back to the present with a guilty shock. He was suddenly aware of the stocky figure of the bosun below. The man was looking at him oddly in an awkward silence. The bosun must have said something, and was waiting for an answer. 'What? What did you say, bosun?'

'I said: "Hands mustered," sir - what there is of them. Me and Chips and Sails and the apprentices.' The man was looking at him curiously; the bosun would know something of what was going through his mind, but the bosun had been most of his life on the jute run from Calcutta, and perhaps hadn't seen a norther yet.

'Very good, bosun. It's going to blow soon - like the very devil. How much cable out?'

'Fifty fathoms on each, sir.'

'Right, we'll put some more down. Veer to seventy-five on both. It's going to be bad.'

'Aye aye ... but begging your pardon, sir ...'

'Well, what is it now?'

'That's plain enough, Mr Grant, sir, isn't it? With the few hands we've got we'll never get that weight of cable up again. We'll never shift the windlass with that lot out - not with the hands we got.'

'I know, but never mind that. Can't be helped. You'd better pray instead that it will hold her. We'll worry about heaving up when it's all over - if we're here to do it, that is.'

The bosun looked sour and sceptical. He'd been told the WCSA was a lousy place, but hell, it could never blow that hard, surely? And after all, they were in harbour! Jesus Christ, you were supposed to be safe in a harbour! The mate, however, had a worse shock for him: 'And when you've done that, get all the hatch-covers back on her and batten them down tight.'

The old sailor stared in disgust, as if at an unreasonable and petulant child. 'The hatches? God's strewth, sir, we got launches coming with the first of the nitrate cargo today!'

'Believe me, bosun, there'll be no launches coming out today. Look at the swell, man!'

But the bosun went doggedly on: 'And them hatch-beams weighs a bloody ton and all... Us being so short-handed... No proper men, neither, only brass-bounders - as much trouble as they're worth.'

Grant found an unreasonable scarlet fury welling up in him at the man's obstinacy, but fought it down, and merely said crisply: 'Mr

Metcalfe, Mr Dunn and I will be down after breakfast to lend a hand. See to it, Winters, and look sharp about it.'

Bosun Winters, too angry to risk an answer, turned and walked away, and when it was safe to do so he spat a stream of tobacco-brown spittle on to the clean deck. Grant, for his part, looked down and saw that his knuckles were white with tension; why couldn't that bastard McMasters be here to take these decisions, and suffer this pressure? He thought bitterly: I'll get no credit or thanks from the owners out of this, whatever happens and whatever I do. Any reward to me would seem like a rebuke to him, and they always seem to think the sun shines out of his arse, just as he thinks it shines out of theirs. I reckon Metcalfe is right: our precious captain has got relations in the right places. What a damned profession it is to go to sea - to take on this sort of responsibility for seven pounds a month, and eat salt garbage too, most of the time.

A small noise from across the silent sea caught his attention; it came from the big Cardiff barque, the four-poster, that had come in the previous night; it was the steady slow clink-clink-clink of the pawls as her anchor chain was hove up, foot by foot. He trained his glass on her: FIGARO, CARDIFF...One of the new sort, a big carrier; made by the mile and cut off by the fathom, as the old-timers would say. Her captain was a lucky Welsh devil, though; a full cargo and a full crew on board. Easy enough for him to up anchor and get out to sea where it was safe - well, safer. Funny thing, though: the capstan up on her foc'sle seemed to be fully manned, and there was no more than a light breeze, and yet the cable was coming in very slowly, and though it was a Welsh ship, not a soul was singing - which was unheard-of with a ship of that nation! He smiled a little to himself - *schadenfreude* had its satisfactions after all. It was not hard to guess why the work was going so slowly: the crowd would have been looking forward to the booze and the senoritas after their long trip, not to beating about in a cold gale fifty miles offshore. They were all just like big children - sulking. Half-a-dozen men were climbing aloft up the ratlines to loose the sails, and through his glass he could see how slowly, how sullenly, they moved. They'd never forgive their captain for taking them straight back out to sea, not even when they knew, deep down, that he was right to be prudent. Not many of them could think straight, not even about their own safety. Being made to weigh anchor without once going ashore - it wasn't the kind of thing they could forgive.

He snapped his glass shut and took a final look round his ship. There was nothing else to be done, except perhaps to clear away the lifeboats later on. He went below for breakfast, sat down and looked round at the good solid mahogany panelling of the mess-room. It was hard to think of it being ground and beaten into splinters along the rocky shore of the bay, hard to think that he might never again sit in this particular chair and stir the coffee in this particular blue cup. The ship seemed so solid, so commonplace, so permanent; as fixed as a house, a street, as the mountains or the sky. But there was fury enough in a black norther to rip it from its anchors and pound it to matchwood in half-an-hour. Old Sam Johnson was right about life at sea: being in a ship is being in a jail, with the chance of being drowned. The sea killed all alike, without respect to rank; he and the bosun and the little makee-learn apprentices might all finish up this afternoon smashed to bloody fragments of skin and bone against the rocks of the malecon.

*   *   *

As more and more of 'Figaro's' cable came in, the load on the cable-holder lessened, the capstan went round faster despite the spiritless push from the hands, and the pawl clinked away smartly. The tops'ls on fore, main and mizzen masts hung in their gear, released from their spars but still looped in bags that stirred and flapped with gentle booms in the light breeze. 'Cable's up and down, sir !' shouted Evans from the eyes of the ship, right up in the bow over the hawsepipe. The anchor was just about to break free.

'Aye aye. Heave up roundly.'

The rhythm of the clinking pawl suddenly accelerated; the chain was coming in fast. 'Anchor's aweigh!'

Roberts roared to the men on the main deck: 'Let go buntlines and clewlines! Sheet home the tops'ls!'

There was a drumming of feet as men sprang to the ship's side, where the sheets were belayed. Getting a big ship under way was a lively business, and the crowd's tantrums were beginning to wear off. With high raucous rhythmic cries the men hauled taut the sheets; ropes squealed through the blocks, and lengths of chain sheet shook and jingled. As if by magic, by a remote hand, the topsails spread out, their bottom corners drawn down and out to the yard-arms beneath. The soft rumple and drumming of canvas stopped abruptly as the breeze pressed the sails back against their masts, the ship slowly gathering way astern. The Old Man, too preoccupied with his craft to be angry now, stood at the poop rail until he saw the water start to move ahead. 'Port your helm - hard over,' he barked to the helmsman, who stood beside the great double wheel of oak. The man heaved on the stiff, dead spokes, and then helmsman and captain watched as the spiny finger of the bowsprit began to slide to the left across the dusty brown slopes, across the rocky northern headland, gathering momentum every second, until it pointed clear out to sea. Roberts walked then to his sacred spot, the for'ard corner of the poop on the weather side. Glancing back, he saw 'Figaro's' stern getting perilously close to the high, ballasted Liverpool barque astern of them. He saw the mate looking aft expectantly, and called: 'Starboard tack! Lee braces - heave!'

There was a brief rush and more high shouts from the hands as they stamped aft, hauling on the braces. Like formal clockwork tree branches, the huge yards on fore, main and mizzen masts ponderously revolved together, ending up close-hauled on the starboard tack. After a few gentle shakes, the three long rectangles of sail caught the breeze and the ship gradually gathered headway. 'Midships the helm,' he called back to the helmsman: 'Full and by, Larsen, and don't pinch her.' He heard the man repeat his order, and then, effortlessly, without apparently raising his voice, he spoke to the mate two hundred feet away upwind, by the foremast: 'All plain sail, mister. Set watches.' When a man had rounded Cape Horn as master ten times each way, as Jacob had, he developed a Cape Horn voice, to be heard over the roar of waves on deck and the fearful drumming and howling of the gale in the rigging; it is a voice he never loses.

'All plain sail, sir,' repeated Evans, and he was relieved to see that the men had dropped their stupid petulant sulking. It wasn't that they'd changed their minds or forgiven the Old Man or forgotten their lost (or at least postponed) liberty. They still held that against him, and most of them would blame and ridicule him for it to their dying day; when you've worked like a donkey, fed worse, and been stuck in a damp wooden bunk with nothing but your own John Thomas for company for three months - well then, a good wet, a good beefsteak, and above all a good all-night-in with a willing tart - never mind what colour – they're things that can't lightly be put off, not for any storm. But then, as the old shellbacks were always saying: Growl you may, but go you must.

Evans shook his head at their foolishness: if the voyage had lasted another week they wouldn't have complained much; it was just seeing the port, smelling the shore breeze, hearing the anchor-cable rattle out, and then being told 'Man the capstan! Back to sea!' – that's what the crowd couldn't stomach. Luckily, they were a goodish crowd for these days, mostly Welsh boys, even if some of them were Gogs - men from far-off North Wales. Thank God they hadn't got a crowd of 'Frisco bums or Liverpool packet rats – they'd have had knives out by now.

Look at them: they'd got caught up in the old familiar routine of making sail, and shuffling out along the footropes attached to the yards, loosing the gaskets, the short ropes that held the furled sails; the voices of the young apprentices came down to him thin and faint, from where they stood on swaying wires, their chests against the royal yards, a hundred and eighty feet up from the deck. Sail after sail fell from its furled state, was hauled down by its sheets, caught the wind with a soft crack, and took up its lovely curved shape, adding every moment to the thrust driving the ship seawards. Larsen at the wheel felt 'Figaro' come alive in his hands, saw her head respond to every spoke of the wheel; the hands up in the eyes, right for'ard, setting the triangular staysails that stretched between foremast and bowsprit, they heard the music of her progress - first a soft chuckle of water at her forefoot, then as some stiffer gusts came in the wind, and more and more sails were unfurled, heard the chuckle turn to a steady roar as the blunt cutwater began to turn a roll of white foam over in front of her - a bone in her teeth, as the old sailors called it. Instead of clumsily wallowing in the swells, the barque attacked their smooth shifting flanks, gracefully nodding, ducking, and tossing her bow. In a few moments her masts had changed from a dense, squared-off, tangled forest of steel, wood, wire, rope and chain to four distinct and elegantly angled spires of white canvas cloth, so steady that they seemed to be carved from ivory. Not even the basest, grossest, most case-hardened man aboard could quite ignore the ship's beauty, nor the lively grace with which she now moved.

Roberts stood, swaying easily to the motion. He felt more peaceful, now that the die was cast. If he was wrong, so be it; he might be master under God, but he was still only a man, and men made mistakes. Better safe than sorry, better almost anything than lose a new ship, only a year away from the Clyde slipway. *Iesu Mawr!* she picked up well from a standstill. Look at the way she was carving ahead now. Not a clipper - not like the sweet-lined tea clippers of twenty, thirty years ago, built like race-horses, like yachts - not a straight line in the hulls, canvas like snow and teak decks nearly as white, slicing like knives to windward through the Malacca Strait. A quarter the tonnage and twice the crew! Compared with them 'Figaro' was a great slab-sided wagon, a huge steel box for getting three thousand tons of coal or nitrate from one side of the world to another. But by God she was powerful and she could go!

He swung his glass to the ship astern; looked like a Liverpool ship - one of Smith's Dales, probably. Got both anchors down, and he could see men busy on the foc'sle. Veering out all her cable, probably. Poor devils, that was all they could do; a bad lookout for them. He scanned the receding anchorage; he wondered whether any other captains were making the same decision as his. If they were it would be comforting, somehow. Yes! He gave a little grunt of satisfaction: the PSNC mail-boat was getting her anchor now, and a tramp steamer further inshore had a great plume of black smoke from her funnel as she got up steam hastily. He could see a big German four-master - one of Laeisz's P-liners - loosing her topsails, but all the other sailers were stuck; half-unloaded, under-manned, they'd have to put up with whatever the Almighty sent.

And that, he allowed himself to think, was not always very pleasant or healthy; somehow, God didn't seem to worry himself overmuch with sailors. Noah and Saint Paul, and even old Jonah - they came through all right, but then they were really passengers, not ordinary old shellbacks like himself. Perhaps a good Christian - and he tried to be one – shouldn't have such thoughts, but sometimes he wondered whether that Psalmist fellow had ever been to sea - not some piffling little puddle like the Sea of Galilee but the real deep sea. They that go down to the sea in ships saw the works of the Lord all right, and his wonders in the deep; and sure enough they reeled to and fro and were at their wits' end, and a good many of them - especially those pious Gogs from Bangor and Porthmadog - they cried unto the Lord in their trouble. But as for Him bringing them out of their distresses unto the haven where they would be – well now, that was another matter altogether, with all due respect to Him and His sacred Word. If you were captain, you couldn't just sit in your cabin and rely on a psalm to get you out of trouble! That psalmist had never seen a norther on the WCSA. And you only had to go to Cwm-yr-Eglwys, to the tiny church by the shore in north Pembrokeshire, and look at the graves of sailors from the coasting ketches and schooners, to see that sailors didn't always reach the haven where they would be. Doubt, doubt, doubt – your besetting sin, Jacob *bach,* and not just in matters of religion. Enough of that! Be still, and know that I am God... Aye, aye, well then, let those rascals in the foc'sle be still and know that you, boy, are capten.

As if to test his new resolve, there came a satanically sceptical comment from Evans, at his elbow: 'Only one or two getting out, I see, sir.'

'Got no choice, mister, most of them. Port watch on deck, is it?'

'Yes sir, my watch until noon. Starboard watch standing by for orders.' Roberts glanced down at the main-deck, where groups of men of the starboard watch stood or lounged waiting. It was a weekday and a forenoon watch, so they clearly expected to be put to one of the endless chores of cleaning and maintenance needed in a big sailer. Without any particular benevolence he said: 'Starboard watch stand down, mister.'

With a wry grimace of silent disapproval, Evans barked down: 'That'll do, starboard watch,' and saw the first grins of the morning on the faces of the second mate's watch. In thirty seconds they had disappeared into the foc'sle. The two men stood for a moment looking ahead; every minute now the wind was freshening from the nor-nor-west. The three spires of square sails, hauled in sharply to drive the ship to windward, were set into taut lines of power, every square inch of canvas drawing, every foot of rope and wire and chain bowstring-tight to lift, trim or support the strong yellow masts and spars; just to their left, at the for'ard end of the poop, the fourth, smaller mast, the jigger, carried only two sails, set like a yacht's, fore-and-aft.

The first mate looked severely at the shut door of the starboard foc'sle: 'There's plenty for that lot to do on deck, capten - any amount.' His thrifty soul didn't like the thought of men lying in bunks smoking when the owners were paying them to chip paint, mend sails or splice rope.

'Aye aye, mister, I know that. But they've had a bit of a shock, I suppose, being brought back out... Like being kept in at school. And there'll be plenty for them to do up here soon.' As if to confirm his words, a strong gust laid the barque over until her decks sloped like a hill-side, and short choppy seas began to spill their tops over the lee bulwark. 'How long shall we be able to carry this much sail, d'you think?' He turned round to look back at Caleta Buena, now barely discernible as a bay, the ships mere toys with matchstick masts. 'I wonder what will that place look like when we see it again? And how many poor buggers will be dead by then?'

3

When the draughtsmen at the famous Sinclair yard at Clydebank had started work on 'Figaro' their task had been simple: to design a carrier. Not a ship to take the breath away with the beauty of her lines, but a carrier - a great long steel box, rather scornfully dubbed a 'windjammer', sharpened at each end just a little, fitted with steel masts kept up by steel wires, and ready to hump great quantities of the world's bulk goods - coal, corn, jute, ore, nitrate - as cheaply as possible so as to outbid and keep at bay the cursed stinking, oily, dirty steamships, with their expensive engines that took up cargo space and gobbled up expensive coal. In the mid-1890s there were still a few trades - there would be for another forty years - where a big sailer, a four-masted barque, could make a profit for her owners: trades where cargoes were chancy, or might not be ready, or where loading took a long time, too long to tie up a costly steamer; trades where cheap bulk cargoes needed hauling across the globe, often being sold and re-sold on the way; trades where time didn't matter too much. Trades, in short, too unattractive for the steam-kettle. Then, once you had your steel four-poster, all you needed was luck and thrift: the luck to find good agents who could get you decent charters and the thrift to run the ship like a floating workhouse.

And so the Scottish builders had paid most heed to giving the barque her giant echoing wombs for cargo; her main hold two hundred feet long, forty wide and sixteen high, a maw which could swallow trainloads of coal at a gulp; and above this the tween-deck hold where smaller, lighter goods could be stowed. Only twenty years ago the tween-decks would often have carried human freight - emigrants from Britain to Australia, coolies from India to the Caribbean, or poor devils euphemistically known as 'indentured labourers' from China to the guano islands of Peru. But now the steam-kettles had the passenger business and sailing ships were just travelling holds.

The ship's crew was, on good thrifty principles, stowed in the spaces unsuitable for cargo. Right up for'ard, over the chain-locker and under the foc'sle head, and sub-divided by the massive anchor windlass, was the wet, wedge-shaped kennel where her foremast hands lived, eating, reading, and card-playing at rough deal tables, sleeping in coffin-shaped bunks that were like cupboards in the bulkheads. The stink of the cable (which often came in covered in mud and silt), the foc'sle's wetness in rough weather and its violent motion in a seaway made it the obvious place in which to house the lowest ranks - the crowd.

The ship's after-end, where there was much more of shelter and a little less of violent pitching and heaving, was devoted to the comfort of her captain and officers, and to the housing of the stores of food and drink which those officials felt they must guard. Under the raised poop-deck were an officers' mess-room, cabins for the mates and the steward, and a kind of flat - a cabin, bathroom and saloon - furnished in heavy Victorian splendour, for the captain. Below that was the lazarette - the after-guard's pantry, remote from, and fortified against, the hungrier members of her complement.

Between these two extremes, socially, hierarchically and physically, were the petty officers and the apprentices, the 'brassbounders', those officers of the future who were the dogs-bodies of today. Both these groups lived in square white boxes built on the upper deck; built, so to speak, as afterthoughts; boxes which were liable to be swilled and penetrated - and even occasionally uprooted and removed - by the ocean seas that savagely invaded the main deck in heavy weather. For, unlike the slow and tubby galleons and caravels which had first come to the Horn from Europe, bobbing like corks over the roughest seas, 'Figaro' and her sisters, laden with thousands of tons of deadweight and racing along at sometimes three times the galleon's speed, slammed and crashed through the waves, like a half-tide rock going at fourteen knots.

Smack in the middle, where they felt they belonged, was the deck-house of the so-called idlers, the petty officers essential to a sailing ship - the bosun, the cook, the carpenter and the sailmaker. The better to ensure their comfort, their box housed also the galley, so they alone got their food hot; they stood no watches, and enjoyed the unbelievable luxury of 'all night in', even at sea, but they worked long hours, and the cook especially might feel that his was the most thankless of all lots - the serving up of a dull, cheap and rubbishy diet to a crowd of twenty-odd hard cases.

Between the mizzen and jigger masts, just in front of the poop, was the box containing the apprentices. It was grandly known as the half-deck. It was wet, crowded, and as grubby and untidy as six over-worked and underfed young brassbounders could make it. It was far enough aft to be under the stern eye of their chief enemy the Mate, and its closeness to the cabins and their stores of unheard-of delicacies made the lads, in their turn, the bane and dread of Isaac Hughes, the captain's steward.

This morning in the half-deck it was as stuffy and damp as usual; the deep-loaded ship, heeling steeply to port, was taking solid seas over her starboard rail which cascaded down the sloping deck in torrents, swilling round the deckhouse in their passage to leeward. The deckhouse door had a high sill or coaming to it, but every now and then it was not high enough, and a spurt of water came from the bottom of the door. The door-latch was defective, so to prevent it flying open and drenching the inhabitants, a piece of codline fastened its handle to a nearby coat-peg. A shallow lake of dirty water slopped to and fro on the lee side, spreading its skin across half the deck as the ship came upright, running back to lee as a gust made her lean again. The hanging oilskins on the windward bulkhead hung vertically, well away from the bulkhead, and swayed together as 'Figaro' pitched into the steep Pacific seas, eerily co-ordinated in a kind of circular stirring motion.

The starboard watch - Mr Leyshon's watch - of apprentices lay or sat about, making the best of the unusual leisure. John Raven, the senior apprentice, the unchallenged king of the half-deck, was bulky, powerfully built, lolling like a banqueting Roman on one elbow, looking down from his upper bunk disdainfully on the other two, enjoying the status that eighteen months' seniority gave him, throwing his opinions like bones to obedient dogs, not bothering to argue with callow inferiors. Like the others, he had shed only his streaming oilskins, for they all knew that at any moment sail would need taking in, and one of the mates or maybe the bosun would thunderously bang the door and shout 'All hands!' The other two lads sat at the plain deal table, each eating part of a rock-hard biscuit - a Liverpool pan-tile - saved from breakfast; Ieuan Davies, the elder of the two, was from St Davids, and was therefore known to the Welshmen aboard as Ianto Tyddewi. He was dark, with a thin, strong Welsh face and a serious manner; in an otherwise English half-deck he was the persecuted minority, the defender through thick and thin of all things and persons Welsh. Jim Robbins, the baby of the half-deck, seemed half-formed: not yet a man, but with the makings of a strong build; still so unsure of himself that he echoed and reflected too much the opinions of all those he'd met recently. The comfort and softness of his Cotswold home still showed in the fresh, guileless face, chubby despite the ship's grim diet of paupers' junk.

Sitting in their steel cube on the main deck, the lads were alive to every motion of the ship, every sound from the deck, every note of the wind in the rigging. Suddenly, the steady hard pitching motion changed; it was as if the ship, rushing through the head seas, had run straight into a wall of soft yielding rock. They first felt the ship's head falling, falling, dropping sickeningly into nothing, until it met the steep wave with a jolt that stopped the barque dead, that made every plate, beam, frame and rivet in her shudder and tremble. A split second later there was a warning yell from the Mate and a blundering rush of feet outside as the watch on deck leapt for safety into the shrouds and on to the fife-rails. At the same moment the two tin plates that had held the biscuits sprang off the table, bouncing over the fiddles, the small raised slats round the table's edge, and clattering to the deck with a tinny alarm that made the boys catch their breath and look at each other as, outside, a huge sea came over the weather rail and slammed against the thin steel bulkhead. Water dripped from the porthole and spouted freely from the bottom of the door as the solid torrent roared down to leeward.

The sardonic Raven was the first to recover from the common lurch of fear: 'Jesus! That stupid old taffy up there'll drown us all yet. Got too much sail up - going too fast into this sort of sea.'

Ianto's patriotism was too much even for his loyalty to a fellow-sufferer; he felt obliged to defend a fellow-Welshman, even if he was one of their oppressors: 'Oh, too fast now, is it? You're always saying he's an old woman, doesn't crack on enough for you.'

'It's all right cracking on when you're going somewhere. We're just arsing about. Must be about halfway to Tonga by now, I should think.'

'Better than being drowned, back at whatever that place was called where we anchored, isn't it? I heard the Mate telling old Leyshon...'

'Telling him what?'

'Well... you know... Like how the glass had fallen.... How it was going to blow like hell.'

'Telling him in Welsh, I'll bet?'

'Of course. That's natural, isn't it?'

'Oh yes, indeed! Jew-jew, borry-da, yessy-mower and all that! But how do we poor English sods find out what's happening on this hooker, when all the after-guard and half the crowd too go in for this taffy gibberish? Nobody tells us anything.'

Davies was stung by Raven's superior air of chauvinism, and reddened: 'This is a Welsh ship -what the hell do you expect them to speak - Hindoostani? I s'pose you think that if you were in one of them big German barques the Old Man'd give you a translation of all he said?'

'Ah, but surely that's not quite the point?' said young Robbins, venturing to support his senior: 'That's a different situation, Taff, because this Old Man, old Jake, could easily...'

He was stopped by a mighty kick at the door and a sharp cry of 'Tins!' Instantly, all three leapt to their feet. Raven snatched the loop of codline from the peg and flung the door open. Perkins, the senior port watch apprentice, sprang over the coaming into the deckhouse and the door was slammed behind him. He was holding the skirt of his oilskin up to his waist, and when he let go of it, half-a-dozen large cans fell to the deck. The boys off-watch snatched them up without a word and spirited them out of sight with a desperate, frenzied speed, which yet took the form of a smooth, well-practised routine. Two tins went into spare sea-boots, to be covered by evil-smelling thick socks; two were thrust into a hole in the casing of the wash-bowls, two were stuffed into the pockets of the swinging oilskins. In ten seconds the boys were, like conscientiously rehearsing actors, back in precisely the same leisurely attitude as before - Raven in his bunk, Davies and Robbins at the table, having retrieved their biscuits from the filthy wet deck. Perkins was dragging a grubby towel from his locker to wrap round his neck.

Raven twitched his head towards the door; he had caught the sound of a quick footstep outside; he nodded to the others. The door burst open, as they knew it would, to reveal the wet and enraged shirt-sleeved figure of Isaac Hughes the steward. He was not dressed for the upper deck, and had clearly collected a good deal of spray, rain and solid water in his dash from the poop, but there was triumph in his face; for this time he had really caught one of those God-damned brass-bounders at it!

Raven rapidly improvised a revision of a seamanship lesson: 'Worm and parcel with the lay, and serve the rope the other way. That's the rhyme you need to remember when you're – Why, Isaac, you're wet through! Just coming to see us! To what do we owe this overwhelming pleasure?'

The steward ignored him: 'Ah! I though I'd find you in here, mister bloody Perkins!'

'Aye, aye, I'm here. I live here, remember. Mister Evans lets us come in for a dry towel, as long as we're quick.'

'Never mind no bloody towel! You know well enough what I means. I means food. *Food!* The bloody captain's food you lot keep on pinching.'

Raven said, in a hurt manner that conveyed deep moral offence: 'You know, Isaac, we really can't have this sort of language in here! We're all young, and not used to it.'

Ianto, at the table, his mouth full of dry biscuit, spluttered an innocent protest: 'Aw, come on now, Isaac *bach*,… *Chwara' teg*, it's only a bit of biscuit, and I saved it from breakfast. I got a right to eat it. It's been down on the deck in the slop, but if you really want it back…'

'Not that food, *twpsyn!* Nobody calls ship's biscuit "food". *He* knows what I mean.' He pointed a finger that trembled with his righteous wrath, at Perkins. 'I means the food he's got in his pockets. In his oilskin… Tins and tins of best salmon.'

Perkins held up his empty hands: 'What tins, Isaac? I've got no tins. Search me if you like.'

'Aye, and I bloody will, too. And after that we'll see what the Mate says. He'll have you up on that royal yard for a month, you thieving young bugger. Now then…'

He went up to Perkins and frisked him. They stood close together swaying to the ship's motion, the young apprentice with his sullen good looks standing half a head taller than the steward. The thin scummy water washed over the steward's polished shoes; the silence was tense. As the man's hands patted him Perkins tittered and squealed coquettishly: 'Hey, steady on, that tickles! Oops! How could I possibly put anything *there*, man? Get your horrible hands away, Isaac. Do you know, boys – I reckon Isaac here is a lecherous old man. He fancies me, and he's been at sea so long he just invents this sort of thing so as to have a good feel. Did you see where he was looking just now?'

Hughes went a dull red with anger and embarrassment. Before God he could swear he had never had such a thought in his life, though you couldn't be at sea all your life without knowing about the sin of Sodom. 'I'll see you suffer for this, you dirty-minded little swine, when I find them tins of salmon. I'm three short at least, and I heard you pick them up when my back was turned.'

'You can't count, that's your trouble. Anyway, what is this salmon you're talking about?'

'All right then, you ain't got them on you. You're all in this - the whole damn lot of you.' He swung round: 'I'm going to search this damn pigsty of yours, and when I find them...' He went over to an empty bunk: 'This your berth?' Perkins nodded. Hughes scrabbled away furiously, not really hoping now to find anything, but set on some sort of revenge. He tossed all the blankets behind him onto the swilling floor, ignoring Perkins' protests. He was about to follow those with the thin biscuit mattress when Waters, another port watch apprentice, burst in: 'Hey, steward! The Old Man's hollering for coffee, and he doesn't half sound waxy. I'd get a wriggle on if I were you.'

Swearing low and viciously, the small, harassed and mystified steward rushed out. That young sod must have had those tins - but he hadn't. And yet he'd been right behind him into the half-deck; even those young devils couldn't have stowed them out of sight, not in that time... Could they? My God, when the Old Man's supplies ran out... And if old Jacob just suspected that his stuff had been pinched, he'd get such a bollocking off him... Might even stop some of his pay... Black eye as well, like enough, the man was so irascible.

The half-deck erupted into laughter as soon as he was clear, but Ianto shook his head: 'Damn, but that was close, Perky - too damn close. We didn't get a chance to stow them properly. He'd have found them in a minute or two.'

'Yes, good job the Old Man shouted for coffee when he did,' said Robbins naively.

'Jesus, Robbins, you are so bloody green,' said Raven. 'Why has the company started taking idiots on as brassbounders?'

'Why? What did...?' said Robbins, red with confusion.

'You've got a hell of a lot to learn, sonny,' said Waters, who was a good eleven months older. 'Still wet behind the ears, you are. The Old Man didn't shout for anything - I just made that up. I thought things might be getting a bit tricky in here.'

'But what about when Isaac gets up on the poop with the coffee? Then he'll find out.'

'My God, where do they find people like you, Robbins? Don't you think old Jake has got plenty on his mind at the moment? If Isaac comes running up with coffee he'll just take it and drink it - probably won't even know he's drinking it. Good God, Isaac isn't likely to ask if he ordered coffee, is he? He knows well enough he'd get Jake's boot up his arse if he asked questions like that ...'

'All right,' said Raven, magisterially, 'that's enough from you two. Clear off on deck now, or we'll have the Mate in here after you, and then you'll get his boot up your arses. How did you get the tins, by the way?'

'Cockroach.'

'Right. Remember then, everybody: keep off the cockroach dodge for a bit.'

Perkins and Waters forced their way out into the wild watery gloom of the deck. Robbins said: 'Cockroach dodge – what's that?'

'I know you're only the nipper here, Robbins,' said Raven, 'but try not to bother us with such utterly wet questions.'

'Oh, come on now, Raven,' said Ianto, ever the friend of the oppressed. 'Fair play, he doesn't know what it is - you didn't know once. So if he don't know, how can he lay off it? Tell you what it is, boy: you go down the galley and scull round a bit, and then, when the doctor - you know the cook – when he's not watching, you pick up a nice big cockroach - no shortage of them in there, see. Only it's no good if the doctor sees you, cos he and Isaac are mates. Right then, you stick it in your pocket and later on, if you're mopping the deck down aft, round the captain's store-room, you drop your horrible cockroach down on the deck near Isaac...'

Raven interrupted: 'Yes, and then you yell blue murder and tell old Isaac he'd better catch it before the Old Man sees it near his store...'

'Um...yes...?' Robbins was still doubtful.

'Well, you cissy-faced willy wet-leg, if you can't pinch a few tins while Isaac's flapping about catching the bug, then you're even more useless than you look. Got it?'

But before the callow nipper could reply there was a crash at the door and a stern summons that all obeyed, a cry which brought them out of their cosy schoolboy world of diddling the steward and back to reality: 'ALL HANDS - IN FORESAIL!' They rammed their feet into sea-boots, dragged on oilskins, and made fast their 'soul-and-body' lashings - the pieces of thick twine around waist, wrist and ankle that made their oilskins at least a little more watertight. Each of them knew that for the next hour or two he would be working to the point of exhaustion on a hideously precarious perch; but young creatures can adjust to almost anything if they have to: furling the foresail in a savage norther or pinching tins from the steward's pantry - it was all part of the same life at sea that they had signed on for. One job seemed pretty much as dangerous as the other. Without a thought they stepped out into the mad world of wind, water, wood, steel and rope - especially wind.

As they clawed their way for'ard, hanging on as the ship plunged and reared, the foc'sle door opened and the starboard watch of seamen came out. The Mate was already among the web of ropes behind the foremast. They could scarcely hear his high bellow above the howl of the wind in the stays and the crash of the seas. 'Fores'l sheets! Buntlines and clewlines!'

'Figaro's' high graceful spires of sail had mostly gone already, and only taut, spray-darkened strips were now left. Foremast, main and mizzen could each set six sails: lowest of all the huge courses, eighty-seven feet across and thirty-three deep - nearly three thousand square feet of heavy canvas, well-nigh as stiff as metal; above this the two topsails, always the last sails to come in dirty weather; above these the good weather sails, the two topgallants and the royal. The Mate had been keeping his watch busy since clearing the land, so that only the lower topsails and the fore-course (or foresail) were left. Now the time had come for all hands to tackle this great brute. It was an all-hands job in this weather.

Each sail could be partly controlled from the deck: the sheets held down the bottom corners, so first these must be slacked off. Then, by means of the clewlines, these corners could be hauled up to the yard above, and the buntlines did the same for the middle of the sail. All these ropes, for all the six sails, together with many more, were led by blocks down the masts to the fife-rails, where they were belayed with figure-of-eight turns on to stout wooden pins. At the foot of each mast, then, a tidy jungle of ropes large and small, each with a vital purpose, each with its rightful place, each to be known and remembered, even in dark and storm.

Under the tough old Mate's direction, the men and boys went methodically from one pin to another, finding the right rope among dozens of others cleated near, each time heaving in fierce unison to the tune of breathless cries of 'O-i-O!' or 'O break her!' until they had transformed the foresail from a lovely curved oblong distended by the wind to a great unhandy, looped-up sausage of canvas, cracking and thundering in the gale enough to shake the whole mast.

With sail reduced to the topsails, the spanker and a few staysails, 'Figaro' now met and climbed the seas more easily, not dashing at them, but yielding as they came endlessly marching at her starboard bow out of the gloomy wrack to the north. Now only the breaking tops streamed over the bulwark and down the sloping decks. But for the boys and men the worst was to come. Evans blew a shrill blast on his whistle and bawled: 'Aloft and furl it!' He, the carpenter and old Jac Davies the sailmaker stayed on deck to help those on the yard by hauling on clewline or buntline as needed; and God knows they were entitled to stay, all of them; they were old men and had gone aloft times without number, times when it had been even worse than this.

All the rest must scramble into the weather shrouds, and climb the rope ladders or ratlines stretched between the huge wire stays, the fierce wind pressing their bodies almost against the wires, until they reached the height of the foreyard where, one after another, they had to make the fearful step (or even, if they were short, the leap) from the ratline to the footrope slung under the tubular steel yard. From now on, their sole means of staying alive was to stand or move on that wire, the chest and stomach up against the yard, the hands (or, when working, the hand) on the metal bar, called the jackstay, that ran along the top of the yard. 'One hand for yourself, one for the ship' was the old foc'sle saying, but when things got difficult enough the ship had to have both, or you'd be up there all night. To a newcomer, furling a sail was a fearful job even in harbour on a calm day; in a storm, in freezing weather, in darkness - worse still, in all three together - it was literally a task for heroes. For a month of such heroism, provided he survived it, the thrifty owners were prepared to pay a man the resounding sum of two pounds, fifteen shillings.

The boys mingled with the men. No-one gave any orders, for all knew what was to be done, and how. For a good hour they fought that sail; they took half of it at a time. Grappling at the board-stiff fabric, fingernails broken, finger-ends bleeding, they hauled it bit by bit, fold by fold on to the top of the yard, and there they pinned it with their bodies. They worked as one up there on that dreadful swaying, reeling, shaking, wind-battered perch, all grabbing a piece of the monstrous balloon, and at a wild cry from the bosun, all hauling together to deflate the bag; their spirits rose as, with each fold, the task grew easier. Sometimes, at the onset of a vicious squall, when the bosun heard - as it were out of the corner of his ear - the pitch of the wind's voice in the stays rising to a sharp edge of madness, then he would yell: 'Hang on, boys!' and then they would stop gathering sail and hold grimly on to what they'd got, the yard and the wire they stood on canting ever more steeply to leeward, until the yard-arm brushed the passing wave-tops in the smother of foam to port.

Away down aft on the poop, the Old Man had got the port watch's two best ABs on the great double wheel, and lent them his own oak-like strength in the squalls, for if the ship's head were to fly up into the wind so that the topsails spilt their wind and flapped - well in this norther they would flap hard enough to shake the yards, to shake every mother's son off the foreyard, to be drowned in the sea or smashed to bits on the deck. It had happened before, often enough - a moment's carelessness or neglect would do it. Staring through the dark midday murk of the norther, Roberts watched the pointing bowsprit, watched the straining topsails, watched the little ant-like figures on the yard with his very soul, and at the least sign of a swoop to windward he would growl: 'Meet her, meet her! Full and by, damn your souls, full and by!'

For some of the men on the yard, the last stage of the battle was the most dangerous. Now that the sail was gathered - spotted now here and there with the blood from torn fingers - it must be secured by the gaskets, the ropes placed every few feet along the yard for that purpose. Jim Robbins found himself by a gasket, so while the men on either side held the bunched sail, he had to lower his body to the level of the footrope (one hand for the ship, one for yourself) to pass the gasket under the sail and up the other side. He had done it before, but it was not a nice moment, with the rope wet and stiff, his hands numb with cold, the wind screaming by and tugging at his bulky, clumsy oilskins, and the AB beside him cursing steadily: 'Come on, you bloody brassbound monkey, you, for Christ's sake get it under! What use are you?' At long last it was done, the sail furled tightly on top of the yard, held in by the gaskets so that the wind could not finger and pry and force the giant oblong of canvas open again. It wasn't a neat job - not a furl to show going up Thames or Mersey - but it was good and tight, the sail tamed down from a raging, flogging, man-killing demon to a long sodden bunch of cloth. It would do until it could be furled properly, Bristol-fashion.

The men were cramped and weary as they shuffled slowly in along the foot-rope towards the security of the mast, then down the ratlines to the deck. They were out of training, for they'd had nothing like this to do since the Horn, weeks ago. All felt they'd earned a little rest, a little while on the firm deck, sheltering from the wind's rage. Must be twelve noon by now - eight bells - time for dinner and a smoke below for the port watch. In terms of determination and courage shown they had each done enough to earn a medal in any army or navy in the world, but all they wanted - all the hundreds of Frenchmen, Germans, Britons, Swedes, Finns and Yankees who served in sail ever wanted - was a belly-full of dinner and time for a kip afterwards.

There was a bellow from Roberts to the mate. A knot of hands going forward to their refuge in the foc'sle stopped abruptly, and Billy John Ffynnongroes groaned: *'Iesu mawr!* What does the old bastard want now?' They had no need to speculate long, for there was a blast from the Mate's whistle and his high cracked voice yelled: 'In all stays'ls, brail up the spanker!' Even the fore-and-aft sails were coming in to ease her, for the savage wind was still rising.

'I never seen nothing like this in all my fuckin' days,' said Billy as he and old Curly Kellock AB strained at the downhaul of a stay-sail. 'Why don't he take her back to Penarth while he's at it? I never seen the like...'

'Don't know, Bill,' grunted the other, between heaves. 'Look at them seas going by. They'll be smack onshore back at Kalaty Bono there. You fancy riding to an anchor in this? P'raps the old boy's right after all.'

4

Up to windward, it was as if you looked at the end of Creation - at the frontier of blind Chaos. The sky - the air itself, so it seemed - was a lowering grey-brown, and so solid and thick that the eye could not penetrate more than a few hundred yards before vision was lost in that dreadful backcloth of dark vapour, spume and spray. Giant waves, approaching shoal water, began to rear their crests steeply, so that they formed into long parallels of dirty sliding wool; the air was so thick that only two or three of those great lines of combers could be seen at any one time, rolling in an endless succession out of the nothingness to the north-west, like the ranks of an army fanatically devoted to the one cause they knew - that of wiping every ship that floated from the face of the earth, of finally punishing the impertinence of all the ships and sailors that had ever presumed to travel, to trade, to explore on the sea's surface. And especially to punish the temerity of those who, like the master of the 'Birkdale', trusted to hooks and chains to defy the open waters of the Pacific; who anchored, who even loaded and unloaded their ships, trapped between a mighty ocean and the barren rocky shore of a sub-continent - like a fly taking his rest on the nose of a giant.

The men of the 'Birkdale' had long forgotten about meals, watches and the normally rock-like structure of ship's routine. With his handful of officers, old men and boys, Simon Grant sheltered behind the midship deckhouse by the door of the galley. Over their heads, streaks of pungent coal-smoke were snatched by the gale from the galley-funnel to be lost at once among the filthy rags of black vapour that rushed overhead. But there was comfort in the familiar warm greasy fumes that wafted by as the doctor within prepared them a hot dinner of stewed salt pork, hashed up with ground biscuit and served - as a special treat - with a solid dollop of dried peas boiled to a yellowy-greeny mush.

When it was ready, the cook cautiously opened the top half-door of the galley and silently handed out the tin plates with the food roughly sloshed on; to the mates first, then to his fellow idlers, Bosun and Sails, and last to the brassbounders, as the lowest form of life aboard, and as his mortal enemies, for 'Birkdale's' apprentices thieved as cunningly, persistently and ruthlessly as did 'Figaro's'. Grant looked with some distaste at the cheap, battered enamel plate pocked with round black chip-marks. No clean mess-room china today! Hadn't eaten off a plate like this since - when? - Years ago, in the half-deck of the old 'Thetis'.

'Eat up, men,' he said. 'Get a lining in your guts. Don't know when we'll - Jesus!' He broke off as the tormented barque's bow was thrown up by a wave so violently that their feet seemed to leave the deck. A second later, the next blue-grey glassy wall hit the descending bow so hard that every plate and rivet shook and her anchor-cable sprang taut as a fiddle-string. It felt as if a giant had casually, brutally, tweaked her forward, and they all swayed and blundered against the galley bulkhead. The old hands looked quickly at each other with glances that said: 'She'll never stand it.'

Grant thumped his fist on the galley door: 'Riley! Grab these plates and keep them warm. We'll come back and finish later.' He turned to his scanty crew: 'Get the spring up from the for'ard tween-deck, bosun. The boys will help you. And Sails, Mister Metcalfe, Mr Dunn, stand by the windlass.'

The petty officers looked at each other in resigned disgust. Why give us a bloody meal, the look said, if we don't get no bloody chance to eat it? The spring can wait ten minutes, surely? If there'd been the usual foc'sle crowd of Liverpool Irish and sullen Russian Finns to back them, there'd have been a good growl or two, and Mr Grant would have needed some of his well-known artistry with boot and fist; but as it was, Bosun and Sails saw the murder in his eye as they hung back. That Grant was a bucko all right, a holy terror. One night, perhaps, ashore, in some dark alley among the knocking-shops of Antofagasta or Cardiff, Valparaiso or Wapping - some time - they'd get even with him. But not now; they'd seen a few buckos in their day, but this one - there was something a bit extra dangerous about him: the way them eyes, like bright-blue boot-buttons, seemed to stare right through you, but when you looked at them you could read nothing about what he was thinking. And the way he seemed to be holding back all the time, holding himself in, like... as if there was someone even worse hidden inside, who couldn't ever be let out. But he knew his work all right, and he'd be first up on a yard in a blow if that were needed. They grumbled in their beards, but wiped their mouths and handed their plates back in sullen silence.

The spring was a huge towing hawser of coir - coconut fibre rope, thick as a man's thigh and full of give and stretch. Getting it up on deck was a hard job for such a weak party. All of them, however, had got cold just standing about, and the labour was welcome. The bo-sun rigged up a block and tackle to hoist the end of the rope up on deck, the boys tailed on to the fall and heaved in unison to the old man's shouts: 'Two-six HUPP! Two-six HEAVY! Two-six HA-HOY!' A foot at a time, they hauled the monstrous python of grass rope up from the hold and along the deck to the for'ard end of the main deck, where the after-end of the raised foc'sle sheltered them. As they worked, the barque's bow repeatedly dived into near-vertical waves, each time striking with a booming thud which sent solid showers of spray clean over the foc'sle to patter on their oilskins. Several times some or all of them lost their footing at the shocks, and the Bosun raised his voice in curses: 'Stand up, ye clumsy young sojers! Stand up and haul, damn ye!' One day these boys would be officers, and he might have to obey them, but not yet.

They found the mates in under the shadow of the foc'sle, look-ing gloomily at the huge anchor windlass. It stood in the space between the two houses where most of the crowd lived, a great horizontal bar-rel, geared powerfully to the capstan above and controlled by screw-on brakes. The anchor-cables, taut as bowstrings, led in from the hawse-pipes, over special toothed drums called gypsies, and down the navel-pipe to the cable locker beneath. Anyone visiting the ship in the still waters of a dock would say the windlass was three times as big and strong as it needed to be; today, now that they were close, the boys could see why the mates looked grim: the windlass was taking all the strain of those savage snatches, and it was clear that it wouldn't do so much longer. Each jerk at the cable shook the massive machine as if it were a gim-crack toy. Flakes of rust danced up, and brakes groaned. Something had to give; before long, if the anchors didn't drag or the cables part, the windlass would be smashed to bits.

The officers spoke quietly, for it was as well if the apprentices didn't hear too much. Grant said: 'You've got seventy-five fathoms out on each, Mr Metcalfe?'

"Yes. There's another twenty-five fathoms on each in the locker, isn't there?'

'Aye, mister, but I daren't let the brake off now to pay it out. Once it starts running...'

'Aye, aye. What about the cable-ends - the inboard ends? How are they fastened, if it comes to that - if the windlass goes?'

'God knows. Captain McMasters should know too, only ...' he shot the Second a meaning glance: 'only he isn't here. He stood by her when she was being built, I believe. I've never been aboard when she was docked, so I've never seen all the cable hoisted out.'

'It should be securely shackled to the keel itself.'

'Should be, aye, should be. But we all know what yards are, and we know what yard foremen are, some of them. May be just seized on with a trashy bit of wire; may not be fastened on at all, for all I know. I can't risk it, not being sure. Come on, let's do what we can - get the spring on her.'

Heaving, grunting, sweating in the cold spray, officers and men lashed the ends of the spring hawser to the chain cable, then laboriously hauled the middle of it - the bight of the rope - to the foot of the foremast, a massive tube of steel going right down to the keel - and made it well fast there. That, surely, would hold anything till hell froze!

'That'll do, men,' said Grant. 'You can lay aft for your hash again. We've done all we can.' The Second came and stood beside him as the rest scampered off aft, and together they watched in silence, listened to the fearful cacophony, and felt in their own bodies the appalling stresses that the ship and its ground tackle were taking. Every wave now struck with the same dull smothered boom, and every boom was followed by the slashing rattle of spray on the main-deck; worse still, she was now yawing this way and that, sheering to and fro almost as if sailing, propelled by the force of the wind on her high empty sides. If only she had a cargo under hatches! Looking out from their shelter down the long sweep of her deck, they could see nothing of the land - there was too much spray for that, but now and then they caught glimpses of other ships at anchor, and could see how much the 'Birkdale' was swinging. The waves, as they passed astern, turned into giant, smooth, whale-backed hills of water, racing towards the shore, throwing up the bows of the anchored ships - their fellow-sufferers - until perhaps a third of their length came clear out of the water, the bottoms gleaming a dull red in the flying murk. Grant shook his head: 'We've done what we can, mister, but I doubt it's enough. She'll never stand it. Neither will the others. This anchorage will be swept bare by tomorrow morning... Swept bare.'

Once the huge rope had been made fast to the mast, Grant had released the windlass brakes a fraction, and with a sudden grate and clank the chains round the barrels had eased out, so that now the ropes had the strain - a strain which made them creak and groan, visibly stretching and thinning under the appalling wrenches. Those ropes had at least a bit of elasticity in them; now there was at least a bit of 'give' when the ship took those fearful blows. Not much, but some.

Metcalfe tilted his head back and stared aloft. The yards had been braced round as sharply as possible to cut down the windage, but every wire, rope, mast and spar sang in the wind; the bigger wires - shrouds, backstays, forestays - drumming and droning a bass note, the small buntlines, clewlines and down-hauls screaming a rising and falling banshee wail. 'My father was in the Blackwall frigates, years ago,' he said. 'He told me once that in his day, if they were at anchor in this sort of blow, they used to lower every yard they had to the deck. Even the upper masts used to come down too - topmasts and t'gallants... That was the way of it then.'

'Aye, but what use is that to us, mister? You're talking about little wooden hookers with crews twice what we've got - or had; rather, but with spars like ours, and the crews you get today? That'd be a long dockyard job nowadays.'

'What, then? What's to be done?'

Grant gave a short bitter laugh: 'Pray, mister, that's about all. And you'd better do it, not me. Him up there – He's not likely to listen to me, I shouldn't think - not if He was watching me upstairs at Rosita's last Friday night. Rosita lets you have two whores at a time if you've got the right equipment and the money and she likes you.'

Metcalfe looked at him seriously, solicitously: 'You may pray, nevertheless. He is not a petty God. Your sins grieve Him, but do not shut you out from His mercies. He listens to anyone... to everyone who speaks to him with a full heart.'

Grant was taken aback momentarily by Metcalfe's earnest sincerity, but soon recovered his customary cynicism: 'Maybe, maybe, though I doubt He'd think I was worth bothering with. You go in for that sort of thing, though, don't you? He might decide to take a stroll on the water for you - though he'd get deucedly wet in this weather.'

'He saves all, even those who mock him,' said Metcalfe, reddening with anger. 'He told his disciples ...'

'Unless...' Grant was now looking aloft with the distant look of one weighing up fearful decisions, a seaman again, not a scoffing Voltaire. 'Unless, we make up His mind for Him... Cut and run.'

The Second looked round sharply, wrenched from his spirituality back into the harsh professional world: 'Cut and run? Slip the anchors? But she'd be on the rocks in half an hour, pounded to bits. Be lucky if any of us survived.'

'Exactly. That is just what will happen, in my judgement, if we do nothing. Sooner or later she'll drag or part her cables; the wonder is she hasn't done it already. Now then, the wind's nor-nor-west, isn't it? So if - or when - the cables part, we shall drift broadside-on through the anchorage on to the rocks along the south shore of the bay... Helpless... Likely enough we'd drift down on top of other ships at anchor, and take them with us. But...' he paused to allow his thoughts to form cogently, 'but if we slipped the cables and got some sail on her...'

'Sail?' said Metcalfe incredulously. '*Sail* - in this weather?'

'Hold on, mister. I don't mean much sail, I mean a few staysails, enough to give us steerage-way. Then at least we'd be able to pick our spot - and - yes, that's it – we'd run her ashore bow-first, not drift broadside-on. We might be able to point her up to that sandy bit of beach halfway round the bay. No rocks there at all.'

'No, but that's where all the nitrate lighters are moored. She'd smash up the lot.'

'Lighters! What do I care about lighters? No-one's aboard them today, for certain. This hooker's made of quarter-inch steel plates, mister; she'll crash her way through those tin boxes and hardly spoil her paintwork. Forget about them. Now if I could put her ashore there we'd walk off at low water... *Walk off!* And later, with decent weather and a good tide, the ship could be towed off.'

Metcalfe looked at him and shook his head slightly, but said no more. There was something about the mere fact of command that set a man apart from others: nothing to do with rank or character, just command - the duty of deciding between appalling alternatives, the duty of judging, and of answering for that judgement afterwards, at the Owners' offices, or a Board of Inquiry, or even at the Judgement Seat itself. He sensed that, in Grant's present agony of mind, it was unfair to argue or carp at his decisions. They were hard enough to make anyway. Clad in black streaming oilskins, Grant was stocky, as fixed as a rock, except that he swayed instinctively as the ship shuddered, flinched, rose in torment at the belabouring of the sea. Metcalfe saw him look swiftly round - at the howling spars, the racing clouds, the seas that surged remorselessly past, at the tortured ropes holding the cables - and recognized it at once as a captain's look, as every captain's look: swift, piercing, professional, and in a way unseeing, in that it didn't just take in the immediate phenomena it saw, but looked through them into the probable future. And insofar as Grant could change things, it was a future he, to some extent, controlled. Grant's eyes saw things his could not see, for as yet the things didn't exist. The Mate stroked a bristled chin with one thick-fingered red hand; some decision was forming behind those blank, very bright blue eyes. 'What's the time?' said Grant suddenly.

Metcalfe started; he'd forgotten about time. 'Just gone half-past-twelve, sir,' he said. He'd never called Grant 'sir' before.

'Plenty more hours of daylight, such as it is. High water's at two. H'm... Hang on for a while, then.' His manner suddenly became brisk. 'Very well: when the hands have finished dinner, put buoys and buoy-ropes on both cables.' It was an ordinary thrifty seamanlike thing to do, but Grant couldn't suppress the bitter thought that once that was done, the precious Owners would be able to recover their precious new cables and anchors, even if he and his men had been smashed to a sodden bloody pulp in the surf. Ground-tackle cost money, men didn't.

Metcalfe said tensely: 'You're not going to slip now?'

'Of course not. Use a bit of sense, man: not much point in putting her on the beach on a rising tide, is there? She'd be pounded for hours. She'll get the very devil of a hammering even on the ebb, but that can't be helped. Very well, mister, I'll have my hash and then turn in for a spell. You and Dunn share anchor watches. Call me at once if there's any change. And don't forget those prayers, either.'

Without waiting for any comment or question he strode off aft, every inch a captain. Metcalfe - not a quick thinker at the best of times - at last perceived the truth: yesterday they had been colleagues, near-equals; now there was, for the time being anyway, a gulf fixed between them. And that last bit about the prayers: was that his usual jibe, or had he been serious? He was such a sardonic devil, it was hard to say.

*　　*　　*

Fifty miles away, in the relative safety of deep water, the barque 'Figaro' pitched sickeningly, but at least steadily, into the huge seas.

She was close-hauled on the starboard tack, heading out into the Pacific, forging slowly ahead as close to the wind as she would go, her sails down to the three lower topsails, the heavy weather rig, three narrow horizontal strips of canvas as stiff as boards, their lower corners held by chains, for no rope was strong enough. Out here the seas might be larger than at Caleta Buena, but they were not so steep, and a ship under way had a freedom to yield to them, to respond to their blows like a live thing, not like a dead passive hulk at anchor.

Jacob Roberts felt things were going well enough. He was satisfied that he'd made the correct decision – hadn't been overawed by the foc'sle crowd and their stupid nonsense. He stirred his stiff arms and legs, and realized how tightly, how unnecessarily tightly, he had been gripping the for'ard rail of the poop; he realized that he had scarcely moved a muscle for the last three hours - not since he'd had that coffee that Isaac Hughes had suddenly appeared with - though he didn't remember ordering it. Funny, that... He had stood in that captain's spot, the front weather corner of the poop, the spray streaming from his black oilskins, as immobile and apparently unfeeling as some bull seal, ignoring the wind, the cold, the lashing spray. Yes, maybe he'd been right, but all the same his was not a good plight to be in, and his treacherous fears stabbed at his composure from within.

For the ship was plunging into a murk of nothingness; he could scarcely see a ship's length ahead, sometimes scarcely to the bowsprit-end. What might be beyond that pointing finger - that was his gnawing worry. There was no land or offshore rocks for a thousand miles, but there might be a ship; it wasn't at all probable, but there might be. There might be a dismasted hulk rolling her hatches under just out of sight there, waiting like a set trap, or worse, a homeward-bounder, a ship from up the coast - from the Peruvian guano islands, - tearing along, revelling in the gale from astern, rolling and yawing her way under topsails and foresail, reeling off the miles to the Horn at maybe fifteen knots. The foolish, disembodied thought had become a part of his mind, a waking nightmare. Sometimes he could almost see her, the ship of his nightmare, could fancy he heard the thunderous roll of water under her steel bow. 'She'd cut us in half - like a knife' he whispered secretly. 'My God, who'd be a bloody sailor, especially a master?' A thought like that had only to slip quietly into the mind - be put there perhaps by Satan to torture you - and straightaway you heard voices in the wind, and every misty glimpse of foam to windward looked like the 'bone in her teeth', the rolling bow-wave, of a big wind-jammer tearing along. *Duw, Duw,* these lawyers, bankers, grocers, safe in their warm offices and shops all the week, tight and snug in their pews on a Sunday or lording it as deacons on the *Siat Fawr*, tucked up nicely at night, pawing and fumbling their comfy willing wives when-ever they pleased – *Iesu Mawr*, they had the best of it! Then, in shame, his solid gritty self spoke up: Listen, boy, don't bloody whine! Put up with it, isn't it? You signed on, you take John Powell's money, you never got yourself a shop or a business, so it's no good belly-aching now. Keep a damn good look-out and leave the rest to the Almighty. No-one's safe, really; after all, Roscoe Hughes Bank dropped down squint dead in Fishguard High Street last summer with the apoplexy and he was only forty-three.

He half-turned and looked over his left shoulder towards the cluster of men by the wheel: the tall gaunt Leyshon, who had taken over the deck at eight bells - twelve noon - and the two seamen at the wheel - for in this weather it took two to master its brutal kicks; every blow delivered by the seas upon the massive rudder was transmitted by the steering chains to the wheel itself, and thence to the man at the wheel in the shape of a wrench that could break his arm or fling him clean up into the air. He beckoned the second mate over to him and bellowed in his ear: 'Getting too far out. Wind might drop. Going to wear ship. Call all hands, mister.'

In good weather, under all plain sail, 'Figaro' would swing handily enough from one tack to the other by simply tacking - turning her head through the wind's eye; but with this sea running and so little sail up she'd never come about, so he would have to wear her round - turn away from the wind, run before it for a while to gather speed, then swing her up into it on the port tack. It was a waste of several miles to windward, and it would cause some nasty moments, but there was no choice. These northers could blow themselves out quite suddenly, and he didn't want to be caught miles off-shore in a flat calm and a north-going current. So it was time to put her on the port tack, the inshore one.

Looking forward along the long, heaving, steeply-tilted per-spective of the main deck, he saw Leyshon's messenger going forward to call the crowd. The man stumbled and slithered, running a hand along the life-lines rigged from end to end of that slippery treacherous level, never letting go of those, except once when he jumped up into the ropes around the mainmast as a great comber struck the starboard side and came slopping, seething, roaring, a foot deep over the bulwarks. Jimmy Protheroe from Dinas, to judge by the way he moved; a handy boy, quick on his feet, a good man on a yard-arm, but - like a good many - as dull as a bat in his cups. A few tots of *aguardiente*, the local firewater on the Coast, and he'd fight the whole Chilean Navy - or the British, for that matter. Roberts' face cracked into a near-smile as he imagined the torrent of abuse Protheroe would get (a few boots slung at him too) as he burst into the foc'sle calling all hands. Fair play to the port watch, they'd only just about finished their dinner after a bitter forenoon on deck. They'd have reckoned on a nice warm stuffy after-noon watch in their bunks, snoozing, smoking, farting from all the peas they got, telling each other what a daft bugger the Old Man was, and how much better things had been done in their last ship. The young ones - after all the sea-time – they'd be dreaming dirty, about pulling up the skirts of a few plump Chilean senoritas... Couldn't blame them!

But they weren't a bad crowd; they came out one by one, struggling into oil-skins as they emerged, mustering at the foot of the poop ladder. Not many smiles, of course, and some black looks from under the sou'wester brims. No point in apologizing or explaining; masters were masters, men were men. He just barked: 'Hands to braces. Wear ship,' and they went for'ard again, dispersing to the ropes that would need hauling. The braces - the tackles that controlled the angle of the yards to the wind - would take some shifting today. As was the custom, the mates left the poop and the handling of the ship to the cap-tain, while they went to the braces on the lee side, to pay them out un-der control while the men of their respective watches hauled in to windward. All knew there was a bad time coming, but they lived with some danger or other every day.

'Hard up the helm!' The two helmsmen, sweating in the cold wind, threw their weight on the spokes, fighting the rudder, the wind and the seas. Roberts himself lent a hand. As the wheel turned, so the ship's head paid off from the wind, her motion became easier, she surged ahead through the water, gathering speed. As the speed in-creased, the pressure on the wheel grew until all three men gasped, scarlet in the face with the strain of holding the spokes.

'Square away!' The spars, the masts, the whole ship jerked and shuddered as, with the men hauling and the mates paying out rope, the yards, those strong level branches of the tree-like masts, came square across the ship. No longer fighting the wind, she was being thrust and urged along by its fearsome strength.

'Steady as you go!' Pointing due south, back the way she had come for the last two weeks, 'Figaro' went storming towards the faraway Horn, racing the huge white-sloped seas, rolling till her lower yard-arms brushed the wave-tops. At each sickening roll great fleeces of white sea came lipping over the high bulwarks, and with yells of warning and obscenities the hands leapt up into shrouds, on to fife-rails, up ladders - anywhere to escape that deadly mill-race. And yet the worst was still to come; that would be when she came broadside-on to the sea, just before she turned to face the wind again on the other tack.

Now the Old Man turned himself about to look astern at the overtaking seas, trying to spot a patch of smaller waves to minimize the risk, for when the wheel was put hard down and her headlong violent career was checked, she would be swept by the seas like a half-tide rock. He'd get all hands on the poop for that manoeuvre, but before that there was work to do on the braces, and that would be risky enough. He glanced for'ard again, saw the black, streaming oilskinned figures, saw the white of their faces as they looked at him expectantly from their precarious perches. 'Come on, Jacob *bach*,' the faces seemed to say, 'get it over with, for God's sake.'

He looked astern again, nearly choking on a burning anger at the risks these poor devils took with their lives, at the dangers he was forced to bring upon them, despite all his care; forced, not by Nature or the sea or the wind, but by the blind, penny-pinching avarice of ships' owners. Skinflints, hard-hearted, ignorant skinflint bastards, all these owners. If John Powell had only done what he'd asked many times, and spent a few sovereigns on a set of Jarvis brace-winches, and then mounted them on top of the deckhouses - why, then half-a-dozen men could have trimmed the yards in safety. The Germans had them, and the French, and even the Yankees; Britishers invented something good, but only the damn foreigners had the sense to buy them. If only... if only he could get some of those soft-handed, leather-arsed office people up on a yard-arm, or heaving on a brace-fall up to their waists in freezing Cape Horn water... Ah, what was the use?

His slitted eyes picked out what looked like a run of three or four smaller seas astern; he dismissed his useless indignation brusquely and roared with that speaking-trumpet, double-bass, double-forte voice of his: 'Port tack! Lee braces, haul!'

Now for it! First Mate Evans and the port watch stood ready at the foremast braces, Leyshon and the starboard watch at the main. The mates took the turns off the cleats, and the watch at the other rail tailed on to the fall - the hauling part of the brace. The men hauled hard, with sharp high cries to co-ordinate their efforts on the rope. The less time on deck the better, by Christ, in this weather. Soon the yards on fore and main masts were swung, braced sharply round for the opposite tack. That still left the third mast of square sails, the mizzen; Leyshon got to the mizzen brace first and when Evans arrived he was flinging the coil to the deck. The Mate picked up the bight of the rope to help him pay it out, but Leyshon gave a characteristic scowl: 'Leave it, mun. Doesn't take two. Think I can't do it?' He jerked a horny thumb towards the poop. Evans didn't stop to argue; damned irritable, bad tempered old.....

He made for the port-side poop-ladder and had just reached the top when the high yell came: 'Look out, boys!' Out of the corner of his eye he saw the huge lump of sea roaring over the starboard bulwark, submerging the men, who, floundering, slithering, rolling in the dreadful white cataract, yet hung on, hung on for their very souls to the brace fall; not, of course, because it was their duty to haul it in, but because it was all that stood between them and death. A sea like that could knock a man loose and take him back out over the rail in a matter of seconds, out into three hundred fathoms of cold Pacific water.

As the clump of men slid sprawling on the end of the rope, the deck suddenly canted with a swift treachery, a deliberate malice, as it seemed, and poured tons of solid water towards the gaunt figure of Leyshon at the port rail. Like a good seaman, he had caught a turn of the rope when he saw his men knocked down; he didn't want the yards swinging out of control. But taking that turn took him a second too long; the water slammed him against the steel bulwark, threw him down flat, picked him up like a piece of flotsam, swilled him back across the deck as the ship rolled back to starboard again, and crashed his spine against the barrel of a halyard capstan. Evans saw, for one instant, the old man bent backwards horribly - wrapped, almost, the wrong way - round that stout steel cylinder in the rush of grey-white water. Then the water was gone, pouring out through the clanking freeing-port, and Leyshon, like a black fish stranded by the tide, lay lifeless.

The Mate clattered back down the ladder and reached his old colleague at almost the same time as the captain. (Afterwards, Evans could never believe that a chap with the Old Man's bulk could have moved so fast.) Leyshon's watch came rushing across, their faces set. They'd never liked Leyshon much, but he knew his work, wasn't vindictive or unfair, didn't carry tales back to the Old Man, wasn't nearly as bad as a good many mates they'd met, wasn't, in short, a bad old bastard.

Roberts knew at once it was serious - not just a matter of a bruise or two. You couldn't hit a solid capstan-barrel with your spine like that and get away with it - not at Leyshon's age, anyway. He must take peremptory charge, not only as the nearest thing to a doctor for fifty miles, but also as the ship's master. 'Don't drag him like that, you fools! Don't touch him. Larsen, get the stretcher from the steward. Tell him to get the second's bunk ready for him. Here, you - Billy John and Kellock - stand by to get him on the stretcher when it comes. The rest of you, get back to those braces, damn you. The ship can't sail itself, can it? Mr Evans, port braces, if you please.' He raised his voice to effortless thunder and addressed the men at the wheel, who had been distracted by the crisis: 'Williams and Johansson, you misbegotten sojers, you! If you let her yaw like that, I will kick your stupid arses all the way from that wheel to Valparaiso!'

Billy John and Kellock, the senior AB, exchanged glances as the furious words boomed in the gale. Billy said: 'Miserable old swine! We try to help and do our job right, and get this old boy safe, and all we gets is a bloody good hazing.'

'Don't you take no notice, Billy-boy,' said the old cockney. 'It's only words. Be fair - the Old Man's got things on his mind, like, ain't he?'

5

Simon Grant of the 'Birkdale' unbuttoned his oilskin coat enough to haul out his watch. Two o'clock; high water. The time to decide had arrived. He stepped out a little from the shelter of the foc'sle to look round at the sea, though with the storm unabated there was little enough to be seen. The cold gusts, more furious than ever, made him stagger, and drew blinding tears from his eyes. It was hard to look round properly, hard to think calmly, hard to avoid giving up - crawling into a shelter - any shelter - until the vile cruelty of the norther had gone. He swept his glasses slowly round the arc of vision astern, stopped, as if in surprise, and tracked back again. That French barque, just off the port quarter and only a few cables away – she'd gone! Less than ten minutes ago he'd seen her labouring bow heaving up again for the thousandth time, water streaming from each hawsepipe and freeing-port. Now there was nothing but empty sea.

Metcalfe saw his reaction, and stared at the same spot. 'She's gone - parted her cables or dragged!'

'Yes. Or else we have - dragged, I mean. Dragged down past her. It's possible; let's see.' He went rapidly in under the foc'sle deck into the gloom, stepped over the bar-taut grass rope and clasped the equally taut chain links. Metcalfe could hardly bear to see him there, so absorbed as to seem unaware of his danger; if anything parted now he'd be lucky indeed to survive - would more likely go out of the hawsepipe with the cable in small untidy pieces of flesh and bone.

Like a doctor feeling a limb, Grant laid his hands on each cable in turn; a dragging anchor would send the vibrations of its movement over the seabed up the straining links. The vessel plunged its bow deep into a sea, and a great spout of water came through each hawsepipe, drenching him, but he seemed oblivious. He stood up abruptly and came back to Metcalfe: 'Hard to tell, with the way she's pitching into it, but I think she's starting to go. Heave the deep-sea lead – that'll tell us for sure.'

Metcalfe lowered the fourteen-pound weight into the water over the starboard side, paying out coil after coil of the light rope until he felt the weight reduced; the lead was on the bottom, the rope leading straight down into the yeasty sea. If the rope stayed straight, the anchor was holding; if the rope started to lead forward, it wasn't. The two mates watched the rope with a silent intensity for five minutes, and then their looks met; it was no longer possible to be in any doubt: bit by bit, a little at a time, the barque was going astern; the thin rope tightened and drew unmistakeably ahead. Grant straightened abruptly: 'Right - that decides it. We slip. I would like you, mister, to remember what you have seen, especially the care I have taken to establish that the anchors are not holding. You concur with that verdict, do you not? Good. I can see a time coming when I may need you as a witness. Unless, of course...' He didn't finish the sentence; Metcalfe saw him gulp with the tension of the moment. The Second wanted to kneel and beg him to wait, to put it off, to take refuge in doing nothing. Stay as we are, for the love of Christ, he wanted to yell. Stay as we are, it's safer. But second mates don't act like that, and his professional self told him that Grant was right. But to cast off. ...! To actually let go their tenuous hold on the solid land, to - above all - hoist sail in this cold, furious inferno! To set off as irreversibly as a toboggan down a snow-slope... That took nerve.

Now that he'd made his mind up, Grant's face was a mask of stoicism. He summoned all hands with him into the shelter of the foc'sle, and explained his decision as calmly as if he were mustering them for an ordinary day's work on the cargo. He ended: 'Does everyone understand all that I've said? Once we slip I'll have no time to give more orders. I shall need one other hand at the wheel, I expect.'

Before Metcalfe knew it, he had raised his hand in a quick, embarrassed gesture - embarrassed because he didn't, in his humility, wish to parade himself as a hero, when he knew that any one of the men and boys around him would have gone to the wheel without a second thought if ordered. 'Very well, mister,' Grant nodded, too absorbed to be grateful. 'And remember, once we're under way the rest of you will get back under here and stay here until I tell you to move. If I'm - if anything happens to me or Mr Metcalfe, you will obey Mr Dunn's orders. Now then: stream anchor buoys and buoy-ropes, then hoist all lower staysails, and stand by to sheet them in on the port tack as soon as she's swung. Mr Metcalfe, put the wheel over hard-a-starboard, if you please. I'll join you there shortly. And good luck to you all; you'll need it. Say your prayers, if you're that way inclined.'

The men, so long and aimlessly idle, sprang into purposeful action. The four triangular staysails crept up the stays to which they were linked, like curtains to a rod; but as they rose, the wind furiously attacked them, slatting them to and fro in a thunderous tattoo, the sheet-blocks dancing murderously above the men's heads. Meanwhile the Mate, stifling the fears that turned his belly to water, put the winch out of gear, unscrewed the cable-holder's brakes to the full, took up an axe, and with a few swift blows severed the stout springs.

Even he was staggered by the resultant din and chaos: hideous noise and an extreme violence of movement filled the windlass room. From each cable-locker below, fathoms of heavy, rusty chain came roaring and clattering up the navel-pipe, hurled itself over the madly-spinning gipsy-winch and disappeared out of the hawse-pipe. The air was full of leaping flakes of rust and sparks; Grant had run back a few paces clear, and was glad he had when he saw the wicked flailing of the cable-ends as they flew over the winch. The end of the port cable caught round the stout brake-wheel and casually twitched it off with a shriek of metal. He caught a brief glimpse of some rusty wire round the end links; ah, so the cable hadn't been properly fastened to the keel; with McMasters as captain that was to be expected. Then there was a sudden shocking silence and the ship's motion became easier as she began to drift with the seas, no longer fighting them.

But there was no time for any respite. Now it was time to sail her - and God help them all! There'd be no second chance if he'd made a mistake. As he ran aft he was pleased to feel the furious wind coming at him over the port bulwark; that meant she'd started to move astern and the rudder was causing her bow to pay off towards the shore. A few seconds later he was with Metcalfe at the wheel, feeling again the full force of the norther. He glanced at the compass in its brass binnacle, and was glad to see the ship's head moving slowly eastward. He stabbed a finger at the compass, looked at Metcalfe, nodded and grinned. He was glad to see an answering smile; a dull stick, old Metcalfe, with his pi-jaw and his soft-hearted way with the crowd, but he'd got guts and backbone all right, unlike their superior, that miserable canting hypocritical old bastard McMasters.

He bawled 'Midships!' and he and the Second laboured, one on each side of the six-foot wheel, to bring the rudder back straight. With a succession of deep thunderous booms the staysails filled, their sheets creaked and stretched with the strain, and the sails began their task of moving the great slab-sided clumsy hulk through the water. Grant crossed the deck quickly to the lee rail and looked down into the wild frothy chaos overside. Yes, she was beginning to move ahead very slowly, but it wouldn't do - she was swinging too fast down-wind and there was too little way on her for the rudder to grip. He yelled into the wind: 'Mister Dunn! Topmast stays'ls!' and saw the scruffy, lion-hearted apprentices scampering up the shrouds to cast off the gaskets securing the sails.

With her sail area now doubled, the 'Birkdale' began at last to feel like a ship, rising and falling to the beam seas, but checked from rolling too wickedly by the bellying sails. Though he could see little through the cloud and flying spray, Grant could feel that the wheel was alive, the ship was moving, responsive. He was soon able to steer a rough course by compass; twice he and Metcalfe had to haul hastily at the wheel when, suddenly, anchored ships loomed up ahead. Each time they put the helm up and drove close under the ships' counters; on both poops they saw oilskinned figures pointing, waving, staring white-faced at them in astonishment. Grant had acquired a strong affection for the 'Birkdale' - her clean Clydebank lines, her tall elegant rig, her beautiful mahogany fittings aft - and a feeling of rage and grief grew in him: rage that another man's folly and negligence had led to this, grief that he was forced to sail her straight at the shore, and couldn't, like that prudent Welsh skipper yesterday, take her out to deep sea and safety. But there, she would never have been able to beat out to sea past the headland to the south; better beach her on sand than do nothing. But - he looked up at the complex web of rope, wire, chain, block and spar above his head; by God, when she did strike, a good deal of that gear would come down - sure to, with the shock. And then there'd be a real shower of lethal missiles. Unthinking, he pulled his blue cap on tighter, and then gave a rueful grin. Some of those blocks weighed twenty pounds or so, and a good many of them were a hundred and fifty feet up! It'd just be a matter of luck for Metcalfe and him - nothing they could do would increase their chance of survival. He looked along the deck to check that at least all the foremast hands were under the foc'sle head as ordered, and as he did so the Second shouted in his ear: 'Lighters ahead! Helm up to miss them?'

'No, never mind the damn lighters, man. Can't possible steer between them. They'll all be empty – they're just old iron boxes. They'll hardly mark her paintwork. Drive straight through.'

'Birkdale', going a good five knots now, blundered and crashed her way through the lighters, the empty iron barges emitting huge, dismal metallic booms as they were struck, to be pushed aside, torn from their moorings or rolled over and ground beneath the barque's keel. Grant cheerfully ignored the expensive carnage and said: 'Shows we're in the right place, anyway.'

Metcalfe stared ahead, and almost murmured: 'There it is - the surf!' and then, as they drove rapidly towards the white desert of furious water under the lee bow, he declaimed in a clear steady voice the words of the Lord's Prayer: 'Our Father, which art in …'

'Never mind that, you fool! Get the hell out of it for'ard, as you were told! I can manage now.' But the firm voice went on without a break, and the Second's strength was added to Grant's at the wheel. Grant looked over his shoulder, and immediately wished he had not. As the huge Pacific seas approached the shelving beach, the sand slowed down their bases while their crests kept their speed; accordingly they were now with every yard growing higher, steeper, more vicious. One monster hung now over the port quarter; he saw every fleck and streak of foam, every etched detail of its tossing white mane. He bent towards Metcalfe: 'Any minute now! When she grounds we'll really be for it. It'll breach clean over us, I shouldn't wonder. Jump for the jigger shrouds and hang on for dear life until you can see a chance to get for'ard. And mind your head too; a lot of the top-hamper will come down, I reckon. You've been a bloody fool, but anyway, well done you, and good luck'

Then it was as if a gigantic brake had been applied, then let go; applied again, let go again; and at last it seemed as if she'd been struck by an advancing stone wall. The barque was in the surf and helpless now, a plaything of the waves; and as the gravelly beach clamped her in place, the waves at last had her at their mercy. The following sea eagerly rose above her quarter, leant forward as if smelling victory, hung - as it seemed - in glee for a second, and then crashed in triumph over her poop and main-deck.

Dunn and the crowd up for'ard had time to leap into the foremast shrouds; the agile Metcalfe reached the jigger shrouds, and the stockier Grant almost did, but the sea joyfully threw him to the deck and drove him against the poop rail, and as he lay there the destruction began aloft. Up there ensued a fearful cacophony of groaning, grinding, splintering and crashing, as a part of the intricately-engineered web of rigging lost its careful balance of stresses, and wires parted, spars fell bodily, ropes flew whirring through blocks, and upper masts - thick and solid pitch pine - broke and fell with the slow dignity of felled timber. Less than a minute after the beaching of the 'Birkdale', Simon Grant was an inert and sodden black shape under an ugly raffle of splintered spars, snapped wires and ropes. A thin rivulet of blood, swiftly diluting as it went, flowed down the sloping wet planks from his bare, wounded head. Beneath the barque's bowsprit-end the surf rolled, no more than waist-deep, up the tawny sand of Caleta Buena.

*   *   *

Next morning the sun was well up, clear of the saw-edged mountain back-cloth, when, with the last breath of the dying northerly wind, 'Figaro' luffed up, the light air gently shaking her canvas, and glided into her former anchorage at Caleta Buena. Once more her starboard anchor dropped from the hawsepipe with a sullen splash and her cable rattled out, suddenly breaking the silence of the bay. She had come ghosting in under full sail and now her tired men went from mast to mast, fife-rail to pin-rail, hauling on the clewlines and buntlines, slacking away on the sheets, until all the sails, all her forty thousand square feet of canvas, hung idly in their gear. Stout canvas, that only twenty-four hours ago had been as rigidly curved by the wind as sheet steel, now only stirred and fluttered with gentle rumpling sounds in the warm zephyr.

'Right, boys, aloft and furl them,' said David Evans, dog-tired, but content to be back in harbour at last. 'Make a tidy job up there too, isn't it? Show these old Dutchies and Frogs and *Saeson* and dagoes what a smart Welsh ship looks like. And you brassbound young devils, you'd better make that mizzen the best of the three, unless you want to be sent up to do the whole damn lot again.' By tradition, the mizzenmast was the domain of the half-deck, and the boys, shouting and skylarking, were beginning to spread along its yards. Evans shook his head in tolerant amusement as he saw how soon they forgot danger, hardship and weariness. They'd be ready for a run ashore tonight, if they got the chance.

Captain Roberts still stood at the poop-rail, staring for'ard at the bustling scene as if in a dream, so tired as to be mesmerized into stillness. All the previous day and half the night they had fought the norther; then, as the wind had eased steadily he had hove-to ten miles offshore, waiting for daylight. And all that time - since yesterday noon - he and the Mate had stood watch-and-watch to make up for the lack of a Second. Poor old Leyshon - a nasty business. The finish for him at sea, that was certain. Let's hope he'd managed to put by a bit of his pay for a day like this, or that he could be patched up enough to get about and perhaps find a job as a harbourmaster, somewhere small and quiet. Roberts roused himself to action, entered the chartroom and grunted an approving *'Da iawn!'* (Very good!) as the barometer needle rose at his rap. *Bendigedig!* Thank God for some peace at last - from the weather, anyway. He went below, and was about to call on the Second Mate when he met Isaac Hughes, neat and spruce in white jacket and blue serge trousers, hovering outside the Second's cabin door.

'I shouldn't go in, capten,' he said officiously. 'He's asleep. *Duw!* his back is painful with him, though, poor old gentleman. Got no feeling in his legs, he says. I have to help him every time he wants to go to the *ty bach.* Anyway, I gave him some aspirins after his breakfast, and that's helped him to sleep. So I wouldn't ...'

'All right, all right, I won't. I don't need telling twice, mun. I signalled for a doctor when I made my number to the shore. They'll send a steam-launch out, I expect, when they can. Things are in a devil of a state there with them, by the looks of it. Mr Evans will be aft in a minute, so get us something for breakfast - something decent, mind. No damned salt junk and biscuit.'

The steward looked wounded: 'God knows I do my best for you gentlemen, night and day, and so does cook. And God knows it's hard, capten, what with the way the Owners provision the ship, and the stuff I have stolen by those wicked limbs of Satan in the half-deck. It's not fair of you to complain, and that I must tell you, Capten Roberts, with all due respect.'

'Just go and get breakfast, isn't it? And stow all that belly aching too. Nobody made you sign on, did they? You can thank your stars you're not standing on a bit of wire at the end of a tops'l yard, like the rest of the crowd. Now - breakfast!'

He went up on deck again, growling softly in irritation as he went. There was always something wrong with somebody. Go and piss up your leg, you whining old besom! But once on deck the warm sunshine and gentle breeze brought relaxation and balm for all the many pinpricks of his existence. He hadn't even had time for a good look round yet. He swung the telescope astern, towards the anchorage, and whistled in sober astonishment. Two days ago there'd been twelve other ships anchored off the port: two steamers - they were back again, the plumes from their funnels showing that their furnaces were still smouldering - and ten sailers. The big German four-poster - one of the Hamburg Flying P Line for sure – she'd gone, finished loading and gone for home, and was five hundred miles off to the south by now, with that fearful north wind to push her. There were - one... two... three... four...*Iesu mawr!* - only four still left! *Diawl!* So five of them must have gone up. He re-focused the glass to look further off at the shore straight to leeward, and saw the rocks there littered with a horrible jumble of hulks, some impossibly high out of the water, some looking intact. From the 'Figaro's' poop they looked to be piled up, interlocking, lying on top of each other like herring in a basket. Some - especially one old wooden ship - were masses of wreckage, their masts gone, their holds split open. A cargo of timber from one of them showed up in the glass like a thick scattering of matches. Rags of grey sail hung from the few masts that still stood, leaning crazily. All the wrecks were clustered on the jagged rocks at the south end of the bay.

'A very sad sight, capten,' said the Mate, at his elbow. 'A lot of poor men drowned and smashed, I dare say. Not us, though, fair play to you. This God-forsaken coast! Hundreds of miles of it, and not one decent sheltered harbour north of Talcahuano. Just bits of bays and coves and creeks. They should never send ships out here - not till they've built us some moles to shelter behind. This trade in nitrate and guano: I suppose the merchants and brokers and ship-owners have made their thousands out of it. Thousands upon thousands, they say; numbers on bits of paper; cheques in the bank; nice tidy office ledgers. They should see what we see, isn't it?'

'They never will, mister, that's certain. It's always been the same, ever since I've been to sea: where there are cargoes to be shifted, there's money to be made. And where there's money to be made the ships will be sent. It used to be copper - you and I both grew up in the Swansea copper-ore men. If there was more money in.... in fetching polar bears from Greenland, that's where we'd be, mun. By damn, I can remember, when I was first at sea, you'd meet slaving schooners sometimes – Portuguese usually - off Bermuda, slipping along in the calms. There's a way to make money, eh, buying and selling poor wretched creatures that God made to live their own lives... And by Christ, the smell of those ships would carry down-wind for miles. Faugh! Never forget it, never. Times are a bit better now - Good God!'

'What is it, sir?'

'Drop squint dead! Look at that - here, take the glass. No, further round to your left - further; further. Got it? That's the Liverpool barque that was next to us - the one high in ballast, remember? Look at her now - standing up as straight as if she was in Gladstone Dock!'

'She's lost her mizzen topmast and main t'gallant mast, by the look of it.'

'Aye, but what's that? Stick and string, that's all. And it looks like there's a tug standing by, waiting for high water to haul her off. By God, her master - or whoever put her there - is what I'd call a seaman, mister, a regular, downright, A1 at Lloyd's seaman. Otherwise she'd likely be washed up and smashed up like all those other poor devils. H'm...' He took the telescope back and trained it on the pier near the stranded barque: 'We'll soon hear all about it, I expect. I can see the harbour-master's launch getting under way, and he'll no doubt be coming out with the doctor to give us our pratique. We're all clear, aren't we, mister? No fevers, measles, spots, John Thomases falling off? I can't remember having anyone aft for medicine in weeks.'

'All clear at present, sir. Let that crowd for'ard ashore a few times, and no doubt there'll be men down with everything in the Medical Guide. Disgusting fools...'

'Aye, aye, always been the same. It's the ports that ought to fly the yellow flag, isn't it, not the ships? . Now then, talking of medicine: the first thing to do is to get Mr Leyshon to a decent hospital here, and get his back properly looked at. It's his legs I'm worried about; got no sensation in them, steward says. So we'll see what the doctor ...'

Evans reacted fiercely, and for the first time in his life interrupted his commanding officer: 'The only decent hospital in this benighted country - as you well know, capten - is the American one at Valparaiso ...'

'Yes, mister, but that's eight hundred miles off.'

'I don't care how many hundred miles it is. We're not talking about a few cuts and bruises, Capten Roberts, we're talking about a man who can't use his legs. You've just said so yourself. A cripple for life, maybe. You remember: two days ago he was a fit man carrying out your orders... your orders.'

'I know, I know ...'

'He went where you sent him, down on to that main-deck, as he always did. He didn't say: "*O Duw,* capten, that'd be too dangerous!" He thought of your ship before himself ...'

'Yes, I know all that, mister. Look, I am doing what I can for him...'

'Shoving him into some dirty pest-hole in Iquique, I suppose, because it's nearer? So that it won't cost your precious Owners so much?'

Roberts controlled himself, pitching his voice low - a great effort for one so naturally choleric: 'Don't you think, mister, that before you say another word you'd better remember who you are and who I am?'

Those solemn words had silenced Leyshon, but did not work for Evans. 'I remember everything well enough, Jacob Roberts. I'm John Leyshon's friend, and I'm taking him to hospital in Valparaiso, and you can like it or lump it, I don't care which.'

The captain went scarlet with apoplectic shock and rage, and yelled: 'God dammit, mister!' and then noticed that two seamen coiling halyards on the jigger fife-rails nearby were listening to every angry word and exchanging grins of amusement, which swiftly faded as they caught Jacob's eye on them. 'You two lazy scrim-shankers! Finish that and get for'ard before I .... Mister Evans, the chartroom if you please.' The seamen took rather longer making up the coils than usual, and cocked their ears towards the small deckhouse chartroom, but had to be content with the muffled and indistinct sounds that could filter through its steel sides.

'Now then, you listen to me, mister,' said Jacob as the Mate closed the door. 'I had a lot of respect for Mr Leyshon, and I'm as sorry as you are that he has been injured. I challenge you to say that what happened to him was through my negligence or folly; you know as well as I do that it was the sea that did it. Another time it could be you or me or the bosun or Davey Jones. And he could easily have been washed clean over the rail and never seen again. Very well: since it happened I've done my level best to make him comfortable. But - now you mind me, mister – I've got a ship to run, coal to be unloaded, nitrate to be loaded, a hundred and one damn things to be done ashore - which you know nothing about. Just a minute, don't you interrupt me in my own bloody chartroom! Now, I'm not unreasonable, and I'm not a callous man. I will find someone to take Mr Leyshon's berth when I can. But this is not Liverpool or Cardiff or London; I can't pick up good officers off the waterfront. I need time, man, you can see that, surely? So that means that, in the meantime, you'll have to stay by here and take your proper place in charge of the cargo and the hands. You can understand that, can't you? I can't manage everything on my own. Now, you calm down and be reasonable, isn't it?'

But Evans' normally cold blood was up, too, and the wattles of his scrawny neck shook with passion: 'Reasonable, is it? Is it reasonable to put your damn lumps of coal before a good man who's served this company for I don't know how many years? You'd look after him better if he was tied up in a gunny-sack with "*Nitrado de Chile*" stamped on it, I suppose. I don't give a.... a .... fish's tit about your bloody cargo: that man's going to Valparaiso, and I'm going with him. I'm going to see him to hospital, I'm going to book his passage on a mail-steamer home, and then we'll see about your damn cargo. And if you don't like that you can discharge me today - Go on - pay me off and go and get two mates, not one.'

'*Iesu mawr!*' yelled Jacob, and gave the chart-table a thump which sent parallel ruler and dividers jumping. The hands outside heard the yell and the thump and leant their ears towards the bulkhead. 'That is refusing duty! Mutiny! Leaving the ship without permission! Disobeying a lawful command! By God, I'll log you for that this minute, and that will cost you a pretty penny off your pay in fines, mister.' He bent down, snatched open a drawer, took out the official log and, all thumbs in his haste, fumbled among the stout parchment pages. He picked up a pen and jabbed it so forcibly into the inkwell that half the rusty nib broke off. With a vicious blasphemy that shocked even himself, he flung the pen down, creating on his Pacific chart a little flurry of hitherto-unsuspected islands west of the Galapagos. The very idea of putting cold accusations on a piece of paper against so good a man as Evans was deeply repugnant - and yet he had a ship to run, a thousand things to see to besides this. He sat with fists clenched, mastering his choler: 'Look, mister, like I say, be reasonable. I wasn't going to send him off alone. I'll send someone with him. I'm not some stony- hearted tyrant like... like...'

'Who?'
'What?'
'Whom will you send?'
'Oh, someone reliable, but someone who can be spared.'

'Who?'

'Christ, man, don't keep saying "Who" like some constipated old owl! I'll send... er... Davey Jones.'

'The peggy! A turnip-headed piggish-dull *crwt* like that! If you was home now you wouldn't trust that boy to take a cow to Cardigan market - you know damn well you wouldn't.'

'All right, then, one of the apprentices.'

'Schoolboys - wicked wild jackanapes, the lot of them!'

'I mean one of the sensible ones ...'

'There's no such thing as a sensible brassbounder. It's no good, Jacob Roberts: out on deck there I respect you as my superior officer - you can't deny that. I have done for six years. But this is different; you are telling me to abandon my best friend to a lot of strangers, - dagoes, I suppose - and I won't do it, because it would be wrong - wrong in the eyes of the Almighty himself. It's only a four-day trip once I'm on the steamer: I could be back in just over a week; it'll take that long to clear the for'ard hold, even if the lighters turn up properly.'

Both men were cooling, retreating from the clash. Jacob slumped wearily down on the leather-padded stool. 'All right, then. You go. Only what old Powell will say about two steamer fares and you losing a week's work I don't know. And not so much about your dagoes and pestholes: I've met a young Chilean fellow in the hospital at Iquique who's as smart a doctor as anyone from Edinburgh.'

'Maybe, maybe... As for John Powell - what do I care about the old cheese-paring miser? Give me my money to date - what I've earned - and I'll pay for all the fares and give you a week's wages for a substitute. Even he couldn't grumble at that, could he - even if he would boil his granny down for soap. I wouldn't take a favour off those Owners of yours for fifty pun.'

'Don't blame me for their ways, mister; I work for them too, God help me. Never mind about a substitute; I'm going straight ashore to see if I can pick up a decent second mate to take Leyshon's place. There may well be survivors from the wrecks stranded ashore, who'd be glad of a berth. And there's something else I've decided, too, after what happened the other day; one other change, and I might as well tell you now, while we're at it. And I'm not discussing it with you, or arguing with you, or anything - just telling you. I'm going to appoint the senior apprentice, Raven, as third mate, to stand his watch with you. No, don't start your damned spluttering again; this time I will have my way. You're a good man with a sextant, you can trim a cargo better than anyone I've met, you keep the men up to their work well, and you've forgotten more seamanship than young Raven will ever know. But you're not... you're not a young man, David. I've got to have mates who can go down on the main-deck or up on a yard when it's "All hands". Now don't tell me you can do those things, because I've seen for myself what can happen, and I don't want to see it again. Come on, it's time you swallowed the hook altogether, maybe - got a shore job. But that's your decision; this one is mine.'

Generally, it was Jacob Roberts' way to look any man in the eye, whatever the situation; now, sensing the bitterness of the blow, he looked down at the table, absently putting the ruler and dividers tidily at the back, examining the points of the pencils.

Evans broke the long silence, leaving all the bitterness unsaid. To be told at last that you were not really up to the job - the only job you knew. To be replaced by a boy, and an English boy at that, and the wildest and most impudent of the whole half-deck into the bargain. To share his watches, his meals, his leisure with such a godless unworthy hooligan! To have to call him 'Mister Raven' in front of the crowd... Mister Raven - that wicked English cub! 'Raven?' he said at last. 'Do you have to pick *him?*'

Jacob felt a little relieved. So that was what had been going through the old man's mind - his long-drawn feud with that young devil. 'Yes,' he said, 'it has to be him. There's not another of them ready to stand up to the crowd yet. It won't be easy for him, you know. Like enough some of them will fancy their chances with him. He'll have to give and take a hammering or two before he's accepted - especially being English. He won't be able to talk to them like we do - in the language of heaven, I mean. No, it's going to be tough for young Raven at first.'

'Aye, I suppose so...But he's such a ...'

'I know well what he's been, but he's ambitious, he's certainly not stupid, and he's being promoted, after all. You'll be surprised what promotion will do; and I'll lay the law down too, never fear. The best keeper they ever had on the Teifi to look after the salmon was Ianto Cwmfelin, who'd been a terrible poacher. If God could change Saul of Tarsus from a persecutor to a Christian saint in a flash of light on the Damascus road, I think even I can alter young Raven a bit.'

Evans grumbled on, not hearing him: 'And as for me, I'm not

quite dead or crippled yet, you know. I'm still ...'

'Accept it, David. Accept. We all have to. Time is in God's hands, not ours. It is He who brings these changes in our lives - not captains or ship-owners...Just time. You were Raven's age once, and no doubt you then thought all masters and mates were senile dodderers, ready for the breaker's yard.'

The Mate turned away, overcome. He stared out through the scuttle at the blue, breeze-ruffled swells of the anchorage, at the horizon line that climbed and fell, climbed and fell, up and down the bright circle of vision. Raven's age...Good God, he'd been at sea five years by the time he was that age. But (unwillingly) he found himself remembering another bright forenoon in... forty-two?...no, it must have been forty-one. *Iesu mawr*, fifty-four years ago! May the ninth, 1841, a beautiful sunny morning, just a gentle sailing breeze; the schooner 'Alert', Captain Alexander Davies, Criccieth, beating to windward over Porthmadog Bar, every stitch of canvas set, with two hundred and fifty tons of slates for Hamburg; his first trip as a fourteen-year-old peggy. *Duw,* the way his Mam had cried the night before he left Aberaeron. But there was no help for it in those days on the Cardigan coast, no other way for a poor man's son to get a living where the farms were so poor and small and stony. Fifty-four years, and nearly all that time afloat; no wonder streets and fields and stones and house floors felt dead beneath his feet, still and lifeless...

He flourished a handkerchief and blew his nose unnecessarily loudly: 'Very well, capten. I must attend to things on deck if you will excuse me. The yards will need a harbour trim, and the hatches - you will want the forward hold discharged first, I take it?'

Both men were relieved to find the exchange was back to its normal professional flatness: 'Aye, aye, for'ard hold first, mister. Get the hatch-covers off, rig cargo-hoists and so on. I shall try to get our first launches tomorrow, but you know how it is on this coast, even without a bad storm: what with the swell and the holy days and the fiestas and the liquor and the strikes and the heat and the women, not to mention these damn great German four-posters coming in and taking priority with the lighters – it's the devil's own job to shift a cargo without it taking months. The Dutchies will take all this trade off us one of these days, you'll see.' (British sailors in those days rather cavalierly lumped Dutch and German seafarers together with the same name.)

Evans swung round with the air of a man about to say something that was hard to say, then abruptly turned again and marched out. Roberts allowed himself a wry smile: that was the nearest he'd ever be to getting an apology from that stiff-necked, sober-sided old stick. Never mind. He raised his voice to a casual bellow: 'Bo-o-oy!'

He heard Davey Jones clatter up the companion-way and a second later the boy burst into the chartroom. 'Isn't that breakfast ready yet, Jones?' he barked.

'Yes, cap'n. Well, nearly, cap'n. Steward's just setting the table. Ready in a minute, cap'n.'

'All right, all right, calm down, boy. I'm not going to eat you, am I? Listen: go to the half-deck and tell mister ...' he checked himself; that would be premature. 'Tell the senior apprentice I want to see him in my cabin at four bells this forenoon. Got that, boy?'

The pale-faced youth nodded emphatically, his lank black hair flopping: 'Senior apprentice, three bells ...'

'Four bells, half-wit.'

'Sorry, sir, four bells. Very good, sir...' He seemed about to go, but after a short silence said with great reluctance and trepidation: 'Excuse me, sir, did you say in your cabin or here?' But the roar from his captain was so dreadful that he did not wait for an answer, but fled wildly, taking the poop-ladder steps three at a time.

What's the matter with the boy, Roberts thought, as he stowed away the unused log and the blotted chart. Behaving as if I was some holy terror of a down-east Yankee bucko. H'm... if I was, David Evans would be down on the deck now, spitting out the last of his teeth. Cross-grained, obstinate, contrary old sod... Leyshon his 'best friend'! Never had a good word to say about him, or to him, until he was injured. 'Best friend' indeed! The sea itself, with all its moods, currents, tides, waves, winds and calms - even that was easier to understand than other people.

6

Some eight thousand miles or so to the north-east, Jacob's daughter also found herself out of her depth, jolted from the dull routine of life with her mother in the quiet little Welsh town of Newport, Pembrokeshire. It was late afternoon on a brisk fine winter day, the air chilling as the sun sank towards the west over the black wedge of Pen Dinas. The smart trap in which she was travelling moved slowly, its metal tyres splitting the road grit, the strong pony's head nodding vigorously as he threw his weight into the collar, steam rising from his flanks into the cold air. On these lower slopes of Carn Ingli – the mountain overlooking the town - trees grew well, and the road was a tilted tunnel enclosed by high grass banks on which grew blackthorn and rowan, ash and sycamore, whose outstretched branches nearly met overhead. The trap climbed the stiff dark slope of the mountain road, and at a twitch of the left rein turned into the track leading up to *Ty Coch Uchaf,* (Upper Red House), the cosy and comfortable home of Jacob Roberts, master mariner, his wife Mair and the trap's passenger, young Eleanor Roberts.

She half-turned to the driver and said shyly: 'Perhaps I should get out? The track is steep for the poor pony.'

'No, don't trouble yourself. Our Billy is a strong young devil who doesn't get nearly enough work. Stay where you are, Miss Roberts.'

She glanced down at her companion's hands deftly holding the reins; so strong, white and smooth, scattered with very black hairs; above those, the white cuffs showing below the sleeves of his smart checked ulster. She felt close to him now, yet she had not seen him or even known of his existence twenty-four hours ago. Catryn Meredydd, a school friend, had invited her to her birthday party on Friday, and (in the manner of siblings) hadn't bothered to mention her elder brother Bryn. And now, a day later, Eleanor had travelled the seven miles from Fishguard alone with him, an odd experience for her, so used to the company of her mother, female teachers, the other girls in school, and the occasional drearily respectable middle-aged visitor at home.

Sitting shoulder-to-shoulder with Bryn in the trap, Eleanor had felt his difference, his maleness. At his home she had noticed and admired his neat, stylish clothes and his perfect manners and polish, the smoothness of his voice, his cultured Welsh and, not least, his tall athletic figure. Only once had there been a jarring note: just as they were leaving for Newport, Catryn had come bounding up, smiling and dressed for the road. Bryn, busy backing the pony into the shafts of the trap, had looked at her irritably: 'Why are you dressed up like that? There's no room for you in the trap.'

'Yes there is, Bryn. I'll squash in the back.'

'Don't be silly. Three's too many for the pony on the hills - you know that.'

His cold air of dismissal had brought an awkward chill into the polite atmosphere, as if something unpleasant had been suddenly and momentarily revealed. But Catryn was easy-going and good-tempered, besides being a little in awe of her masterful brother: 'O, very well then, I'll stay. I'll see you back at the prison for girls on Monday, Eleanor.'

As soon as she had gone, Bryn's urbanity returned like the sun after a shower. 'Do allow me to help you up, Miss Roberts. And take care, for the step is a little worn and slippery.' She felt his strength through the firm clasp on her upper arm. 'The air is cold today. Allow me to help you put the rug across your lap.' He did this by adroit twitches, his hands carefully avoiding all contact with her legs.

His words were equally tactful: polite, friendly and charming, yet cool - quite free from flattery or flirtation - quite different from her last experience with a young man. She still remembered with hot embarrassment the evening walk back from Ebeneser Chapel with Hywel Morris blacksmith. Full of strength, vigour and simple lust, he had taken her guileless acceptance of his company as a permission for bearish hugs, forceful kisses and brisk exploration of the more available parts of her body, the small of her back wedged painfully against the top bar of a stile. The best-suit-and-high-collar restraint of Chapel and the ordeal of a lengthy and dull sermon in difficult Welsh seemed to have produced in him an access of lechery not to be found on a weekday. It had been an encounter she didn't want to repeat, yet it had nevertheless shown her her subtle, unsought power over men. Frightened at first, she could now smile secretly at her struggles for chastity; secretly, because if her mother knew, she would have had, as the English said, forty fits. Quite apart from the moral issue, Eleanor guessed that Hywel Morris blacksmith would not feature on her mother's list of possible suitors.

She was grateful for Meredydd's cool restraint, and enjoyed every yard of the journey; it was intriguing to meet, to be alone in the company of an unusually handsome young man who was yet old enough to have acquired experience, a gloss, a bloom that came from confidence and professional skill. Yet for all his sophistication, he was perhaps just the same as Hywel Morris blacksmith under the skin. After all, he had deliberately got rid of his sister to be alone with her. Why do that if he had no desire for her? Perhaps only the veneer of class divided the two men!

'Catryn tells me,' she said, 'that you work for Jones and Watts, the auctioneers in Fishguard?'

'Yes, that's so - for my sins! It's my uncle's firm, of course.'

'But that must be so interesting! If I become, as I expect, a teacher, I shall have to spend most of my time shut up in a room with noisy children, but you must meet so many people, and see the inside of so many little worlds.'

'Yes, that's acute of you, Miss Roberts, we do. But some of those worlds are very humdrum and often distasteful. Why, sometimes at a clearout sale on a farm, I have to take rods and tapes and measure out the cubic volume of a manure-heap - a charming occupation! But it is not all so earthy; when we sell up a mansion we must strive to value its pictures, objets d'art, books and wine-cellar.'

'That must take much skill and knowledge.'

'Yes, but alas, I am a mere beginner, with so much to learn on a hundred topics, from dry rot in houses to the London prices of rare first-editions.'

'How I wish that we women too could enter such a profession! It seems unfair that we should be so confined...'

He shook his head tolerantly: 'Don't envy us. The work is often rough and unpleasant, out in the rain, conducting country auctions of pigs and heifers smothered in mud, and half the bidders revoltingly drunk. The sellers, you see, often encourage the bidding by giving beer away at farm sales. I shouldn't like a woman I respected to be present at that sort of degrading affair.'

If Meredydd had shown politeness and charm to Eleanor, he (astutely) showed twice as much to her mother when they arrived at the door of the pretty pink house. Hearing the wheels approaching, Mair Roberts, tall and striking like her daughter, had come to the door in some anxiety.

'This is Mr Bryn Meredydd, Catryn's brother,' said Eleanor, blushing much against her will, and adding, rather unnecessarily: 'He's brought me home.'

'I see. We're both obliged to you, Mr Meredydd. Will you take tea with us before you go back? I have a kettle boiling on the hob.'

'That would be most kind. I fear I cannot stay long, as the trap has no lights, and it gets dark very early now.'

'I did think I might see your sister Catryn too... I have heard so much about her from Nell- from Eleanor.'

'Yes. Unfortunately there was no room for her in the trap, and besides, the hills are so steep between here and Fishguard, particularly Gelli.'

'Very well. Do come in and sit by the fire to warm up after your drive. Eleanor, take Mr Meredydd's coat for him.' Out in the kitchen making tea, Mair closed her lips tight in disapproval, and said to herself: H'm! He gives two reasons why his sister couldn't come. People who do that are always concealing a third. We all know what *that* was. The young think we are so dull; he might have hoodwinked that foolish Nelli, but not me!

Later, over tea and Welsh cakes, she took in his glossy appearance: the well-cut brown suit, the high white collar, the carefully-trimmed whiskers and pomaded hair. Smart, but a bit too smart; a handsome, successful young fellow, but a bit too pleased with himself for her liking. She fancied she saw a shifty, treacherous look in those clear dark eyes. He wouldn't do for Nelli, that was certain, but the silly minx seemed captivated by him. It was intensely irritating to her to hear Nelli chatter on about him, as if she had swallowed the bait whole: 'Mr Meredydd is studying for his articles as an auctioneer, mother. He is hoping to have his own business one day.'

Meredydd cut in disarmingly: 'Ah, that is a long time in the future, if ever, Mrs Roberts. I still have much to learn. But business is not everything. I am excessively fond of music as well, for instance. Which reminds me: may I have your permission to take Eleanor to the *Gwyl Fawr,* the big eisteddfod in Cardigan next month? I have every hope of being staged in the tenor solo event. We have to sing Handel, a favourite composer of mine.'

Mair's guard was up at once: 'That might be difficult. Eleanor cannot always get home at the weekend. After all, it is over twenty miles to her school in Haverfordwest. And besides, eisteddfod competitions sometimes go on so late. I've known them not finish till one o'clock in the morning, the way the adjudicators ramble on.'

'Yes, they do, but fortunately that does not matter too much. I have an aunt living in Cardigan who I'm sure would be delighted to put us up if necessary.'

The idea of Nelli spending the night in a house eleven miles off, in the company of this smooth young man and an entirely unknown - and perhaps non-existent - aunt once again rang a loud alarm bell in Mair's head. She would need to know a lot more about Meredydd's and Meredydd's aunt's characters before allowing that. However, she did not want to embarrass Nelli or cause a scene in front of this dubious young man, so she merely temporized: 'Well, that is for Eleanor to decide, but it's too early to say yet... she has a great deal of work to do for her German and French examinations later next year.' And in the meantime, she added to herself, I will see she decides on the right course - of prudence and refusal. When Meredydd had gone, and Eleanor had come in from bidding him a chaste farewell, Mair at last spoke her mind: 'You didn't tell me Catryn had an elder brother living at home who was such a swell.'

'No, I didn't know myself.'

'H'm. If I had known, and known what he was like, I'd have been against your going to this party.'

'Why, for Heaven's sake?'

'Because he thinks too much of himself, and I don't really trust him.'

'Don't trust him? Why? He seemed to me to behave like a perfect gentleman all the time.' Bryn's curt snubbing of Catryn flashed into her mind, but she chose to ignore it.

'O yes, he knows all the tricks of the trade, but he's a bit too clever for my liking. He made sure he got you on his own for the journey, didn't he?'

'He explained that. The trap was too small.'

'Trap fiddlesticks! It was quite big enough for three. Eleanor, you're getting to the age when you go about and meet people – that's natural. But you're only nineteen, so you must be careful, especially of young men. Sometimes you seem to me to be much too interested in

them, and not nearly careful enough. And don't blush and look innocent and indignant, because you know perfectly well what I mean.
Some young men are just looking for the chance to take... to take... liberties with you ...'

'What liberties?'

'I tell you, don't play the innocent with me. I can tell that you
know exactly what I mean. You know that certain things happen between married men and women, as a result of which children are born.
You know enough of Nature to know that. Very well, then: we humans
are not beasts of the field, and it is the declared will of God that this
union of man and woman should take place only within marriage.'
There was a long awkward silence, and Mair looked at her daughter
with a touch of pity: so tall, so good-looking, with her regular features,
her combed-up dark hair high on her head. So grown-up and attractive
to men, and perhaps attracted *to* them, and yet such a child in the ways
of the world!

'Mother,' said Eleanor, still furiously blushing, 'I don't know
why we're talking like this. I have just been brought home a few miles
in broad daylight by a perfectly respectable young man from a good
family, and he has been polite and gentlemanly to me – that's all.'

'Yes, well, all I'm asking, *cariad,* is that you'll listen to my advice, which is kindly meant, and that you'll be very careful about being
alone with unattached young men. Believe me I have seen so much
trouble - just in this little town - when girls aren't careful. And when a
wrong thing is done, it can't be undone.'

'Very well, Mam, I do understand,' said Eleanor, privately
thinking: What a mercy she doesn't know about Hywel Morris blacksmith and his antics!

Her mother crossed to a writing-table and came back with a
letter: 'I'm sorry if I've been a little impatient with you, Nelli, but I had
this letter while you were away on Saturday, and I've been worrying
about it ever since.'

'A letter? From whom?'

'From your father's old Uncle William over at Mathry. You
can read it if you like, but it's pages and pages of old rigmarole, half of
it nonsense and lies.'

'What does he say to trouble you?'

Mair spoke with deep bitterness: 'O, only that we've got to
clear out of this house by next Lady-day, that's all.' Her handsome face

grew red with anger as she explained: 'You know this house belongs to him? And that he married that scheming piece Bronwen Lewis from Caerfarchell a few years back? Old enough to be her father, nearly! I knew no good would come of it, but there's no fool like an old fool. Well, now madam has decided that one of her cousins - on her side, I mean - shall have Ty Coch.'

'But why? I thought all her cousins had good jobs in banking in London and Cardiff?'

'So they have, but this one must have made a pile of money already. Now he wants to come to Newport and set up as a country gentleman. That means he needs our house. He talks to our beloved Bronwen, she twists Uncle William round her little finger, so have it he must.'

'But can Uncle do this? What about the law?'

'The law wouldn't help us, and well he knows it. It would be just throwing money away to get lawyers arguing about it. That wicked old man - God forgive me for using such a word about Jacob's kin - promised us faithfully when we first rented this place fifteen years back that we could stay as long as we liked, provided that we kept the house and garden up well. The house looks better now than it ever did, thanks to us, and this is our reward. Thrown out! We've nothing on paper to prove our case. We trusted him, God help us!'

'But mother, whatever shall we do? This has always been our home.' Tears started in Eleanor's eyes as she looked round the cosy parlour. Every stick, every inch of cloth, every gleam of the firelight on polished wood or brass was utterly familiar and beloved. She could not remember another house, and felt that her whole world was being wrenched away from her.

'Don't cry, lovely. We won't despair and we won't give in. Let the old fool keep his house! Do you know what he had the impudence to suggest? That we moved into Pencnwc - you know, that hovel of his up on the Bedd Morus road? Half the slates off, the last time I saw it. It would finish us off the first winter - especially you, with this bronchitis you keep getting.'

'But then what are we to do? Could we buy a house, or have one built? Or rent another one?'

'I'll never rent a house again after this. As for buying, we've not got quite enough money for that yet. In a year or so, yes.'

'Mother, I'm so sorry you've had all this trouble to yourself, and I'm sorry too for arguing with you about Bryn Meredydd. But I didn't know then ...'

'Don't worry and don't feel sorry. As long as the three of us stick together we can weather any storm. Ever since I had the letter I have been praying to the greatest Helper of all, and He has given me his guidance; it came into my mind before I went to sleep last night, and it came from Him, I'm convinced. We will go to Dadi and share his quarters aboard ship. He has a fine large barque with plenty of room aft. We can save all our rent money like that, so that soon we can come back with enough to buy a house.'

'But how do we - how can we...?'

'I did a lot of voyaging with your father before you were born, don't forget, so I understand these things: by now "Figaro" should have reached port at Caleta Buena. She will be there for weeks probably, as she has coal to discharge and nitrate to load. These little ports on the West Coast are so slow. If I send a cable on Monday - as soon as the Post Office in Fishguard opens - Dadi will cable back in a day or two to say yes or no. I'm sure his answer will be yes. Then, if we can get a PSNC ship from Liverpool soon, we can be out on the coast long before he's ready to leave. I'll wire the company's office as well for a list of sailings.'

Eleanor sprang up and impulsively hugged her mother: 'O mam, you're so wonderful to have thought of all that! I shouldn't have known what to do. It will be quite an adventure after that stuffy old school and stuffy old teachers.'

'Mind, we're not out of the wood yet,' said Mair. 'Dadi has to agree, and we have to find whether there's a boat leaving soon. Otherwise we'd be too late - he can't wait for us. But God has helped me so much already, I feel certain He will make our way easy.' She smiled and looked out of the window, her eyes seeing something far away. 'You know, in some ways this may turn out to be a blessing in disguise - God has made me feel that. Your father and I have lived so far apart for so much of our married life that sometimes I feel that we are only half-living. We should be together - all of us. I have such happy memories of the voyages I took with him soon after we were married, when he had his first command on the Australia run. You will love the sea-life too, I'm sure. God knows what is best for us - even if his agent is that dreadful old Uncle William!'

'But Mam, what about the money for our passage?'

Mair abruptly dropped her air of spiritual exaltation: 'I'll find the money all right. I've got the rent saved right up to next Lady-day - you know, in March. Well, I'll pay William Roberts Mathry exactly to the day we leave, and he can whistle for the rest. Not another penny-piece will I pay him. Anyway, girl, we're not beggars; your father is the master of the finest and biggest four-masted barque out of Cardiff, and don't you forget it.'

Eleanor smiled, dabbing away the tears: 'I'll catch the pony first thing on Monday, brush the mud off him and ask Twm Ty Gwyn if we can borrow his trap for the day. Then we'll be off to Fishguard Post Office to cable Dadi.'

'You've got to get yourself to school tomorrow, my girl, don't forget.'

'School?' cried Eleanor gaily. 'What's the point of talking about old school? Getting the cable off is much more important, surely? I'm going to be a sailor in South America soon, and sail the great blue oceans in the best ship afloat! And by the way what's the PSNC?'

'Don't you know that? That's the Pacific Steam Navigation Company. They run beautiful liners out to the West Coast round Cape Horn.'

'Liners! Cape Horn! Mam, you are wonderful to know about all these things!' Being young, she had already replaced the pain of leaving Ty Coch Uchaf with the glamour of high-seas voyaging. Her normally pale face was flushed with excitement.

The practically-minded Mair said: 'Yes, well, as I said, I am no stranger to the sea and ships. And it will do you and your poor chest a lot of good to be out of this wind and rain. The bottles I've bought of ipecacuanha syrup this autumn, and still you're coughing. It'll be the making of you.' And as the girl flew out of the room to change her dress, the mother added grimly to herself: Yes, and it may prevent the undoing of you too! I didn't like the look in that clever young fellow's eye one bit. There was that line in the English hymn about 'those in peril on the sea', but sometimes the sea could be the safest place of all!

7

'Figaro's' half-deck was a peaceful place; the morning sun streamed through the ports and warm, soft, dry air came benevolently in through the open door, drawing a fetid reek of wet wool and serge from the storm gear and the thick socks and jerseys hung up to dry. But no stink troubled the denizens of that cramped and villainously squalid metal cube very much. Though all six apprentices were present the place was miraculously quiet, save for the clink of spoons on enamel plates as six large helpings of burgoo were shovelled down hungry throats A good burgoo today - a thick oatmeal porridge enriched with plump squashy raisins and laced with a slosh of condensed milk. The cook, to celebrate their return to the rest of the world after three months' isolation, had been busy opening tins; as well as the milk, the boys had a new tin of soft yellow grease, labelled 'Peabody's Superior Preserved Farmhouse Butter' and even a tin of Dundee marmalade to put on their biscuits after the burgoo. A similar largesse was spread on the tables in the idlers' mess and both foc'sles. Steam arose from six mugs of some hot brown liquid; a fierce debate had decided, on the senior apprentice's casting vote, that it was coffee. There was no debate however about the fact that whatever was put on the half-deck table would be wolfed or swallowed by the six ravenous brassbounders.

Perkins, the eldest of the port watch apprentices, was the first to finish his plateful of porridge and laid down his spoon with a thunderous belch of appreciation: 'Whew, pardon me! The doctor's come up to scratch today. That wasn't half bad.'

The doorway suddenly darkened as Davey Jones came rushing in over the coaming, exclaiming abruptly as he came 'Oy! Which one of you lot is senior? You, Raven, is it?'

Perkins, a tall, fair, reckless extrovert, half-turned on his bench in some irritation. 'You miserable worm, peggy, who said you could come barging in here without knocking?'

'How could I knock, mun? The bloody door's open,' said Davey, quite unabashed. He might get kicked around by all the afterguard, but he wasn't going to knuckle down to these brassbound buggers as well.

'What's that got to do with it?' said Raven, also much concerned with matters of status. 'Open or shut, you knock it, or I'll damn well knock your ears off.'

'Don't see why,' said the puny but defiant peggy. 'You lot ain't officers, nor petty officers, nor nothing, only makee-learns. That's what the mate calls you.'

'Not officers yet,' said Perkins, 'but we shall be some day, and you won't, and anyway, you're not the mate.' He reached out and seized a handful of the cabin-boy's grubby shirt: 'P'raps you'd like to come out on the main-deck now and fight me? Settle it that way?'

'Naw thanks,' said Davey, still not noticeably terrified. He looked along the table and saw the pale studious face and scrawny build of Waters, the first-voyager, and said shrewdly: 'But I'll fight him - him with the spots. Waters, isn't it?'

Raven looked on with the bored indifference of the accepted cock-of-the-walk: 'Shut up, you two; you're disturbing my breakfast. Anyway, what have you come for, young Taffy Jones?'

'You're senior, en't you? Right, well the Old Man wants to see you. Four bells this watch, in the chartroom...No, in his cabin.'

'Which, you bloody oaf?'

'Cabin, definitely...I think. Anyway, it was four bells for sure.'

'What about? What does he want me for?'

'Ow should I know? Think he'd tell me?'

'Did he seem annoyed? You know, out to raise hell about something?'

'No good asking me, mun. He's in his bloody temper with me half the time about something. Listen I got to go, or old Isaac will be after me. I'm s'posed to be swabbing out the mess-room now.' He went to the door, giving Perkins a wide gappy smile and leaving him with the vague but irritating feeling that somehow apprentices' status had not been well asserted. Davey caught the eye of his fellow Welshman Ieuan Davies, and said cheerfully: *'Twll tin bob Sais!'* (Arseholes to all Englishmen) and shot out like a rabbit.

'What was that he said?' asked Perkins suspiciously.

'Oh nothing,' said Davies, with a sudden attack of patriotism, choosing to ally himself with an oppressed fellow-countryman: 'Just... goodbye, sort of thing.'

'I bet it wasn't that,' said Perkins. 'I bet it was some bit of damned cheek. You Taffies stick together, don't you? Jabber, jabber,

jabber...Might as well be on a Chinese junk, for all I understand.'

'Will you shut up, Perkins?' said Raven. 'Never mind that little oick - this is serious.'

'What is?'

'What is? Old Jake wanting to see me, that's what is, half-wit.'

Robbins put in mildly: 'But we don't know what he wants, Raven. Might be anything.... Might be something good.'

'Don't be so appallingly wet, Robbins. When the Old Man sends for me it's always for a bollocking about something one of you young swine has done. If he doesn't know who it is he always sends for me. I cop it because I'm senior. Right, well, can anybody think of anything good we've done? No, neither can I, so it can't be that.' It was totally characteristic of windjammer sailors that he didn't even consider the sheer heroism of their deeds on the yards in the storm. That was an ordinary day's work, which they and the captain would take for granted.

'Hey!' Waters had jumped up, pale and staring. 'The tins! All that salmon!'

'Exactly,' said Raven. 'Glad to see there's one other intelligent being in this pigsty. The tins; which a certain smart aleck not far from here thought it would be such a good idea to pinch. Very clever, Mr Perkins... Brilliant. Now old Isaac's had a proper count-up and has got Jake to believe him. So now we'll all be stuck up on the royal yards every dog-watch for a month. You goddam idiot!'

'You're getting in a panic about nothing, Raven,' said Perkins. 'All guesswork. You don't know. Nobody's found anything.'

'If Jake himself starts looking,' said Raven, 'he'll find them. He'll take this deckhouse to bits until he does.'

'All right, all right,' said Perkins with an attempt at nonchalance, brushing dry biscuit-crumbs from his moustache and overalls. 'If you're going to wet your trousers about the bloody salmon, I'll go and own up. Jake doesn't frighten me.'

'Chuck them overboard!' said Waters suddenly, as if amazed at his own genius. 'Don't own up and get into a hell of a row – let's just chuck them over the side. Then there's no evidence against us.'

'0 *Iesu mawr,* boys, you can't do that!' said Ieuan plaintively, a wild Celtic pathos in his voice. 'You can't. Not six pound tins of prime red salmon... You can't!'

'I don't know,' said Raven, the responsibility of rank giving him caution. 'I don't know ...Maybe we should. Old Jake's no fool.'

Robbins, even fonder of food than most of them, put in a de-spairing plea to echo Ieuan's: 'Oh but Raven! Six pounds of salmon! We've never had a haul like that. It'd last us for weeks'

'Shut up, Robbo,' said Raven mechanically, hardly listening. 'Snotty-nosed little fat sprog - who asked you for your opinion?'

'No, but he's right,' said Perkins, sitting down again. 'We'd be balmy to chuck them overboard when we don't even know what the Old Man wants. We'll never get the chance again - old Isaac will see to that.'

'I've decided,' said Raven. 'They go, like Waters said. I've been racking my brains, and I can't for the life of me think of anything else Jake might want to see me about. It's too chancy. By the time I find out what he wants it'll be too late. I know him; he'll ask me what I know; I'll say I don't know anything. He'll give me the father and mother of a hazing and come straight back here poking around. Look here, I want to sit for my Second Mate's ticket soon. I don't want this kind of stupid trouble' He stood up abruptly: 'All right: everybody take one tin. Stuff it down your shirt and chuck it overboard when you can this forenoon. It might sink slowly, so heave it well clear. Robbins, that box of figs you pinched: that'd better go too. And for God's sake make sure Jake does-n't catch you at it, or the Mate, or Isaac, or the doctor, either – he's pretty thick with Isaac.' He looked round the table at the appalled and depressed faces: 'It's no good looking like that; Perkins ought not to have swiped so many all at once. If we're copped we'll lose shore-leave as well as being mast-headed. Is that what you want? I'll sling one of them on my way to see the Old Man.'

He left the littered table, threw some water over his face from a bowl, rubbed it with a grimy towel, and tugged a comb through the tight black curls of his hair. Behind him, as with Browning's Hamelin rats, the muttering grew to a grumbling. He paused on his way to the door: 'All right, you can grumble as much as you like, but I say it's got to be done, and when I come back, anyone who hasn't slung a tin over-board gets a good smash in the mouth from me. That clear enough?'

*   *   *

Tongue slightly out with the effort of concentration, Jacob Roberts care-fully wrote the page heading for yesterday's log:

Barque "Figaro" off Caleta Buena WCSA January 19th 1895

Then, copying from his scribbled chartroom notes, he began his cool, bald narrative of the previous day:

Noon: Begins whole gale from NNW. Tremendous heavy sea and cross-swell. Shortened down to lower topsails and staysails only. Course W by N.
2pm: Ship labouring something terrible, as bad as I have ever seen. Decks full half the time. All hands on poop deck for safety.
3.30pm: Wore ship to eastward to close with land. While running before wind, ship struck by tremendous sea on starboard quarter. Hands at braces on maindeck. I gaved clear warning but John Leyshon Second Mate knocked down by sea and hit his back against port after capstan. He was hurt bad and I fear he may have broken bones. Sent him to cabin in care of Steward.
4pm: Ship head-reaching under lower topsails, course due East.
6pm: Wind clearly modurating. Set upper topsails, topgallants, topmast staysails and spanker. Set course to return to anchorage at Caleta Buena. Gaved Steward ordors to issue tot of rum to all hands, in regard to there excellent work in storm.

His lip curled gently in amusement as he wrote, and he allowed himself the complacent thought: You're a crafty old bugger, Roberts, when it comes to handling the crowd. When we weighed anchor yesterday morning they were hard cases and like as not to mutiny. But when the rum was dished out last night they were lining up for their tots, happy as a lot of nippers at a chapel bun-fight. That's what they are, most of them - big children. Live for the moment – that's all it is with them. Still, old Powell will probably stop the price of that much rum out of your pay, as it's not prescribed in the Board of Trade regulations. With a sigh, he plied his pen again:

8pm: Set all plain sail to royals.
6.45am: Came to anchor at Caleta Buena. Tremendous damage done in anchorage by storm. Many ships ashore. Consider my action in riding out storm at sea well justified. Second Mate Leyshon worse. Find he has no use in lower limbs. It was decided...

Then he stopped and thought: No, dammit, I'm captain here; I decide everything. He crossed out the last three words very emphatically and wrote instead:

I decided to send him by next coast boat to Valparaiso in care of the Mate David Evans, for return to UK by passenger steamer. Regret los-i   *n*   *g*
an excellent...

There was a rap at the door and he called irritably: 'Yes?' He hated writing the log, and even more he hated being interrupted while doing it.

'Raven, sir. You asked me to see you.'

'Wait.' He finished off the log, fighting off a heavy drowsy wave that attacked him - a drowsiness compounded of yesterday's violent struggle and worry, a largely sleepless night, and the warm benevolence of the tropical breeze wafting through the open ports, the quiet lop and pluck of wavelets under the barque's counter, the gentle, ever-changing light-patterns on the white deck-head as the sun was reflected by the glancing water. What a climate - that could change so fast and so much in twenty-four hours! Not to mention a *terremoto* - an earthquake - every now and then. Let's hope that was the last of the northers anyway, for a season or two. His mind wandered just enough for him to bark out his order in the wrong language - *'Dewch mewn!* so that as Raven entered he felt a shade confused and said: 'Oh yes, it's you. Come in then. Sit down.'

Standing there stiffly in greasy, salt-stained dungarees, expecting an almighty bollocking and dire threats, together with a long homily on theft, Raven too was thrown out a little. He muttered: 'Thank you, sir', drew a chair out from under the table and sat. Both of them looked up for a moment as hasty and obviously youthful footsteps were heard on the poop-deck just above them. Then the captain began: 'Well, I know what you apprentices are like for buzzes and rumours, so I suppose you know about Mr Leyshon?' He broke off as there was a loud splash from outside the cabin port: 'What the devil's that?' Raven felt a lurch of dread, followed by a surge of anger. He knew well enough what had just landed in the drink. What goddam young idiot was it that had no more sense than to sling his bloody tin of salmon overboard just by the Old Man's cabin port? If only he could get his hands on him... He thought quickly, rose to his feet, and briefly stuck his head out of the port. 'Just a bucket, sir. One of the boys must be getting water for washing-down paintwork on the poop. I'll nip up and tell them not to disturb you, sir.'

'Very good, only look sharp, isn't it? I've got to get ashore on business... Damn brassbound monkeys - more trouble than they're worth...'

Young Robbins, who had been feeling relieved at getting rid of his tin, though grieved at losing it, was surprised to be rewarded by a heavy clout to the side of his head and a brawny hand on his collar Raven, red with fury, first hissed: 'You bloody idiot! Jake heard that!' and then called out officially and even officiously: 'Don't do that aft here. You're disturbing the captain.'

'It's bad enough losing all that lovely grub,' said Robbins five minutes later in the half-deck, nursing an aching head, 'but on top of that I have to take a hell of a chance ditching my tin and then I get a thick ear from Raven for my pains. Doesn't seem fair; I didn't pinch them or decide to ditch them!'

'Now then, young man,' said Jacob, when at last Raven was back, panting somewhat, in his chair: 'You're no doubt wondering why I've sent for you?'

Raven was silent, but thought: Am I not! He was beginning to suspect that he'd made a giant error of judgement, which the half-deck would find unforgivable.

'As I expect you know, Mr Leyshon is now badly disabled. Permanently, I fear. The mate will be escorting him to Valparaiso in a few days to catch a mail-steamer home. I shall be appointing a replacement to the post of second mate, and Mr Evans will, of course, be resuming his duties when he returns.'

Oh Christ, Raven was thinking; I don't know what the hell Jake is leading up to, but it isn't going to be tins of salmon. What a bloody fool I was! What a waste! Can't stop them ditching the lot now. They'll never let me hear the last of it. 'Yes, sir,' he said politely, his face a blank mask.

'Well, there is a great deal of work to be done in discharging and loading cargo, and of course on the voyage home. So I shall have to strengthen the afterguard a little: I've therefore decided to offer you the post of Acting Third Mate...'(Good God - so that was it!) –'for the remainder of this voyage. You're due to sit for Second Mate's ticket then, isn't it? Done your four years? Yes... Now then, I can offer you a salary of three pounds ten shillings a month; the appointment would be for this voyage only, of course. You can move your dunnage into the spare cabin - port side next to the pantry - this morning, and from now on, of course, you will mess aft. Is that acceptable to you, Mister Raven?'

Thunderstruck, Raven was just able to gulp: 'Yes, sir. Thank you sir. And I'll do my best...' The captain's words had all along been more in the nature of an order than that of an offer, but Raven was an ambitious young man and didn't for a moment contemplate turning it down.

'Very well then, I will amend the Crew Agreement later today and you can sign it tonight.' He stood up and offered his hand ceremonially across the table. Raven shook hands in a daze, a whirlwind of feelings and ideas. Shaking hands with the Old Man himself! And he called me *Mister* Raven!

'I will call the hands aft at eight bells to tell them of this. As you know, I am not a bucko or a martinet – don't want a lot of gold braid and bullshit. But I expect firm discipline in my ship, and it will be your job to help to maintain it - you understand what that means?'

'Aye, aye, sir.'

'I wonder if you really do. It won't be easy, you know. You've been one of the half-deck crowd - one of the boys. As bad or worse than the rest of them... No better, anyway...Now that's all got to change, isn't it? You've got to handle the foc'sle crowd now, and your half-deck cronies and all. And set an example to all of them.'

'I'll do my best...'

'And another thing: you know what St Paul says: "When I became a man, I put away childish things"?'

'Sir?' Raven was genuinely at a loss.

'I think you know what I mean: raiding the stores in the lazarette, pinching tins from the pantry, tormenting the life out of the steward... I know what goes on. The steward tells me we're suddenly short of tinned salmon, for instance. Now you've got to put all that behind you. Like, be a gamekeeper, not a poacher any more. You've got a splendid chance to show the company what you're really made of.'

Amazing, thought Raven: I really had forgotten all about those damned tins. All that seems like another existence now - a lot of stupid kids' nonsense.

'Now then,' the captain's manner was brisk and professional. 'You'll assist the other mates about the deck while we're discharging and loading. When we're at sea you'll stand a watch with the mate and help with the work aloft. Of course, I don't need to tell you that Mr Evans is perhaps a little too... well, it wouldn't do for him to lay aloft in bad weather. You understand, don't you, what that means? When it's necessary, you've got to be first aloft, not last, and when things are bad – dangerous, like – you've got to be in the worst place, not the easiest or the safest. We've got a decent crowd for'ard - a lot better than most, these days - and by and large they know their work, but they've got to be kept up to it, and by God they will watch you, mister, for a month or two, to see if you're up to it...Very well then, get your gear together and say goodbye to your former fellow-criminals in the half-deck. And by the by, mister....' Raven paused in the act of stepping over the high coaming of the door. 'You'd better smarten yourself up a bit. Have a good wash and shave, get rid of those greasy duds. You'll have to use your apprentice's uniform until you can get to a decent tailor ashore.'

*   *   *

'Cigar, Mr Grant?' Captain McMasters pushed the box across the polished desktop.

'Thank you, captain.' Grant, his mind elsewhere, took one, rolled it close to his ear to hear it crackle, and lit up, drawing in the rich smoke with relish. 'H'm... Havana... Very good.'

'Aye, straight from Cuba. The very best... But don't thank me, thank Senor Rodriguez, the company's agent here. When he very kindly gave me the use of this office he told me to help myself to anything... There's a few bottles of the right stuff in yon cupboard behind you, by the by. Later, maybe?'

'Not for me, sir. The doctor did say...'

'Oh aye, your head. Is it fairly comfortable now? No concussion? And what about your ribs?'

'Still very sore when I breathe. Got pretty bruised under all that gear. Head's passable, thank you... Just aches a bit.'

'Good, good.'

'And I gather there's nobody else hurt on the "Birkdale"?'

'No, nobody, thank God.'

It'd be more to the point, thought Grant, to thank me. God (if there is one) sent the norther; I was the one who saved the ship and her men. There was a prickly silence between the two men, for they had scarcely exchanged a word since the storm. McMasters had arrived back in Caleta Buena at mid-morning to find his ship ashore and his mate being treated by the young Chilean doctor at the small hospital run by the nitrate company. The doctor had been glad to see him: 'Ah, captain - you have come for your brave officer, Senor Grant. That is good, I think. I have done what I can for him, and he will recover, but this is a poor place for an English gentleman - a poor, bare, dirty place. My patients are only mule-drivers with kicks, and *lancheros* who have falling - no, pardon, have fell - into holds, or have been with bad women. It is no place for an officer. I will send a *peon* for the cab - yes, captain, we have one cab in Caleta Buena - and he shall take you where you wish.'

They were silent in the cab, for there was much to be said on both sides, and neither wished to start. Grant, besides, was still dazed and sore, though astonished at his luck in being alive. He waited for some word of praise and gratitude from McMasters, and when none was forthcoming he spoke only to ask: 'Where are we going? The waterfront is down that way, surely?'

'Aye, but there's no hurry. The barque's well enough where she is for the bye. The company pilot and tug are coming at high water - about three - to haul her off, if she'll come, and berth her in the tier ready for refitting and loading. They've sounded the well and she's not making a pint of water, thanks be. That's the Clyde for ye - they know how to make a ship there. We need to have a talk, and we'll have it at the company office; my quarters being in the state they are, we'd find nowhere to sit, I believe, in the cabin.'

So now Grant sat back, drew steadily on his cigar, and looked about him at the elegant office - its solid desk, bureau and horsehair couch in highly-polished mahogany, the deeply comfortable leather-upholstered chairs, a natty new swivelling office chair behind the desk, slatted blinds to shut out the fierce sun, rich satin curtains loosely furled, as it were, with gaskets of gilt tasselled cord; on the desk a complicated metal gadget which he supposed was a typewriter with 'Made in Milwaukee' on the back in gold letters. All first-class stuff, worth a pretty penny too. And here it was, smack in the middle of a small dreary tropical hell-hole, choked with blowing sand, rock-dust, nitrate-dust and coal-dust. Somebody was making a copper or two out of the trade in dust. He said coolly: 'Do themselves pretty well here.'

'Oh aye, pretty well, pretty well. All these places along the coast are going ahead fast. Ye can't blame them. After all, the Chilenos have not long finished fighting a war with Peru and Bolivia over the nitrate mines, and now they've got them they're not the people to sit on their hands. Most of this stuff' - he waved a hand round the room – 'is imported from Europe in German ships. From Germany, most of it, too, I'm afraid. They get the business...A canny lot, the Germans. D'ye know, up at his house where I've been staying - inland a wee bit - Rodriguez has a grand piano for his wife and daughters to play? A Bechstein grand - the finest in the world, they say. One of Laeisz's ships brought out a cargo of them a couple of years back. Just fancy – a hold full of pianos! There's civilization for ye. And all we get to sell them is coal, coal, coal, with a few railway lines now and then.'

'You wanted to talk with me, sir?' Grant cut in. 'Not about pianos, I take it?'

'No, that's so...We must get to business, mister. Once they've got the ship berthed in the tier, moored bow and stern, we can go ahead with getting her back into shape...'

'Yes, I was working that out while I was in that hovel of a hospital,' said Grant. 'The bosun and sailmaker and myself - we can rig her well enough. May need a bit of blacksmith's work, but Metcalfe's a fair hand at that. But there's only the boys to help, so we shall need a few decent ABs off the waterfront to do the donkey-work - fixing blocks, reeving the running rigging and so on. Four or five would do - Swedes if you can get them, or Russian Finns, maybe.'

McMasters looked uncomfortable and shuffled an inkstand about, for unconsciously as they began to talk business, he had sat down in the chair at the desk: 'Thank ye, mister; I'm glad to see energy and enterprise, but that won't be necessary.'

Grant flushed with annoyance: 'Look here, captain, a few hands wouldn't cost the Owners much. You could hire them by the week, come to that.'

'No, it's not a question of that, mister. The fact is I've had a word with the nitrate company's agent - with Senor Rodriguez - about the refitting. He's in charge of all the shipping side of their business here, you understand...And we've more or less agreed that his men will do the re-rigging.'

There was a tense silence, in which Grant stared at his captain incredulously. McMasters met his eye briefly, then looked down again, his face suffused with a flush. Despite his knocks and bruises, Grant leapt from his chair and came to the opposite side of the desk, leaning over it, grasping its edge. 'You've *what?* His men will do it? What men? What men has he got here who could rig a... a clothes-line?'

Now the captain's handsome face was deeply flushed with anger, and he too raised his voice: 'He doesn't need to have men here, mister. He is the agent for the biggest nitrate company in Chile! He will get the necessary new spars and cordage, and the men to fit them, from Iquique.'

'Huh! I've no doubt he will!'

McMasters stood up abruptly, and the two men stared level, face to face: 'And what, pray, do you mean by that sneer, mister? I don't like your tone one little bit!'

'Has he given you an estimate of the cost?'

'No, I've not yet had...'

'Have you signed a contract for the refitting?'

'No, but I've more or less...'

'Then legally there's nothing to stop you changing your mind, sir. May I say this, with all due respect: if you let Rodriguez go ahead, let me assure you his bill will be nearly as much as the whole ship is worth. I know these small ports – they're the same the world over for overcharging. Port Stanley in the Falklands – that's another den of thieves.'

'Mr Grant, I will thank you not to interfere. I have as good as given my word of honour to Senor Rodriguez that the job will be his. As for the cost...'

'As for the cost, it will be hundreds - no, thousands, - of dollars thrown away. Let me get four decent ABs, and we can do the job ourselves, sir. There are good men sitting about on the sack-bales on every waterfront on this coast, just waiting for a homeward-bound berth. The bosun is an ex-Clyde rigger, as you know, and I myself am no fool at it, if I may say so. As for the spars and cordage, I heard in the hospital there are five ships ashore; do you mean to say we can't find all the rope and spars we need there? We can salvage them - get them for a song. Then it's just a matter of adzing the spars to fit. We'll have her ready well before she's finished loading.'

The force, the truth, of every word he said showed in the urgent thrust forward of his stocky body over the desktop, but McMasters summoned what dignity he could and held up his hands in a gesture of arrest: 'Very well, Grant, that will do. You have made your suggestions, but the ship is my responsibility; it is for me to decide, and I have decided. I do not have to explain my reasons to a subordinate officer, but I may tell you there are many considerations in an affair such as this which someone in your position cannot appreciate.'

'Oh, that I don't doubt,' said Grant ironically, and added suddenly: 'What about the Owners?'

'The Owners?'

'Yes, the precious Owners! You have many times impressed upon me and the other mates that we must always act in their interests. We mustn't waste a rope-yarn or a scrap of soap or a penn'orth of paint. What will they think when they find you've spent five times as much as you needed to?'

McMasters was too ill-at-ease to think carefully, and replied unguardedly: 'The Owners are insured...' Then he tried to improve it a little: 'The Owners have always placed their trust in my judgement, and I'm sure they will do so in this instance.'

Grant sank down into his chair again, and stared full at his captain, his face expressionless: 'Yes, sir, I dare say they will. And I assure you I am beginning to understand very well the "considerations" you mentioned just now.'

His cool manner riled McMasters to the point that he spluttered and fumed: 'I've already said, mister – *that'll do!* Don't worry about work; I've plenty of work in hand for you and the hands aboard. You, I take it, haven't seen the state of the ship yet? All the accommodation aft has suffered, but especially my cabin. The spanker gaff fell down through the skylight, and no doubt several seas came clean over the poop after that. My cabin is wrecked - utterly wrecked, and many of my display cases smashed to bits. So to begin with, you can get to work, under my supervision, salvaging what we can of my collection from the cabin and bringing it here for restoration.'

'Jesus Christ Almighty! We're to footle about with *your butterflies?*'

'Yes, sir, my collection. It happens to be a life-time's work on my part, from every corner of the globe, and it is reckoned by many experts who have seen it to be the finest international collection in British hands. If, like me, you were a Fellow of the Royal Entomological Society, you would know that, and know its financial value, and its value to Science. Perhaps you would not then take this philistine attitude.'

'Sixty men died in that norther yesterday, I hear. Sixty-two to be precise. All of us on the "Birkdale" might easily have died too. And all you can think about is your goddam butterflies!' Despite his anger, Grant had difficulty in suppressing his grim delight that the captain's quarters had suffered by far the most. Serve him bloody well right for not being there!

'Let me tell you, Mr Grant, that your manner - not to mention your disgusting blasphemies - seems to me impertinent and insubordinate in the extreme. But I will make allowances for your experiences yesterday, and for the head injuries you sustained. Perhaps you have not quite recovered your mental balance yet... However, I must come now to the point I wished to discuss with you in the first place: namely, your action in slipping the anchors and grounding the ship. That is an extremely serious matter, and I trust you have thought out your position, and considered how you will justify yourself, if need be?'

'Justify? Justify? I saved your ship and the lives of all those aboard her.' And he added bitterly: 'The butterflies, of course, had been killed already by you in the sacred cause of Science.'

'We are not discussing my collection now, mister, we are discussing your future in this profession, and I think you have a great deal to justify. For instance, an experienced assessor at a court of enquiry might well ask why, since all the ground-tackle was new and in excellent order, you had to slip the cables. You could have paid out more cable. Four other ships hung on successfully.'

'They weren't stuck up out of the water like a haystack, in ballast, I'll wager. And five other ships were not so lucky. I could not pay out cable because I couldn't trust the cable-holder brake to control it - Oh, and by the by: you were saying the ship was your responsibility. I believe you even stood by her while she was being built? Did you ensure that the bitter ends of the cable were shackled to the keel in the proper way?'

'Of course.' The reply was prompt, but the man's confusion and uncertainty were written on his face.

'Remarkable! When I last saw them they had scraps of rusty wire round them. That would interest the assessor too, I suppose. I slipped the cables, captain, when I found she was dragging both anchors...'

'When you *thought* she was dragging, you mean. From my much greater experience, I think it highly unlikely that she would do so.'

'Perhaps you could have judged that better if you'd been aboard. We put a lead-line down – that's how we knew. Metcalfe will confirm what I say.'

'H'm...The Second is a very young man, and no doubt was influenced by you.... There is also the matter of the lighters - six of them - that you rammed and sank. They will all have to be replaced by new craft from Valparaiso, and the third-party claim will be very considerable. An assessor might think you could have beached the ship on sand without causing such wholesale destruction of other people's property. Why, man, it's a wonder you didn't smash up the loading pier while you were at it!'

Grant got up abruptly, and went to the window, which looked west, out over the bay. Of 'Birkdale' he could see only the ruined masts over the shimmering tin roofs of the loading sheds, but looking straight ahead he could see the ships that had survived the storm lying quietly to their anchors, rolling and nodding to the ceaseless blue swells. Here and there a lighter crawled painfully, beetle-like, across the bright blue, her sweeps swinging slowly, their wet blades sometimes catching the sun to send a quick spark of light. Business as usual: out with the coal and timber and railway lines - and grand pianos too, perhaps - and in with the everlasting nitrate. It was hard to grasp - never mind convey to another - what it had been like the day before - that howling cacophony of wind, surf and driven spray.

'You weren't there,' he said quietly. 'You didn't see it or feel it. You can't imagine what it was like. I've never seen weather like it, and I've seen plenty of dirty weather in my time. I've been round the Horn six times. You, sir, and any assessor who thinks he could have done better, should have been there yesterday. Damn it, I only had old men and boys! I dared not send them aloft on the yards, so that meant I could only use the stays'ls. And you couldn't see past the bowsprit-end, most of the time, for spray. There's only a hundred yards or so of sandy beach between the rocks; wasn't it better to hit the lighters than miss the sand?'

'Aye, that's all very well, but yon was a pretty expensive little trip, mister, when ye add it all up. You were complaining just now about the size of the repair bill; you just wait till the third-party claims start coming in.'

'The lighters couldn't be helped. They're only tin boxes anyway - they don't compare with the cost of an A1 at Lloyd's, Clyde-built, two thousand ton barque, do they? Never mind the lives that might have been lost. But I suppose those don't count for much with the Owners?'

'Well, speaking strictly financially, no, they don't - not *financially,* ye understand. The Company has no actual legal liability to any widows, offspring, next of kin and so forth, beyond the deceased seaman's back pay and personal possessions. Of course, on the other hand, the Owners are humane men, Christian gentlemen....'

'Oh yes, I've always noticed that. You've only to see the provisions they buy for the men they love so much.'

'Mr Grant, if you'd kindly leave off these mannerless interruptions, perhaps I could get on to saying what I've wanted to say all along. It is this: you and I don't always see eye to eye, maybe, and I think ye've been hasty, precipitate, in this instance - slipping the cable and so on. On the other hand, for your age you're a capable officer, and good with the men, and I accept that, whatever the consequences may have been, you acted for the best as you saw it. So I've no wish to lose you, and I'm prepared...' he paused, licking his lips, to allow his incredible magnanimity to be appreciated and given its due weight – 'yes, I'm fully prepared to stand by you if there should be any ... any difficulty.... any unpleasantness.... at some time in the future.'

He tailed awkwardly to a halt and the mate, outlined blackly against the sunny window, studied his captain in silence - the plump red features over the brilliantly-white starched collar, the portly figure in smart shore-going blue serge and brass buttons leaning forward in (now he saw it clearly) a kind of eager, pitiful, supplication. McMasters was frightened - frightened of what the Owners might think of his absence from his ship in a crisis; frightened maybe about other things Grant didn't know about. This last speech of his was an olive branch, thrust at him. But why? For what? Nothing was ever for nothing with McMasters. Look at his fat hands grasping the ebony ruler, twisting it round and round; look at the beads of sweat glistening on his jowls. The certainty suddenly came to Grant from nowhere - from thin air - that he could never sail again with this man. To do that, to sit at the cabin table, to say 'Aye aye, sir' twenty times a day - for that there had to be some respect, and now he had none. That being so, there was nothing to hope for from McMasters, and therefore nothing to fear. After a pause, which was intolerable to the captain, Grant said: 'I see. That is most kind, captain, I'm sure. Like your Christian Owners, you are forgiving me for saving your ship... And in return?'

'In return? I don't understand.'

'There must be something in return; with you there always is.'

'Once again, mister, I don't like your manner one little bit... But since you put it so... so crudely, I will explain. I shouldn't have thought that between gentlemen it was necessary to explain, but it seems I must. Very well then: if I show loyalty to you, is it too much to ask the same in return? That you should show to me the same... eh... loyalty and... eh... discretion that I am extending to you?'

Grant advanced to lean over the desk, a sardonic grin on his face: 'Aha! Now I understand! You're worried, and you want me to be worried too, don't you? You're saying "You tell lies for me, and I'll do the same for you".'

'Mr Grant, I must ask you...'

'You went off to Iquique, didn't you, on some footling errand that could easily have waited, when the glass was falling and dirty weather expected? And not content with that, you didn't even come straight back, did you? You put in some time - some nice civilized shore-time - with your precious crony Rodriguez at his nice comfortable house with his beautiful whatsisname grand piano. You just thought: 'The ground tackle's good and Grant will manage. It's a lot nicer here - good brandy, good cigars, beef steaks, fresh fruit and whatnot.' So you left it all to me. But you see, I couldn't manage after all - not in the way you'd hoped, so now you're right in the shit, aren't you, if I breathe a word to the Owners?' Grant suddenly straightened and flung an arm up to point out of the window. His voice was thick with scorn and anger: 'See that ship out there - the Frenchman? The one with grey topsides with black ports? Her skipper tried to get aboard her from a tug in the early part of the storm. He'd been ashore to see his agents too, only *he* thought he should be aboard his ship in a crisis. The trouble was, he fell between the tug and the ship and got crushed to bits. They'd got what was left of him under a bit of old sail in the hospital - not much, by the look of it. "Ah well," you'll say, "he's dead and I'm not, so I was right." Yes, he's dead, but at least he died as a man and a captain, and a credit to his nation, whereas *you*...'

'Very well, that is enough from you, Mr Grant. I have been very patient, but that is *enough!* You will kindly leave; I will discuss your conduct with you when we are back aboard.'

'I'm not leaving, and neither are you, by God, until I've finished. I've put up with four months of whining and belly-aching and hazing from you since we left Middlesbrough, so now you can listen for a change. You thought that if you frightened me with bogeys like courts of enquiry I'd back you up with a few discreet lies - about your absence from duty and your rather expensive bargain with Rodriguez. I suppose you expect to do quite nicely out of that, one way or another? Five per cent, is it - or ten perhaps? Should I have had to keep quiet about the ballast at Valparaiso too?' It was a shot in the dark, but Grant felt a surge of triumph as he saw McMasters go first a deep crimson, then a muddy greyish-yellow at the word 'ballast'. 'Ah, so I was right about that! We both know that "Birkdale" needs about five hundred tons to keep her safely upright at sea; no doubt that's what the ballast company will have charged the Owners for, but how much actually went in? Three hundred? Three-fifty? Not an ounce over three-fifty, I'll bet a year's pay! I'm not some stupid young cub straight from Conway, you know. I know what five hundred tons of ballast looks like when I see it, and I know about the rackets some captains fix up with the sharks ashore. You sign a delivery note for five hundred tons, he puts in three hundred, the Owners pay a damn sight more than they should, and you and the shark split the difference between you. You'll be able to buy yourself some more pretty butterflies.'

'That is enough! I will not listen to another word of these disgusting libels! You are no longer an officer of my ship, and what is more, I give you a bad discharge, so no-one else will have you.'

McMasters, now thoroughly frightened and furious at the same time, made for the door, but Grant made three tigerish strides across the room, seized the collar of his smart shore jacket, hauled him backwards, and flung him into the chair he had just left. Several brass buttons were torn off, and bounced about on the rich crimson carpet. He stood over the dishevelled captain, an almost dangerous madness in his eyes.

'You won't, you fat Scottish swine, you won't do anything of the bloody kind! I'll tell you what you'll do: I'm going back aboard the ship to get my dunnage packed and brought ashore. I'll see you at ten o'clock tomorrow morning at the British Vice-consul's office. You will bring my discharge form signed, with "Discharge by Agreement" entered on it. And I'll have a "Good" for character and another for ability. And don't forget the ship's official log. I'll see a good discharge written in that by you, stamped and countersigned by the Vice-consul, and then I'll be only too happy to wash my hands of you. And by Christ above, if you are not there by ten I will start making a formal statement of complaint against you, McMasters.' He limped to the door, feeling his injuries now that his passion was gone, and paused with his hand on the knob to speak almost calmly, objectively. 'The trouble with you is that you're a pathetic bag of piss and wind, even as a blackmailer. You never stood any chance of frightening me, because I'm a seaman, and I know my job, and I did my job - better than most. What I did yesterday I would do again tomorrow in the same circumstances, and fifty courts of enquiry wouldn't frighten me, because there I'd be judged by decent seamen, not by cheating, canting hypocrites. And talking of cheating, don't forget my four months' back pay either. Six pounds ten a month, plus a few extra days. And I'll have it in gold sovereigns, if you please. And then good luck to the "Birkdale" and all the poor bastards who sail in her - with *you*.'

8

'Oh, and Raven!' Jacob Roberts called as the young man's steps began to fade beyond the door.

'Sir?'

'Ask the mate to get the bosun to rig the gangway and get my gig hoisted out. Right away; I've got to get ashore.'

Self-consciously, as if his new exalted status were blazoned all over him, Raven hurried for'ard past the half-deck, ignoring a puzzled look from Ieuan Davies, who stood in the doorway expectantly. He climbed briskly on to the foc'sle head, having passed through a group of foremast hands, who paid him about as much attention as they would a bluebottle. He was to them still just the biggest of the scruffy band of adolescent nobodies who lived in the after deck-house.

The tall cadaverous frame of the mate was bent studiously over the cable of the port anchor, and he was in earnest conference in Welsh with the bosun; the hands were mustered up for'ard as the ship was to be properly moored for a 'full due' - for many weeks, perhaps months - while the coal was unloaded and the nitrate loaded at a leisurely, tropical, Chilean pace. It would all be hot slow work. So the port anchor would be dropped ahead, and another anchor laid out astern to hold her securely. For many weary and monotonous weeks 'Figaro' would be part of the port, one of the more-or-less fixed points in the Caleta Buena seascape.

When Raven passed on the captain's order Evans looked round at him sharply. He obviously knew about the promotion, but said nothing directly about it. Raven felt a twinge of disappointment; it wouldn't have hurt Dai Dome to say, 'Well done' or 'Welcome aft' or something. It seemed he didn't approve of the promotion; he just sniffed and said: 'The boys taking the captain ashore in the gig, is it? What about you? Are you to go in the boat?'

'He didn't say, sir, but I should think not - five is a crew.'

'I know that, young man. Very well then - you come up here and help.'

'Captain said I was to shift my dunnage to...' he caught a

111

wide-eyed look of amazement on the bosun's face, and went on, flustered - 'to shift my dunnage, then to change.'

'Change?'

'Into - into uniform.'

'Diawl! A bloody admiral now, is it? You stay as you are, mun; I'll explain to the capten. We got to get seventy-five fathoms of cable up from the locker - all rusty; then we got the stern anchor to lay out - the tug will be alongside soon for that. Then we're taking the hatch-covers off the for'ard hold and rigging hoists. That's not brass button and gold lace work, is it? It's just ordinary work, so you stay as you are...I know what: you can make a start by getting the gig overside yourself. Use those dratted boys to help you. Know how to do it, do you? Davits may be stiff - may need a drop of oil to get them turning. And mind, mister: I've just had that gig painted lovely; any paint that gets scraped off, you'll put it back yourself.... personally.'

'Aye, aye,' said Raven, who considered he was now justified in dropping the 'sir'. After all, Dai had finally called him 'mister', the title universally applied to mates, and mates only, in sailing ships. He walked aft, to where Perkins, until an hour ago a near-equal and rival, was plying a deck-scrubber. 'Right, Perkins, belay that. Muster the other apprentices to launch the gig. Get the covers off her and let go the gripes. Look lively, and don't argue either; the Old - the captain's just made me third mate, so I'm telling you, not asking.'

There had never been much love lost between Raven and Perkins; they had always been too near rivals to be friends, and the former's slight seniority had always been a bitter pill to the jealous Perkins. This abrupt and uncompromising order from someone who had slept last night, and even breakfasted this morning, in the half-deck was too much for him. Raven couldn't be allowed to get away with this throwing his weight about so soon - especially not after the great tins debacle. All right for him – he'd get all the decent food he wanted now, but the half-deck boys had lost a gastronomic treasure, thanks to his stupid and unnecessary panic. No, he wasn't going to let him strut about already; he was now shrewd enough to realise that Raven's abruptness arose, not from vanity or conceit, but from insecurity. Perkins said: 'Third mate, eh? Good God! Well, Mister Raven, *sir,* we're swabbing down – mate's orders. Haven't finished yet.' He was about to turn away when his broom was snatched out of his hand and pitched for'ard to clatter on the deck yards away. It landed at the heels of the unfortunate steward, who leapt in the air with a feminine scream and dropped two real china plates on the unforgiving deck.

'I said "lively!"' yelled the new third mate. The young men glared at close range, red-faced with rage, and for a moment there was a tense silence in which anything could have happened. Then a voice rapped out from the break of the poop above them: 'My boat, mister! Is it ready yet?' The captain had an instinct for appearing at the right moment and for saying the right thing.

'Aye, aye, sir!' said Raven. 'Ready in five minutes. Robbins, get the oars and rowlocks from the bosun's store; you two sweat up that after fall and get her off the chocks!' He felt grateful that Jake had so firmly and yet tactfully upheld his authority, while appearing to reprove him for tardiness, and yet a part of him was frustrated; it might have been better, that part said, to have had an out-and-out showdown with Perkins. If he'd flattened him the foc'sle would soon have known about it; as it was...

The smart little white boat was freed of the chocks and gripes and cover that had held it tight and protected it from the crashing seas, swung out over the bulwark and lowered, the blocks of its falls squeaking from disuse, to bump and nuzzle gently at the ship's side. Her crew of five boys went hand-over-hand like monkeys down the life-lines into the boat and hauled her aft to the gangway. As he was about to descend (with a great deal more dignity) into her, the captain called: 'Mister Raven, I want this boat sent back for me at eight bells this afternoon. And by that time I want its crew to look like decent indentured apprentices and Christians from a decent Welsh ship. I've seen gangs of poxed-up greasers who looked smarter than that lot do now.'

The boys laid into their oars with suppressed glee, despite the virulence of his criticism; if they were to look like a smart boat's crew they couldn't be given dirty jobs to do down in the hold amid the coal-dust. The stay at Caleta Buena looked like being a good loaf; the Old Man would probably need (or at least want) to go ashore every day. That would mean plenty of boating in the sunshine and hanging about ashore waiting for him - better than cargo work any day!

Perkins, as senior, had taken the tiller and sat in the stern-sheets opposite his captain, whose attention was taken by the hideous tangle of wreckage - smashed painted hulls, littered cargo, ruined masts and spars - crusting the southern end of the bay over on their starboard side. Perkins headed the boat for the Company jetty, and was looking conscientiously ahead at his course, when, to his dismay, he saw, nodding in the little wavelets ahead, the stolen and ditched box of figs, horribly conspicuous and (probably) instantly identifiable. He was appalled to see that it would pass down Jake's side of the boat. He could not fail to notice it! Damn these tideless anchorages - it was like being becalmed: anything that went overboard - tins, trash or even turds - stayed alongside for hours.

Holding his breath for fear, he brought the tiller gently towards him, so that the boat would turn a shade to starboard, and the box would pass down his side. But it was no good: watching a course was in the Old Man's blood. He noticed the turn - though thankfully not the box -and said irritably: 'Duw, boy, can't you steer a course in a fourteen-foot dinghy? There's the jetty, over there!'

Robbins, one of the starboard oars, understood at once, and, though not generally noted as a great intellectual, saw what was to be done; he made a move which combined self-sacrifice and genius: instead of raising his oar at the end of the next stroke, he kept it clumsily in the water, catching a tremendous crab, fighting the loom of the oar as it pressed into his chest. The boat slowed and swung right round to starboard, putting the offending box well away from the captain's line of vision. That worthy potentate was in any case in a paroxysm of righteous rage over the humiliating incompetence of his boat's crew. People ashore and in other ships would have seen that pathetic failure, seen and sneered in contempt; captains of ships on the West Coast took pride in having a smart boat's crew, in racing them against other crews, even in putting a few dollars on their success. And then there was the prestige of Wales to be upheld - or rather, restored - too.

Jacob snarled furiously at all of them: 'What in hell is wrong with you snot-nosed young sojers? One can't steer, one - whatsyer-name -Robbins – can't even row! Don't they teach you anything at your fancy bloody colleges these days? Iesu mawr! I suppose you'll all be captains one day, and then God help the British Merchant Service, I say. Listen, boy,' he stabbed a blunt forefinger painfully into Perkins' chest, then pointed to a barque anchored a good mile off to the southward. 'See that grey barque there - the Frenchman? Right, when you come back after putting me ashore you go round her first, understand? Give you a bit of practice, won't it? And I'll be bloody watching you too, so no shenanigans.'

The boys sighed silently, philosophically; miles of extra rowing on a day that was getting hotter and more windless all the time; but at least it was better than being caught out with the stolen gear; better than being stuck on the royal yardarm for hours on end, for weeks on end. Robbo's crab had been worth it!

*   *   *

'Very well, captain, that seems to be all in order,' said Aloysius Martin, British Vice-consul in Caleta Buena, pushing the official log and ship's manifest back across the desk. 'Crew's health all right - no fever, no contagious diseases? Good…. Now then, a glass of sherry perhaps? I can recommend the fino… or perhaps you'd prefer schnapps? The P Line ships from Hamburg bring us plenty of good German liquor and wine.' He uncoiled his lanky white-suited figure and opened a cupboard. 'Or brandy? The French ships are useful when it comes to claret, cognac and so forth. All the British ships seem to bring us is coal and carbolic soap and very elderly copies of "Punch" - no great assets to civilized life, don't you feel?'

Jacob opted for schnapps, but declined to toss it back in the German style. Martin sank back languidly: 'Good, eh? I'll say one thing for nitrate: it may be revoltingly dusty stuff, and it may keep some of us stuck in these horrible little holes between the Atacama and the sea, but at least it softens the blow a little - brings us a few little luxuries, what? Cigar?'

Roberts accepted gratefully, and with a grunted 'Excuse me', rose from his roomy chair and went to a window that looked across the wide blue horseshoe of the bay. He gave another grunt of mingled satisfaction and amusement; far out across the bay lay a grey French barque, one of the Bordes Line ships, and as he watched, from under her bowsprit appeared a small white boat which was steadily, laboriously, painfully, crawling its way across the matchless blue sea.

The official looked over his shoulder: 'Your boat? You sent her aboard the "Jeanne d'Arc?"'

'No, not exactly. Just getting my apprentices into shape a bit. Spot of boat-pulling in the sun won't do them any harm. Forgotten how to manage a boat, by the look of it. And they've got away with about half the cabin stores, if the steward's to be believed. Can't be bothered to investigate all his tittle-tattle. So today I'm smartening up their rowing and getting a bit of my own back, isn't it? Sweat some of the devil out of those cubs.'

Martin nodded and smiled urbanely. He was used to adjudicating in the often bitter and tedious disputes between ships' masters and their subordinates. That duty was, after the dust, the heat and the isolation, the most tiresome aspect of his job. He was glad to find a master who could deal with his own troubles. 'I was sorry to hear about your second mate, captain. Most unfortunate accident...Shocking storm, what? Fortunately, the coast boat is due in from Arica, bound south, tomorrow. She stays only an hour or two, so it would be best for you to arrange a Company tug to transfer your patient straight to her. Then he will be in Valparaiso in four days. I will telegraph the hospital for you, to reserve a bed for him, and I should advise you to wire also, to secure a berth for him on the next PSNC mail-boat home. I have a list of sailings in my desk.'

'Thank you, Mr Martin, thank you. You are most kind. Now then, there is...'

'Ah, I think I know what you're about to ask, captain, and the answer is yes, I do know of a possible replacement for your second mate. I had a Mr.... what was his name now? Ah yes, Grant, that's it, here this morning taking a discharge from the barque "Birkdale", the ship that was beached near the jetty.'

'Was he the first mate or second?'

'First, captain. Indeed, it was he who beached her, I believe.'

'Indeed? *Diawl!* Her master not aboard in weather like that?' Roberts was incredulous. 'And that man - the man who saved her - is now discharged?'

'Er, yes, captain.' Martin remembered the silences between the 'Birkdale's' captain and mate, and the almost palpable hatred that had filled the air of his office. Obviously, there was much about that blandly-worded 'Discharge by Agreement' that he did not understand. But he also remembered that, as a young career diplomat in Her Majesty's Consular Service (however seedy and humble his present post) it was not for him to gossip or speculate over things that didn't concern him, nor to make any statement that was not totally proven, verifiable and unavoidable. His long, sallow, yellowish face (he'd had some bad times with fever when he was up at Callao) took on a professionally 'shut-down' look. 'I couldn't say why, of course - not in my province, you know.'

'That's a damned rum business then,' said Roberts. 'But anyway, I fear a smart first mate like that will hardly sign on as a second.'

In sailing ships there was a great gulf of rank and status between the first mate and the second or third; the former was the captain's right-hand man, the others (at little more than half his pay, and often valued financially less than the cook) were more like senior petty officers.

'As to that, too, of course I couldn't say. He did however express to me a strong desire not to... er... remain long at Caleta Buena, a most understandable desire, I feel. In the meantime, he is staying at our one and only hotel, such as it is. He was knocked about somewhat in the stranding, but I could send a message there and ask him to meet you here this afternoon, if you wish? Shall we say two-thirty? Until then, may I offer you lunch, captain, at my lodgings?'

'Lunch? Oh, you mean dinner, is it? Yes, yes, very good of you, very kind indeed. Make a nice change from ship's tack, I dare say.'

'Ah, captain, let me implore you not to raise your hopes too high. We are, as it were, virtually at sea here, since all our provisions must reach us by sea.' He waved a hand towards the back window of his office, that looked out at the steeply-rising, lion-hided foothills, parched, splintered and trembling with heat. 'Last rained here in 1886, they say - a twenty-minute shower.... Nothing grows, not a blade of grass, unless you count the cactus inland a little, in the desert. "I think I never saw such starved ignoble nature; nothing throve..." That sort of thing, you know.'

Jacob was at a loss. Martin gave a disarming laugh: 'Poetry.... My apologies for launching into it without warning.... Fellow called Browning. One of my enthusiasms.' He waved a hand at a well-filled shelf to his right. 'My fond mama in Winchester keeps me well supplied with books... The time goes by slowly here sometimes, even in office hours. However, one mustn't grumble - one could easily have been sent to Vladivostok. A ship calls here once a week from the south, where they have fields, cattle, sheep, vineyards and so on...Ah, delightful, what? Come along, though. I expect my capable senora will be able to find you a fair beefsteak. Would that be agreeable, captain?'

Nice enough chap, Roberts thought, and does his job well, but by damn these Saison talked funny, especially these posh ones, with their 'lunch' and 'as it were' and 'what?' and this funny way of saying 'A-ah'. He said aloud: 'That'd be very nice, sir, very nice indeed.'

*　*　*

The afternoon encounter between the two seamen was a brisk, brief affair. Each began with a strong professional admiration for the other for his conduct in the storm, for each approved totally of the other's course of action. Each liked, too, what he saw in the other, for they were of the same Cape Horn pedigree - stocky, powerfully-built, square of face and shoulder, with large, capable, blunt-fingered hands. Both had the self-confidence of the skilled professional who was used to commanding men, demanding obedience from them, and facing the worst that they and the elements could do. There were contrasts too: Grant's face tanned a handsome brown and his light-brown hair bleached by the sun; Jacob's a leathery brick-red with lines sunk like deep ravines, especially about his eyes, after forty years of screwing his eyes up against the sun's glare, against the lash of rain and the blinding sting of snow. His hair, still thick and strong for his age, a grizzled black, well plastered down across the wide skull with glossy macassar oil. Despite the heavy grim lines downward from the mouth and the parallel wrinkles of age and worry on his forehead, there was yet a warmth and kindliness (almost a softness) about Roberts' dark eyes, and a reluctant humorous twitch about his lips that contrasted with the blue, intense stare of Grant's eyes and the hard, poker-player's inscrutability of his features.

They talked in brief professional sentences for less than five minutes before Roberts held out his hand and said: 'Very well, Mr Grant: I offer you the post of second mate for the remainder of the voyage. We are to load nitrate here, then to Falmouth for orders to discharge in a UK port. Can't offer you more than four pounds ten a month, I'm afraid; the Owners, you know...'

Grant took his hand: 'I accept, captain, and thank you. I'll do my best to give satisfaction.'

'Mind you,' said Jacob, 'speaking just man to man, there are things I find hard to fathom: I should say you did damn well in your last ship, and yet you leave her - and take an inferior post. You'll admit it's a bit odd-like? I don't want to pry, of course. Your discharge is quite satisfactory - perhaps it's none of my business.'

'With all respect, sir, I think the least said, soonest mended. Let's just say Captain McMasters and I didn't exactly see eye-to-eye on some matters.'

'McMasters? I've heard that name.... Isn't he one of the Compass Line captains...from Liverpool? Wait a minute.... Isn't he the one who collects bugs wherever he goes?'

'Indeed he is, sir, only it's butterflies.'

'And he left the ship with you? How long had the glass been falling here?'

'Three days. One thing I will say for the norther: it gives you plenty of warning - not like a *pampero.'*

'Very well, Mr Grant. Now I think I understand everything on that matter, and I'm bound to say that in your place I think I'd have done the same. Of course, it's only fair for me to point out to you that you might find a mate's berth if you were to wait...'

'I've no wish to hang about on this coast, sir.'

'No? Well, that is your affair entirely. Of course, I can make no promises, but my present mate Mr Evans is an elderly man. He may well decide to swallow the hook after this voyage; I think Leyshon's accident was a shock to him. If he does, I may - with my Owners' approval - be able to offer you something better than second mate quite soon, at the end of this voyage. But I can't tell yet. Right, then: my boat will be at the Company jetty at four. Take a couple of the lads to collect your dunnage if you like. I have to see the Company agent now about launches for tomorrow morning - want to start shifting the coal if I can. Hope there's not too much swell running.'

'Using a donkey?' said Grant hopefully. The donkey was a small steam engine housed for'ard, which could be used for heavy tasks like weighing anchor and hoisting out cargo.

'No, mister, all by hand, I'm afraid – Armstrong's Patent, as they say. My Owners - the Powell Line of Cardiff – won't stump up for engines or coal, not with men at two pound fifteen a month. Uneconomic, that's their word for it.'

Grant shook his head. 'By Jove, sir, they should come out here and see the way the Germans do it. They know what's economic all right. They've got donkey-winches rattling away all the time - one on each hatch. They get loaded in no time at all. They'll be the finish of us out here one day.'

'Aye, very likely - one day. In the meantime, I have mail to collect, and a cable to send, as well as seeing the agent. Wait for me at the jetty, if you please, when you've got your gear into the boat. You'll have the great delight of meeting our brassbounders - the usual collection of loafers, idiots, ne'er-do-wells and criminals.'

*   *   *

By six o'clock that day, 'Figaro' was like a ship of the dead. Securely moored fore and aft, she gently rolled her masts in eccentric swoops and circles against the darkening sky. A few seabirds squabbled over a patch of floating galley refuse close alongside; ropes, chains, wires and blocks groaned a little as the huge swaying masts put strains upon them in turn. The anchor cables shifted, clinking quietly in the hawse-pipes as the bow rose and fell, rose and fell endlessly.

All hands were free from toil after a hard day mooring ship, lifting hatches and rigging cargo-hoists and chutes. Even Wellington Jones, the ample Jamaican cook, a man who seldom had a moment of leisure from his endless drudgery, had left his pots and pans and his stifling galley fire. Dabbing his glistening face and neck with a pad of cotton waste, he sat at ease on the main hatch with his friend Isaac Hughes, and, like every man-jack aboard, he read his letters. For the captain and boys had come back, not only with a new mate, but also with something of much more immediate interest - three months' mail for the entire crew. Many nitrate ships were manned by careless, feckless, friendless sea-gypsies who seemed devoid of any secure bonds ashore: no wives, mothers or fathers, children, brothers or sisters, uncles or cousins to care how they were or where they were. Such men looked for no letters, and generally could not have read them anyway. But 'Figaro' was a Welsh ship; nearly all her foc'sle hands were from the tight, interrelated communities of the West Wales seaboard from St Davids to Borth; nearly all were steady men with tidy wives, children and homes in those snug, stone-built warrens; most of them had served in John Powell's ships for years. Each had a fistful of letters, and sat spell-bound at the unaccustomed exercise of reading, their lips moving silently in time with the words on the page, unconsciously breathing soft exclamations of surprise, pleasure, sorrow or sympathy at the homely news, the paper sheets flimsy in their great brown clumsy hands. Kellock, the elderly Cockney AB, known ironically as 'Curly' because of his total baldness, had a sheaf of newspapers and political pamphlets besides his letters. The Swedes Larsen and Johanssen, even the Russian Finn Seppinen from his tiny eastern Baltic island, all had their letters. To all these hard, simple men the letters brought, for a while, a magic softening of their hearts, a humanizing touch that eased the pain of their exile - for all were fugitives from the grinding poverty of their seaside towns and villages. It was a moment which not even the most downright, Down-East, big-booted bucko of a Yankee mate would have dared to interrupt.

The half-deck was silent too, its denizens having left its solid simmering fug of sweat and old socks to sprawl on the after hatch with their letters, in which mothers, aunts and grandmothers exhorted them to be good and pure, to bath frequently, to change their vests at least once a week, to say their prayers every night, go to church when they could, and not on any account to swear or get themselves or their clothes wet.

Down aft, not an officer was to be seen. The mate was keeping Leyshon company in a sort of surly, taciturn sociability. Each was absorbed in his letters; neatly-rolled copies of the 'Fishguard Echo', the 'Teifiside Advertiser' and the 'Western Telegraph and Cymric Times', rich garners of local events and gossip, lay ready to succeed the letters for their attention. Poor Leyshon lay helpless, propped up with pillows in his berth, his lean face muddy-pale with pain, his mouth and chin marked with the lines of his despair as (in every blank moment) he looked down the prospect of the long wretched years ahead - the certainty of an age of pain, helplessness and near-beggary - his reward for a life of dogged, conscientious service to seaborne trade.

Most of his gear - his lifetime's humble accumulation of possessions - lay strewn about the cabin, for when the steward had finished reading his letters, he and Davey were to continue Leyshon's packing, to be ready for the coast steamer tomorrow. Down the passageway, muffled thumps and dragging sounds announced that the new second, Grant, was shifting his gear into temporary quarters in the after spare cabin. Having no sudden access of mail to read, he was the one man bestirring himself aboard the otherwise silent barque.

As for the captain, in his more spacious quarters, right aft on the starboard side, he sat at his desk, staring down at the flimsy cable form, which he had ripped from its envelope in the office ashore. He looked and pondered over the laconic message; 'Evicted from house from next Lady-day. Suggest store furniture and join you aboard. Mair.' His mind in a whirl, he carefully flattened the form on the brown leather of his desktop, smoothing out all its creases. His human family feelings, long dammed up, shut away by the pressure of his job, broke out and flowed full, like waters finding out their former bed, dried and forgotten. That Bronwen Lewis Caerfarchell she was behind this, he'd bet a sovereign. Old fool, Uncle William had been, to marry that jumped-up flibberty-gibbet, half his age and putting on airs like a damned duchess. Yes, she was behind it! Whatever she wanted, that was law to him; he was too lazy, too 'come-day-go-day' to do it himself. Well, be damned to him and his Ty Coch. 'We'll do without him,' he heard himself growl aloud. 'And we'll do it now.' But there was a pull of regret too. He saw himself perched on a ladder in his old clothes, happy as a schoolboy with a pot of lime-wash, the sun warm on his back, blackbirds in the orchard trees, the little grey town stretched out in the July warmth below him. The name Ty Coch Uchaf - Upper Red House - meant that every year he must mix red dye with the lime-wash for the walls, adding another parchment-thin skin to those of his predecessors. So many years, so many men, so many crackly layers of dried pink lime. A nice snug house - he would miss it, but it couldn't be helped. Sometimes pride mattered more than where you lived; the house was lost anyway, so why demean yourself by whining?

Impulsively he opened a note-pad and wrote on it: 'Roberts, Ty Coch Uchaf. Newport, Pembrokeshire, UK. Take passage first PSNC boat to Iquique. Advise me date of arrival. Jacob.' There, that was done - no point in a lot of humming and ha-ing. Send it as soon as the cable office opened in the morning.

Then Roberts sat for a long time, as the brief tropical twilight descended, hardly noticing when the steward came officiously bustling in to light his brass hanging oil lamp. 'You'll ruin your eyes, capten, reading letters in this light... Ruin them. And I suppose someone had better put all your official letters tidy on your bureau, before half of them get lost.'

Jacob, like a man married to a woman at once shrewish and ineffectual, said 'H'm' mechanically and picked up the cable again. His wife's words had touched off his own reminiscences: those happy boat trips at Newcastle, New South Wales - himself cheerful and hot in shirtsleeves, splashing the oars more untidily than a sailor should (but then real sailors don't often row about in boats; landsmen didn't realize that!). Mair reclining, laughing at him, in a long lilac dress and a big wide straw hat; and the picnics at Waratah with John and Bronwen Griffiths from Port Talbot; and all those breezy hospitable Aussies they'd met. The old 'Dryslwyn Castle', his first command, and in the first year of their marriage; everything, all of life, every possible and impossible thing in front of them: good, clean, profitable freights out and back every voyage, more money in his pocket than he'd ever known or imagined; making love in his ample berth on quiet nights in the trade winds, when all about the ship was peaceful, the breath of the wind so steady that not a brace, a sheet or a halyard needed touching. The strong lift and fall of the ship's stern below them like a participant, another dimension in the intense, spellbound rhythm of their own naked bodies. Lying moist with sweat and half-awake afterwards to hear the Atlantic rushing by, only the thickness of a steel plate away from them. The quiet tread of the mate on watch about their heads and his occasional word to the helmsman, quiet too, for the presence of Jacob's strikingly-beautiful wife had inspired a discretion and gallantry among the officers and crew alike; they wouldn't disturb her rest if they could help it, though, being normal men, they had also the envious feeling that by God the Old Man was a lucky devil! One especially magic evening in the south-east trades off Brazil: the off-watch hands all at supper, the ship close hauled on the port tack, leaning slightly and shouldering her way quietly over the great shadowy seas, her bow now pointing to heaven, now falling, falling, falling, until it seemed it must vanish into the next advancing roller, then, with creaks and shudders from the keel to the mast-truck, heaving itself up again. He and Mair sitting side-by-side silent, hands clasped, in the bowsprit netting, watching - from outside and ahead, as it were - the ever-changing beauty of the ship's gentle struggle with the ocean. No sign of the solitary lookout, the mate and helmsman distant and invisible many yards away, the ship seeming alive as a sentient creature, not a machine controlled by men. The sharp bow was now deeply buried, now uncovered to the red forefoot, but always the water rolling over and over in her bow-wave as steadily she pushed her way from Penarth Dock to Melbourne. 'O Jacob,' she'd whispered, 'isn't she beautiful? Isn't it a wonderful world... and we're so lucky too, isn't it?'

When the steward had gone Jacob sniffed and knuckled the corner of each eye. That's all twenty years back, Mair *bach,* he thought. Twenty years... It'll be grand to have you here, but it can't ever be like that again... not like it was... not quite.

Later, up on deck, when letters and supper were finished, and one man told off for anchor watch, it was a time for ease and gossip. Taking advantage of a flood of lamplight from the galley, two men sat on the main hatch in middle-aged dignity, enjoying a sociable game of cribbage, the greasy battered cards flimsy in the grasp of their huge crooked brown hands. A love of peace and silence had drawn them together: the elderly Londoner, Curly Kellock AB, and his friend and contemporary the sail-maker, Jac Davies, called by his fellow-

Welshmen Jac-y-Bont-Bach (Jack Little Bridge), since his home was in a wooded dingle, along a winding lane, at the point where the lane crossed the Nant Hafren brook by means of a ford and a wooden foot-bridge. No place could have seemed further from the world of ships and docks and ocean passages, yet within a few miles of that spot ketches and schooners unloaded anthracite and lime on the Parrog beach at Newport, and men chatted in the village pubs about the coolie girls of Calcutta, the bars of San Francisco or the fevers at Bahia Blanca. Curly, by contrast, had grown up among the sights, sounds and smells of big ships. His home was one of a little huddle of back-to-backs built for dockers at Cubitt Town, Isle of Dogs, and sandwiched between the forbidding spike-topped walls of Milwall Docks and the dirty, busy Thames. The streets of his boyhood often led over swing-bridges, and many a time his errand or his journey to or from school would be held up while smart full-rigged ships, rusty barques, brigs, ketches and barges – ships of every rig and size, ships manned by every colour and race under the sun - glided slowly past under tow, or steamed by with a whiff of coal-smoke and engine-oil. In the rare moments of quiet in his little riverside school you could hear not only the peremptory hoot of tugs and the long siren warnings of the big steamers, but also the clink-clink of engine-room telegraphs and the deep thunder of turning screws; sometimes, from a sailing-ship, the cries and curses of busy mates and a snatch of shanty from a crowd hauling on hawsers or chain cable. 'I bin a sailor all me life, reely,' he used to say. 'Can't change nah.'

Peaceably, the two men shuffled, dealt, and shifted match-sticks in the scoring board, but their peace was not to last: an argument that had echoed vaguely back from the foc'sle now ceased, and two of the participants, Billy John Ffynnongroes and Jimmy Protheroe, came hastily aft with the air of lawyers seeking a ruling from a panel of be-wigged judges; 'Here,' said Billy John, 'you two been at sea a few years, isn't it? You settle an argument for us. We says a capten ain't allowed to make a brassbounder up into a mate on the same ship - overnight, like. The others say he can, so what do you think, Jac? I says it's not right, promoting snot-nosed English kids; just because their mams and dads have paid a premium for them.'

'Yeah,' said Jimmy, 'there's bosun - the Old Man could have made him up to mate instead. He's a better man for the job. It's bloody well not right.'

'And another thing-...' said Billy.

'Can't you see me and my mate Curly is having a quiet game o' cards?' said Jac indignantly. 'What do you want to come bothering us with your damn sea-lawyering for?'

'Because it's not right, that's why,' said Billy. "And some of us ain't afraid to tell him so.'

'You explain it to him, Curly,' said Jac. 'You're better with all these English rules and regulations than I am. Give me a palm and a needle and some twine and some canvas, and I'll soon knock you up a good topsail - but as for all these words...' He spat his contempt into the nearby scupper.

'Nothing much to tell,' said Curly. 'A captin's a captin, and that's that. "Master under God" they used to say. He's got all the guv'ments and all the bleeding coppers of the whole world behind him. He can have you slung in the calaboose in any port in the world – that's how many rights you got. Once you've shipped aboard, and signed or made yer mark on the Crew Agreement, he can bloody nearly do what he likes. Gorblimey, we had a skipper once, up in the Chinchas there - you know, them islands off Peru - loading guano on the old "Beatrice": he pulled a revolver on us because we couldn't stick it in the hold, what with the stink and the dust and the heat. And he was a hard old bastard too - he wouldn't have given a fish's tit about firing it into yer guts.'

'So what happened?'

'We loaded the bloody guano of course - what d'you think?'

'Why don't you damn *crwts* grow up a bit?' said Jac. '(That's fifteen-one, fifteen-two and one for his nob.) I've seen many a brass-bounder made up to mate before - good ones and bad ones, you take your chance. This young Raven don't look to me no worse than most of them. God damn, mun, if you don't like the Old Man's doings, just get over the side with yourself and your dunnage into a coal lighter one evening and bugger off ashore. You wouldn't be the first, would you? Only you'd be a bloody fool if you did, because this hooker's a paradise compared with a good many I've seen.' He added, growling half under his breath: 'Pair of half-hard wankers...'

'Look at it another way,' said Curly diplomatically: 'You remember signing the Crew Agreement when we shipped at Cardiff? That didn't say nothing about brassbounders and third mates, did it? So you ain't got a leg to stand on, even if you had some proper lawyer geezer here on your side. Half a mo: let's have a look at them matches you got in yer hand. Thought so – they're vestas. Now that *is* in the Crew Agreement - the Old Man could have you for that: "Safety matches only to be allowed on board", it said. See, they got you - and me - all sewn up where they want us, my son. Seagoing slaves, that's what we are... Slaves of the capitalist system.'

'Aye,' said Jac, 'and times like this, it ain't too bad, is it?' He laughed, scornfully and yet affectionately: 'You and your slaves and systems, Curly, and your workers of the world and your pamphlets and manifestoes! Why, mun, you're the biggest sea-lawyer of the lot! *Diawl!* things have always been much the same for people like us, and I can't see no bloody chance of them changing.'

'You'll see, Jac my son, you'll see. Things will change - some time, one way or another. They'll have to, or there'll be rivers of blood all over the world.'

'Aye,' said Billy John hotly, 'we'll pull all them bloody *crach-ach* down off their perches one day... But meantime, we got to show that old fool aft he can't do just what he likes.'

'Aw, come on now, boys,' said Jac impatiently, '*chwarae teg* now; he's a tidy enough old boy, even if he is a capten. And he's no fool, neither. You can see what he's up to, can't you? It makes sense to me: after what happened to poor old Leyshon he don't want no more old men down on the main-deck or up aloft in heavy weather - except Curly, of course - so he's got himself a couple of young mates, so he and Dai Dome can stay up on the poop and shout at us.'

But Billy was not quite done with his grumbling: 'Ah, that new second - that son-of-a-bitch: now there's another thing. He looks to me as if he might be a bit of a bucko...'

He was interrupted by a kind of suppressed, whispered shout from aft: 'Hey, boys, what d'you think?' and the rapid, rather mincing approach of Isaac Hughes the steward, almost falling over himself with self-importance. 'Drop dead, boys, you'll never believe it: the Old Man is having his missis on the ship!'

'What, when we get back?'

'No, now - coming out on the next mail-boat to Iquique - at once.'

Jac spat in disgust: 'You and your damned old woman's tat-tling, Isaac! How do you know what the Old Man wants his missis to do? Ask your advice, did he? Or come to you for permission?'

'No, but he gets this cable from her today, and he sits there reading it and reading it again and thinking about it all through the dog-watches. He hasn't even looked at his official letters yet, and there's two there from Mr Powell himself; then he writes a cable to her out on a note-pad. Then he goes off to his *ty bach* for a leak.'

'Yes, well...?' said Jac persistently.

'Well, while I was tidying up, like, I couldn't help... you know... catching sight of what was on the pad - what was written there - just out of the corner of my eye, you understand...'

There was a general laugh at Isaac, whose prying and meddling ways were well known. 'What's he on about, fer Gawd's sake?' said Curly testily, for Isaac had been too excited to speak anything but Welsh.

'He says the Old Man is having his missis out to join him aboard.'

'Oh yeah? Very nice for him...Don't see it matters much to us. Might make him a bit more contented if he's getting a spot of how's-yer-father every night.'

'Every night? At his age?' said Billy John, with all the scorn of youth. 'Poor old bugger'd fall to bits.'

'All right then, my son: whenever he fancies a bit of greens and she's willing.'

There was a laugh among the ABs, but Isaac was still indignant: 'It's all very well for you boys for'ard to laugh - you won't see nothing much of her except when you does your trick at the wheel. She won't be bothering round you all the time, bossing and complaining about every dratted thing, finding dust and grease and bits of rope-yarn all over the place. I wouldn't have signed on this damn ship if I'd known she was coming. I know what they can be like, these women.'

But he got little sympathy from the foc'sle men; 'You know what your trouble is, don't you, Isaac?' said Protheroe. 'You don't want another old woman aft besides yourself, do you?'

'No,' said Billy. 'You come to sea to get away from the women, didn't you, Isaac *bach?* I mean, they're not much use to you for nothing, are they?'

At this baiting, Curly's sense of fair play came to the surface; he had little time for the sea-lawyering Billy John anyway. 'Never you mind, Isaac my son,' he said acidly. 'You get Billy here to have a quick word with the skipper. Billy'll put a stop to his capers, woncher, Bill? He'll tell the Old Man that he's decided he ain't gonna let him have no third mate, nor no old woman neither. That should do it; the Old Man, see Isaac, he's shit-scared of our Billy. We all saw that the other day.'

Jac picked up his neglected cards with a flourish and said: 'Right then, shove off, the lot of you. I've heard enough tittle-tattle and bullshit for one evening.' He turned on Curly with mock hostility: 'I s'pose you hope I'll forget this game, seeing as you're getting such a hiding? Well, I damn well won't, because when I win it you'll owe me another plug of tobacco. So come on, it's your go, mun.'

'All right, keep yer shirt on, mate.' Curly looked reflectively at his burnt-brown clay pipe. 'I ain't so sure old Isaac ain't right, y'know. Women are trouble on board a ship. Can be, leastways, if they're the nagging sort. They git at the Old Man about something, he gits at the mates, and they git at us lot for'ard...No swearing on deck, no spitting, mustn't sing no shanties with naughty words in them when you're git-ting the anchor or the tops'ls up. No more "Maid of Amsterdam" when you're tramping round the capstan. No more going round bollock-naked when it rains in the tropics and you want to git all yer clo'es dhobeyed. Women kind of... disturb things, Jac. They don't mean no harm, I daresay, but they upset the way we all go on, us and the after-guard. It's a pity; this has been a nice peaceful sort of ship up to now. No argy-bargy, except from our Billy and his pal; nobody slinging knives about; no hard-case mates with big boots nor bosuns with ropes'-ends. Of course, on the other hand she's full of you bloody Taf-fies, and I can't understand a word of your jibber-jabber, but that suits me all right, because I got me books. Gives a bloke a chance to think and read a bit in the dog-watches.'

'Aye, well, come on then; think about your damn cards, mun! That's plain enough talk even for a heathen *Sais*, isn't it? As for peace-ful, don't you be too sure that'll go on. That new second – don't like the cut of his jib much, I can tell you. Too big for his boots... Barks away as if he was in the bloody Navy.'

'Never mind, my old son. I've been in the Navy, so I've met his sort before. You know what they say: "Growl you may, but go you must". We're all slaves, and the officers are all slave-drivers of one sort or another. But then again, they're slaves as well, even the captin; - slaves to the Owners and a bunch of fat idle shareholders who don't know one end of a ship from another, and who lie soft in their feather-beds every night. It's Capital at work again, my son, and it does just what it likes with us working men, only you won't see it - none of you.'

9

One morning, a fortnight or so after 'Figaro's' arrival at Caleta Buena, the new third mate sat slumped over the table in the mess-room, sleepily stirring a mug of muddy coffee, yawning and watching the dawn light strengthening through the port-hole. His body still slack with sleep and torpor, he allowed himself to sway sluggishly to the slow rhythm of the ship's eternal rolling; he felt some of his weight transferred from one elbow to the other, saw the liquid in his cup climb and fall, this side and that. The monotony of the motion, the dull grey light in the room, the everlasting creak and groan from hull and rigging - all these settled upon and strengthened the deep early-morning gloom of his soul.

Twenty-five past six. Five minutes to swallow this hot gritty sludge, and then it was time to start the endless work of cleaning and maintenance of the ship and her rigging, time to stand by for the first empty lighter of the day to come crawling across the shifting lumpy swells. Washing down decks just before starting to heave out baskets of dusty coal? Balmy, really, but ship's routine for all that. You washed down every morning, at anchor or at sea, even when the decks were streaming with spray already! Routine, routine.... Talking of routine, where was Grant? He was a bit late this morning - not like him.

Raven drained his cup, and as he did so, Grant shouldered in the door, followed by the mate, who took out a ponderous silver watch and frowned at it: 'Very near time to turn-to, gentlemen. Two minutes of the half-hour, I make it.'

'Coffee,' growled Grant, slumping to the bench opposite his brown mug-full. He was clearly in an ill humour. 'Got to have some coffee - if that's what this is - before getting into all that goddamned dust.'

'I've had mine in my cabin,' said Evans, with a kind of smug severity, 'so as to be out on deck in good time. Sets an example to the crowd.' He left his reproach to Grant unspoken. 'I shall be busy with Sails today, mister, helping him measure out canvas for a new mizzen t'gallant stays'l. See they do a good wash-down.'

'Ready for a two-inch coat of coal-dust,' muttered the second into his coffee.

'Never you mind about coal-dust,' said Evans. 'That'll only be round the for'ard hatch. This is a tidy Welsh barque, not a Chinese bumboat. D'you think we leave off washing down just because we're...'

'All right, mister, all right. We're going, we're going. Raven, nip along and turn the crowd out, will you? I'll be along in two shakes. It's barely half-past yet.'

Raven went out on deck, hoping to find the straggling knots of men already out of their quarters, for he still had some diffidence about exactly how to turn them out on his own. But the main-deck - still gloomy, for the sun had not yet shown over the snow-caps of the Andes - was empty and silent. The huge continent, split into planes and gradations of grey, like stage scenery, stretched along the ship's starboard beam. Neither among the huddle of white buildings at the shoreline, nor among the patient lines of ships was there the slightest sign of movement or life, save for the endless slow tilting and swaying of the ships. His hand, casually sliding on the t'gallant rail, brushed cold dew from the polished wood; the only sound was that of his boots on the planking; the only sign of life aboard was the feather of blue woodsmoke from the galley funnel. His nostrils caught the sharp, pleasant piney reek of it. Homely, that... His father's study fire on a winter morning, just lit by Elspeth and breathing little wisps of smoke into the sunbeams.

He drew level with the galley amidships and was aware of a dull clunking sound, as of a man chopping wood; he gave an unconscious wry smile: that wasn't wood the doctor was chopping - though very similar in appearance and texture. He glanced sideways, and saw, framed in the galley door, the burly form of Wellington Jones, wielding a shiny cleaver with skill and energy. Today was Tuesday, and every man and boy for'ard was therefore due for his duly prescribed and measured Board of Trade ration of beef - one and a half pounds. One and a half pounds of beef! That would sound lavish, splendid, if you said it ashore... Until you saw and smelt the grey, leathery, gristly, shapeless lumps of salt meat, dredged from the slimy brine of a great cask, well soaked overnight to soften it and rid it of some of the salt, but still strong, stringy and indistinguishable by flavour from the one and a quarter pounds of salt pork due tomorrow.

The cook was hacking the beef into smaller fragments, ready for stewing with some good leaden dumplings for dinner at midday. He glanced up from his work, and his white teeth gleamed in a brief grin; but he was a grossly overworked man, proud of his skill, a stickler about his status, better paid than a junior officer like Raven, and no great friend of recent ex-brassbounders.

Most mornings he would have been chatting as he worked with his crony and fellow-idler the bosun, Reuben Mathias, who, most mornings, would have been sitting with his coffee on the coaming of the galley door. Today there was no sign of him, and Raven felt it would be a lowering of his dignity (like most young men, he was very worried about his dignity) if he were to ask the doctor where the bosun was. Normally, Reuben, a slightish, tough, taciturn man from Aberaeron, would have kicked on the doors of the two foc'sles and bellowed something harsh and incomprehensible in Welsh to bring the crowd out, wiping coffee off their lips, yawning, stretching, scratching and farting, a few breaking away to spit tobacco-quids over the lee rail, coughing at the cool freshness of the morning air.

But today, no bosun... Well, what of that? He'd roust them out himself... everybody was late today. The Old Man sometimes took a stroll round the poop in his pyjamas at this time of day; if he found nothing happening there'd be fireworks, and the most junior officer about was always the one to cop it. Not bad, being a captain: once you'd seen everyone turn to, you could duck down below again for a cup of decent tea made in a proper pot, before dressing up to go ashore, to while away the time with brandy and cigars in the cool back-parlour of the ship's chandler's shop. That was called 'Going ashore on ship's business.' Ah well... one day maybe....

He stopped outside the door of the starboard foc'sle, his hand on the spring latch of the door, vacillating. He looked back.... Still no bosun. Grant would think him a very wet sort of greenhorn if he did nothing. Making his mind up, he gave a thump on the door with his fist, opened it wide, and stepped over the coaming to call, with some semblance of gruff confidence and authority: 'All right, men! Look lively, then! Time to...'

He said no more; his first words had gone into an astonished silence - the silence of incredulous outrage; then there was a general growl of rage, several blasphemous Welsh oaths and a clear voice saying in English: 'Sod off, you! This is our bloody foc'sle!' An instant later he fell out backwards with a yell of pain as the heel of a flying leather sea-boot struck his right eye. He tripped on a ringbolt and fell flat on his back to the sound of a yell of fierce laughter from the open door. His head thudded hard on the unforgiving planks, and for a second or two he was too flustered and stunned to know what had happened or where he was.

Then he felt strong hands under his armpits and looked up to see (upside-down, as it were) the lean brown features of the bosun, who was hauling him to his feet. Then the foc'sle door shut with a bang, and at the same time the port watch of seamen came crowding out of their door to goggle and guffaw at the spectacle of the new Third scrambling to his feet, pawing tenderly at a red and rapidly-closing right eye. Then, somewhere near, he heard Grant's voice: 'What the hell is going on here, bosun? Raven, what the devil have you been at, boy? Who hit you?'

'Nobody.... A seaboot... Some bastard slung a seaboot at me.'

'What - on deck? Who was it? I'll give him seaboots, by Christ!'

'Don't know - it was too dark.'

'Dark?'

'Yes.' There was an incredulous silence. Grant was staring at him, those light-blue eyes popping from his head. Raven realized he had been an egregious ass. 'I went in, you see...'

'You did *what?'*

'Well, there was no-one on deck, so I went into the foc'sle to... to roust them out.'

'You idiot - nobody ever does that! Nobody from the after-guard, anyway. You've never seen me put my foot over that coaming. Even bosun just bangs the door, don't you, bosun?'

'Aye sir. That's their place, see; they don't like intruders.'

'I didn't know... I thought....'

'Well, you damn well should have known. Anyway, you know now.' He looked at the huge throbbing bruise, the eye closed down to a slit. 'Shouldn't think you'll forget in a hurry either. Come on, we're not going to stand about all day yapping. Bosun, go and tell them to turn out now, and no more shenanigans, or they'll get some sea-boot from me.' When the bosun had gone he said quietly to Raven: 'Any idea who threw it?'

'No, no idea. It just came out of the dark.'

'Starboard watch… that's my crowd. Haven't had them long, but I bet I know who did it - that Billy John!'

'The loud-mouthed trouble-maker?'

'Aye, him. Billy John Finnan-something, they call him. Now look here: you've been an idiot, and you've got what you asked for. No-one in the afterguard goes into the crew's quarters except on orders from the Old Man, to make a search for liquor or weapons - things like that. But we can't let them get away with it altogether. Thanks to your idiocy, they've got the better of us, made us both look stupid; being English doesn't help, either, on this hooker – can't understand what the beggars are saying to each other. But that precious Billy John'll find he's been a bit too clever. You leave it to me – I'll get even.'

'Mr Grant!' There was a loud bark from aft; the Old Man, with the mate beside him, was hastening for'ard towards them. 'Mr Grant, what in the world is going on? Nearly quarter to seven, only half the hands on deck, and nothing being done, by them or you. Won't do, won't do….' He suddenly took in Raven's swollen cheek and closed eye: 'And who the devil have you been fighting, mister?'

'My fault, sir,' said Raven, blushing. 'I went to turn the hands out, and as I went into the starboard foc'sle…'

'Someone slung a boot at you!' said the Captain abruptly, and with a total lack of sympathy. 'H'm! Expect I'd have done the same when I was a young AB. Bloody fool, boy! That's their home - the only one they've got, some of them. I don't come shoving into your cabin every morning, do I? When are you going to learn, eh? You've been aboard this ship long enough to know better; you're not a brassbound nobody any more. Now I shall have to make a damn fuss with them - give them a good hazing - just because you've been *twp.*"

Summoned by the bosun, the starboard watch was beginning to straggle out, grinning furtively, when they were electrified by a huge Cape Horn bellow from Roberts: 'STARBOARD WATCH ON DECK!'

While they gaped in sudden silence the Old Man turned on his heel and strode off abruptly, saying over his shoulder to the mate: 'All hands lay aft, mister.' He sprang up the poop-ladder two steps at a time, and stood like a preacher in a pulpit grasping the thick mahogany rail at the for'ard end of the raised poop. Like a godly minister with an erring flock, he looked down with the withering glare of outraged morality. What genuine indignation he felt was directed against Raven for having stirred up this silly, irritating, tedious commotion; but the crowd below wouldn't know that, and he certainly wouldn't tell them. Men were men, mates were mates, and black eyes were black eyes. He watched in silence as the hands, silent too now, straggled aft like chastened schoolboys. With a keen grasp of the drama of the moment (born as much from his Welshness as from his long experience as a ship's master) he waited impassively while they shuffled into a rough semicircle below him, all in grubby shirts, vests and dungaree trousers. Neither he nor they found his striped flannel pyjamas and mule slippers in the least incongruous to the solemnity of the occasion. He did not speak until they were quite still, cowed, all the bounce gone out of them. He needed no thunder in his voice now; standing there below him, heads flung back, they found the level quiet of his tone more chilling than a bellow

'Right. Now listen, every man jack, and remember my words, for I mean every one of them: one of my officers has just been struck and injured by a boot thrown at him by some man in the starboard watch.' He paused and raked them with his eyes. 'Now then: I am not going to waste my time or your working time asking who it was, because I know for sure that I won't find out. But I will say this: I am not going to tolerate men who behave like gaol-birds.... hoodoos... hooligans. That plain enough? Such a thing had better not happen again, or I will stop all shore-leave for the whole watch concerned until I find out the culprit, and when I do I will disrate him to ordinary seaman for the rest of the voyage, and he will never sail with me or with this company again... ever. That plain, is it? You don't know, some of you, you younger ones, how well off you are in this ship.' He made a quick angry gesture to the other moored ships: 'Hell ships, some of those - boots in your ribs, ropes' ends across your arses twenty times a day for nothing. Isn't that right, Johanssen? You know, don't you? You've served on some Yankee Down-easters.'

Johanssen, a great shy ox of a man, dropped his gaze, flushed, and looked sidelong at his mates around him, embarrassed to be thus singled out. Then he raised his head and nodded: 'O yah, cap'n. Dey voss make us yump to it all right. Handy mit de boots.'

'So there you are, you see!' said Roberts triumphantly, intending to close the scene on that note. But he was to regret having called the Swede as a witness to his words, for Johanssen's mind was as slow, as thorough, and as painstaking as his hands. Having been called as a witness, he was now determined to tell, not just the truth, but the whole truth, as he saw it. Without a trace of impertinence he broke in on Roberts' peroration: 'O yah, cap'n, dey voss hard, but de Yankee grub voss bedder, I t'ink... Yah, lod bedder dan dis Limey stuff. Day voss givink us proper spuds all time, und fried johnny-cake und proper bully-beef from tin, all same as cabin.'

All the tension that Jacob had so carefully prepared was snapped, as the crowd roared their laughing approval of Johanssen's evidence. Now genuinely angry with both himself and them, he had to shout for silence: 'All right, all right - we don't want to hear all that rigmarole, Johanssen.'

But the Swede was not to be so easily deterred from ploughing on with his scrupulously fair testimony, and he also had the foreigner's perennial problem of selecting the right vocabulary for the occasion: 'Und de cook he made us real Brazil coffee, and he have a big barrel of red apples by de galley door. You have one any time you like... und dey voss fokkink good too, I t'ink.'

Looking down in helpless frustration, Jacob was aware of nothing but rows of wide-open jaws, of men clutching each other for support, almost falling down for laughter. The whole affair - all his careful staging and timing - had been ruined by that goddam half-witted square-head! 'ALL RIGHT! That'll do, Johanssen!' As the laughter subsided into moans and coughs, and as the Swede coloured with offended bewilderment (he had been asked for the truth and he had told it), the Old Man said, with an attempt at the restoration of dignity to the occasion: 'As for the rest of you - you can laugh like bloody jackasses if you want, but any more shenanigans like this and you won't be laughing, I promise you. So act tidy, isn't it? Like I said just now, I don't want anything like this again. There'll be no occasion for it again.' As he said this he gave a quick involuntary glare at Raven, who stood to his left, fervently wishing himself elsewhere - anywhere. The look was not lost on the more seasoned and discerning hands; Curly Kellock and the bosun exchanged discreet winks. Jacob decided not to prolong a mismanaged scene. He snapped to the mate: 'Turn to, mister, if you please. We've wasted half-an-hour already.'

Evans sang out: 'Both watches of the hands muster!' and clattered down to the main-deck. Grant and Raven made to follow, but Jacob called them sharply back: 'Mister Grant, Mister Raven! One word if you please. I've rebuked the hands; I think they'll pay heed to what I've said, despite all that damn nonsense from the square-head. Now I want that to be the end of it - you understand? Finish!' He looked straight at Grant: 'I don't want anyone trying to get his own back on the crowd, or anyone in the crowd. The trouble we've had is enough. We'll never find out who did it in a month of Sundays.'

'I think I could have a very good guess, sir,' said Grant coldly.

'Aye, you could guess - any fool can guess. I can even guess what your guess would be. But I've got to *know*. I can't put guesses down in the Official Log, can I? So just leave it at that. They're not a bad crowd, and after all, this young man did ask for it. Now I want to hear no more about it. I've got more important matters to attend to ashore.' He strode off and went below, and a few seconds later they heard him bellow: 'Hughes! This damn tea is as cold as a witch's tit - go and get me some more and shift your arse about it! And get me my shaving water while you're at it.' They did not hear him, moments later, settle into his big cabin chair and sigh: *'Bobl annwyl!* Sometimes I think I've got the biggest load of half-witted *crwts* in all South Spain...Just like bloody kids - squabble, squabble, squabble...'

*　　*　　*

The cafe society of Caleta Buena was small and less than metropolitan in its sophistication, but it was lively, and it functioned with a cheerful democracy, salted with a healthy pinch of common sense. It reflected a highly hierarchical society without being snobbishly restrictive; it relied on custom and price to classify its customers without proscriptions or shibboleths. No-one was admitted or excluded because of the wearing (or not wearing) of any particular piece of apparel. Sailors, mostly youngish, of most nations, arrived at its quays with a rabid thirst for liquor, with their stomachs mad with desire for food that tasted like food and was not doled out in penny-pinching portions, and with their libidos starved of womanly contact and titillated by foc'sle and half-deck chat, banter, boasting and pornography. None went away dissatisfied, though many lived to repent their various indulgences.

One evening, when his eye had had a week to recover from its contusion, John Raven sat with Simon Grant at a table (with a cleanish cloth on it) in Il Palazzo - known as Giuseppe's - while 'Figaro's' starboard watch roistered in their own less elegant way at Conchita's, two streets away on the quay-side. The two young mates had demolished a huge portion each of a delicious peppery beef stew, served with a massive plate of spaghetti; together, they had downed a very passable bottle of Chianti as well as a couple of *piscos* before the meal. Gastrically speaking, John was content - and yet somehow the evening was empty of cheerful fellowship and fun; only half over, and yet dragging already. A high screech, followed by a roar of bawdy laughter went up from the long table by the end wall; some of the 'Figaro' apprentices had chummed up with some boys from the 'Breconshire', and together had joined a quartet of fresh-faced German lads from the P Line ship 'Pisagua'. Their table groaned with bottles as an informal beer-drinking contest developed. Two plump, dark and apparently willing Chilean girls who sat with them were being explored under the table in ways that they and the boys found uproariously funny. John Raven longed to be with them, but now he was a third mate, in theory above such immature horseplay, and stuck with Grant as a companion.

He tipped the last of the Chianti into the Second's glass and tried to strike a little life into the evening: 'Don't make it obvious you're looking, but there's a real bobby-dazzler at the table behind you who keeps smiling at me. The one in red - really nice bit of skirt.'

Grant tipped his glass back and looked discouragingly at him: 'One of Guiseppe's resident whores, no doubt. They are a shade above the average, I admit. Not for captains, maybe, or the owners of *oficinas* (nitrate factories), but at least whores for mates. That's something, I suppose.'

'No, I don't think she's on the game. All the real tarts are over by the bar. And she's got another dolly with her who's all right, too.'

Grant was scarcely interested enough to turn round: 'Smiling at you, eh? That settles it; any woman, young Raven, who smiles at a mug like yours when half of it is still black from Billy John's sea-boot must be a whore - and a pretty desperate one too. However.... On my port quarter, eh?' He swung casually round, stared coolly without any sort of tact or discretion, and swung back to face Raven: 'H'm.. Can't say I can see anything that I'd care to risk my reproductive organ for.... But you go ahead, old son, if you've a mind to it; get the dirty water off your chest, as they say in the foc'sle. Plenty of spare third mates about on the beach, if anything should drop off.'

'No, it's all right,' said John, his spirits flattened by Grant's cold, ironic jeering. I'm not that keen...Let's have another bottle of this Italian stuff.' He waved to a waiter, who jostled his way across between the crowded tables sweating profusely, his lank black hair stuck in hanks across his forehead. A raucous hullabaloo drew Raven's attention to the brassbounders' table where one of the German lads was searching -pretending to search - for something between the breasts of one of the girls, who was becoming more hysterical and more décolleté by the minute. 'My God, look at that randy young bugger. Strewth! She'll finish up being rogered by the lot of them under the table, I shouldn't wonder.'

'Doubt it - not in this place. To start with, Giuseppe would think it lowered the tone a bit, but more important, he expects to get a rake-off from all the shagging that goes on under his roof. He'd make them rent a room and - Hey! Look at that!' He broke off suddenly, indifferent to the lascivious horse-play, and tapping Raven on the arm, pointed out of the window. 'Over there - those chaps across the street, under the gas-light.'

John peered casually: 'Two drunk sailors - what of it?'

'They're not just sailors – they're two of our beauties. That one with his back to us is our friend Billy John, I'd swear to it. The other one's Protheroe; the starboard watch has got shore-leave tonight.'

'All right, but what of it? Don't you see enough of them round the hatch all day?'

'Aye, but watch. They're looking at something in that grog-shop window... Just watch.'

The two men, lurching and clutching at each other, were pointing at the bottles and casks in the shop-window, and dredging coins out of their trouser pockets. They disappeared through the door, and came out shortly after, laughing gleefully, each holding what looked like a huge black sausage.

'Thought so,' said Grant. 'Treepas! - one each. They look like two-bottle treepas.'

'What the hell are they - sausages?'

'No, those hoodoos wouldn't be interested in anything so nourishing or sensible as sausages, would they? No, the grog-shop owners all down the West Coast, they know about foc'sle hands, and they know about ships' regulations about liquor on board, so they cater specially for their customers. Those things are wine-skins specially designed to be smuggled on board the nitrate ships; but they haven't got wine in them, of course - that wouldn't be strong enough for a foc'sle thirst. They've been filled with the local fire-water - *aguardiente* or *pisco*. It'll make those blokes very popular in the foc'sle, no doubt, once they've got them on board... See the way they're made? Tapes fixed on each end for tying round your waist or down your trousers. Now you watch.'

They watched in silence as the drunken pair, guffawing and tumbling against each other, opened their jackets, pulled up their shirts and tied the *treepas* round their waists. When their shirts were tucked in again and the clumsy, ill-cut jackets buttoned over them, there was no obvious bulge to a casual onlooker. Grant grunted with satisfaction and smacked his hands together: 'Right! We've got them - Look out! Turn your back on them quick! They're gawping all round - I don't want them catching sight of us...Now then, we need to get back aboard before them - and that shouldn't be difficult. They won't have spent much on those things, and I can't see them going back until they've spent every cent of their advances. We've got them. But there's no hurry; here comes the johnny with our second bottle. We've got time for that - it'll just put me in the mood.'

'The mood...? The mood for what?'

'What do you think? Get aboard and nab these birds as they come up the ladder, of course. They won't have a leg to stand on.'

'They won't like it - there'll be trouble.'

'Of course there will - I'm counting on it. So much the better. Time some of these Welsh scrimshankers were taken down a peg or two.... And time I made my mark on them, too. I haven't forgotten that boot, and you shouldn't have, either; if you swallow that sort of thing they'll be all over you before long. You were only a brassbounder a fortnight ago, so you've got to establish yourself; so have I, because I'm new to the ship.'

John looked glumly out of the cafe window as the two Welsh-men staggered off down the street and disappeared into the garishly-lit open door of a fandango hall. He said: 'What about the Old Man?'

'What about him? Where does he come into it? He'll be in his bunk. I shan't ask him to do anything. I'll settle with those two -you'll help if necessary, I presume? I should bloody well hope you would.'

'Oh yes, of course. But he didn't want us to do anything more, did he, the Old Man? Didn't want us to try to get our own back on them.'

'Yes, but don't you see? (Come on, drink up, don't sit there sipping like a bloody old duchess!) Don't you see, that's what's so lucky about seeing them buying the *treepas*. Smuggling liquor aboard is dead against the Crew Agreement. They signed that, and so did he, so he has to back us, whatever happens. He can't say, "Oh, I let them do that." And it will be totally separate from the sea-boot business – he'll just have to back us.'

'Yes, I suppose... All the same...' Raven was no coward physically, nor weak-willed either. When he'd been made up to third mate, he accepted that sooner or later he'd probably have to fight it out with some obstreperous jack from the foc'sle; that was part of a mate's job - you did it when you had to. But this Grant - he was different; he enjoyed it a bit too much. His eyes! Now that he'd got trouble to look forward to, they'd gone bright and fixed. He was excited, happy; yet when John had taken a fancy to the pretty girl at the table opposite, he'd not thought it worth while turning round to look at her. He wasn't natural, somehow. Any chap of his age who didn't get more excited about girls than about scrapping with foc'sle roughnecks must be a bit odd somewhere.

Grant was exasperated: 'What do you mean, "all the same"? Christ, I'm telling you, young Raven, this is not the time to be dragging your feet. After all, the whole thing wouldn't have happened if you hadn't been so daft. The least you can do now is to back me up. Listen, I'll tell you something that you ought to know: you were saying the other day, weren't you, that every time you went past one of my starboard watch Welsh boys they whistled the same tune - Tum-ta-te-tum, ta-tum-ta-re-re? Well yesterday I cornered that old fairy of a steward and got it out of him - found out what it was. That tune is a Welsh folksong called "Die rozin" something or other – anyway, the first line in English is: "Two red roses and two dark eyes". So now you know: they've been rubbing it in, taking advantage of you, ever since it happened. The Old Man might want to forget all about it, but they don't. You see what it is: being English, and not understanding their damned lingo, we're sort of... outsiders. They think they can just take the piss out of us and get away with it, because they can do it in Welsh. And the Old Man's not too bothered about backing us because he comes from the same damned village, probably. Knows half their mothers, uncles, cousins and grandads. Goes bawling out Welsh hymns in the same bloody chapel. They're like a great big family of weird bible-punching yokels, and their jabber keeps them together and keeps us poor buggers out. We don't know what's really going on, any more than we would among a bunch of Hottentots.'

'Well, to be fair, I suppose you can't blame them for using

their own language – it'd be just the same on, say, a French ship among the Johnny Crapauds. We'd be outsiders there too.'

'Aye, but the French don't allow that to affect the discipline, from what I've seen; nor do the Dutchies. It's this Welsh "all one big family" business that I don't like. Because of that, the whole ship's too slack, if you ask me. You can't run a foreign-going four-poster barque as if it was a chapel outing.'

'All right then, I see what you mean.'

'Still half-hearted about it, though, aren't you? Well, I don't care. You can be a wet-leg if you like and let them walk all over you, but they won't do that to me. I was made to look an absolute chump that morning too, so I'm settling my own account anyway. Nothing would give me greater pleasure.'

*   *   *

Those last words of Grant's went through John Raven's mind as he waited uneasily with him on the poop-deck an hour later. Like all the ship's libertymen, they had bargained noisily with a Chilean boatman - a *lanchero* by day, no doubt - for the half-mile trip out to the barque in his leaky battered skiff. Now they leaned on the starboard rail, looking out for the boat carrying the two spirit-smugglers. Grant had lit a cigar, and between puffs whistled tunelessly between his teeth. 'Nothing would give me greater pleasure,' he'd said. Raven could sense the suppressed excitement in the man's alert tension, in the drumming of his fingers on the taffrail; Raven felt, underneath the glow of the Chianti and the heavy weight of the good shore food, the slightly sick feeling of life running, for the moment, out of his control; here he was, committed to a line of action he didn't really agree with, in alliance with a man for whom violence seemed to be a kind of need. For clearly the impending fracas had little to do with the professional maintenance of discipline. 'Nothing would give me greater pleasure' - that was the real truth of it.

There was no sound but the creak and groan of the standing rigging as tons of steel and wood and wire swayed through perhaps twenty degrees of arc above their heads, and the quiet wash of the water as the ship rolled her side into and out of it. The smoothly-ridged water reflected the starlight in shimmers; nearby ships were like black holes in the dark, glancing backcloth. The ships' riding-lights, the lights of the little town, and the red lamps on the end of the loading jetty twinkled at the top of long, slender, shifting columns of gold and blood-red.

'Listen!' Grant held up a hand; from far off on the starboard beam came the faint sound of voices raised in song and the steady clunk-clunk of oars in rowlocks. Grant sent his cigar shooting out and down to end with an audible hiss: 'It's them, I'll bet,' he said quietly, as a small dark blob detached itself from the black hulk of the next ship in the tier. Now the splash of the oars could be heard; after a short pause for argument, the voices were raised again; over the silent swells came a slurred but passably tuneful rendering - tenor, baritone and bass - of the hymn *'Blaenwern'* - sad, wistful, yet lilting; alien to the great dark hills behind, a defiant claim to be a part of this immensity of desert and mountain and ocean. The hymn was a sound which said that even when drunk, broke, and seven thousand miles from home, a Welshman was still a Welshman, and different from all other men. On a more practical note, it seemed to Raven that he was hearing more than two voices, but Grant gave no sign of noticing that.

The officers stayed silent and motionless as the boat approached, and as the boatman's fare was fumbled out of pockets, collected, counted and handed over. Then, as the men began to climb the ladder, Grant motioned to Raven to follow him down to the main-deck, where the ladder hung. They arrived as the first man breasted the rail, rolled awkwardly over it, and landed with an undignified thump on deck. Grant moved quickly to confront him as he hauled himself upright on a coil of rope hanging from the pinrail. Both Grant and the drunken boarder were surprised and taken aback: Grant because the new arrival turned out to be the Wellington Jones; the cook, because when one rolls aboard after a good night's wet and a very satisfying bout with a high-toned whore, one does not expect the Second Mate to appear from nowhere like a malevolent zombie. The doctor's eyes and teeth flashed white for a moment in alarm, and he stooped forward for a closer look, for he was a man of some mettle: 'Jee-sus, Mister Grant sir, if you din' give me the goddamndest fright! What you at, sir, prowling round like some fuckin' *obeah* man (witch-doctor)?'

Grant took a step back in confusion, then, recovering, did his best to get rid of Jones without alerting anyone in the boat below. 'Ah, Jones, it's you! Off to your bunk then, doctor. The hands'll be wanting their coffee in a few hours.'

But the portly Jamaican was too genial, too expansive, too

pleased with his male prowess that evening to be so dismissed: 'Hands my arse, mister mate, and coffee my arse too. Hey, you should a' come with us...'

At this point another man landed heavily behind the cook, belched resoundingly and said with a mocking irony: 'Good evening, mister mate, sir!' in a Cockney accent which labelled him as Curly Kellock. In his irritated frustration with the two first arrivals, Grant was vainly trying to see who else might roll over the topgallant rail; if Billy John and Protheroe heard his voice they might jettison the *treepas*, and all his trouble would be for nothing. So he added to the absurd confusion by muttering quietly to conceal his presence: 'Right, that'll do. Away you go then, men.'

The cook grabbed his arm: 'Eh? What you say? Why you talk so quiet, man? Listen, you should a' come to that fandango hall – Pedro's ... near the church. Upstairs, man, they got the dandiest bunch a' whores you ever seen in your life - yeah, in your *life!* All shapes, all sizes... You can have it any way up you want, s'long as you got the dollars. Listen, mis' mate sir: tonight I had me a gal there with the smoothest, roundest, tightest little white arse I ever handled, an' I'm tellin' you I've handled a few...'

'White!' cried Kellock indignantly. 'You big black liar, you! More like coffee-colour – mulatter, sort o' colour. I was upsides with her before you, my chav, so I knows what I'm talking about, remember.' He too became voluble and confidential to the exasperated Grant, and laid hold of his other arm: 'I was up there in her caboosh having a few sharp rubs while mooshti here was bargaining with the madam, the bloody skinflint.' He glared across at the cook with the friendly aggression of an old friend: 'Skinflint - thass what you are, Welly - fat black ole skinflint. You git six-pun-ten a month - pri-nigh three times what I git - and you'd still skin a gnat for its hide. Judging by the way you black coves boast about yer wedding tackle, and how long it is, and all that, you oughter pay extra, not less!'

'Consuela, her name was,' said Jones, totally ignoring his chum's tirade, and still clutching Grant's arm as another man came aboard. 'Consuela... Consuela... That's a real nice name, eh? And what a lady she was too! She tickle me so pretty with them long soft fingers, she make my ole dick stand up like a spike jibboom.. Yes, sir, like a real big ole spike jibboom...And her snatch, man, that was as smooth inside as a...'

'Yes, all right, all right,' said Grant in quiet fury. 'Good for

143

you. Now away you go... Bosun, that you?'

'*Ydy, ydy, ydy, dim ond fi.* (Yes, only me). *Beth sy'n bod?* (What's up?)'

'I was just telling Mister Grant here about my Consuela,' said Jones. 'You din'see her, Reuben... Them lovely white legs, she wrap them all round me real tight.'

'Not white, brown,' said Kellock automatically, 'and she ain't yours, neither, nor yet mine. She's anyone's - any cove's who can stump up a dollar-an-a-half, ain't she? No good getting no silly ideas about her. Come on, doctor, you an' me better give our mutton-guns a good wash if we want to still have them next week.' He went to the rail and called down: 'Jimmy, Billy! Come on up, you pissy-arsed taffies! Whass up with yer? Can't climb a ladder?'

Grant peered cautiously over, watched curiously by Kellock. The two young Welsh ABs, much drunker than their seniors, were making floundering and hilarious attempts to scale the ladder, and fluent Spanish curses came up from the boatman, who was by now tired of their buffoonery, and anxious to get to his home and bed. By seven tomorrow morning he would be back at the heavy scull of a nitrate lighter. These *gringo* sailors, always stupid or snarling with drink - what a painful necessity they were!

Grant stood back and motioned to Raven to keep silent; drunk as they were, the three senior hands were curious to see what would happen; they had shuffled a few paces for'ard, but now turned to watch. Irritated as he was by their presence, Grant could not get rid of them quickly or quietly, so had to ignore them. He stood in the shadow of the half-deck bulkhead while the ABs struggled over the rail, laughing and joking. Most of their talk was in Welsh, but Grant looked quickly at Raven when Protheroe called up: 'Look out, Billy *bach* – don't squash it on the t'gallant rail for Chris' sake.'

At last the men reached the rail and flopped over on to the deck. In the moment of quiet, Raven noticed the clunk-clunk as the skiff made off back to shore. The two men were shambling off for'ard when Grant stepped into their path: 'John, Protheroe, stay where you are. I want a word with you both.'

The men were startled, astonished and puzzled: Billy John Ffynnongroes exclaimed, with no particular disrespect: 'Eh? Who the fuck's that? Oh, Mister Second, and yer brassbounder chum too. What you want? We come aboard tidy-like; we ain't late an' we ain't fighting no-one, is it? So what you want, then? I wants to get my head down, I do.'

'So you shall, John, when I've done my duty. Under Clause Two of the Crew Agreement you are forbidden to bring on board any spirituous liquors. The penalty for so doing is a fine of five shillings. I have reason to believe that you and Protheroe are carrying such liquors, and I am therefore about to search you.'

'You ain't bloody searching me!' said Billy John fiercely. 'No, not if you was the biggest bucko in South Spain. You ain't searching me, nor Jimmy here. You can see we ain't got nothing on us. Just picking on us, you are.'

'Don't be a fool, man! Think I don't know about *treepas?* Own up, chuck the things overboard like sensible chaps, and we'll say no more about it - though you should be logged.'

Billy John must have known that the game was up, but sense and discretion were not his main qualities, and he was not the man to give in tamely - not with the others watching. 'How the hell can I throw away what I ain't got, mun? Talk sense.'

Protheroe had a good deal less stomach for a hullabaloo with this mate, but he felt he had a reputation for sea-lawyering to keep up: 'Listen, mister, we ain't got nothing on us, see? An' you ain't allowed to search us without the capten being by here... And another thing - you got to settle disputes in port in front of the British Consul - I knows that. Well, I don't see no capten, nor no consul neither, so you can't do nothing. Come on, Billy.'

He made as if to go for'ard, but Grant stepped firmly in his path. 'As a sea-lawyer, Protheroe, you're nearly as useless as you are as a seaman, and that's saying something. It's only disputes about fines and discharges that go in front of the Consul. We're not talking about fines now. I'm just acting lawfully on the Captain's behalf to prevent your smuggling liquor aboard, that's all. So cut the cackle and pull your shirts up – *now!'*

There was a tense silence; Billy John stood facing the second, Protheroe facing Raven. Billy was beginning to feel sober enough to think. He no longer cared much about the liquor or a fine from the Old Man; he glowed and seethed with a desperate hatred of this jumped-up English prick of a second mate. Never give in to him, no matter what! He was aware that behind his right shoulder, gleaming faintly in the starlight, was a row of heavy metal belaying-pins to which the starboard mizen braces were made fast. Grant, his fighting instinct strung taut, caught the half-glance, and was ready for what followed. The three older hands, cold sober now, stood by helplessly.

Billy growled into the tense silence: 'I'm pulling up fuck-all for you, mister. You pull it up if you want.'

'Right, then. You asked me to, mind!' Grant stepped forward and with his right hand ripped the seaman's jacket open. He at once saw Billy's right hand go back over his shoulder to grasp one of the pins and tug it from the rail. As the pin came out (the coil of rope flopping to the deck) and before the crunching blow could be struck, Grant's left hand flew up to knock the blow aside, and at the same time he drew his right arm back and delivered a short savage jab at the seaman's bulging midriff. There was a wet, farting, bursting sound, followed by a patter of liquid to the deck and a pungent reek of strong spirits as the *treepa* burst, deluging Billy John's lower half with a quart of *aguardiente*. The wineskin absorbed some of the force of the vicious punch, but not all; the force of the blow threw Billy John bodily backwards against the pinrail, then he folded inwards with a cry of pain, and sank to the deck, grovelling at the second mate's feet, and painfully retching all the evening's good food and liquor into the scuppers. Jimmy Protheroe, white and sick-looking, all his fight and bluster gone, looked down in horror at his friend.

Grant too looked down with a satisfied scowl. He said: 'Had enough?' and Raven could have sworn that his right foot drew back ready for a kick into John's face; but the kick was never delivered, for an instant later Curly Kellock stood between Grant and the seaman, confronting the second with a kind of calm, natural authority. 'Yes, sir, he's had quite enough - more than enough. He's lost his booze and his supper, so I'm taking him to the foc'sle now to put the poor bugger in his bunk. Jimmy, sling your liquor into the drink, and let's have no more of this, for Christ's sake.'

He began to haul Billy John to his feet, taking care to keep between Billy and the second. Grant had felt a primitive and ugly joy in smashing John to the deck and uncovering his pitiful fraud at the same time; now he felt a twinge of resentment that it had all been over so quickly and painlessly - that there'd been pathetically little fight from Billy John. Grant had been braced for a good long, knock-down, bruising scrap that would really settle things, finishing off with a few good boots into John's ribs. Now there was this old nobody, this old buzzard from the back streets of Wapping, butting in where he wasn't wanted, and with plenty of lip too. He remembered the mate mentioning Kellock as an odd fellow, always on about Karl Marx, that mad anarchist chap. Curly Karl, the hands called him sometimes, he'd heard. Some bloody old wind-bag revolutionary - a ship was no place for the likes of him!

'Just a moment, Kellock! I'm in charge here, and I don't like your tone one little bit. You'll kindly leave me to deal with violent offenders in my own way.'

But the bluster, which might have worked with a young hothead like Billy, was of no use against the older man. Kellock replied coolly and reasonably, with no trace of either deference or insolence: 'Aye sir, you're in charge, and I should say you've had your way all right. You've waited for him, you've belted him, and now he's spewed his ring up, so what more d'you want? Now if you'll excuse me and my mates... Bosun, cop hold of his legs, will yer?' The three men closed round the still limp Billy John, physically, as it were, bringing the scene to an abrupt end Then they lifted him, and made off for'ard. Protheroe stood for a moment irresolute, then snatched off his *treepa* and flung it over the rail. Wellington Jones called to him irritably: 'Hey, Jimmy man, what you at? Come an' open the foc'sle door for us, chop-chop!'

Grant and Raven suddenly found themselves standing alone and feeling foolish. Grant covered up his embarrassment at the way he had been coolly bested, and in effect, overruled by Kellock, a mere AB. 'There you are, you see? They had got them. So perhaps Mister John will have learnt a lesson or two about me.'

'Possibly,' said a firm voice above them. 'I certainly have, by God.'

Both officers turned quickly; the Old Man stood above them at the poop rail in his pyjamas, as still as if he'd been carved in oak. 'Captain!' said Grant, and thought: How much of that did he watch? Bloody well spying on us now!

'Come up, please, gentlemen,' said Roberts quietly. As before, the incongruity of his voluminous striped Welsh flannel pyjamas was cancelled out by the aura of authority and strength that came from him. 'Trouble with the hands coming aboard?' he asked, with an ominous calm.

'A little, sir,' said Grant uncomfortably. 'Nothing we couldn't settle here, though. It was that man John in my watch.'

'William John Ffynnongroes? I thought so.'

'That's the one, sir. The usual thing - bringing liquor aboard. Got ugly when I tried to search him. Had a swing at me with a belaying- pin. He'd got a *treepa* of *aguardiente* under his shirt.'

'So I can smell, mister, from by here...And you happened to be on deck, on the spot, when he came aboard?'

Grant, for all his years and toughness, began to feel like a schoolboy hauled up before the Head, and he had too much respect for Roberts' perspicuity to try to lie: 'Well, no, sir. Actually we - Raven and I - saw these two men ashore buying the *treepas*. So we knew they had them.'

'So you waited up? I think I heard you two come aboard some while ago? That shows great zeal, Mr Grant - great zeal. As I recollect, the mate is in charge of the ship this evening, so officially who or what comes on board is his responsibility, isn't it?'

'Yes, sir, but we thought...'

'You thought you'd save him the trouble?'

'Well, yes, sir. I - we, that is - thought we'd better... I mean, we don't want that stuff handed round the foc'sle, do we?'

'Indeed? You feel strongly about that?'

'Well, yes, sir. It is in the Crew Agreement, after all... smuggling liquor aboard.'

'Ah indeed... the Crew Agreement... Do you believe in taking that seriously, too?'

'Why yes, sir, of course. I mean, it's the signed legal basis for all the crew's discipline.' Grant was puzzled at the way he was being led on. Some sort of blow was coming, but he couldn't for the life of him think what.

'Good, good; as I say, I'm always glad to see devotion to duty in officers.' He made as if to turn away and close the interview, then suddenly swung back and snapped out: 'And what about Kellock?'

'Kellock, sir?' Grant was floored.

'Yes, Kellock - he came off in the same boat, didn't he?'

'Yes...'

'Stone cold sober - a total abstainer, would you say?'

'No sir, hardly that.' Grant smiled uneasily. What on earth was he working up to?

'Right. So how much liquor was he smuggling on board? Or the cook? Or Reuben Mathias bosun? You didn't look, did you? Didn't even *ask?*'

148

Grant and Raven both felt the same sense of schoolboy guilt; they didn't need to reply, for the captain took a pace towards them, and spoke with great energy: 'No, you didn't even think of searching the others, and I'll tell you why: because you knew none of them threw the sea-boot at Raven here, and you think Billy John did. Well, you may be right - like enough he did. It's the sort of wild, stupid thing he would do. I've had trouble with him myself, as Raven will tell you. But we shall never know for sure about the boot, and this kind of damn petty grudge-bearing is no way to run a ship.'

Grant had recovered his composure and gift for sarcasm: 'Do I understand, captain, that I am being reprimanded for acting against indiscipline? Are the men to be allowed to hump barrels of liquor aboard?'

Jacob was nettled into letting his anger go: 'No, mister, I hope shall never be fool enough to reprimand any officer for keeping good discipline. But you were just using that damn piece of paper, the Crew Agreement, to give you the chance of hitting a man in the guts - and you'd have given him a kicking too if Kellock hadn't chipped in. No, don't deny it, man, you know you would. I saw your foot move. Now listen to me: you're young men and you've still time to learn. Remember what the Bible says: "The letter killeth, but the spirit giveth life." Your mistake was in following the letter of the Agreement, instead of trying to foster the spirit that makes this a happy ship - not all the time, of course; we're only human, we have our rascals and our fools, and we all make mistakes on times, and these things bring our troubles. But on the whole I challenge you to deny that this is a happy ship. Now understand me: I've little enough sympathy for William John; he would have clocked you one with that pin if you hadn't hit him first; I've been a second mate too, and I've had to be handy with fists and boots on times. I picked up a crimp's runner in San Francisco last voyage and chucked him clean over the side, as this young man here will confirm. But this crowd aren't jail-birds or Liverpool packet-rats – they're just ordinary Welsh working men - country boys, mostly. John went to pull that belaying-pin because you goaded him to it; you gave him the choice of belting you or looking like an idiot and a weakling in front of his mates.'

'But he was committing an offence, captain, a serious offence.'

'An offence, yes. But listen, mister: this crowd are not scum or hoodlums. Suppose you'd let John go without a search; what do you think would have happened?'

'I think that's obvious: the foc'sle would have been full of drunks, maybe out for trouble. I've seen it happen.'

'Not in this ship you haven't, mister. Unlike you, I've lived for years in Welsh ships' foc'sles, so I'll tell you. Those *treepas* would have been passed round the whole lot of them, especially among the port watch, who haven't been ashore tonight, and there wouldn't have been that much liquor each. So the whole bunch would have had a tipple before turning in, and we wouldn't have known a thing about it, most likely. Tomorrow night, someone in the port watch might do the same for Billy and his mate. If - if, mind you - we ever get a foc'sle full of fighting drunks - well then will be the time to act, and I can tell you, mun, I shall be the first to go in there and bang some heads. So I'm not saying "Act soft", I'm saying "Be reasonable". I've never seen any good coming from feuds. Now I want some sleep, so off you go and remember my words. I don't want anything like this from you again.' He stumped off, disappeared into the companionway, and then shoved his head back round it to say: 'By the way: this precious Crew Agreement, mister: did you ever read what it says about the crew's diet? "Sufficient without waste" it says. You ask that young man beside you how often the brassbounders get "sufficient" on their plates. No good ever came out of sea-lawyering; you keep that in mind.'

10

'Right,' said Senior Apprentice Perkins to his boat's crew, 'they'll be coming in a minute, so smarten up a bit. Robbins, for Christ's sake wake up and hold her in with the boat-hook. What do you think it's for? You're about as handy as a cow with a musket.'

'Figaro's' apprentices, looking monstrously transformed - almost smart, in square-necked white fronts and crisply-creased white duck trousers - sat in the gig alongside the gangway of the Pacific Steam Navigation Company's ship 'Magellan' and waited in the hot afternoon sunshine for their captain and his family. The beautiful long white liner lay, like a distantly polite aristocrat, well clear of the dusty loading tiers, rolling with ponderous dignity at her anchor. Launches full of cargo and ships' boats from the nitrate fleet went out of their way to pull past her, and glasses were trained on her from every poop, for such a ship was not often seen at a benighted backwater like Caleta Buena.

As the great smooth swells passed under the liner, the boys in the boat struggled to keep the gig alongside without damage to Dai Dome's precious paint. The scrubbed-white teak grating at the foot of the gangway ladder rose and fell five feet or more, sometimes almost submerging. One moment, the grating was level with the boat's top strake, the next, as the steamer reeled gravely to starboard, it rose high above their heads; exposing a band of smart red boot-topping with scarcely a barnacle to be seen on it. The lads used the starboard oars to fend her off, and Robbins, standing in the bow, used his boat-hook (scrubbed, polished, and ornamented by Curly Kellock, the old Navy man, with an elaborate turk's head in white codline) to keep in contact. It was not easy.

The boys, accustomed to dungarees encrusted with the tar, grease and paint of the seaman's trade, felt hampered, inhibited, in everything they did by the cleanness and newness of their clothes, and by the urgent need to keep them clean and dry. The urgent need sprang from their fear of the new Second. Almost as soon as he had joined, Second Mate Grant had been taken aside by the captain and told: 'Now see here, mister: you look a smartish fellow to me. I want you to knock those apprentices of ours into a bit of shape, like. They've been treated too damn soft lately - turned into a pack of idle, greasy, loafing sojers. Don't shave once in a week, by the look of them, can't row a boat straight, about as smart aloft as a lot of pregnant nuns. I can't help noticing some of the other ships' brassbounders - especially the Germans. Knock spots off our miserable *crwts,* they would. So I'm putting you in charge of them: drill them aloft - nothing dangerous, mind, no racing about. And teach them how to pull a boat with a bit of style. Now listen: you know Gomez' place - the chandler in the main street? Well, he was showing me some decent duds yesterday - white fronts (you know, Navy-rig shirts?) and white duck trousers. Got them off some chiselling Navy purser, I shouldn't wonder. Gomez runs the only half-tidy bunch of whores in the town. As for the rest, they'll give you a dose fit to finish off an elephant. He caters for the senior officers, you see, so we can guess what the purser got in return for the duds, eh? Where was I? Oh yes: take those damn boys in there and get them fitted up decently. Tell Gomez to put the duds down on the ship's account, and tell him to put them down as sailcloth. After all, that's what they're made of, more or less. Saves a lot of argument with the Owner.'

'Surely he wouldn't jib at white ducks for the gig's crew, sir?'

Jacob was in a relaxed, expansive mood, despite his stern and perhaps rather unfair tirade about his apprentices: 'Jib? He'd cry the bloody place down! *Duw,* boy, let me tell you something that perhaps I shouldn't: old John Powell would jib at an extra currant or split pea or copper nail. It's pound-and-pint on this ship - just the bare minimum the Board of Trade says and not a crumb or a rope-yarn beyond. Good God, the damn boys could row round stark bollock naked for all he'd care.'

Fortunately, John Powell was many thousand miles away and no such indecorum prevailed. 'Figaro's' boys, after weeks of hounding, driving and hazing from Grant ('Gorilla' was the politest of the names they used for him) were now as smart as any in the port, and a better boat's crew than most. Even old Curly Kellock, profoundest of sceptics when it came to officers and their fads, was reminded of his far-off Navy days, and commented to Jac: 'I'll say this for our snotties: they're a middling tiddley bunch now, thanks to the bucko. Good enough for a Home Fleet cruiser, nearly.'

The boys waited a long time in the afternoon sun; the heat

throbbed out from the liner's plates, there was not a breath stirring, and there'd be no land-breeze to cool the stifling ships for an hour or so yet. Their mood sagged from an excited curiosity to drowsy boredom. Ieuan spoke listlessly: 'Jake's taking his damn time; he's only got to collect his missis and daughter.'

'Getting pissed with the captain, I expect,' said Smith, the burly, red-faced second-year apprentice of the port watch. 'They're old pals - shipmates, - Isaac says. That's why he's anchored here. He's not supposed to.'

'We know, Smutty, we know,' said Perkins wearily. Like Isaac, Smith was a great gossip.

'And Isaac says old Jac the sail-maker has seen the Old Man's daughter, and he says she's a nice piece of skirt.'

'Jesus! What would an old nancy like Isaac know about skirts? Never been up one in his entire life, I'll bet.'

'Well anyway, that's what he says,' said Smith with a knowing leer, 'so we shall see in a minute, shan't we?'

Ieuan turned half-round to look at him: 'Oh yes, we shall see. And I suppose you think, with your wonderful English good looks, she'll be sure to fall for you as soon as she's in the boat?' There was an edge to his voice; somehow he resented the unknown Welsh girl - his compatriot - being talked about so coarsely as a piece of something, and by a gang of foreign boys. After all, 'Figaro' was a part of Wales, even if she had been built in Scotland and named after a barber who, he gathered, was some sort of dago. The ship was still Welsh, and the boat was a bit of the ship.

All these undertones eluded the crude mind of Smith, who was unabashed: 'She might - depends on whether she's got taste or not. Can never tell with people born and bred out in the wilds. Shouldn't think she'd want a weed like you, even if you are another taffy. Even she must know a man when she sees one.'

'Shut it, you two,' said Perkins mechanically. 'Robbins, keep hold of that bloody ladder, will you? What makes any of you think the Old Man's daughter will even look at a pack of louts like you? Anyway, they're coming now. I can see the officer of the watch at the top of the gangway. So shut up, and let's have a smart shove off from here, and keep your damned ears open for orders. Get it together from the first stroke; Jake will go barmy if we make a balls-up of it alongside a liner, with his pal and his missis watching. And Robbins!' He raised his voice cautiously: 'Don't you go gawping up the women's skirts as they come down the ladder. This ain't a fandango-hall.' There was a quiet snigger among the boys at this; they all remembered Robbins' wide-eyed, incredulous stare at the woman in the smoky cantina ashore a few days ago, as she listlessly, to the raucous music of guitar, accordion and castanets, wriggled her way out of her grubby clothes, finally presenting to the cheering, hooting assembly a globular and surprisingly white pair of buttocks. A Welsh voice, thick with the fiery local *pisco,* had yelled: '*O diawl, bois,* she's just like the missis!'

On deck at the head of the ladder the group of officers in immaculate white was breaking up, with a flurry of smart salutes, bows, and cordial handshakes between the ladies and the 'Magellan's' afterguard, who had been their hosts and companions for six weeks; the two seasoned captains watched, listened and understood all, for they had been twenty not so long ago.

'Well, capten,' said Jacob, offering his great brown paw to his exalted counterpart, 'I shan't forget this act of kindness. Very, very good of you to put in here specially.'

'Not at all, not at all,' said Captain Morris of the 'Magellan'. 'The least an old shipmate and fellow-Welshman could do. Nice to have a yarn about the old days. And it's been a great pleasure to have your charming wife and daughter with us. We shall all miss them a great deal, I assure you. Wouldn't like to think of them jolting and frying and choking to death on that infernal railway between here and Iquique... Dust and heat and nothing but sand... Crowds of peasants spitting and breathing garlic all over you – that's the Longitudinale Railway for you. I've had to travel on it myself - for my sins - and it's not the vehicle for decent Welsh ladies, I can tell you...Bugs in the seat-cushions, I shouldn't wonder. I think we've done a little better than that aboard the "Magellan", eh, ma'am?'

Six weeks ago, Mair Roberts, fresh from the small Welsh town, might have been nonplussed at being the centre of such social attention; but now she had picked up enough of the ways, the 'outward habit of encounter', of that island of sober luxury and bourgeois gloss, the liner's saloon. She smiled and inclined her head gracefully, and murmured 'Indeed, captain.'

'Besides,' said Captain Morris, with his very best professional smile, 'it's given us the pleasure of the ladies' company for a few more days. It has done my heart good, captain, I can tell you, after all my years in England, to hear the language of heaven spoken aboard my ship.' The smile disappeared as he turned casually to his Chief Officer: 'Cable party to the foc'sle, Mister Attwood. Ring down "Standby engines." Steam on the anchor-winch.' Then, like sun succeeding shower, his bonhomie beamed forth again. He felt especially genial towards Jacob Roberts of the 'Figaro' because he was comfortably aware of having done rather better in life than Roberts had. The airy reference to being old shipmates glossed over the fact that when they last sailed together on the Melbourne run in the old 'Bucephalus' he had been a senior apprentice, having been top of his year at Conway, while Jacob had been the bosun, struggling upwards through the ranks - climbing in through the hawsepipe, as they said in the Navy. The social gap between them was as wide as ever; all the same, young Bosun Roberts had done damned well for himself, even if he would never quite count as a gentleman.

'No trouble, you see, captain,' he said smoothly. 'Simple enough in steam to drop anchor and weigh it again - the machinery does everything. I'll easily make up any lost time before we get to Callao.'

'Aye, but the stop will be in your log. What about your Owners? Shouldn't like to land you in any trouble with them.'

'Owners! Parcel of money-grubbing pen-pushers, chair-polishers! What will they know about it? As I say, I shall make up the time. As for the log: if they ever trouble to read it they'll see that I made a brief stop at Caleta Buena for minor engine repairs.'

'Captain!' said Mair Roberts, almost flirtatiously, 'you didn't tell us poor passengers you had problems with the engines!'

'No ma'am, nor have I, as far as I know. But I'll tell you this, and as a captain's wife I know you will understand: as soon as you get into a steam ship you find that your engineers - a strange breed, all of them - are always repairing something. Hammer, hammer, hammer, all day long down there, covered in grease most of the time, and happy as sand-boys to be so. So the log won't be lying- not exactly.' He laughed easily, like a relaxed emperor among his court, and such of his officers as were listening to him echoed his mirth politely. Those who were not - and they were notably the younger ones - were looking, discreetly but with the keenest regret, at the tall dark girl, turning aside from them towards the ship's rail. Ah, that profile! That chiselled chin, making such a delicious angle with the neck! That glorious high bosom, so... so... Words failed them, even in reverie.

155

Eleanor stepped towards the upper platform of the ship's ladder, her hair combed up neatly from the nape of the white neck, its curls crisply confined. No wonder the 'Magellan's' officers had christened her - not in the least satirically – 'The Duchess'; no wonder that all of them, looking from Eleanor to Jacob and back again, were dumbfounded that this delicate, demure, exquisite creature could have come from the loins of the tough, red-faced, whiskery old shellback skipper of a Welsh nitrate barque, with no class at all about him, by the look of his baggy, ill-cut blue serge suit. That was never a proper bespoke suit - and what a cloth to wear in this heat! A nice crisp white drill - that was better for summer in twenty degrees south latitude.

It really was extraordinary: the Duchess looked such a lady; she wouldn't be out of place at Ascot or Henley or in Bond Street. And yet when her father had spoken to her in some gibberish that was presumably Welsh, she - even she - had understood it, and replied in kind. By Jove, they'd miss her, especially her singing in the saloon after dinner, with her mother playing for her on the ship's piano. The old girl had been a looker in her day, too - you could see that. But by God, look at the way she - the Duchess - stood waving to them! Beautifully frilled and starched blouse, with ruffled neck and leg-of-mutton sleeves; the blouse drawn in at the high waist above the light, dove-grey skirt, so that her figure formed two subtle interlocked triangles. What a creature to be wasted aboard a grimy, slab-sided fourposter full of disgusting dusty nitrate bags and a motley crew of salt-junk-eating, limejuice-drinking, hairy-arsed ABs from all the dirtiest corners of the world, most likely. What a waste! And what a shock for her, after the civilised life she'd been used to with them!

As the disembarking party descended the ladder, the young officers moved to the rail, looking with polite, despairing lechery at the girl, and with mixed feelings of contempt and envy at the apprentices waiting in the boat; contempt, because their own raw apprentice days were behind them, and they belonged to a liner; envy because what they had lost, the lads in the boat had gained. She would be aboard that beastly Welsh hooker for months, and maybe not shut away in a cabin and chaperoned quite so zealously by mama as she had been on the voyage out. Not one of them, for all his efforts, had managed to get beyond the barrier of cool, charming, friendly aloofness; each knew the others too well to even boast that he had. And now she was going, and when would they get another passenger like that? There weren't usually more than a few dozen, all told, most trips, and they were mainly dreary middle-aged engineers, diplomats and officials and their acid-faced, bored, bridge-playing wives.

As the ladies descended the ladder, Jacob Roberts touched his peaked cap in an awkward salute: *'Wel, dioch yn fawr, capten, diolch yn fawr iawn!'* (Thank you very much, captain).

When he reached the foot of the ladder, he found Eleanor looking nervously at the plunging boat alongside; she had not been to sea since childhood, when she had been unceremoniously tossed like a bundle in and out of boats. Now it was different: she was a self-conscious but fiercely independent young woman, and some at least of the apprentices in the boat were of her own age. The boat was close alongside, yes, but rising and falling several feet, and the part of it directly opposite the little platform where she stood was occupied by young men in white sailor shirts, who sat silent, staring at her curiously. If she jumped into the boat, she'd just land sprawling on top of one of them, and though she'd had a respectable and sheltered childhood she could guess the kind of jokes they'd make about that when Dadi wasn't there to make them behave. Already she could see some furtive grins being exchanged; she went hot and scarlet with embarrassment and frustration. She saw the grins disappear rapidly as her father reached the lower steps of the ladder and said irritably: 'What's the matter, girl? You've got into a boat before, haven't you?' Jacob was not a stupid man, but imagination was not his strong suit; accustomed as he was to getting in and out of boats in conditions ten times rougher than today's, he did not stop to think how it would be for a virtual beginner, clad in a long skirt and petticoats. Even his love of his daughter, and his pleasure at seeing her again, could not quite prevent that little stab of professional choler - the twist of impatience in the face of delay and diffidence. He of course turned his wrath on the boys: 'Perkins! Use your wits, boy, for God's sake! Haul the gig for'ard a bit so that we can step into the stern-sheets. Robbins! Wake up, you...' He checked himself, remembering the ladies, and was lost for a suitable noun. 'Bear a hand, boy! Haul ahead on that guest-rope, can't you?'

When the stern of the boat was alongside the platform he had the wit to say to his wife: 'Now then, Mair, show her how it's done. Perkins, pass your boat-hook to your stroke oar and stand by to steady the ladies as they step aboard.'

Perkins stood up, self-consciously aware of the other boys'

covert amusement, and spread his arms ready to clasp dutifully and firmly anyone who might come his way. He was startled when, almost at once, he found himself holding the upper arms and shoulders of the captain's wife. With an experienced eye, she had waited for the boat to sink to its lowest pitch below them, and had then half-stepped, half-jumped, to land nimbly, without a lurch or a stagger, precisely in the centre of the boat. She was relieved to have managed so well before that critical audience, but did not show it. With a polite smile and a 'Thank you, Perkins,' she detached herself and took her place on the side bench away from the steamer, so as to leave more room for Nelli. She needed no imagination to sympathize with her daughter, for she remembered from the 'Dryslwyn Castle' days how hard it was at first for a woman to get into and out of small boats with any dignity.

Her husband's face creased into an approving grin: *'Da iawn, cariad!* That's the way of it. Now you, Eleanor *bach.* Nothing to it.'

Mair looked at her daughter's concentration - the grip on the platform rail, the fixed gaze at the boat's heaving, the teeth biting firmly at her lower lip. Mair suffered vicariously, but dared say nothing; the bit of coaching she had given her down in the cabin would have to do. Nelli would be furious if she fussed now - in front of these lads. There was a moment's pause; Eleanor missed one rise and fall of the boat and was angry with herself; Perkins stood ready, his awe at the captain's presence and his determination to do a job properly distracting him from the delightful, frill-clad breasts that moved before his eyes as the gig rose and fell. Then suddenly she was coming at him; with a flash of slightly-too-much white cotton stocking, and with a leap that was a little too impetuous, she landed in Perkins' arms. He staggered back one pace, but instantly recovered his balance. He was aware of the wide brim of her hat striking the top of his cap and becoming comically tilted over her left ear; for an instant she was very close to him, so that he sensed (most agreeably) the pressure of her breasts and the coolness of her arms inside the thin blouse, caught the fragrance of eau-de-cologne about her, felt the warmth of her breath against his face and neck.

He had done his job well, but all the same he flushed crimson, said, 'Sorry, miss,' and at once let go of her arms. No brassbounder dared to make a sound, but he felt the sudden surge of ribaldry among his fellows in the boat. Now that his hands had touched her, they seemed to him curiously large, grubby and sweaty. Unconsciously, he wiped his palms dry on his duck trousers.

Copying her mother, Eleanor said: 'Not at all. Thank you, Perkins,' in a very polite, correct Welsh English. She had used the English language mainly at her boarding-school for young ladies in Haverfordwest, and hardly at all at home, so she unconsciously associated it with formality, etiquette and education. She seated herself in the sternsheets, facing across at her mother, grateful that she did not have to look straight at the apprentices, of whose wicked and unruly ways she had heard much over the years. Her mother smiled back with her eyes and nodded minutely to say 'Well done!' Perkins took his place at the tiller and the boat gave an abrupt lurch as, without any kind of pause or thought or finesse, her father dropped his fourteen stone casually into it and sat next to Eleanor.

He gave no order, but the apprentice at stroke laid down the boat-hook and took hold of his oar, Robbins in the bow doing the same. Perkins growled 'Shove off, star-board... Give way....*together!*' He barked out the last word like a drill-sergeant, so that in perfect unison the four oar-blades bit the water, the light boat leapt forward, and the passengers swayed backwards, the women momentarily startled by the force of the stroke. Jacob swayed easily and thought: That Grant has done a fair job with this bunch of sojers; not bad now, not bad. He hoped the steamer's people might have noticed, but said nothing in the way of praise to the boys; no point in giving the young devils swelled heads. Instead, he beamed a welcome to this little fragment of his command to his beloved Mair. *Iesu mawr!* It made him feel ten years younger just to see her looking so brown, so spry, and as beautiful as ever.

As the boat went swiftly clear of 'Magellan's' bow, he heard shouts from above, heard the clank of the winch, and saw the links of her cable rising slowly, dripping, out of the water. He nodded towards it and said to his wife: 'Smart fellow, Morris - always was. Doesn't waste much time, does he? *Duw,* the way he's got on...'

As for his daughter, she sat in the spotless boat as it climbed the round blue swells, taking in everything in this new world, her senses vitally awake and alive. The quiet, ordered life of the little, grey-stone town - that world seemed remote indeed, in space and time; even the comfortable cocoon of the saloon passenger's life aboard the 'Magellan' was dropping rapidly astern. The liner had got her anchor now; Eleanor could see a spray of water cascading from her foc'sle head as her hands hosed the mud from it. A cloud of dazzling white steam came from her siren-pipe and a moment later the long vibrant blast reached them in the still air. The beautiful ship was swinging, turning seawards, her masts and funnels opening out, a small white fleck appearing at her bow as she gathered way; there was a distant tinkle of brass bells, black smoke poured from her two high funnels and a livid white lash of racing water shot from under her counter as her captain rang down 'Full Ahead'. Soon she would be gone for good into the blue hazy vastness of the Pacific.

Her father leaned nearer and touched her knee, smiling and pointing ahead: 'There she is – "Figaro". Just beyond that big German barque. Not looking her best, of course, being so high out of the water, and in the middle of loading. But you wait till we've got her ready for sea, in a few weeks' time.' Jacob left his wife out of this conversation, not from any coldness, but because he knew she didn't need telling. Years of her life had been spent on and among ships, and she would have picked out his ship long ago.

The barque stood high and awkward, the expanse of red bottom-paint spoiling her looks, her nice lines lost. Her huge rudder, normally submerged, stuck up now like a high, narrow barn door. A grey-white cloud rose from among the clumsy sheets spread above her for'ard hatchway; her lower yards were cock-billed - turned upwards out of their normal horizontal - to assist the loading, and cargo-hoists cluttered the orderly web of her rigging. A big, blunt-ended lighter or launch lay alongside for'ard. Jacob sensed his daughter's disappointment and said: 'She's not a liner, of course; the poor old girl has to work for a living, but wait till you see her sailing. Give her a good breeze on the quarter, and she doesn't plod along stinking of coal and grease, she flies like a bird!'

Eleanor pressed his hand and said tactfully: 'She's lovely, dadi. Better than any old steam-kettle... All that black smoke....' And Jacob thought: By damn, it's going to be good having them both aboard!

Her eyes gleamed affectionately at him, but he was not to know that some of the gleam was from her excitement at the strangeness and newness of it all. She was no stranger to the sea; it lapped placidly or roared thunderously at the edge of her home-town, depending on the season and the weather. Sometimes, on a spring tide, she launched her father's little dinghy and rowed on the smooth waters of the Nevern estuary; sometimes, in the summer, a friend or relative would take her and her mother to sea for a half-day sailing or fishing trip along the rockbound coast. But now she herself was launched; launched into a world where the sea was everything, where nothing counted but ships and crews and cargoes and rope and canvas. And then to be surrounded by so many men! Of course, she met young men in Newport too: the polite, respectable, dark-suited, high-collared callers who were teachers, clerks or ministers - like that poor pathetic Gwilym Davies Ebeneser with his begging puppy-dog eyes; or else they were the young men who didn't call - who would never be invited to do so: rough boys, *crwts* from Preseli farms, hands from the trading ketches, who came stumbling out of the public-house to vomit their evening's beer into the gutter. But now she and Mam would be living in a man's world. She thought with scorn of the way some of the girls at school had gone on giggling and tittling and tattling about men and what they might do to you if you weren't careful, and what they'd look like with their clothes off. Silly lot of little hussies! If only they could see her now, in this beautiful boat, on a magically blue tropical sea, with those grand snow-topped mountains in the background. And these fine fellows - the apprentices! So smart, so disciplined, so strong! As brown as coffee-berries, with such big hands and arms; they'd been rowing for a good twenty minutes now, and yet every stroke was as firm and as perfectly together as the first one. Those stupid girls at Hill House College wouldn't see anything like this in Haverfordwest! Mind, she couldn't help noticing that the boys smelt a bit sweaty, but then they'd been working hard in this hot sunshine, and she supposed they'd got very little chance to bath or anything in their quarters. Even on the 'Magellan' fresh water had been quite scarce. And their hands too: they weren't gentlemen's hands, like Bryn Meredydd's. She flicked a glance down at Perkins' hand on the tiller: very big, heavy and strong, the skin cracked here and there and the cracks and finger-nails dark with grease and tar; the palm horny, the back scarred about the knuckles and tanned a deep red-brown; the nails split and broken off here and there. A hand that had suffered more pain, strain and knocks than any labourer's at home - a hand like her father's.

Never mind, they were still the sons of gentlemen - they weren't labouring class. And some of them (her eye flickered discreetly among them as she looked ahead, pretending to study 'Figaro'), some of them did look very handsome; some even had quite good sets of whiskers.   Funny to think that they came, probably, from rich English families - the real *crachach*, the nobs, as the girls in school used to say - and yet her Dad could order them about just as he liked, and (she could see) they regarded him as God. In awe of him, they were! Of her Dad! And Dadi too - he seemed different here - so silent and stern and... majestic. These boys, they'd have a shock if they could have seen him giving her piggy-backs, or wearing a funny hat at Christmas, or dozing in his big chair after Sunday dinner, with his mouth wide open, or in the woodshed, chopping up kindling-wood. He was like two men, really, one for home and one for the ship: a Dadi Ty Coch and a Capten Jacob Roberts 'Figaro'.

'Easy-all!' cried Perkins, as they swung in under the shade of the barque's counter. 'Stand by for'ard, Robbins.'

*   *   *

At the for'ard hatch Perkins' predecessor, John Raven, had perhaps more cause to feel disgruntled than any of the apprentices. He was learning, in the hard school of experience, that there was a high price to be paid for the meagre authority and scanty pay he had acquired by his promotion. Instead of the relatively carefree open-air boating existence of the brassbounder - in port at least - he was condemned to the twelve-hour grind of cargo-work. He also now realized fully that, though the mate had some status in the ship as the captain's right-hand man and deputy, the second and third mates had very little. When cargo was to be worked, they were little more than working foremen, labouring sweatily at the ropes as hard as the foremast hands, while the mate, clean and cool, strolled about the decks, supervising, and the captain, spruced up in white linen suit and panama hat, disappeared ashore in the gig every morning after breakfast on 'ship's business'.

Every day except Sunday, apart from a few blessed local saints' days and fiestas, there was a lighter alongside; every day, from six till six, with short breaks for meals, the hot, filthy, dusty monotony of unbearably slow unloading and loading went on. Every morning, soon after dawn, they would see a black lighter crawling across the gently-heaving water towards them, the two *lancheros* at the stern swaying from side to side as they sculled with long sweeps, the steady clunk-clunk of their progress sounding dully in the stillness.

For weeks on end the hands had worked all day in the stifling cavernous holds, shovelling into puny baskets all those thousands of tons of Welsh coal so casually tipped in by the truck-load at Penarth. As each basket was filled, a yell to the men on deck set them cranking away at the handles of the dolly-winch, hoisting the basket clear of the hatch-coaming. Then Raven hauled on a tackle to swing the derrick across to plumb the lighter, the winch-men let the hoist pay out until another yell came from the lighter, where a *lanchero* would capsize the basket of coal with a dull rattle. The empty basket would be tossed up on deck and back down into the hold; Grant would heave the derrick back over the hold, and down would go the empty hook, by which time the hold party had another basket full.

The job had been unbearably slow and long, for when the men began to shovel they were standing on a mountain of coal, cramped up close under the hold's ceiling. A whole day's work had seemed to make little impression on such a quantity, and it was galling, in their few moments of ease, waiting for a lighter, to look across to the next ship in the tier, a huge Laeisz Flying-P barque from Hamburg, and see the lighters waiting, clustered alongside each hatch, and the cargo whirring up from four holds at a time, in great buckets and slings, hoisted by furiously-rattling steam winches.

'Look at them lucky square-head bastards!' Billy John had said one day, wiping the runnels of sweat from his face with a filthy rag. 'Two winches to each hatch - bugger-all for them to do but scull about in fancy white shirts and work the donkey-winches.'

'Not lucky,' said Curly Kellock sententiously. 'No luck about it, my son. They're capitalist robbers too, but at least they know how to organize their robbery prop'ly. We're in the hands of English incompetents.'

'Welsh, you means,' said Billy angrily. 'Old Powell is Welsh; everything about this ship is Welsh, not English.'

'All right, my son, have it yer own way: Welsh incompetents, then. Couldn't manage a piss-up in a brewery. When was our Owner at sea? How many of his clerks and shareholders have even seen the ship, or know where she is now? Nearly all the lime-juicers (British ships) I've been in are the same - owned by people who don't know nothing about them, and don't care, so long as they get some miserable dividend every year for doing nothing. Christ, even lazy robbers should know their job.'

The political philosophy was totally lost on Billy, who rapped a stinking black dottle from his clay pipe and said: 'I'm going to ship aboard one o' them big Dutchmen, one day.'

The cockney shook his head and grinned: 'You never will, my son; you like it here too much, gabbin' away in Welsh to yer mates. And if you did sign on one of them, you wouldn't last a dog-watch. Run like battleships, they are; they'd work your arse off, and as soon as you started your sea-lawyering capers they'd stick you in irons, mate. They don't mess about, y'know. Any case,' he added pedantically, 'she ain't Dutch, she's German.'

'Germans, Dutch, Swedes, Finns – what's the difference? Damned Dutchies, I call them, all that square-head "jah for yes" crowd. And there's getting to be a sight too many of them about on this coast.' The shrill sound of the mate's whistle had brought a sudden end to this rather academic conversation. Another empty lighter had boomed hollowly alongside, waiting for its hundred tons of coal.

When the last lighter had gone, the hands were set to the even filthier task of sweeping the holds clear of the remnants of the coal. There was, however, a better side to this job: it was tacitly understood, for'ard, aft, and even in the Owners' office, that whatever oddments of burnable coal they found in small corners of the hold could be bagged up for the ship's own bogie-stoves that warmed the foc'sle, the idlers' mess, the half-deck and the cabins aft. It looked as if they'd have to face a winter rounding of the Horn, and in those wild and bitter latitudes it would be some comfort to have the bogie red-hot, cracking and spitting in the corner of the foc'sle, when the crowd came down off the yards frozen stiff and soaked.

Before the last of the coal was gone from the after hold, nitrate had started to come into the for'ard one, for the barque must always have a 'stiffening' to keep her upright; somewhere at the bottom of her holds there must always be a few hundred tons of something, to balance the leverage of her sixty tons of lofty masts, spars and rigging. Now the for'ard hold was perhaps a quarter full, and the pattern of the work was reversed. The lighters came deep-laden with two-hundred-pound gunny sacks of the acrid, grey-white *nitrado de Chile*, the precious desert dust over which Peruvians, Bolivians and Chileans had fought murderously for two years and more. Slings of sacks came creaking up from the lighter, swaying and swinging over to the hatchway to drop down in controlled jerks as the rope was allowed to slip back round the winch drum.

The hold was vast, cathedral-like in its proportions, gloomy in its far corners, but in the middle, under the open hatch, it blazed fiercely in the broad shaft of light from the eternal West Coast sun. Seen from the dark recesses of the hold, the angled pillar of afternoon sun was livid, alive, teeming with motes of the whitish dust, and its light fell full on what seemed at first like an altar, a roughly-formed altar of gunny-sacks. But it was a secular altar to the very human god of the Chilean stevedores, the *capataz de cargadores,* the chief stevedore, the most exalted, respected and iron-muscled man among that hardy band. While his followers grouped themselves like acolytes about the platform of sacks, he tramped, bent-backed, to and fro, to and fro, at a near-trot, and personally laid every sack in its proper place. There would be forty-thousand-odd sacks to lay before 'Figaro' was down to her marks; nevertheless, the chief alone could decide where each sack was to go, and the chief alone could put it there. No gringo bosun or mate, or even captain, dared to trespass on his office, for fear of a prompt and uncompromising strike; as for his Chilean subordinates, they would as soon curse their Redeemer or spit upon the Blessed Virgin as touch one gunny sack that the *capataz* had laid. Their task was to unsling the sacks as they landed on the platform, and to place each sack across the herculean shoulders of their leader. While at work, he never spoke to them, or they to him; he was simply their reason for being in that hold, and earning a wage to feed their families. On a day when he was ill or drunk or in jail they remained ashore idle, dozing on the beach on a pile of empty sacks, under the shade of the loading pier, earning nothing.

Slowly, day by day, with infinite effort and skill, he built his cargo; at first he covered the whole floor of the hold with sacks, right out to the turn of the bilge, but the next layer was drawn in a little from the ship's sides, and the next a little more, until, in each hold, he would make a long low pile, pyramidal in section. Only a low pile, for the nitrate would absorb moisture from the sea air and become immensely heavy, so that a full cargo would not half fill the hold space. As the sacks grew in weight and dampness, they also stuck together, so that the unloading stevedores in Liverpool or Bristol or Dunkirk or Antwerp would need crowbars to prise them apart.

The stevedore's work was pure folk art. This afternoon John Raven and Grant, taking a short spell from their hauling, joined the mate at the hatchway, looking down on the *capataz* and his minions. It was a new experience for Raven, and he watched with interest and grudging admiration the amazing strength, skill and authority of the Chilean. Scarcely lifting his head, he took the weight of each heavy sack as if it were a pillow, then a few quick, crouching steps and a deft sideways shrug, and the sack landed with a soft thud exactly in line with the last, never requiring more than a kick to align it precisely. Raven wondered why he grudged him his full admiration: the fellow was good at his job - there was no getting away from that - and yet... he was only a dago stevedore, after all. Probably couldn't read or write, or understand a word of English. But it wasn't quite that - it was the sort of airs he gave himself. Went around as if he owned the ship and the port, looked right through you. Yet the odd thing was that Grant, who was pretty touchy, and old Dai Evans, and even Jake himself seemed to almost defer to him, as if it were not for them to comment on his workmanship. And that certainly wasn't because Jake was naturally timid or polite or gentle - the boarding house runner in San Francisco had found that out, and serve him right for trying to get decent British sailors into his foul clutches!

Grant said: 'He's making a good stow, mister.'

'Yes,' said Evans. 'Diaz.'

'I beg your pardon?'

'Diaz, Antonio Diaz. That's his name. He's one of the best from here to Iquique, they say. We were lucky to get him.'

Strewth, thought Raven, he even knows his name. It'll be Senor Diaz next! Raven was at an age when the raw race prejudice and snobbery of his upbringing and public school were not yet modified by experience, or mellowed by age or indifference. His prickly resentment could not be bottled for long: 'I suppose it's just a knack he's picked up,' he said dismissively.

'Oh, indeed?' said Evans, straightening up suddenly with indignation. 'Knack, is it? Well, I shall be very pleased when you've got the knack of your job half as well, boy.' He pronounced the last word with stinging contempt, for he felt nettled at this young English upstart. He felt too a bond of empathy with the stevedore: they were both working men who'd done well, who'd risen above the crowd by sheer dogged merit, not through a father's sovereigns or an old school tie or an uncle on the board of directors. He walked off aft a few paces, then turned: 'Tomorrow morning, Mister Raven, you can take two port watch hands and shift those spare spars in the tween-decks. Lash them

166

securely fore and aft, outboard of the stanchions.'

'Aye, aye,' said Raven stonily. When the mate had gone, he muttered to Grant: 'Sometimes that old man makes me sick. He gets offended about nothing, so he gives me a stupid useless work-up job as revenge. Just petty spite!'

Grant's cool blue eyes looked at him blankly, weighing him up. Grant said: 'The mate's right about you - you have got a lot to learn. I'd better lend you a few of my books if you ever hope to sit for your second mate's ticket. Don't you know that some of the nitrate has got to go into the tween-decks? That's why he wanted it cleared - not just for spite, you young idiot.'

'Nitrate? Heavy stuff like that, up in the tween-decks?' The tween-decks were the upper storeys of the hold, small upper holds, each like a giant shelf filling in the space just under the deck. Normally, with a general cargo, it would be for light goods.

'Don't you know anything about cargo stowage, young Raven? Listen: if this chap were to put all the nitrate down there, in the bottom of the hold, the ship would be too damn stable. Every time she rolled, she'd whip back like a spring. You wouldn't be able to live aboard her in heavy weather – you'd be battered to bits. And she'd snap off her masts like carrots. So he puts some cargo high up to make her roll gently - well, more gently, anyway.'

'All right, I see.' Raven's face was dully flushed with sullenness.

'Right then; I don't want to be pompous, but remember, you don't know everything yet. When you were a mere brassbounder, I don't suppose you even thought about the way the cargo was stowed. That Chilean chap down there probably couldn't explain anything much of what he knows, not even in Spanish. But he knows it all the same.'

Shouts from overside of 'Hey Johnny! Hey mister, you take a line, eh?' followed by a dull shuddering thump, announced the arrival of another loaded lighter. Raven went back to his place at the ship's side with the simmering, almost guilty resentment of a confident young man who has been firmly put in his place by his elders. It might be good for him, but he didn't have to like it. Anyway, as for their precious *capataz,* he looked more than half Indian.

He noticed that the mate had disappeared aft, and, while the first sling of cargo was being assembled by the *lancheros,* he saw that the men at the winch were pointing and grinning with interest at something on the poop. He remembered hearing at lunch in the saloon that the captain was expected to bring his wife and daughter aboard today. H'm: two fat, prudish Welsh chapel-going frumps, probably. What a bore! Damned interfering nuisances on board, just as he was beginning to feel his feet a little among the afterguard. He was the son of a weak, doting, put-upon martyr of a mother; his only surviving sister was so much younger that she was never a companion; and his spell at boys' public school and Conway had confirmed his lofty and patronising detachment towards the female sex. Of course, good-looking young tarts, amateur or professional, were all right for a bit of fun on a night ashore, but you could pay dearly for that, too, he'd found. You had to hire the best.

However, anything was a distraction from cargo work, so he too craned his head to look aft. But from his viewpoint, the bulkhead of the midship deckhouse and the dense web of shrouds, backstays, lifts, halyards, braces and clewlines obscured his view, and he caught only a fleeting glimpse of two figures in light-coloured garments crossing to the companion and disappearing down it. The next moment he started guiltily as one of the *lancheros* bawled up: 'Hey mister! You tell them hoist away chop-chop! What you wait for, eh?'

Grant heard the shout and flashed him an irritated look, but said nothing to him, preferring to haze the winch hands: 'Come on, come on, at the winch there! Pull your fingers out, you sojers! Heave up roundly.' The men bent their backs and brought the sling of sacks swaying up from the lighter, but what they had seen was enough to make them defy the normal sailing-ship rule about not talking when on duty: '*O bobl annwyl, bois*, did you see the young one, though? What a bloody bobby-dazzler, eh?'

'That's never one of Jacob's breeding, Jim. Can't be, surely? Not with a clock like his!'

Even the stolid and taciturn Johanssen, gathering the subject from their looks and tone, said: 'She nice good strongbody vooman, I t'ink.'

'Don't know about strongbody, Jo, but *Duw,* I'd like to be down among her frills, mun, specially after all this time at sea; I'd get a stand like a spanker-boom.'

'Shut it, both of you,' said the first man. 'I can see the bloody bucko looking this way. Don't start him off again, for God's sake.'

Sack after sack, sling after sling, in a stolid resigned silence, the nitrate was hauled aboard; tirelessly Antonio Diaz, grey with dust from head to foot, went to and fro, to and fro in the stifling hold, the pile of sacks growing imperceptibly. An inch or so of 'Figaro's' red paint disappeared as she felt the weight of the cargo. Ashore, shovels rang in the lighters as the last of the Welsh coal was winched up into little railway trucks on the loading bridge. Tomorrow, two engines, their fires gleaming with that coal, would haul the trucks to the *oficina*, the nitrate factory high up on the desert altiplano. Once there, the coal would drive the machinery used to crush the rocky ore ready for shipment. The sacred cycle of Trade would be complete.

11

In the saloon, too, there was silence, the silence of stiffness and embarrassment. The four people at the mahogany table - Jacob, Mair, Eleanor and David Evans - sat waiting for their tea in a silence which stretched and stretched, becoming more painfully oppressive as the time passed. The brass clock on the bulkhead had a loud tick, which somehow made the time seem longer and the surrounding silence more deadly. The mate, earnestly pressed by the ladies to join them for tea, and too gauche to be able to conjure up a plausible excuse in time, suffered the most. His worst fears were being confirmed: bad enough having women aboard (unlucky too!), without having to make silly smalltalk to them the minute they came up the gangway. *Diawl!* It was too damn bad of Jacob! What did he want them here for? He'd never said. Couldn't be the flesh, surely, at his age, after all the time they'd spent apart? Mind (he raised his eyes warily to look at the captain's wife) she was a fine-looking woman still; well pulled-together, plenty of go. Well, whatever, that was all very well for him; didn't do the rest of them any good.

He longed for a reason to push his chair back and leave; if only they'd been at sea, where the flap of a sail or a suggestion of a lurch would have enabled him to jump up and go with a clear conscience. But the ship was as dead and still as a house, except for the constant sluggish rolling and dipping.

Mair felt impelled by his unease to try to be winning and sociable, as her husband was clearly - and typically - oblivious of the problem: 'I understand you had a good voyage out, Mr Evans?'

'Oh yes, ma'am, pretty good. Except for the Cape, of course.'

'Ah, Cape Horn, yes; That is nearly always... um...'

'Troublesome. Yes, ma'am, very troublesome.' Good God, a bitter fortnight of beating about in mountainous seas, sometimes among ice, the wind scarcely ever anything but a westerly gale in their teeth; hardly a day when someone didn't nearly lose his life; several days when they might all have perished, like so many that travelled that dreadful way. And all he could think of to say was 'Troublesome'!

The silence stretched out again.

'And I was so sorry to hear about Mr Leyshon.'

'Yes, ma'am... A great pity indeed...yes indeed.'

'Yes, my husband used to think a great deal of Mr Leyshon, didn't you, Jacob?'

Jacob's thoughts were elsewhere for the moment: he was mentally cursing himself for having forgotten in his anxiety about Mair and Nelli to check up on tomorrow's lighters. For all he knew, it might be one of their damned Popish fiestas tomorrow; they seemed to have about fifty of them a year - any day of the week. And if it was, the dagoes would all be off to mass, then off to a cantina to get drunk as skunks on *pisco*... Then they'd need another day to get over that. Two more days of harbour dues for nothing, and his own hands sculling about idle and restless. God, the way time could drift by in these South Spain ports! He'd expected that they'd be loaded by the time Mair and Nelli arrived, but that was still a long way off. And the way the damn German ships came in and collared all the lighters with their 'special arrangements'. 'What?' he said. 'O - Mr Leyshon. Yes, great pity. Very capable officer.'

The mate seemed incapable of not continuing the monotonous liturgy: 'Knew his work well, he did, and handy too, for his age.... Yes, a pity indeed.'

Mair decided she could not bear it any longer: 'And Mrs Evans; is she well?'

'Very fair, ma'am, when I left, very fair. Of course, she's getting on, like the rest of us. Suffers with her chest in the winter.'

'Really?' This seemed at last to be almost a conversational opening: 'My daughter here is just the same, just the same, every winter.'

Eleanor blushed, annoyed as well as embarrassed now; she wasn't some exhibit. Evans was not exactly responsive to the new topic. 'Oh, indeed? I'm sorry to hear that, ma'am.'

'Oh yes, her chest is quite a trial to her.'

Unconsciously and inevitably, Evans found his eyes sliding to the offending chest, across the table from him; it was half embellished, half disguised by the crisp starched frills of her blouse. Quite unbidden, there came to his mind the goatish thought: I've never seen anything that looked healthier, or less of a trial, than those beautiful titties. His guilt at the wicked thought made him lift his gaze quickly to meet the girl's eyes, and at once he read in them that she had seen his glance and knew his thoughts. She blushed deeply. In something approaching panic he jumped to his feet and said: 'Ah, ma'am, capten, miss... You must excuse me. Got to go for'ard and see to the... er... the er...' By this time he was out of the door, so saw no reason to attempt to finish the sentence; in a few seconds he had burst thankfully out of the door at the break of the poop and into the heat and dust of the main-deck.

In the cabin, Jacob was at last aware of the unpromising social situation; he chuckled as the door closed, and shook his head: 'Never mind him, *cariad*, he's a funny old stick, but good at heart. He meant no harm in the world. Set in his ways, he is. He'll come round in time, you'll see.'

Eleanor stood and walked about to conceal her confusion, annoyed with herself at being so foolishly self-conscious, so easily embarrassed and put out by someone who was clearly a decent and respectable old man. Dadi was right - he meant no harm; men just were like that - even old ones, apparently. Couldn't help looking at women's bodies in that sort of way. If she was going to bridle up like that at him, what would it be like when she met the younger officers - for apparently there were two much younger mates aboard, and English too. The best thing now was to do something. She said: 'If you'll show me where the pantry is, dadi, I'll make us some tea.'

'No, Nelli, indeed you won't. That's the steward's job. He won't be long. He'll only get into his old temper if you go out there. It's his pantry, you see.' He was beginning to be aware of some problems he hadn't foreseen. Dai Evans was bad enough, but that old woman Isaac would be worse. If he wasn't careful they'd be at each other's throats all round him, like Kilkenny cats. There was enough trouble running the ship without that as well.

"Well, I must say,' said Mair, with just a trace of irritation, 'that he's taking his time. We've been sitting here twenty minutes now. It's not a seven-course banquet he's...'

She stopped abruptly as the door was opened and Isaac Hughes came in with a tray of the ship's best china, and a pot of real tea. He sensed, it was clear, that he had been the subject of conversation and the object of some unfavourable comment. He glanced quickly from one to the other and put the tray down, smiling an ingratiating smile at Mair: 'Afternoon, ma'am, and welcome aboard. And you too, miss... Very welcome, I'm sure.'

'This is the steward, Isaac Hughes, my dear,' said Jacob unnecessarily.

Isaac bobbed his head in something like a bow, wiping his hands on the front of his white linen jacket in case either of the ladies offered him a hand to shake. They didn't, but merely smiled formally and nodded, so he was left with an awkward pause to fill: 'I hope you'll be very comfortable, ladies; I've given the capten's cabin a good spring clean, so far as I was able, and I've put the young lady in the spare cabin, port side aft. We had to clear a lot of old ship's stores out of it to start with,' he added, with a look of severe reproach at Jacob. 'Bolts of spare canvas, log-lines, hanks of spunyarn - all sorts of things that should never have been there by rights. Anyway, I've had Davey Jones painting it now all that junk is gone. I hope the paint smell will have gone off by now, miss – I've had the port wide open. Now if there's anything you want, ma'am and miss, anything, just let me know.'

Mair seemed to find something she did not like about the steward; she replied frostily - in a tone quite unlike her customary one: 'Very well, since you ask: there is something I'd like - a duster and some beeswax polish. This table is not looking its best by any means.'

Isaac flushed with annoyance and his smile disappeared: 'O ma'am, there's really no need for you to trouble yourself; I've got a tin of polish in the pantry, and dusters; the table is normally polished every day, but as I say, Jones and I have been very busy getting ready for your arrival...'

'Very well, then.'

'And of course the capten and the other officers are very busy too. They have to have their meals on time because of the cargo...'

'Yes, I see, steward. Very well.'

'And then again, ma'am, a ship's not a house, is it? By no means, ma'am. There's all this coal and nitrate being moved about - into the holds, out of the holds.' He spoke of the cargoes as if they were trivial, unimportant nuisances in the life of the ship. 'Terrible dusty cargoes, both. Not like a nice clean load of timber or rails. We never seem to get a clean cargo these days.' This with another barbed glance at the captain.

'I understand. I will leave it to you, then,' said Mair. Her tone added: For the present, Isaac Hughes. Then she said abruptly: 'You're from Eglwyswrw, aren't you?'

'Yes, ma'am, that's correct.'

'I thought so; your mother's Mrs Hughes Siop Fach?'

'Yes, indeed ma'am. Had the shop for years now.'

Mair said no more, and Isaac ducked his way out of the door again. After a brief silence, Mair said quietly: 'I thought so. I remember going into that shop once or twice when I was staying with Auntie Gwen Llain-fawr - years ago now. That fellow used to be there sometimes, when he was home. Used to stare at you, as if he was... you know, calculating. Nasty sly fellow - and you remember about his mother, of course?'

'No *cariad*, not a thing.'

'No, I suppose not... you're always away. Well, she was up in front of the Eglwyswrw magistrates not five years ago, for giving short weight. When they tested her scales, well, it was disgusting. She'd only been giving folk fourteen ounces in the pound - for years, they said. So you be careful of that fellow; that sort of thing runs in families, you know. She'd have gone to Swansea prison, only a lot of old cackling deacons and ministers got up and said what a good Christian woman she was really, and how she gave pounds of butter and jam every year for the Baptists' Good Friday tea, and all that sort of nonsense. *Duw,* she could afford to be generous!'

'All right, Mair, all right,' said Jacob soothingly. 'But, fair play, Isaac does have a hard job with all the dust there is from the nitrate.'

'Maybe, but you can take it from me that this table hasn't been polished for a fortnight or more - and don't argue, because you blessed men would never notice, not if the dust was an inch thick... Heavens, the taste of this tea!'

'You know how it is on the Coast here - you can't get fresh milk for love nor money. And old skinflint Powell buys the tea we use, so I don't suppose it's the best quality. You'll find the food's the same - no great shakes. Still, we must be thankful we don't have to eat what the crowd for'ard have to put up with, poor fellows.'

'That old John Powell! I don't know why you...'

Eleanor tried, very unsuccessfully, to be diplomatic: 'The food was very good aboard the "Magellan", father. Delicious... D'you know, they'd even got one of these special cold rooms for carrying meat without it spoiling. One of the engineers showed me round, one day in the Tropics. It was so strange on a hot, hot day to go down into this huge, white, clean room, and feel so cold. He called it a refrigerator, I think. So of course we had fresh English food for a while; and then we called at Lisbon and Rio de Janeiro, and they took on fresh stocks.' She became carried away by her rhapsody on modern times, to the point where she did not notice the increasing impatience and testiness in her father's manner. 'And, dadi, in our cabin we didn't have a lamp, we had an electric light. You only had to push down a little brass lever on the wall...'

'The bulkhead, girl.'

'All right then, the bulkhead; and then this beautiful bright light just flashed on at once - as bright as day. You could read and read, and your eyes wouldn't get tired at all, not like they do at home with the oil. And in the saloon there was a big fan on the ceiling...'

'Deckhead!'

'O hush, dadi - and that went round by electric too, they said.'

It was all too much for Jacob; every word offended his conservative soul, and he spluttered indignantly: 'Just like floating hotels... Like damned great brothels sculling about. People won't even know they're at sea, soon.'

'Really, Jacob!' said Mair, 'there's no need for that sort of language in front of your own daughter...'

'Language! *Duw, Duw,* if you call that language, wait till the crowd have to furl the foresail in a storm! Then you'll hear some language to make your hair curl, I can tell you. *Twt,* she'll have to get used to a few words you don't hear much in chapel – can't be helped. Sailors are sailors and mates are mates.'

'And another thing,' said Mair, skilfully switching the attack, 'I think it's foolish, the way you go on about steamers and liners. You can call them what you like, but they're the thing nowadays. It's no use your being a stick-in-the-mud, all behind the times. Why you don't...'

Jacob laughed, and lifted his hands in protest: 'O *Duw,* no! Not that one again. We've had that argument ten times a year for the last twenty years. Look, I've learnt a trade; it cost me a long time and a lot of hard knocks, so now I'll stick to it. Those that like the steam-kettles, they can have my share. I'm not ready to give up the sea and go into steam yet - not while I've got enough life left in me to do a proper man's job.'

'No, but dadi...'

'Listen, Nelli girl: in fifty - or a hundred – years' time, long after I'm gone, there'll still be ships - proper ships with sails on them - to be manned. The blessed steam-kettles can never take over the whole trade of the world – it's just laughable to think of it. There's been sailing ships ever since time began, by what I've read. I mean, old Paul in the Bible - he went round in one, and struck some dirty weather too, so he says. They'll never get rid of sail, no more than they will of walking... Now come on, I'll show you your cabin, *cariad,* and I'll show you my bathroom, in case you want to wash before supper. You'll soon get to know your way round. Your cabin is over on the port side aft - next to the steward's. But never mind, he won't bother you – he's a quiet fellow, and not a bit of harm in him, I'll say that for him.'

* * *

The short tropical dusk was deepening by the time John Raven got back to his cabin. He walked heavily along the gloomy passage, weary, sweaty and filthy with dust after the long day at the for'ard hatch. He shouldered his door open and stepped over the high coaming. Only the captain had a bathroom; the mates had to be content with a wash-stand in their cabins and hot water brought from the galley by the peggy.

Raven slumped down an his bunk in irritation; normally the brass cans of hot and cold water would have been waiting by the wash-stand, but tonight there was only the cold water. All day he'd been looking forward to his sluice in warm fresh water to get rid of this horrible, chemical-smelling nitrate dust. That bloody boy! Probably the damn women had been ordering him round with their fal-lals, so he didn't even think about the people who did the work. Christ, even the foc'sle hands would have their water by now! If he and Grant didn't kick that boy's arse a bit, they'd get no more attention from him, now he'd got the women to run round after.

Raven decided that even cold water was better than nothing. He couldn't stand the grime any longer, or the gritty feel of his dungarees. Wearily and stiffly, he stood up and peeled off his shirt, dungaree trousers, vest and underpants, and slung them in a fetid heap, ready for the morning. He went naked to the wash-stand at the ship's side and, his back to the cabin door, poured his cold water into the bowl. By Jove, even that felt good when he threw handfuls of it over his face and head, He heard the door open behind him; that bloody boy at last, and about time too! He swung round, blinded by the water streaming down his face, and said: 'You idle young bastard! If I have to wait again for my hot water like this, I'll have your balls for a necktie - got it?'

The only reply was a smothered, horrified gasp, a girl's voice saying: 'I'm so sorry!' and a bang as the door closed again abruptly.

*　　*　　*

'Now then, boy,' said Isaac to Davey Jones, 'you've laid the saloon table for six - right?'

'Yes, Mr Hughes,'

'And you've given it a good polish - not your usual spit-and-a-wipe?'

'I always gives it a good polish every day - honest.'

'Don't lie to me, boy. And you haven't forgotten the soup-spoons?'

'No, and I've polished them and all.'

'Right, boy. We'll show her....'

'And *Duw*, it doesn't half look a lot of places, Mr Hughes. We only used to have three in Mr Leyshon's day.'

'Aye, aye, never mind that now...Let's look at your jacket... right. Now your finger-nails... *Bobl annwyl*, they're clean! Now, mind you look like that every meal-time, from now on. No more wiping the snot off your nose with your sleeve, is it? Now listen, boy, are the mates in the saloon?'

'Only Mr Evans and the Second.'

'That dratted brassbounder not there yet? He'd better get a move on - capten won't like having to wait, not for the likes of that young whipper-snapper, especially now his womenfolk are aboard.'

The time-honoured hour for cabin supper in harbour was two bells in the second dog-watch - seven o'clock; but tonight, for various reasons, no-one was anxious to be early. Perhaps the least concerned was Simon Grant; despite his forceful manner and rough tongue when roused, and his summary ways with foc'sle hands, he could be urbane and charming when he liked, with a great deal of southern English middle-class assurance and savoir-faire. He was not in the least over-awed by the forthcoming social occasion; on the other hand, he was determined to show that he wasn't eager or curious to meet the ladies either. They could come or go as far as he was concerned. So he would arrive at the table at five-to, just early enough to be polite, but not so early as to appear impressed.

He straightened his tie in front of his mirror, allowed himself one more pass of the comb through his hair, regarded his sun-bleached set of whiskers with some complacency, twitched at his drill jacket, brushed a little dandruff from one shoulder, and was ready. As he passed the mate's door, it opened to reveal Evans emerging self-consciously in full blue serge, his face burnished rather than washed, his detachable collar of a startling whiteness and a neck-sawing stiff-ness and height. Perhaps through agitation and haste his necktie was a trifle awry. He made a determined effort to be casual and everyday: 'Nearly five-to, is it? After you, Mr Grant.' Heroically, with stoic, leaden steps, he followed the young second to another social Calvary, to another scene of ghastly, frozen embarrassment and horror, like tea-time, only much longer and quite unavoidable; there could be no sud-den retreat from formal supper.

They entered the mess-room, and even the caustic Grant stood for a moment and whistled in surprise. The mess-room was a large, comfortable, rectangular room stretching across the centre of the ship between the bulkhead forming the front end of the poop and the cap-tain's saloon. As in all Clyde-built ships of the time, it was beautifully panelled in mahogany and bird's-eye maple, the wood grains elegantly matched and patterned, every joint fitting like a silk glove. The table and its side-benches, as well as the large sideboard against the for'ard bulkhead, were all of the same richly-dark mahogany. Even the luxuri-ant potted palm –Isaac's pride and joy - had leaves of a heavy sombre green. The only frivolities in this rather serious, impersonal, room were the crimson patterned carpet and the pictures. The latter, how-ever, were neither outstanding aesthetically nor calculated to add much gai-ety. On either side of the side-board, as if keeping an eye on their in-vestment, and more especially on their employees, the Owner John Powell and his wife Eluned Bronwen Powell (nee Evans-Davies) stared stiffly down in framed sepia portraits, John looking shrewd and enig-matic, Eluned (as befitted her origins among the Montgomeryshire gen-try) distant, stately, and socially above all this wretched parvenu striv-ing after money. This pair of portraits was a compulsory feature of all of Powell's ships' saloons, and contrasted sharply with the cheerfully disgusting pornography usually favoured in foc'sle and half-deck bunk spaces. On the port side was a painting of 'Figaro's' sister-ship 'Carmen' in full sail, executed in smudgy oils by Powell's unmarried sister; this was another compulsory decorative feature, and one which caused the officers more suffering even than the first two, since, to any seaman, a mere glance revealed a dozen glaring and ridiculous errors in the depiction of the sails and rigging, errors which operated as a kind of visual irritant to the professional eye. Jacob was, of course, as irritated and scandalized as his subordinates, but after all, it was done by the Owner's sister, and was hence above criticism, so (using his own characteristic form of tact) he pretended the picture was not there, and no steward or mate was ever so foolish as to refer to it in his presence. On the other side was a large coloured engraving of their eponymous barber, in the form of an ample Italian baritone in elaborate eighteenth century stage costume and eloquent but epicene attitude. To Davey Jones, who did not quite understand his relevance to the barque, he was simply 'that old dago puff', and even Grant, who had some taste for opera, felt that this description would do very well.

Tonight, even Grant was somewhat shaken out of his sophistication: My God, he thought, the place is clean! The panelling, the sideboard, the table, all shone with polish; much polish had evidently been used, and the pleasant spirity tang of it hung in the air. The big brass oil lamp and its glass funnel gleamed and twinkled unnaturally; its wick had been trimmed and burned clear and bright. As for the cutlery and glasses, he could not believe they were the drab tarnished articles they normally used. 'Whew!' he said at length, 'You've been busy, steward. All credit to you both.'

'Aye, indeed,' said Evans, quite dazed. 'Very good, very good.'

Hughes beamed with pleasure, and ducked his head and shoulders, more to the Second than to the Mate, for the former, despite his lower rank, frightened him more. It'd be good to have him on your side. Then a slight unease appeared on his face as he heard Jacob's laugh and a general sound of movement from the captain's saloon next-door. 'Capten's coming, gentlemen... Is Mr Raven...?'

Grant growled impatiently and crossed rapidly to the port side, shoved his head into the passage and called abruptly: 'Raven! Pull your finger out, the Old Man's coming.'

Of all the officers, Raven was the most reluctant to face the ordeal of the meeting and the meal-table. An hour ago he would have been quite indifferent; he took no pleasure in the prospect, but he had none of the mate's paralysed dread either. But after his hideous gaffe he had been filled not only with shame and anger (with himself and her) but also with dread of what Jake would say. Christ, he'd go off his head! For sure, she would run to Mama, no doubt weeping, and Mama of course would run to Papa - and then look out! It was so bloody unfair! How could she be so stupid as to blunder into the wrong cabin, and how could he help what she heard - and saw? Strewth, there was no law against a bloke showing his own John Thomas in his own cabin, surely?

He had hastily dragged on his uniform trousers and sat on his bunk shaking, expecting every second to hear Jake's fearful Cape Horn bellow. Oddly, he felt more frightened than he had been that night off the River Plate, when, in a squall, a vicious flap of the sail had nearly flung him off the main royal yard, a hundred and eighty feet up. But the minutes had gone by and nothing had happened. Davey had come rushing in at last with his hot water, expecting a hazing and a clout, but had been pleasantly surprised to find him still sitting silent, and dressed only in trousers and braces.

Raven was now fully dressed, but waiting irresolutely for the last possible moment, when Grant's voice roused him. He slipped rapidly into his customary place at the bottom end of the table, murmuring to the others: 'Sorry. Couldn't get washed... That damned peggy!' He had barely seated himself when the captain's door opened, and all three mates jerked to their feet and stood looking somehow rather absurd in such a geometric row, graded by age: the mate tall, bald-pated, lean-faced, his skin a reddish mahogany; Grant half a head shorter, stocky and broad, fresh-faced with curly blonde hair; Raven nearly as tall as the mate, hair dark as his namesake's feathers, his skin tanned olive.

Raven, whose dread of the unknown possible revenge of his skipper had been rising, forgot all his fears at the first sight of the captain's party. Jacob, who led the way, was in so genial a humour that he had clearly been told nothing; as for his womenfolk, they were so far from what he had been expecting that he felt ashamed of his shallow prejudices: the mother so tanned, shapely, with a lively intelligent eye and brisk manner; the girl such a stunner - so tall, dark, like himself; her features were a bit delicate-looking, but the long ocean voyage, the sunshine and unlimited leisure had given her an underlying suffused healthy pink, and she too had all the marks of sensitive intelligence. And he had expected - on no evidence save prejudice - two stolid, dull, plain, bible-punching, chapel-going puddings! You jump to too many conclusions, old son, he said to himself in contemptuous reproof.

Mind you, the girl had been a bit of a fool; and now she was obviously ill at ease. When introduced to him she said, coolly enough: 'How do you do, Mr Raven?' (he recognized the voice!), but she blushed scarlet, causing him to do the same, and scarcely raised her eyes to his face. He tried to put a nuance of apology into his tone as he replied: 'Very well, thank you, Miss Roberts. Welcome aboard the "Figaro".' He owed her that much for not being a namby-pamby; his sister, he knew, would certainly have gone blubbing to Ma.

Mair, while chatting easily to Grant, at once spotted with a mother's unerring eye that there was something a little odd about the young people's meeting, but as they could not possibly have met before, she dismissed it as mutual shyness. Silly things - but heavens, it would be nice to be that silly age again!

Supper, in the end, was not the horror that some of them had been expecting. Jacob produced two bottles of Chilean red wine given him by Captain Morris of the 'Magellan': 'Got a wine cellar down below, they have. Buy the stuff by the case. He says their first-class passengers drink it with their meals - so why shouldn't we? We're as good as they are, and a bit more useful too, isn't it? Steward - corkscrew! Of course, it's not quite like a nice port or sherry... Now then, if we're all ready I will say grace.'

The officers were a trifle nonplussed by this sudden and casual announcement; the Old Man had never before been heard to say grace on any occasion whatever, but he clearly wanted it to appear to be a normal custom among them, and they were discreet enough to lower their eyes reverently and clasp their hands before them in attitudes of pious silence. But Raven could not quite suppress the impious thought: Could even the most frightful God imaginable expect us to give thanks for the sort of food old Powell provides? In any case, the captain's pretence was in vain; out of politeness to Grant and Raven, all the conversation so far had been in English, but without thinking Jacob plunged into a lengthy and florid grace in Welsh, at once revealing to his shrewd wife that the 'custom' had just been invented, and probably rehearsed.

Then they all sat, Jacob in his heavy round captain's chair at the head of the table, the others on the upholstered side-benches: Mair round the corner to his right, Eleanor to the right of Mair; David Evans at his commander's left, then Grant, then Raven. This placed Eleanor opposite Grant and Raven, and it did not take long for Mair to assess the effect of her daughter on the young men. When her husband wasn't booming away about the ship and the cargo and the delays and the harbour dues, and the infinite turpitude and corruption of the harbourmaster, Grant chatted coolly and charmingly to the ladies about their voyage out and the climate and the life on the Coast generally. Thanks to the wine and Grant - in that order - supper was, after all, a cheerful and pleasant occasion.

Raven ate in silence, envying Grant his easy, lubricating chat; none of it meant much, but it did help people to get along. As for himself, he answered questions politely, but embarked upon nothing. Now and then, he raised his eyes quickly from his plate to study the girl a bit more. Once, he caught her in the act of glancing at him; blushing, she gave a faint embarrassed smile before resuming her devout attention to her plate. Mair thought: This fair one is the obvious charmer, but somehow the young dark one seems to me the one to keep an eye on. Still waters... That dunce Jacob didn't realize the problems there might be in having such a smart girl as Nelli aboard a ship among these droves of men - some of them so close at hand. It wasn't like being at home, where you could close your front door on the rest of the world and tell the maid to inform every caller that you were not at home; and it certainly wasn't like the time when Nelli had lived aboard as a small child.

As was the homely sailing-ship custom, Jacob served them all, ladling out the pea-soup, carving the lean and scraggy fowls that Isaac had managed to find in the market ashore, cutting slices of a leaden plum duff more appreciated by the ravenous young mates than by the others. He was blessedly unaware of any incipient sexual problems, and more jovial than ever as the strong, brisk Chilean wine went down; like most fathers, he doted beyond all measure on his beautiful grown-up daughter, and had thought out amusements to prevent her becoming bored, much as he would if she had still been a child. Mair had to suppress a small sting of jealousy at the new light in his eyes as he talked: 'Of course, it won't be like being a passenger on that liner: we don't go in for deck quoits and deck tennis and bridge in the saloon and all that old flummery for the *crachach* This will be more like being at home. Being on a liner – that's like being in a hotel or a spa or something.'

'Don't worry, father,' said Eleanor, wishing very much that he would not make her the topic of conversation and the centre of everybody's attention: 'I've brought my books... I have plenty of studying to do. And Mama bought a lot of dress material in Liverpool, so we're going to make some clothes for this hot weather out here. I didn't know it would be so hot.' She smiled at her father, turning her head away from the young men opposite, who, at the mention of dress, seemed to be making an involuntary study of what she was wearing at present.

'Hot? *Duw,* this is nothing to what it's like ashore, Nelli, nothing. But there's one good thing compared with Newport: you don't have to worry about it raining. Last rained here in sixty-four, they say - thirty years back! I tell you what: you're a great one for the boating, I know. Well, we've got a smart little gig - a sixteen-footer - goes like the wind, and Mr Evans here has got her painted real Bristol-fashion. Well, you've been in her already, of course. The brassbounders could take you up the coast a bit when they've nothing to do, couldn't they, Mister Evans?'

The mate scowled back, as Jacob had mischievously known he would. The very idea that anyone below him in the ship's hierarchy should ever do anything but work during working hours caused Evans acute spiritual pain. It was bad enough already, the way capten kept them sculling about in that gig half the day, all dressed up in those damned white shirts, when there was so much to do aboard. The boys came in handy for the maintenance work - tarring, greasing, splicing - up on the very high, slender yards, the royals and upper t'gallants, but the young devils were hardly ever available. And yet it was the mate's sacred duty to maintain the ship and her rig. He grunted, to indicate disapproval, if not actual dissent. Great Heavens, he thought, I wish poor John Powell were by here now to hear all this - to hear how his money was being thrown away! But what could you expect once you'd got women aboard? He'd never known any good come of it; Jacob had already gone soft in the head - that was the first result.

'And now I think about it,' went on Jacob, 'you used to keep that bay pony over at Dwr-y-Felin, didn't you, Nelli? Dai Bach, he was called, wasn't it?' To Eleanor's utter fury and embarrassment he addressed the mates: '*Duw,* you should have seen her a few years back on that pony. Used to hitch her skirts up and jump astride him, just like a boy. She used to gallop about the mountain like the wind... hair flying... jump anything in front of her. Could damn near keep up with the hounds, she could, when she went out with the Teifiside Hunt. You never saw anything like it! Remember, Mair, that day when he bucked her off in the deep bog above Tafarn-y-Bwlch? Damn, you should have

183

seen her! She came back dripping wet, and black with mud right through to her skin, head to foot. I remember you pulling every stitch of clothes off her in the back yard. I never laughed so much in all my life!' He roared again at the memory of it; Eleanor reddened, lowered her head, and mentally, un-filially, consigned him to an eternity of hellish torments.

Mair, sensitive to Eleanor's confusion, tried to head him off: 'Indeed, but of course, that was years and years ago. We sold Dai eighteen months back at least. Eleanor hasn't...'

'No, but listen, Nelli: Gomez, the main chandler ashore here, was telling me the other day, his uncle has a small livery-stable on the outskirts of town. We could hire you a horse, and you could have some capital fun exploring the desert and the hills round here, I should think.'

Mair was prompt and severe in nipping this scheme in the bud: 'Jacob, she couldn't possibly go careering round some godforsaken desert as if it was Carn Ingli! Anything might happen. You don't know who might be out there - Indians, bandits... Anything could happen.'

Jacob laughed heartily: 'O, don't worry, I've thought of that, Mair.' Then suddenly, to the utter dismay and confusion of the two youngest present, he swung round on Raven: 'Didn't I hear you talking to Grant about horses the other day? If you can manage a horse you could go with my daughter to keep off these bandits and Indians, eh?'

Eleanor closed her eyes and clenched her teeth with rage; was Dadi completely tactless, or was he trying to tease and upset her? That awful Raven, of all people! A dirty-mouthed, stuck-up English snob... To be landed with him all day! But, paradoxically, Raven's reply infuriated her much more: 'What? Me, sir? Oh, but I've only hacked about a bit, at my cousin's, on a quiet old hunter they had. That was years ago and I was never any good at it.' Floundering, he had a flash of inspiration: 'Now Perkins – he's a good horseman, so he says. He was born and brought up on a farm - Hereford way... Rounding up cattle on the hills, hunting with hounds... he used to tell us about it.'

'O no, you'll have to do, young man,' said Jacob. 'You'll manage. Now I've got a decent boat's crew together, I'm not letting Perkins out of it.'

The steward bent deferentially at Mair's shoulder: 'Would you and the young lady like a nice cup of tea in the saloon, ma'am?'

Mair, who strove like the best of Christians to be fair even to those she detested, smiled civilly: 'Yes, thank you, steward. And the meal and the table were excellent.' She rose, almost regally; the young men sprang to their feet; the mate and her husband, a little dazed by the sudden outbreak of etiquette, half-rose with a minimum of alacrity. Eleanor turned away from the men in a passion, her hands clenched. To have someone like Raven foisted on you, and then to hear the conceited ass trying to get *out* of being with you - it was too humiliatingly awful. She was young, and it did not occur to her that her rage was not very logical. If she didn't want Raven with her, wasn't it better that he should decline too? No, it was *not* better, not if you were nineteen and a woman, and aware of making an impression on young men, and aware from your mirror that they had something to be impressed about. That you might decline their company was only decent and proper, and a woman's right; that they should decline yours was a disgusting, puppy-like impertinence.

* * *

Later that night, Jacob lay on his back in his spacious captain's berth watching a beam of moonlight from the cabin port moving restlessly over the furniture as the barque pitched and rolled gently to the smooth swells. The light gleamed dimly on the white of a petticoat flung over the back of a chair; now there was a lovely sight to see! By damn, it was peaceful: not a sound in the cabin but the quiet give-and-take of his wife's breath; not a sound in the ship but the regular ticking groan from wire and hemp as the standing rigging took the strain of the masts and yards aloft, leaning first this way, then that: port... starboard... port... starboard... As regular and gentle as the tick of a grandfather clock. Now and then, from only a few feet away, came the lap and gurgle of the sea as it rose under the ship's sloping counter and swilled around the lifeless rudder. Now and then there was a clank of chain as the heavy stern mooring tightened or slackened; once he heard the footsteps up above of the solitary hand on anchor-watch, making his quiet rounds. A few weeks' time, and what a difference! They'd like enough be running, with all the sail she could stagger with, before an icy gale; the water would be roaring past at fourteen knots maybe; the whole cabin, the whole ship, would be full of the torment of wind and sea - every shroud, brace, lift and back-stay adding its own peculiar whine, wail, scream or deep, bass-fiddle drone, the rudder being struck such hammer-blows by the rushing hills of water that two good men would hardly be able to hold the wheel. He smiled to himself; it wasn't likely he'd hear those cabin noises himself then, for in such weather he'd be on deck, or snatching forty winks on the couch in the chart-room, handy to the deck and the wheel.

The moon picked out and rested for a moment on the silver backs of Mair's hair-brushes. He turned his head to look at her as she lay asleep in the crook of his arm; she lay on her side, facing him, one full breast slanting down to rest on his chest; he gently stroked the silky skin of her shoulder, and she murmured a sleepy protest. He felt a sudden stab of sorrow for all the other men aboard - mostly younger than himself - who must sleep alone, poor dabs.

The soft beam of light glanced across the petticoat again. Nice to see signs of a woman about - to see and feel the softer side of being, to smell her scent, her skin, her hair. H'm... not like Mair to just throw her clothes down like that, but after all the time apart they'd both been as eager for bed as any young honeymooners. And by God it had been good to feel himself moving, sliding deliciously inside her body again, and to feel and hear her so stirred as well. The warm, dull, pleasant after-glow of their fierce love-making was still with him; just recollecting made him stiffen again. It had been a long time; he shifted to face her, and ran his free hand - a hand thickened and made crooked by hard labour, rough rope, seawater and bitter winds - down the smooth sweet curves of back and buttock and thigh. Once again she protested drowsily 'O Jacob *bach*' but the protest softened to small sighs of pleasure, and her body pressed against his with the same long rhythm as that of the Pacific swells. Right against his ear she whispered: 'Randy old goat of a sailor... Not *again*, is it?' She giggled like a girl, then said more soberly: 'You will be careful, won't you, *cariad?* You know...? I'm not too old yet...'

'All right,' he whispered back, 'I'll be careful.' Easy enough to say that, but Hell, it was hard sometimes to come out in time; as bad as clawing your way off a lee shore in a gale of wind under lower topsails.

'Right then, bosun *bach*,' said Mair, giggling again. 'Hand me that marlin-spike.'

Jacob leaned on his elbow above her: '*Duw*, Mair, but it's grand to have you aboard again.'

12

Next day, the work of the ship seemed to slide back into its inevitable routine as if the ladies had been, as it were, quietly swallowed without a trace. The heat of South Spain was oppressive on deck, and they had much to do settling into their cabins and making them - according to their standards - habitable by human beings. The cleaning, tidying and painting done by Isaac and Davey, on which the former had so plumed himself, came a long way short of Mair's notions of comfort and civilization. To her eyes, Eleanor's cabin was nothing but a bare, spartan steel-and-wood box, smelling of paint and Stockholm tar, while the captain's cabin was a stuffy, dusty museum of lumber, sun-rotted fabrics, moribund ferns and tarnished metal, to say nothing of Jacob's chaotic boxes of books and papers: pilots, nautical almanacs six years out of date, a ready-reckoner, a Spanish dictionary and innumerable back numbers of Lloyd's List of shipping. In the first few days there was much mutely indignant to-ing and fro-ing by the steward and peggy, as rubbish was taken to the galley for burning, or slung overboard, while new purchases from Gomez' store were humped aboard from the chandler's boat and taken below: a new green velvet table-cloth, a set of cutlery, a sofa and a brightly-patterned carpet being the chief among these. Isaac's lips were permanently compressed in a pious and martyred expression of disapproval: 'We're only servants, Davey *bach*... Skivvies, like,' he would say. 'It's not for the likes of us to reason why all this perfectly good stuff should be thrown away. Better than some jumped-up people have got at home in Newport, I'll be bound. But what poor Mr Powell would say if he saw this extravagance and waste of his money, I don't know.' His mind, ignoring historical realities, began to conjure up an idyllic picture, both of a benign owner and of the ship's womanless past: 'We was all happy before *she*... they... before we was interfered with by women... happy, we was. We knew where we was... Things went like clockwork. We all got on. Women! Nasty, prying, interfering creatures, I say, for all their damn airs and graces, and paints and powders...I told you how it would be, didn't I? And I was right, see!'

Only at early morning and evening did the ladies take the air, strolling on the long flush deck of the poop, well away from the painting and nitrate-heaving. The officers saw little of them, and the crowd nothing, for in harbour the poop was an empty idle place except for the early morning deck-washing, and maybe an apprentice doing a little painting or brass-polishing. At sea, it was the ship's control centre, where the captain and the watch officer strode or leaned; where a silent helmsman steered; where brassbounders came every watch to heave the log, and where at times men swarmed to work the mizen braces or the sheets of the spanker sail on the jigger mast.

Now, in harbour, the long expanse of snow-white teak deck was a mere seaside promenade, where one could look astern at the huge links of the stern mooring stretching down lifelessly into the clear water, or for'ard at the beautiful order and symmetry of yellow mast and spar and the converging, pinnacle-shaped web of shrouds and backstays, lifts and halyards, buntlines and clew-lines. The huge double wheel, its varnish gleaming, and the stout tower of the binnacle, where the compass now slept unmoving, stood useless and ignored like exhibits in a museum - devices for which no-one could now find a use. And yet on the three months voyage out, not a second had passed, day or night, in which the wheel had not been handled; moved, nursed with skill; gently shifted, a spoke at a time, on tropic nights; wrenched savagely to and fro in storms by the combined strengths of three men. Every few minutes, for those three months, some pair of eyes had glanced, peered or stared into the hood of the binnacle at the tilting, floating compass card, which embodied the answer to the most important question for the ship and her company: 'How's her head?' - in other words, where are we going?

Mair and Eleanor existed in a warm, rather dull limbo; apart from Jacob, the man they saw most was the one they liked least - the steward. At meal-times in the mess-room they met the three mates, but after the first festive cabin supper the atmosphere had settled into a polite, stolid dullness. Jacob felt inhibited - by the presence of the two Englishmen especially - from unbending into the informal jollity and homeliness that were natural to him at Ty Coch; Evans was a glum and disapproving cadaver for the most part; and the two young mates were usually dog-tired from their ten hours at the hatches. Between Mair and Grant there flowed a reasonably flourishing exchange of views on topics of common interest, like the novels of Dickens, Thackeray and Trollope; each was pleasantly surprised to find the other so well-informed. Yet the conversation never prospered fully, for they were both too polite to leave out the other diners for long, and both equally remote from real scholarship, or the literary world of gossip, reviews and back-biting, so that their talk lacked substance and ammunition. Further, Grant's rather tactless enthusiasm for Hardy, Flaubert, and even Zola - of all people! - made Mair shrink from the discussion: there was no telling where a conversation about such godless writers might lead, and she did not want to hear them recommended to Eleanor; Mair had, of course, never read their books; the scathing and horrified reviews of them in the Ladies' Home Journal were quite enough to rule them out.

Raven and Eleanor were unwilling to contribute, the former out of total ignorance, and the latter because she didn't want to reveal to her mother how she had furtively trembled, thrilled and wept over a copy of 'Madame Bovary' which a friend had smuggled into school last year. As for the Mate, he closed his ears to the irritating buzz of point-less chatter, and calculated how many bolts of canvas he and Sails would need for a new fore upper t'gallant, and how he could find a hand to slush down the jigger topmast on Monday without hampering the loading or the manning of the Old Man's confounded shore-boat.

Jacob could not, of course, produce Chilean wine every day, and as for the food, El Norte - the northern desert region of Chile - was, as the young vice-consul had pointed out, little better than the ocean itself as a place for the gourmet. Mair had produced some new minor refinements to the cabin food, but she had had to negotiate delicately with Wellington Jones, for the doctor was a proud and manly man who knew his worth and his status; only the captain and mate were better paid. Mair soon sensed that he could not be put in his place ruthlessly, as Isaac Hughes could, and besides, he commanded respect as a man, as a fellow human being, in a way that the steward could not, with his furtive ways, his petulance and his petty spite. Jacob had warned his wife: 'Listen now, *cariad;* for God's sake be careful what you say to that cook, or he'll be off over the side in two shakes. And there's half a dozen captens I know who would snap him up tomorrow, given the chance. Knows his job, does Jones, or he'd never be able to feed the crowd on what old Powell gives us, and not have a mutiny. Now mind - don't upset him!'

One Saturday night, a week or so after the ladies' arrival, Jacob, as if sensing their *ennui,* sprang his surprises as they all sat din-

ing under the eyes of Beaumarchais' fantastical barber and the two sepia Powells: 'Well then, Sunday tomorrow. The Sabbath - no nitrate, no
launches. The only chance we'll get of a change from cargo-heaving
and all the shore business. I thought in the morning, Mair, we might
have a little service for the crowd. No other Welsh ships in the anchorage, so it'll just be ourselves. Mister, while the hands are washing down
tomorrow, get a couple of them to roust out the old harmonium from
the cabin, will you? And you'll play, Eleanor, won't you?'

'Well, I would, Dadi, only I'm not in practice.'

'Practice fiddlesticks! Don't start that, girl. Don't be so modest.
Anyone who can take first prize in open piano at a big eisteddfod like
Cardigan can surely play a few hymns for us poor benighted shellbacks, isn't it? The crowd would love it; no-one's played that thing
since I don't know when.'

Evans' face was brighter at the thought of something godly
happening aboard: 'Harmonium just for'ard of the break of the poop,
port side, is it?'

'That's it - between the poop and the half-deck, so those
wicked young limbs of Satan in there will at least have to hear something sacred, even if they don't join in the worship.'

Grant said helpfully: 'If you want those young swine to worship, sir, just say the word. I'll see they worship all right.'

Evans broke in, looking reminiscent: 'Like being Bethel ship.'

'Bethel?' said Grant, puzzled.

'Aye, the Bethel ship in the anchorage invites all the other
Welsh ships to their meeting... Remember that Sunday in ninety-two in
Valparaiso, capten? Over a hundred and twenty men on deck... boats
moored four deep at the ladder. And *Duw*, there was singing for you
that day! It was in the evening, you see, ma'am, and when we all sang
"Hyfrydol" and gave it a bit of *hwyl*, like, well, the music rolled right
across the harbour, echoing... It was dead calm, you see. All the other
ships - Yankees, Dutchies, French, English - they all went quiet and listened. Made you feel proud, down here' - he put a fist over his heart –
'to be a part of something... something greater than yourself; something from the spirit.'

There was an awkward silence; Evans seemed embarrassed at
his own display of emotion; Eleanor was touched at the flash of fire and
passion, at the glimpse of a soul, of a love of beauty, unattainable
beauty, buried in that dry, humdrum, spindly frame.

With much more than his usual tact, Jacob allowed the feeling to subside, to be absorbed and enjoyed, before he continued: 'Aye, I remember that, David - a wonderful evening. Well now, after our little meeting tomorrow, I thought we might pack some food and take the gig up the coast for a trip, Mair. Up to the cove at Pisagua, maybe; there's a nice little beach there. Do a bit of fishing, perhaps.' He was like a boy now, in his enthusiasm. 'You see, one of the ships that went up in the norther was a real old clipper - the "Philoctetes" - famous, she was once, in the tea and wool trades. She got sold to the Chileans here years back. Anyway, out of one of her old topmast stunsails and booms Sails and I have made a mast and a dandy little standing lug and yard, and a little foresail too.' He caught the customary look of pained severity in the mate's eye. 'All right, mister, all right. It didn't take him long, did it? He's finished now, so you can start on your blessed fore t'gallant on Monday.'

'But it might be too flat calm to sail, Jacob. Then we'd be stuck, maybe miles away.'

'No, Mair *bach*, God's generally good to the small boat sailor on this coast. You get a sea breeze in the daytime and a land breeze at evening – soldier's wind both ways. You know what I mean: so easy to sail, even a soldier could do it! Anyway, we'll have the brassbounders with us. They'll enjoy a trip. They can row us back if the wind should fail us.'

'But isn't it their day off - the Sabbath?'

'Day off?' Jacob chuckled and looked at the two young mates, who grinned back. 'A day off for those young heathen savages? I'd like to see them Sabbath me if I order them away in the gig.'

'Seventy-three it was,' said Evans, speaking as if from a world away. 'April seventy-three...'

Jacob looked puzzled: 'What the devil...?'

'The "Philoctetes"... I thought I knew that name; I remember her now. This day in April seventy-three...I was second mate of the "Elsinore" - one of Ferguson's wool clippers. We were coming home with the first of the season's clip. Seventy days from Melbourne. We fell in with her just after dawn in a calm off the Lizard. We'd sighted two hundred ships the day before, all becalmed, all drifting - up the Channel on the flood, back down on the ebb. We two clippers ghosted right through the lot of them. Then it started to pipe up from the south-west and *Duw*, the Old Man let her rip - a real driver he was. Up the Channel we went, the pair of us, everything set up to the royals. Left everything else behind. "Crack on, boys," says the Old Man. "What she can't carry she must drag!" And by God those two ships were a sight. Neck and neck, we were, all the way to Dungeness, not a cable's length between us. Wind just on the port quarter - half a gale at least. Rolled both rails under, we did, when the following sea got up - both rails clean under. You could hear the spars creaking and cracking with the strain, but we didn't part a rope-yarn or a stitch of canvas. Very near an acre of white foam round each ship. Nothing could keep up with us, not even the steamers - not even a P and O liner! Not a man went below all day, even in his watch below, it was such a sight. Ah, ships were ships in those days.' He paused, awaking from his spellbound trance from the past to the less-than-perfect world of the present. He vigorously attacked the somewhat durable slice of Chilean beef on his plate and said, with a meaningful look at Jacob: 'Like I said, ships were ships then. Properly run with proper crews and proper upkeep - and proper discipline too. Men had to work to earn their pay.'

'O yes,' said Jacob mischievously, 'I remember those days well. The mates used to complain because they'd just been stopped from using the cat-o-nine-tails on the crowd. Terrible shame, wasn't it?'

Mair intervened tactfully; it was too bad of Jacob to tease the old chap like this: 'Two clippers racing.... that must have been a wonderful sight to remember, Mr Evans... As for this trip to Pisagua, Jacob, it sounds very nice, but I think it might be too far for Nelli and me.' Just like a man, she thought: not a bit of forethought or common sense in his whole head. How in the world did he think two decent women were going to manage all day in a boat with a lot of young men? Didn't he ever think of the problems he was creating? So used to arranging things for nothing but a lot of men, he never realized that there were times every day when a woman needed to be private. All very well for these men, just standing up and doing it in a bucket, or over the side...

'Too far?' said Jacob. 'Not a bit of it, girl, we'll be there in two hours. Don't worry about that. And anyway, I never said Nelli was coming in the boat with us. I've got a special treat fixed up for her - better than any old boat, eh? I've hired two horses for tomorrow morning up at Gomez' uncle's place. It's only a short step out of town along the Calle Major. He's just bought two really smart Creole ponies from a farm down south. Really strong, good turn of speed, surefooted as cats, he says. You could climb a blessed mountain on them.'

Eleanor's face was a dull, hot, suffused red; she was too confused and angry to speak. 'Two horses' - that meant he was sending her
off with... That a well-meaning father could be so *stupid!* Mair sensed
her plight without looking at her: 'O I don't think so, Jacob. They sound
a bit wild - don't sound safe to me. I mean, she hasn't ridden
for months.'

The captain roared with laughter; his will was like a genial
juggernaut: 'Safe! They're safe as houses, *cariad!* Take a bombshell to
move them. Lots of the ships' captains have had a jaunt on them, lots of
times.' He caught a knowing glance between the first and second
mates. 'That is, of course, when they could spare a few moments from
all their shore business. And some of them were no great jockeys, I can
tell you. No idea how to ride - hardly knew which end was which.
Make a cat laugh to see them. Why, our Nelli's an expert, after all.
Damn, she's ridden with the Teifiside hounds scores of times.'

Eleanor sat, still blushing and simmering with resentment, but
tongue-tied. Her father meant to be kind, she knew, and she couldn't
hurt him by just blankly refusing, but all the same he was a stupid old
mule. It was no use protesting; it was like arguing with a steam-roller.
He'd got it arranged, and that was that. It had been bad for him, in a
way, becoming a ship's master; it made him treat all of them like brassbounders. Besides, inwardly she was divided; half at least of her was
longing to be released from this hot, cramped, wallowing steel prison.
To be free, out of this floating box, out on those endless buff hills and
sandy plains that you could see rising behind the town, with a strong,
living, breathing creature under your seat, moving between your legs,
responsive to your wishes! Before you a strong neck, flying mane and a
head with two intelligently-cocked ears, and beyond those, nothing but
space - space to gallop in until you and he were tired; space to turn this
way or that, a blue sky above, uncluttered by masts and yards and trac-
eries of taut wire and rope. If only... If only she could be alone in that
silent wilderness! But she knew what her father would say next.

'You'll be needed ashore along with Miss Roberts, of course,
Mr Raven. I've told young Perkins to be alongside with the boat at six
bells. You know Gomez' shop in the Calle Major? His uncle's place is a
little way outside the town along that road, on the left. You'll see a
wooden arched gateway with a steer's skull - horns and all - nailed up
on top of it. Mention my name and the ship – it's all paid for.'

And she knew what Raven - that wretched Raven - would

say next.

'Very good, sir... But as I said before, I've no great experience of horses. I wouldn't really call myself a rider.'

'What? What are you mumbling about, mun? Good God, I'm not asking you to gallop to Patagonia with her, am I? Or up over the Andes? The Gomez horses are dead quiet, I'm telling you: I've seen fat old square-head captains ride them - men twice your age and weight. You'll be all right. I mean, fair play now: it's better than being told to lay out on a t'gallant yard off Diego Ramirez, isn't it?'

At that precise moment John Raven didn't think it was, but he too lapsed into helpless silence. He caught Eleanor looking searchingly at him, but when their eyes met she looked away, as if in contempt.

Roberts went on obliviously: 'Yes, cowboys' mounts they are. Clever as cats on their feet, wonderful stamina, they say. The Spaniards brought them over, centuries back. And they've got African blood in them too. Funny-looking beasts, though... got stripes like those other African whatchemaycalls.'

'Zebras,' said Grant suddenly.

'That's the ones. By the way, Mr Evans, fair's fair. You and Mr Grant can have next Sunday off if you like. And tomorrow the off-duty watch can take the long-boat off for a bit of a spin if they want. Got to be back by evening muster, though. O, and that reminds me, Raven: we'll be away in the gig tomorrow so you'll have to come off in a shore-boat. I'll give you a dollar or two for that before you go.'

Evans raised his eyes to the deck-head in resigned sorrow; let the crowd take a boat, and they'd row straight to the nearest *pisco*-seller, get into fights, come back late and as tight as fiddlers' bitches, half the oars and rowlocks gone, half the paint scraped off – he'd seen it all before. Great Heavens, the folly of captains!

Raven occupied himself with his helping of figgy duff - plum pudding - a dish he would have slavered over and gulped down ec-statically only a few weeks ago in that grubby, carefree, elemental world of the half-deck. Now it seemed soggy, heavy and greasy, though he was hardly attending to it. He forked at it moodily and looked at the face of the girl opposite him: her eyes downcast on her food, her blush dwindled to two rosy spots in her lightly-tanned cheeks. By God, she was a bobby-dazzler, no mistake; beautifully regu-lar features, especially her mouth and her eyebrows. Funny: he ought to be pleased to be sent off riding with her, with a looker like that... But it wasn't so simple. To start with, she was the Old Man's daughter, and an only child too, he gathered, so that put her really out of bounds. Christ, if Jake caught him up to something with her! That'd just about be the finish of Raven, J., Third Mate! And anyway, it wasn't as if he really wanted to try – didn't even want to go riding; he'd made such an almighty fool of himself at their first meeting, he didn't fancy doing it again. Yes, he could ride a bit, but there were horses and horses. Uncle Theodore's schoolmaster cob on the farm at Islip - gentle, lazy, sluggish, good-natured - was not quite the same thing as some young bucking devil of a dago cow-pony. He didn't want her to have any more reasons for despising him - the first was bad enough. Mind, she had been good about that. Hadn't said a word, seemingly. But some of the looks she'd given him! Well, after all, the Welsh were a chapel-going, Bible-punching lot, so he'd given her a bit of a shock. Very pure-minded, no doubt; wouldn't say cock for tuppence, as the saying went. Suppose he ought to be a bit pure and pious too, with his father being a vicar, but somehow it wasn't like that. It was a pity about her being who she was and what she was. If he'd just met her ashore somewhere, if she'd been just another girl and a bit willing, well then, he could imagine her as a hell of a goer. And then again - he eyed her most casually over his empty plate - what a shape she must be under all those frills! Be quite a wheeze to pay her cabin a return visit some time and see if he could catch her in the buff! Nice and slim, long straight legs. He suddenly caught the mother's eye; she was looking at him oddly, and he suddenly realized that all the conversation had stopped. Jesus, she must have asked him something in the middle of his lecherous fantasy, and he hadn't heard a thing!

'I beg your pardon?' he said, wretchedly confused.

'I just asked, do you ride often when you're on leave, Mr Raven?' said Mair, her mouth just beginning to smile.

'I? Er - no, no - Well, very little, that is... Not much. We live in Oxford, you see. St Ebbe's - that's my father's church – is right in the middle of the city. It's just when I visit my uncle out at Islip, that's all. That's a village a few miles out to the north - in the country, you know. That's when I ride... He's got a horse, you see.' He drew his hand back nervously, sending his fork and spoon clattering to the deck, and as he stooped to retrieve them, he missed the faint wink that Mair gave to her daughter.

Eleanor was not much amused by the wink. It was all right for her mother to be so blessed humorous about the whole thing; she wasn't going to be involved, and after all she was forty-six. All this sort of thing - men, sexual feelings - must be more or less over for her; couldn't matter much at her age. She'd got Dadi, and that was that. She herself had it all to experience and get right. It wasn't easy. She wasn't exactly nervous about going riding along with Raven; after all, she could just be polite, as she was on board - just polite and distant. He wouldn't dare to actually do anything, she was sure of that. She'd seen enough of her father's other self - his brusque imperious manner of command, his unthinking certainty of being obeyed - to set her mind to rest about that. No, the weak spot might be in herself; it was her own flesh that she didn't altogether trust. Apart from his almost foreign dark good looks and cultured accent, there was something about his deep reserve in her presence that made him intriguing - a mystery, something quite beyond her limited experience of men. And somehow Mam and Dadi made it worse by the fact that they seemed determined not to discuss him if they could possibly help it; and when they did there was an under-current of dark hints and warnings, vague but sinister, about his morals. Like all such warnings to the young, their effect was precisely counter-productive; had they striven with all their might to make Raven interesting to her, they could not have done better. And then there was *his* flesh: that incident in his cabin had been ludicrous and embarrassing enough, and his language positively disgusting, and yet... and yet... she had already begun to have personal feelings of guilt about it - as if she had connived at it - simply because she had never breathed a word about it to her mother, and knew that now she never would. It had started as just a confused newcomer in a dark passage, opening the wrong door; now it had become a secret shared between herself and Raven, a thing they hid in common - almost a betrayal of her loyalty to her parents. And as if that wasn't bad enough, she couldn't get the image of his body to disappear permanently from her subconscious mind. It kept appearing unbidden: tall, white, with an elegant tracing and symmetry of body hair, the shoulders, arms and legs slim and hard, the organ you weren't supposed to see just - *there* - obvious. It was how half of mankind was made, of course, and therefore nothing to get excited about, if you could look at it coolly, scientifically; but she found that hard to do - it was too oddly disturbing for that.

She remembered giggling with that silly, puddingy Rachel Pugh over photographs of Greek statues in that big red book – Mac-Dougall's Illustrated Encyclopaedia of Greece and Rome - in the library at Hill House College; and joking about fig-leaves and what you might find if you chipped them off with a chisel. So pathetically childish it seemed now - but low and vulgar too. Now she was being low and coarse in her thoughts again, and that was nearly as bad as being sinful in deed; she'd listened to enough sermons to know that. There was that bit from Jeremiah that old Haydn Jenkins of Ebeneser used to thunder at them: 'The heart is deceitful above all things...' His voice used to rise to a terrible crescendo on 'all things', and then he used to go on, in a throaty whisper, peering keenly into every face before him: 'and desperately wicked' - as if he longed to make the congregation's wickedness apparent to all. She must rise above these low thoughts of the flesh! Tomorrow was Sunday, a chance to be her proper self and pray for better ideas and impulses.

And then, unbidden, forbidden, the thought popped up in her mind: if covering such things with a fig-leaf was weird, what about Raven's even weirder threat: 'I'll have your balls for a necktie'? She shook her head severely, and had to compress her lips to prevent a smile at the strange, savage grotesquerie of the image: the Reverend Jenkins' scrawny neck, his high starched white collar, and those things where his cravat should be.

'Eleanor?' said her mother, with the same smile she had given Raven.

'O,' Eleanor blushed crimson with embarrassment again, and was startled into replying in the wrong language: *'Mae'n ddrwg gennyf i...',* and stopping short in even worse confusion.

'Dim byd, cariad,' said Mair, to help her out a little. 'I only asked if you'd care for another slice of pudding?'

'O no thank you, mam - I've plenty, really.' She focused on her plate, and realized to her dismay that it still displayed a generous hunk of the stolid duff, and that all the men had finished, and were waiting politely, rather obviously not looking at her and her plate. She wished she could make the food disappear by magic.

Her father came to her rescue with what he saw as marvellous tact: 'Too much for you, is it, girl, the doctor's duff? Don't blame you, neither. It'd make better ballast than anything else I know, properly stowed. Thinking about getting on a horse's back again, I'll bet, weren't you? Excited, like? Listen, you leave the old pudding, *bach.* It won't be wasted, I guarantee. Davey Jones peggy will scoff that, double quick, the minute it goes out of that door.'

She smiled gratefully at him and laid down her spoon and fork; the steward appeared (as if telepathically) and whisked the plates away. Eleanor was immensely relieved when the mate, as if in protest at all the chat, returned the conversation to the safe, dull tramlines of ship's business: 'The launches are arranged for Monday, capten?'

'Yes, mister - I told them six at least. First one alongside at eight bells sharp.'

'Very good, sir. And we're getting low on drinking water. Perhaps when you're ashore you could arrange the water-boat for Tuesday?'

'I will, mister,' said Jacob, with a touch of irritation at being bothered with humdrum details on a Saturday night. 'Just remind me on Monday morning, when I go ashore.'

'And if you're going to the chandler's I shall need more sail-maker's twine - three balls, I should say - no, make it four. And bees-wax too. And when the coaster comes on Tuesday we need more vege-tables; we need to put an order in with the agent, or they'll all be gone.'

'Yes, all right, mister. On Monday.'

'You see, ma'am,' Evans went on inexorably, 'after all the time at sea I believe it's essential that the men get some proper fresh cabbage and potatoes and so on, as well as their usual lime-juice. I was reading an article in the "Western Mail" when I was back home, about the pre-vention of scurvy, and it said there...'

'Yes, Mr Evans,' said Mair, as gently as she could, 'I remem-ber. You were telling me about it last week, if you recall, one evening after supper.'

'O, I beg your pardon, ma'am,' said Evans, irritated at the loss of a chance to mount one of his hobby-horses.

'O no, it was very interesting, very interesting. I think it's wonderful what these men of science have found out about... well, all sorts of things. And it's certainly right that these poor men should get a change from salt meat, rice, peas, and those dreadful dog-biscuits. I wonder if Mr Powell would like his family to be fed like that! I'll wager he wouldn't hear of it.'

Evans detected a vein of subversive heresy entering the con-versation: 'Well ma'am, Mr Powell is no worse than any other owner I've come across. The crowd for'ard don't expect to live like... well, like gentry. Wouldn't know how to. Salt horse and biscuit is what they've been used to all their lives. It's the same as they've always had, and the same in every ship nowadays.'

'Yes, but you say yourself it's bad for them. There's no reason on earth why Mr Powell shouldn't supply you with potatoes at least. They'd keep - they do at home, after all. And so would carrots and swedes and onions and.....'

'You misunderstand me, ma'am,' said Evans, smiling indulgently, shaking his head, and sharing his amusement at her simplicity with Jacob and Grant. 'I was just talking about their diet in harbour. As for the voyage, where in the world would we stow all those vegetables, and whatever would it cost to stock up like that? Mr Powell has to make a profit, after all.'

All the men were smiling complacently and Mair, pink in the face, was stung into indignation: 'Where there's a will there's a way. Good gracious, this ship is the size of a cathedral down below. There'd be room to stow a trainload of vegetables. But you men - all of you - are so hidebound, like a horse with blinkers. It's never been done, so it can't be done, that's your way of thinking. And another thing: you could call in now and then for fresh provisions, as the steamer did. That's what would happen if women ran shipping companies. Then everyone would be happier, the men would get a decent diet and they'd live and work better.' She looked at her husband: 'You're always telling me that half the crews these days are just riff-raff; well, what do you expect, if you don't give them humane treatment?'

Jacob, oblivious of the clear danger signals, beamed now with a magnificent, patronising indulgence: *Duw,* Mair, the crowd would like you to be the Owner, especially if they had you to come and cook for them as well. But there, you can't run proper working ships as if they were fancy liners, can you? Before you knew where you were, you'd have the men asking for port wine and cigars after dinner - and then they'd want some nice little stewardesses to make their beds and tuck them in every night, isn't it? What d'you say, gentlemen?'

But the mates could all see that now he'd really overstepped the mark, could see the flush of anger in his wife's cheeks at all this superior male banter, and they prudently looked down and shook their heads non-committally, with only the most diplomatic of smiles. Each thought: You'll pay for all this, my boy, when she gets you alone in your cabin, and you'll be sorry. You'll find out who's really captain aboard this hooker.

The captain and the mate exchanged nods, and the three men rose, taking a polite leave of their reckless commander, his beautiful troubled daughter and his tight-lipped wife.

*   *   *

Calle Major, thought Raven next morning, is not quite as grand as it sounds. What on earth would it be like if it ever rained? The road itself was a mere strip of hard sand; only the larger buildings - the church and the bigger stores - were of dressed stone. All the rest - the little box-like houses, the wretched shops and cantinas - were hasty concoctions of adobe brick, roughly plastered smooth, with bowed flat roofs of rough tile or straw thatch - anything to keep out the fierce sun; rain, of course, did not have to be catered for. But it was not unpleasant to be walking, stretching his legs, along a quiet Sabbath thoroughfare, free of the dust of traffic, the sun warm, the sky cloudless, the only sound the shrill, ragged singing from the church, where morning mass was just beginning. Two men whom he vaguely recognized as stevedores, their faces washed clean of nitrate dust, their hair plastered smartly down and raven-black, dodged quickly up the church steps with their stocky, broad-faced Indian wives, furtive in their lateness. The harsh tangle of voices suddenly boomed and died as the church door opened and shut.

In a polite, embarrassed silence the girl and the young mate walked on through the scatter of dust, past a fandango hall, ghastly in its garish paint and pitifully voluptuous curtains, past Giuseppe's Palazzo with its dreary memories of Billy John, Protheroe and the *treepas*, past the long, low, well-built establishment known simply as 'Gomez' place'- the timber house, the chandler's shop and the snug, comfortable, discreet captains' lounge where Gomez daily dispensed free liquor, coffee and excellent cigars in return for a great deal of lucrative business. In the midst of a barren desert he could supply anything from a thousand tons of ballast or a new topmast to a cabbage or a ball of whipping twine, and made more than enough out of his dealings to finance his modest largesse to the idle captains; for his guests, though not wealthy men in themselves, had the authority to spend thousands of dollars, pounds, francs, marks or pesetas on behalf of their distant owners. And all money was money, wherever it came from and whatever national emblem or monarch it displayed. When it came to cash, Gomez was a true citizen of the world.

His relatively splendid establishment, sensibly placed far from the bustle of the quayside and inquisitive brassbounders, was almost the last along a road which led off into the Atacama Desert. At first, Raven could see, the road was as flat and level as the town streets, but the town itself was built on only a small shelf between the steep slope of the Cordillera and the sea; soon the track would begin to tackle that slope, struggling up through a deep rocky ravine down which, millenia ago, some scarcely-to-be-imagined river had poured into the sea.

There was steady silence between the two young Europeans in this fearsome South American wilderness; its savagery seemed to compel awe and even fear - an utter deadness of dry, jagged rock and sand; a deadness that was of many colours - grey, buff, white, black and deep brown - yet every colour was one of death, of utter drought. Nothing grew, nothing moved in that desolation; once the stir of the little shabby town was left behind, they might have been alone on another planet, or in another era of Creation. To the girl from the vivid green shores of West Wales, to the man from Oxford and the deep, lush, elm-treed river pastures of midland England, the Atacama came as a shock, almost a blow, of unease, a haunting reminder of primal chaos and hellish disorder. How could any humans possibly bear to live their whole lives here, on the edge of this arid Gehenna?

Yet the silence between them was by no means the silence of good companions: the unease produced by the desert was only the margin of a deeper discomfort shared by both. Each felt put-upon, badly used, thrust into an impossibly embarrassing situation. The tension between them had been there since they had met on the poop after the service, which Raven, as a feeble protest, had not attended. Eleanor had appeared, rather self-consciously elegant in a light-grey skirt, high-necked white blouse and a straw boater, to which she had sensibly added a chinstay of white silk ribbon. Any delight Raven might have had in looking at, and even accompanying, such exquisite femininity was more than eclipsed by his general feeling of inadequacy, and by his specific certainty that he, in comparison, looked fairly absurd. The night before he had ransacked his meagre wardrobe for something he might wear on an expedition on horseback with the captain's daughter, and had found nothing but his brassbounder's uniform, dungarees, and a crumpled blue serge suit. After all, when he left home, his kit had had to fit into one wooden chest. In desperation, he had gone to Grant, who had good-naturedly lent him a white drill suit and polished calf-length boots. Raven soon found that the boots were too small, and that the suit, which looked fine on the stocky Grant, was decidedly tight at the armpits and crutch, and short in the leg, for himself. And Grant's mild, amused irony hadn't helped, either: when Raven thanked him, Grant had murmured: 'Not at all, old boy. We must all help to accoutre the bold young squire to the fair Eleanor - the quite delectable Eleanor, in fact... But do remember old Juvenal, my dear chap.'

'Juvenal - Latin, you mean? That Roman chap?'

'The same: *"Quis custodiet ipsos custodes?"* Have a care, young squire... Forbidden fruit and all that, you know.'

'I slept through all my Latin lessons; what does that mean?'

'It means, somewhat ambiguously: "Who shall guard the guards themselves?" you young Philistine.'

'Ambiguously...? I don't follow.'

'A dunce as well as a Philistine! Work it out for yourself. I want to get my head down now.'

Raven's evident discomfort, and his barely-concealed pain in walking, gave Eleanor a spurt of triumphant and vindictive glee, which she tried, unsuccessfully, to dismiss as unworthy of her. He looked so absolutely ridiculous, whereas she knew she didn't, and she divined that his reluctance about the horse-riding - which had so nettled her - arose from his inability to ride decently. He was afraid of cutting a poor figure in front of her; but then she'd had to put up with weeks of being a tyro, a raw intruder, in the male sea-going world, unable to understand half the conversations she heard. Had she been a little more reasonable, she might have reflected that, after all, she was only a passenger; that Raven had nothing to do with her being there, and that she was not asked to 'lay aloft in a howling gale', as it said in that nice Mikado song. But she had been too stung by his gloomy rejection of her company to forgive him easily. She had twisted the knife a little in his wound by giving him a sunny smile and greeting: 'Good morning, Mr Raven. A nice sunny morning for a hack.'

Raven had managed a forced grin: 'Yes, miss. It's always a nice sunny morning on this coast.' She did look an absolute stunner right enough, but what comfort was that? He still sullenly contemplated backing out of the affair; he'd sworn to obey all Jake's lawful orders, but was this a 'lawful' one? Almost certainly not; it had nothing whatever to do with the ship or its crew. Then the Old Man appeared from the cabin companionway; all togged up in his chapel things and looking at him with faint impatience: 'Morning, mister. Boat's alongside. Best get under way, isn't it, before it gets any hotter.' And any possible rebellion evaporated before that brisk glance.

The boat trip too was an ordeal for the luckless third mate; the apprentice crew dared not actually rib him openly, for he now carried his rank, and therefore the captain's authority, like a shield; but there was an air of suppressed mockery and hilarity, which broke out openly once as, approaching the quay, Perkins called out 'Whoa there! Sorry, I mean, easy oars!' And as they turned the first corner from the quay, both Eleanor and Raven heard the falsetto cry: 'Do have a nice ride, Mister Raven, sir!' Raven wondered whether she was aware of the lewd ambiguity of the word 'ride' and guessed by the sudden scarlet in her cheeks that she was. H'm... perhaps not such a little goody-goody after all! Still, the jeer was hardly likely to make her more amicable towards him.

It was indeed partly the indignation arising from this adolescent crudity that caused the long silence to simmer between them as they walked the dusty street. True, it hadn't been Raven who'd said it, but those louts in the boat were his friends, and no doubt he was laughing up his sleeve in that beastly male way about it: such was Eleanor's highly erroneous view of the affair.

Finding at last that the silence was more than he could bear, Raven remarked fatuously: 'Dreadfully dusty ashore, I'm afraid.'

Eleanor answered coldly: 'Yes, I'm so sorry.'

'Sorry? I don't see...'

'Yes, sorry to be the innocent cause of your being here. No doubt you'd much rather be elsewhere, and no doubt in different company.'

'Oh, good lord no, miss. I didn't mean that.'

'As far as I am concerned, Mr Raven, you can return to the ship here and now. I'm perfectly capable of riding by myself and looking after myself.'

'Good God, no - the Old - I mean your father - wouldn't hear of that. If I did, he'd be...'

'I know what he would be - but it's not my fault you're here. I don't altogether blame you for being disgruntled, but it doesn't make you good company when you sulk like a little schoolboy.'

Now Raven bridled and was stung into a little candour; even Jake's daughter was not getting away with that: 'No, I daresay not. But I'm a sailor, and not a bad one either. I didn't sign on board your father's ship to be some kind of groom or flunkey - having to traipse about like a nursemaid.'

She went red with annoyance, not at the implied criticism of her father, but at the sneering suggestion that she depended on a puppy like Raven. But before she could reply, he cut her short by saying coldly: 'Anyway, we're there now, Miss Roberts. This is the place. And I do so trust you will enjoy your ride.'

They had been walking for some time past enclosures of level sand, corralled off from the road and the desert by stout wooden rails. Inside the fields - if one could grace them with that name - were bunches of mules and lean scraggy cattle munching away at heaps of dried alfalfa grass. They were the survivors of the long and dreadful trek from the Argentine, up through the Andean passes, across the interminable salt flats, over the Cordillera, down to San Pedro and then across the Atacama. Now they rested and recuperated and fattened, ready for their new Atacama destinies - to be respectively transport and diet at *oficina* or port. The cattle raised their heads from their hay and looked mournfully at the walkers, as if reproaching them for the long agony of their journey, the loss of their grassy native pampas and their dull stony exile here. The smell of their hay and their dung came gratefully to the two as homely reminders of a more normal countryside.

They came to the horned gateway that Jacob had described and turned into the track that led to a solid wooden house and a quadrangle of stables and sheds. They approached in silence, Eleanor having decided that it was more dignified and much less boring to ignore Raven than to wrangle childishly with him over something that neither of them could change. She was determined, besides, to enjoy the outing and to manage everything so well that next time she would be allowed to come alone. When they were a hundred yards from the buildings a man appeared, wearing the thick shirt and baggy trousers of a gaucho. Seeing them, he put down his bucket and hobbled stiffly towards them with the awkwardness of a lifelong horseman. It occurred to Raven that as he himself knew no Spanish and this man probably no English, there might be more irritation in store, but his anxiety was groundless, for the man raised his hand and called: 'Good morning senor, senorita. You come for ride, no?' Despite the welcome, he was a daunting sight at closer quarters: lean and stooping, his shoulders bowed forward with age and work. Indeed, it was hard to guess his age; he might be anything from fifty to seventy. Because of his stoop, his face seemed to thrust itself forward like that of a snake poised to strike. His face, his scrawny neck with its skinny wattles, his huge strong hands, all had skin as brown, thick and scaly as the armour of a lizard. He seemed fashioned out of the hardest, darkest leather. His eyes and his nearly toothless mouth, wide and thin-lipped - they too reminded them of a predatory lizard, and so did his tongue, which now and then flicked out to moisten the painfully cracked lips. He was an Atacama of a man - dry, repellent, and with an undertone of malignity. All this they felt, and yet he was cheerful and polite enough.

'You from "Figaro", hey? The Limey packet? English barque?'

Simultaneously, Raven said, 'Yes, that's right,' and Eleanor said, 'No, Welsh... Welsh barque.' Had they been friends, they might have enjoyed the quibble; as it was, they both felt foolish.

The old man's reptilian eyes - small boot-buttons of gleaming black - glittered with amusement, and he flicked them over Eleanor's tall body with a rapid, searching lechery. 'English, Welsh, all same. All limeys, eh? I sailor too, many years gone by. I sail in Yanqui clippers, New York to Frisco, round Cabo de Hornos. Plenty bully beef, plenty beans, plenty biscuit. I know all about sailor's life. Cold goddam weather, rope's end, boot up your assole - I know it all.'

Both young people flushed slightly, and Raven intervened: 'Yes, well, my captain has arranged with Senor Gomez that this young lady and I...'

'Ah, you *teniente* - officer - senor? And the senorita, she Old Man's daughter, eh? You very pretty lady; you like Frisco lady. No have ladies like you in Caleta Buena, I think. Very pretty...'

Raven persisted, eyeing the old gaucho and his greedy looks with some disapproval: 'As I say, my captain - Captain Roberts - has arranged for two horses to be ready for us this morning.' Even Eleanor was beginning to admit to herself that she was glad Raven was there, though she still detected a reluctance on his part to be her gallant protector.

Quite unperturbed, the old man turned and gave Raven an outrageously lascivious wink, as if to include him in his own climate of mental lust. 'Yeah, okay, *teniente!* I Miguel - I fix you up, give you the best *caballos* in E1 Norte. You like to start pretty quick, eh? You like to take the lady up the mountains, eh? Is grand up there, I tell you. Is nobody there - nothing, nobody but rocks and sand. You follow the track, you go up high, high. You t'ink you in heaven, eh? These horses, they good ole Creole cow-ponies; if you want to get off an' rest, they stand as long as you like. You don't need tie them none. They don't go no place.'

With another sly reptilian twinkle in Raven's direction he led them to the corner of a corral where two strong ponies stood motionless, only their ears and tails flicking and whisking at the flies. They were of a dark cream colour, and strangely marked, as Roberts had said, with a dark ridge-stripe and zebra stripes on their legs. There seemed no vice about them, for they lifted their heads and watched the new-comers approach, allowing their muzzles to be stroked. They were already wearing huge cowboy saddles, almost like armchairs, with high silver-decorated front and back rests and water-bottles stowed in leather holsters. Miguel tightened the string girths with casual ease and fetched the bridles from where they hung on a fence-post.

The heavy, silver-mounted bits looked murderously powerful to Eleanor; she felt pity for the animals who worked every day with such iron in their mouths, and she resolved to be gentle with her hands; would this clumsy Raven fellow be the same with his great paws? She would have to warn him to take care. She looked at the huge high saddle; getting into that was going to be worse than she had thought, and would certainly have to be done in private.

Miguel finished bitting the horses and led one to Eleanor. 'You like this one, lady? Nice quiet horse.' When she assented, he took the bridle in his left hand and held his right hand towards her left leg. 'You like Miguel help you up?' he asked, parting his few brown teeth in a grin.

'No, I would not, thank you,' said Eleanor firmly. 'I will lead the pony off into the yard, if you please.' She marched off with it determinedly, and disappeared round a corner. Raven, out of his depth in this equine world, looked nonplussed.

'It's OK, *teniente*,' said the old man with a conspiratorial grin. 'She got to get up into saddle, and she no want you and me to see her *bragas* - how you say that? - her drawers.' He gave Raven (to that young man's great unease and annoyance) a friendly punch on the arm. 'What the hell, eh? You maybe see them soon, no? Pull them off, no? You smart young man; this *mujer*, she like you maybe, though she don't say. So she capitan's daughter - so what? They all like to jig-a-jig sometimes, eh? They all same inside. The fancy high-tone ones no different.' He drew so near and spoke so confidentially that Raven inhaled his breath's fearsome blend of stale tobacco, garlic and rotting teeth:

'Women, *teniente!* I just poor *huaso* - cowboy - now, but I fuck plenty women in my time: Chilenos, Indios, nigger gals, high-tone gringo women... plenty nice white Yanqui whores...In Frisco, Portland, Valparaiso, Astoria, Boston, the Bowery - wherever I go I screw them hard. They like Chileno sailor pretty good, I t'ink. But I give all that up and come up here to El Norte - you wanner know why?'

Raven certainly didn't, but had no chance of saying so, for the old lizard was launched into his malodorous rodomontade: 'Listen,' and he moved sickeningly closer. 'I tell you, because you good feller and you no tell anyone. This big bucko mate in my last ship, he give me bad time; plenty boot up the ass, plenty rope's end, plenty big fist. He knock out these teeth, here. So I wait for him one night in Valparaiso, when I got my *curva* with me.' He slapped a hand on a wickedly curved knife that hung at his belt. 'I give him my *curva* under his ribs - just here.' He dug two stiff fingers into Raven's middle in a way that made him start with something like fear. Then he chuckled evilly: 'He no do any more kicking after that, I guess. Then I light out for Atacama; I no hang around with no Yanquis no more. If the *carabineros* find me - finish! Garrotte!' He grasped his throat and made a hideous face. 'But that ten, fifteen years back. They no find Miguel here, not now. Is not bad life being a *huaso*, with the mules and the cattle and riding good horses. Senor Gomez, he good to me too. Ships! The hell with ships, eh? Now then, senor,' he said in his normal voice, drawing back and lapsing into his role as a groom as Eleanor appeared, riding the horse astride, but with her voluminous skirts modestly down. 'You jump up, *so!* You have good time. Only you remember now, this Chileno cowpony, he not fancy gringo *caballo*. He walk good, he canter good, he gallop very damn good but he don't like to trot none. Lady, it look like you ride horse good. You folks come back to Miguel when you've had good time - no?'

He watched them out of sight, his smile dying as they turned their backs; he lit a thin, ragged and villainously strong cheroot; he sighed, shook his head, muttered, 'Gringos!' then spat in the sand and returned to his chores.

*   *   *

Half an hour later the riders emerged from the rock-strewn defile of the little valley on to the level *altiplano*, the true high desert plain which fell sharply to the sea to the west, and gently to the foot of the vast Andean peaks to the east. Here they were truly alone; nothing else stirred in the cloudless heat but the eddies of sand stirred up by the horses' feet. It was a dead accursed land where no man would stay, were it not for the streaks of colour in the dark sand which betrayed the presence of enough minerals to awaken the cupidity of maritime Europe: chemicals to fertilize the gringos' land or help them to murder each other, for the Chilean nitre made excellent high explosives too. The only sign of life here was that of departed life - the casually-scattered white bones and skulls of horses, mules or cattle that had strayed and perished miserably, or foundered under cruel loads.

But as for these two riders, topography and economics did not occupy their thoughts. The horses, as the old *huaso* and Jacob had promised, were swift walkers and amazingly sure of foot. The sweet smooth gait and the rhythm of a willing horse between her legs had purged Eleanor's mind of its petty irritations; Raven, a few yards behind, seemed content enough to follow her lead and even her advice at times. He seemed fairly competent, but seemed also to be *on* the horse, rather than *with* it, a part of it.

Now, with a wide desert track in front of her, she longed to let her horse go free, to feel its suppressed power, to feel the desert wind blow out her hair, to see the horse eating up the miles to the horizon. She turned in the saddle and reined gently to let Raven catch up. 'Shall we canter? It's smooth going now, and this is a bit tame. Can you manage?' Her tone was unmistakeably patronising.

John Raven had known this would happen. It was a bit like his first climb to the main royal yard, a hundred and eighty feet up. He nodded, tight-lipped, unwilling to show his fear to this girl; she'd only mock him. 'Yes, I think so. Don't know about a gallop, though.'

Her irritation returned; what a wet blanket he was! 'All right, I'm not going to gallop. I just said "canter", didn't I? Come on, for Heaven's sake!'

She clicked her tongue and squeezed with her legs, and the pony smoothly bounded straight into an easy, steady canter, which sent rocks and dunes flying by on either hand. She glanced aside at Raven and saw that, thanks to the beautiful gait, the secure saddle and the big leather stirrups, he looked as comfortable as in an armchair. A sudden yearning for real speed grabbed her like a heedless passion, an irresistible urge. She squeezed again, harder, drew in the rein and confided her passion to the horse; in two seconds he was in a flat-out gallop, his flinty unshod hooves drumming on the beaten sand. Raven gave a despairing 'I say!' and tugged clumsily at the savage bit to prevent his mount from following. The double outrage of frustration and rough treatment was too much for the creole, and he expressed his feelings in a buck which no horse in Europe could have emulated. Down and back under went his head, as if to inspect his own back feet, except that these were now some six or seven feet up in the air. When they came down again, his front feet left the ground in a wild, up-ending forward leap, ending in a jarring, stiff-legged landing on all fours. The young mate, of course, stood no chance whatever of staying in the saddle; he was catapulted in a long, lazy parabola, to land on his face in the needle-sharp sand, striking his right temple on a small rock. His cry of alarm just reached Eleanor as she flew along, a hundred yards ahead now. She felt a spurt of renewed irritation at his pusillanimous incompetence; she firmly reined the horse down to a canter and wheeled him stylishly round in a shower of sand, expecting to see Raven floundering behind on his horse. Instead, she saw the riderless horse, its bridle swinging, cantering off into the desert, and Raven still flat on his face. *Bobl annwyl!* It was only sand he landed on - why couldn't the great mammy's boy get up - he couldn't be hurt! What a pitiful pansy he was, with all his posh English airs! Full of scorn, she ignored him, and set off after the loose horse, who allowed himself to be caught, and came penitently back with her. But scorn became horror when, several minutes later, she saw the man still stretched out flat, and saw too, as she halted the horses, a stone the size of a biggish cabbage beside his head, saw his dark hair matted with blood, which dripped off to run into the thirsty sand.

She flung herself out of the saddle with no regard for modesty, and abandoned the horses, who stood, heads drooping, to await their next duties. Her face was drained of the fiery red colour of her exertions as she knelt beside him, appalled and full of the deepest guilt: '*O Iesu Grist!* Don't let him be dead! It was my fault, my stupid, wicked fault. I only did it to show off, and show him up. Mr Raven... John... John... are you...?' Whimpering with fear, she shook his shoulder. No response. She grasped his shoulder and upper arm with both hands and hauled backwards. He was a dead weight, but she was strong and desperate, and managed to roll him over to lie face upwards. She brushed the sharp sand from the damp, yellow-white skin of his face;

his eyes were closed and the big bloody graze on his temple looked horrible. 'O my God, what shall I do?' she whispered to him. 'I'm so sorry, but what's the good of that to you now?'

Then the panic left her and she became practical. Was he alive? That was the first thing to find out. She opened his dusty white jacket, took off her hat, and put her ear to his left breast. Relief flooded through her as she felt, as well as heard, the steady thump-thump of his heart through the thin shirt; moving her ear to his mouth, she could hear and feel the faint fetch and return of his breath. 'Thank God he's not dead. He will come round - but suppose he's cracked his skull?'

She got the water-bottle from her saddle-holster, wetted her handkerchief and began to wipe his face, still whispering to herself: 'That's it, girl, plenty of water... cool him down. Put your hat on and get between him and the sun, you stupid, nasty little fool, you...'

So it was that the first feeling Raven was aware of, as consciousness came back to him, was of tepid water being liberally applied to his face, and trickling down his neck into his collar, tickling him. He opened his eyes to see, not the blinding sun, but Eleanor's face, haloed by her boater, very close to his and looking taut with worry; he was even aware of the sweetness of her breath. She moved back a little on seeing his eyelids open, and smiled nervously. 'Are you all right? I'm so terribly sorry - it was my fault.'

He was still half-stunned, and didn't choose his words as well as he might: 'I'm all right... Wasn't your fault...It was the bloody horse that that goddamned old dago gave me... Pity they didn't garrotte him...'

'John, what on earth are you talking about?'

'Oh, nothing... I'll be all right in a minute, honestly. Still a bit woozy. I'll try sitting up.' He pushed himself to a sitting posture, but was immediately struck by a wave of deadly nausea, so that he was forced to turn away from her and retch painfully into the sand. He lay back when the spasm passed, his face a dull yellow. She wiped the mess from his mouth and cheek, and he smiled feebly: 'Thanks. Sorry to be so revolting.'

'It's all right. You're not revolting. I'm the revolting one, really. Wait a minute, I'll make you a bit more comfortable.' Moving him to and fro, she pulled his arms from his jacket sleeves and then, using all her strength, raised him enough to slide the jacket from under him. She rolled it into a pillow, raised his head and pushed the jacket under. 'There, that better, *cariad?*' The affectionate word – "darling" - was out before she knew it, but she reflected thankfully that he wouldn't know what it meant. It came out only because she was looking after him as if he were a child, not because... And yet he was a lovely young fellow to look at, no mistake. She'd never really looked at him before - not really looked. Unnecessarily, she placed both hands on his shoulders, pressing him down. 'Now you lie quite still, till your head clears properly.' His body was so hard, so solid, so, square when you felt it... Must be all that hard work, aloft and on the cargo. It was strange, this first voluntary physical contact with a man of her own age.

He lay in grateful silence for a while, halfway between dreaming and waking. The sun, the throbbing in his temple - they were real enough. But just now, when she was so close, with the feel of her hands and arms round him, moving him as if he were a baby, and her face so close to his - was all that real too? She'd always been so cool and distant, and now - still - she was so close. A slightly painful constricted twitching told him that he was starting to get an erection. God, that was just ridiculous at a time like this! But every man knew that your John Thomas lived, as it were, a life of his own; unlike all the other bits of your body, he couldn't be controlled! It was as if you had to drag round with you some very selfish companion with an absolutely one-track mind: Never mind about your troubles, it said, what about me? Raven thought: A hard like that must show up a bit in these tight trousers - hope she won't notice. No, too pure and well brought up for that... All that chapel... But godfathers, what a time to pick, when he'd bashed his head, got covered in sand and had just puked up his breakfast right in front of her! What a time! Just perfect for romance!

Eleanor was glad to see signs now of the blood returning to his cheeks, and when he opened his eyes again they seemed more focused, more like *his* eyes. He smiled again: 'Don't look so worried. I'll be fine soon, when my head clears. It's pretty solid, you know... durable. We often get awful belts across the head from the rigging blocks, up aloft. Especially the staysail sheet blocks. Then you've got to hang on if you can. This is better, safe on the ground with you...' He stopped, seeing her blush brightly, and went on: 'You know, looking after me. No-one bothers to do that aboard. You're more likely to get a boot in the ribs, and someone shouting, "Get up, you lazy sojer!"'

'I can't believe it's as bad as that,' she said, smiling back warmly; both of them enjoyed the sweet relaxation of the cold tension.

'And I really am sorry, Mr…'

'No, call me John.'

'All right - John. I was so wrong and stupid to go galloping off like that. Spiteful and selfish too; I was only showing off because I was annoyed with you.'

'I'm not surprised you were. I'm sorry too that I was such a miserable wet specimen, sulking like a spoilt brat. Only I knew I wasn't much of a jockey; that's why I told your father…'

'Him! I was pretty cross with him as well. I suppose it was his fault, really, if you think it all out. He shouldn't have forced you onto a horse'

'Oh well, he's the Old Man. He meant well. He wanted to please you, and he thought you needed an escort, and he picked me.'

'But that's partly what made me cross – he'd no business to make you come with me. It's not part of your - what d'you call it? - sailorizing.'

'No, but as I say, he's the Old Man. Anything he tells me to do is my duty - unless it's absolutely criminal, or endangers the ship - anything. Ships wouldn't work if the crowd and the mates could pick and choose and argue what they'd do and what they wouldn't. Anyway…' he smiled broadly at her and was astonished to hear himself say: 'I'm glad he did, really.'

'Glad? But you can't be! Look at you! You've had a nasty fall, you've been injured and you've been very sick. That must have been a dreadful blow on your head. I'm still quite worried that your skull may be fractured.'

'Not it, I assure you! What's a bit of a crack on the nut - especially a thick nut like mine? I used to box a bit at Conway, so I'm used to knocks. Listen, I think I'll try sitting up now; we can't stay here all day.'

'Very well, but let's be more careful this time. And you must lie down again if you start to feel poorly.' She helped him up into a sitting position, kneeling behind him to support him, one arm across his shoulder. 'There - that better? Look, there's still blood on this graze.' She dabbed at it again with her drenched and ruined handkerchief; thin, pink, diluted blood ran on to her crumpled sandy blouse that had been so pristinely white.

'Thank you… Now who's the nursemaid?'

They both laughed, and he felt her arm tighten in a gentle

squeeze. He said, once more surprising himself - his tongue seemed to be out of control as well as the other, lower, organ: 'That's why I say I'm glad. All I've got is a bit of a headache, but on the other hand we're friends now. We can talk. We weren't before, so that's worth a sore bonce.'

'No, we weren't before, that's true enough. You seemed so... English... and superior, the way you looked and talked. I used to feel you were just looking down on Mam and me... Welsh yokels... And then...'

'I know - our first meeting! That wasn't exactly a well-planned social occasion, was it? In the buff, covered in nitrate dust – and I was sure you were the peggy, and I was wild with him.' Laughter shook them again, this time heartily, and it acted, as so often, like a powerful aphrodisiac potion. Through his thin shirt he felt the delicious pressure of her left breast against his back; her cheek was close to his. She, re- minded by his words, glanced at his lap and saw the thin drill fabric stretched tight by his penis, which seemed unbelievably long and big and strong.

She was seized by a sudden new desire to stretch out her hand and stroke it, caress it lovingly. But that would drive him mad with lust, wouldn't it? There could be only one end to that kind of conduct: he would want to – he would be desperate to – put it into her. And that was unthinkable, too dangerous to contemplate. And besides, all her upbringing, all her Sundays in chapel, all her faith in God, told her that was not how decent young Christian women behaved. Not until they were married, anyway. Then, presumably, you could, whenever you liked. She shook her head to clear it of such thoughts, and said gently: 'If you're well enough I think we should try to get back now. We've a long way to go and it's getting late.'

For a moment he too was seized by the almost overbearing desire to swing round and grab her, lay her flat, kiss her lovely fresh lips and explore with his hands under those all-concealing skirts; but he too, for all his half-deck vaunting and talk about women, was out of his depth. He too had a strong streak of caution. She was (dammit!) Jake's daughter, after all. He was supposed to look after her, not take her out into the desert and shag her. That was what Grant had been hinting at, with his Latin tag, he supposed, 'Yes,' he said, with much lingering re- gret, 'I suppose we should. The sun is getting very hot.' He struggled to his feet and walked a few experimental steps; Eleanor nearly laughed aloud to see that his excitement, combined with the tightness of his borrowed trousers, was forcing him to hobble, not walk, but she dared not laugh and risk another wave of longing in him and herself, for she too felt strangely warm and melting *down there*, and didn't trust herself to resist anything he might try. That was a new feeling too.

'Are you all right now, John?' she asked.

'Yes, thank you.' He took her hand in both of his, and she felt a wave of weakness at the feel of their square hardness and roughness – their difference. But he was back in control, and said only: 'And thank you for looking after me so well, Eleanor, even when it was so beastly for you.'

She just smiled, drew her hand gently back, and went to the horses. But some barrier had gone down between them, for when it was time for her to mount, she unceremoniously hauled skirt and petticoat to her waist and hitched them there, exposing a surprising (and, to Raven, delicious) length of leg and crisp white drawers with lace at the knee. A nimble hoist, a quick glimpse of a shapely behind under the taut *bragas*, and she was up in the saddle, letting her skirt down again with a blush and a smile.

'You men have no idea how awkward it is to be a woman when you want to do anything except walk about or sit in a chair. I wish Mam would let me wear bloomers, but she never will. Now then, we just walk the horses, isn't it? And *carefully!*'

'Aye, aye, ma'am. But I'll get the hang of this riding business. I'll manage better next time.'

*   *   *

At cabin supper that night, however, John's equestrian hopes received a fatal blow when he said much the same thing to his captain: 'What d'you mean – "next time", mister? My wife's had to spend half a dog-watch patching you up, and you might have laid yourself up from work for a week too. You're not up to it, mun – you said so yourself, and you were right. I'll make some other arrangement.' He took another fork-full of beef and said, with the total unreasonableness that made him at times maddening: 'Good God, your job's working the ship, not riding about, using your head to flatten all the rocks in South Spain.'

There was the faintest of sound, like the start of a 'but' from Eleanor, unnoticed by her father, but instantly perceived and understood, not only by John, but also by Mair. Each was a little gratified, though in opposite ways. Mair made no comment, but reflected silently: Thank God the old donkey sometimes makes the right decision, even if it is for the wrong reason!

Then the Mate pitched everything into a sump of dull normality by remarking: 'Aye, working ship… They should finish that for'ard hold tomorrow, and maybe we could rig hoists at the main hatch too, after. If you could, sir, manage to send the brassbounders straight back tomorrow, as soon as you get ashore, they could sweep out the main hold. That'd be more useful than them sculling about round the quay in their fancy duds, isn't it?'

Eyes downcast, John and Eleanor swallowed the tough beef with a remarkable lack of zest, not daring to let their eyes meet, for it would have been hard indeed to conceal their bitter disappointment at this casual shattering of their newborn dream.

13

At eight o'clock next morning the foc'sle crowd, yawning and scratching, mustered at the for'ard hatch, drearily aware of the prospect of six more days of cargo-heaving. The men of yesterday's watch ashore had thick heads into the bargain, after an afternoon and evening swilling Chilean beer and the fiery *pisco*. However, as they peered down into the blackness below, there was something to show for their weeks of heaving; the neat pyramid of gunny-sacks full of nitrate was now complete in the lower hold and today the *cargadores* would finish off the smaller mound in the tween-decks. When that was done, two-thirds of the cargo work would be behind them, and they could begin to think about sailing day, and beyond that, to arriving home with their cargo and a pocketful of sovereigns.

'One hold full, boy,' said Billy John Ffynnongroes to the bosun. 'Two more, and we can get the hook up and we're off back to them lovely Tiger Bay tarts.'

'Tiger Bay?' said the old man gloomily, wincing at the brilliant light and the morning heat on his tender skull: 'Don't count your chickens, boy. With our luck it won't be Cardiff we fetch up at; it'll be Hamburg or Dunkirk or some other Godforsaken foreign hole.'

'What if we do? It'll still be the end of the voyage, so old Powell will have to pay our steamer and train fares back to Cardiff; we'll still be back there in a couple of days.'

'Who wants your dirty whores, anyway?' said Dic Meredydd, a quiet Cardigan man. 'My Gwenny's due in a couple of months. My old girl and her new babby – that's who I'm looking forward to seeing.'

The crowd's gloom, however, was nothing compared with that of the apprentices when, an hour later, they landed the Old Man at the quayside; he was togged up quite smartly for him in a drill suit which Mair had nagged him into buying, a new panama hat and a glittering black walking-cane. Expecting a morning loafing in the shade of the jetty or fooling about with the brassbounders from other ships, the boys were chilled and horrified when the Old Man paused on the stone steps of the quay to say casually: 'Shan't need the boat till eight bells this afternoon, Perkins, so get straight back to the ship - straight back, mind -and get those duds off. The mate wants you to sweep out the midship hold, and after that the after hold. And the two tween-decks, of course. Now get a move on! I shall check with the mate what time you got back, and if you've dawdled - look out! Shove off then, boy! And bend your backs too. You had a damned good day yesterday; right, well today's a working day.'

And, rolling slightly with his seaman's walk, he made off with great dignity towards the agent's office and Gomez' parlour; he had arranged for a photographer to come and immortalize himself and some of his fellow-commanders; after that, there would no doubt be fresh-ground Brazilian coffee, Havana cigars and very good French brandy going.

* * *

But it was true enough: they had had a glorious day yesterday - even they couldn't dispute that. The gig had been beautifully rigged by Sails and the bosun with a lug mainsail and a headsail of light canvas, which set in elegant curves, with not a wrinkle. She went like a yacht in the fresh sea-breeze, heeling her lee gunwale to the water, nonchalantly climbing the slopes of the long blue swells, a steady chuckle of water under her bow. The Old Man enjoyed himself at the tiller; he never touched the wheel of the barque, except in an emergency, and he loved to feel the live pressure of the small boat's tiller as she heeled to a gust and tried to fly up into the wind. Once, he showed his virtuoso skill as a helmsman (as well as his immature sense of humour) by ordering the innocent and gullible Robbins to sit on the lee bench and then -with a wink to the others - tightening the mainsheet, so that the lee gunwale momentarily dipped below the surface, sending a thin, refreshing stream of seawater on to his victim's backside. He enjoyed the hoots of laughter and applause from the other boys; damn, these *crwts* were a nuisance sometimes, but they did keep you young!

Mair smiled indulgently, but a bit loftily, thinking: Why is it that men never grow up? She said sympathetically: 'Are you very wet, Robbins? I expect it will soon dry off in this wind. Jacob, let me take a trick at the helm; perhaps I can do better.'

'Certainly, *cariad*. Wet your trousers, is it, boy? Too old for that, surely? What are you sitting down there for, anyway? Get up to windward and help to sit the boat level.'

Jacob clambered his way forward to the little locker in the bow, where he had stowed a treat for the boys, but he paused with his hand on the catch to look back along the boat at the bunch of happy, tanned lads in their shirtsleeves and the elegant figure of his wife, bare-headed in a long flowered dress with high shoulders and puffed sleeves, sitting in the stern-sheets, the tiller in the crook of her right arm, her lips slightly parted, her eye professionally cocked aloft to watch for a flap of the mainsail... Every inch a sailor!

To her, it was as if the boat were a bird, riding the wind, and she were a part of the creature, balancing it there by subtle, almost imperceptible movements, feeling the vibrant life of the boat passing into her body from her arm on the carved ash tiller. Sensing Jacob's eye on her, she lowered her gaze to smile at him, and his heart nearly burst with pride at her beauty, at her wonderful look of youthful complicity - the look that said: All right, let's all be silly youngsters for the day. He felt the sheer joy of having her as a wife, and of having her here now. *Duw,* what right had a common, plug-ugly old shellback like him got to have such a woman for a wife? Damn, she wouldn't be out of place among the richest of the *crachach* in Wales!

A moment later he was startled out of his pleasant reverie by a sudden chilling of his back and shoulders. Mair had spotted a steep little wavelet ahead and to windward; by quickly releasing her pressure on the tiller she made the boat's bow fly up towards it, so that the little lump of water rapped against it, flinging a small but solid portion of the Pacific over her stooping husband. She called out, 'O sorry, Jacob!' and the boys, swiftly sensing that it was safe to do so, once again crowed with laughter. Jacob exclaimed: *'Diawl!* Look what you're doing, gel!' and then grinned as she said: 'Wet your shirt, is it? Never mind, it'll soon dry.'

He blundered his way back to her side, carrying a paper hag, which he opened as he sat down. 'You nearly made me drop these overboard with your dull tricks. Come on then, boys: stop your cackling and let's have some respect, isn't it? How about some apples to keep us going?'

Apples! The gleaming red fruit looked and tasted like nectar and ambrosia to these hefty lads, starving on a pauper's diet of salted and dried junk. 'One good thing about Chile,' said Jacob, 'it may not be very wide, but it's so damn long, they can grow almost anything somewhere.'

Half an hour later he pointed over the lee bow: 'There you are, Mair. There's the cove - where those rocks stick out. Up helm and head for the last of them. Come on then, you sojers, don't sit there dreaming! Free the sheets, can't you? Wind's on the port quarter now, isn't it? Damn, who could make sailors out of such a crowd of loobies?'

They landed Mair in the little cove, Jacob gallantly carrying her through the surf to save her dress. She picked her way up the pebbles to the tideline to collect dry driftwood for a fire (and, of course, to disappear discreetly behind a rock for a while) while the skipper and the boys pushed off again to fish for their dinner. 'If you want a leak,' said Jacob, 'you can piddle in the bailer, only don't you spill any in the bilge, or you'll scrub the whole boat out in the dog-watch tomorrow. Now then, Perkins, get out the fishing tackle.'

Their method of fishing, as usual on the West Coast, was brutally simple and drastic: the captain took from his pocket a stick of dynamite - easy enough to buy at one of the mine stores - lit the fuse and slung it overboard. The boat jolted with the shock of the explosion, and a pool of white foam appeared on the surface, flecked with the shapes of stunned fish floating helplessly. The Humboldt Current was a rich larder for millions of anchovies, and they in turn were prey for larger fish - bonito and tunny especially. Jacob luffed into the wind and let the sheets fly, while Perkins and Smith reached over the side with landing nets, scooping up the catch. 'Look sharp,' said Jacob. 'They won't bide there long – they're only stunned, not dead. Get all the anchovies you can; they may he small, but they're the tastiest of the lot. Two of you, get the oars out quick and pull ahead – that's a bonito over there, and a beauty too.'

By the time they were back ashore with a good basket of fish, Mair, using paper and old candle-ends, had got a brisk little fire blazing on the pebbles and a pile of driftwood fuel for it nearby. Jacob produced from the locker a big stone bottle of ginger beer, which Mair had made for the occasion, and the lads took turns at swallowing rapturous draughts from it. The Old Man had, in his twenties, served aboard a Brixham trawler out of Fishguard, and made short work of beheading and gutting the catch; he produced wooden skewers which he had wheedled from the cook, and once the fire had burnt up well, the boys grilled the fish over the hot embers, competing for the honour of presenting well-cooked morsels, first to Mair and then to their captain. There was even white shore-baked bread to eat with the fish, and the glorious tangy fizz to wash it down. It had been a good catch, and the apprentices stuffed themselves to repletion, their hands and faces dripping with the fish-fat.

Mair watched them with odd maternal longings. They were togged up sometimes in smart uniforms with brass buttons; they lived such hard and dangerous lives; they were made to work harder than navvies at all the most dreary and distasteful jobs because they were, to the Owners, useful cheap labour - yet they were only big schoolboys, really - schoolboys seven thousand miles from their mothers, made to grow up too fast, too solitary. Sometimes, when she saw them hungry or dirty, injured or smarting from some harsh rebuke from Jacob or one of the mates, she had to restrain herself from running to put her arms round them and giving them the comfort of a cuddle. Somehow, it would have comforted her too for the lack of a son of her own, a son that she knew Jacob had always longed for, but was too kind ever to mention.

But it would not do - she realized that. She was only a passenger, a supernumerary. A ship is a ship, and it runs on discipline, and discipline means distance between the degrees of the hierarchy, not gentle motherly pampering. It had always been the same or worse. Still, it was lovely to see them so happy today - and happy in the way of ordinary youngsters. They'd remember this day when they were Jacob's age, captains with ample paunches and greying hair, walking the bridges of Atlantic liners; they'd remember it as a part of the magic golden kingdom of their youth. They might even remember her giving the Old Man a wet shirt, when she herself was under a green mound in Ebeneser graveyard.

Jacob lit a cigar and reclined his back against a warm smooth rock to enjoy it; she relaxed too in the comfort of the sun and the tempering breeze. Mair snoozed luxuriously, a little section of her mind just slightly uneasy, wondering how Nelli was getting on with the horses and that young Raven, whom she seemed to dislike so much. As she dozed, this picnic became confused with others she'd had under another sun among the dry sheltery dunes of the Traeth Mawr back home.

The boys dozed too, for a while, but then Mair was faintly aware of whisperings and scufflings and quiet receding footsteps in the shingle. Then silence, followed by distant wild high-pitched yells. Sitting up sleepily, she looked along the beach and saw a group of naked figures leaping, running, plunging, swimming and wrestling like puppies in the surf. She smiled to herself, slipped an arm through Jacob's and nestled against him with a sigh of pleasure. He grunted and pitched away the end of his cigar: 'Brassbounders!' he said. 'Look at them - like things from a zoo! Dull as bats, the lot of them... Still, they did have the grace to go off a bit from us.'

Mair half-turned and raised her eyes to him: 'I should hope they would, if they're going to run about stark naked. After all, they are young men, really, and I am a woman.'

'So you are, so you are,' said Jacob, and he kissed her upturned lips long and deeply. 'And if it wasn't for those damn boys I'd prove it to you.'

As the sun began to dip towards the horizon they launched the boat again in a breathless silent calm, and the lads bent their backs to the oars to make the boat fly over the glassy heaving surface. As soon as they were out from under the cliffs, they felt the warm land-breeze come away, lifting the masthead burgee gently at first, and then with a gathering force. 'Easy all... ship oars. Make sail, boys.' The little boat came alive again as the sails climbed the mast and forestay, flogged briefly in the wind, then filled with a snap, tugging at their sheets. The gig picked up her heels, leaned her shoulder right down, and flew back to the anchorage, the boys taking turns at the tiller. It was almost dark when they arrived back, and the ships nothing but silent shapes, dipping and rolling, lit only by the solitary gleam of their riding-lights and the glow from lit port-holes.

*　　*　　*

Now, in the acrid choking clouds of coal-dust raised by their brooms, that blissful day seemed to the apprentices far off already. Only the slight tenderness of their skin under their shirts reminded them of their idyll in the sun; they yearned for the feel of the cool clean sea-water. But at least it was quiet down in the midship hold and the work wasn't hard; no officer could see them, so there was no-one to silence or haze them.

Smith, the most gossip-loving of them, called out to Perkins: 'Hey, did you see our precious Raven just now? All bashed round the head and looking as black as thunder? What's up with him, d'you think?'

'Couldn't say... Looks as if someone has belted him into the middle of next week.'

'Fell off his horse and hit his head on a rock, Isaac says.'

'God, Smutty, I don't know which is more like a tattling old woman, you or Isaac.'

'What I mean is, Raven would say that... But what if she hit him with a rock?'

'Why the hell should she?' said Ieuan Davies scornfully, coming again to Eleanor's defence.

'Why? Use your loaf, Taff: she maybe had to, to defend her beautiful untouched thingummy from old Raven's horrible hands, not to mention other bits of him.'

'Don't be more stupid than usual, Smutty,' said Perkins. 'He wouldn't dare.'

'I don't know, Perky... They were all alone in all those miles and miles of sand. She's such a ducky, and he's such a dirty dog – you've seen what he's like ashore.'

'Maybe, but I bet she's been brought up strict chapel and all that. She wouldn't be willing, for sure. And he wouldn't have had the pluck to try anything on. I bet you she came back with everything she started out with. Make a good nun, she would!'

'You mean - had none and wants none?'

'That's it. Jake and his missis will take her home and marry her to some holy Welsh preacher or Sunday-school teacher, and she'll only get it every second Saturday in the month, and then only after a couple of Welsh hymns.'

'You're disgusting, you are, both of you,' said the Welsh boy indignantly. 'She's a nice girl, she is... Decent... Not one of your cheap cantina tarts. How would you like someone talking about your sister like that?'

'Haven't got a sister, Taff,' said Smith. 'And she ain't yours.'

'And you had a real nice day out yesterday with Jake and his missis - you wouldn't get that on an English ship, I'll bet... And you don't bloody deserve to, neither. It isn't fair after that to talk like you do about a girl you know nothing about - and who's too good for any of you - or Raven, come to that.'

*   *   *

The two subjects of this debate were meanwhile both settling down to their workaday Monday tasks with very mixed - and preponderantly gloomy - thoughts. Both were in a state of electric excitement. The moments of accidental intimacy in the desert had transformed their dull routine lives by opening a window on to a field of joy and pleasure that was new to both. And if the visionary joy was limitless, so of course was the despair at their exclusion from tasting it again, and more fully. Jacob's few blunt words at dinner had slammed shut, apparently for ever, a door to an ecstatic land which they had only just found, and had not even known about before, for neither had ever previously been in the first fierce stages of love. Now they were trapped in this wallowing Clyde-built jail, in sight of each other but barred from ever meeting alone, from ever touching each other's bodies, from ever finding each other in the way that other young people did. Both knew how violently their parents would object, and Eleanor's father wielded the deadly double power of father and Captain.

Mair sensed the change in Eleanor next morning, though her daughter tried hard to be cool and detached. After breakfast they had, as was their custom, brought their sewing up on to the poop deck, where an awning stretched over the spanker boom provided a pleasant shade from the fierce sun of South Spain. She noted that Eleanor had, with an elaborate display of casualness, placed her chair to face for'ard, and that every now and then she raised her eyes to where, between all the shrouds and backstays, she could see glimpses of the tall figure of Raven at work on the cargo-hoist. She noticed the quick fiery blush on Eleanor's cheek when she herself said coolly: 'Mr Raven seems better this morning after that nasty knock. But I don't know that he should be working so hard out there in that glare and heat.'

Eleanor bent studiously over her work before replying in an offhand way: 'You'd better tell Dadi that... But it wasn't such a very bad knock, was it?'

'Wasn't it, though? I saw it when I put the bandage on. It was bad enough. Don't know what your father was thinking of to make the poor fellow get on a horse when he can't ride properly... It wasn't fair.'

'I wish you'd listen, Mam; I've explained all that. It was all my fault, letting my horse gallop off like that. He managed all right most of the time. Another time it would be all right, because I wouldn't gallop off like that again.'

'H'm... Well, I think this time your father is right for a change - to try to get Senora Gomez and the groom to go with you.'

'I've met the groom, and he's the most disgusting old man I've ever seen... I can't tell you how disgusting.' She shuddered as she remembered those old reptilian eyes sliding, flickering, across her body, those thin leathery lips and their lewd sly innuendoes.

Her mother went on steadily as if she hadn't spoken: 'And of course it saves you that other embarrassment – of being forced to go out riding with a young man whom you dislike so much.'

Eleanor rose instantly to the bait, confirming all her mother's fears: 'But I don't - not now. Not now we've met and talked a bit. He wasn't at all rude... .He seemed quite...'

Mair thought: O heavens, the Bryn Meredydd affair all over again! Well, in for a penny, in for a pound! She went on: 'Yes, well, your father and I have talked it over, and we think the new idea is much better. I'm sure you'll find Senora Gomez a pleasant lady. You can practise a little of your Spanish with her. As for the groom, he's only a servant - why bother about him? With his mistress there he wouldn't dare to be impertinent.'

Eleanor stabbed her needle viciously through the fabric on her lap. 'Senora Gomez! Never met her. She's a hundred years old, I expect!'

'You really are being very silly and difficult, Nelli. Yesterday morning you were flouncing about because you had to ride with Raven; now you're in a stupid old temper because you can't! It's not a bit like you to be so childish.'

The girl threw her sewing to the deck, now openly furious: 'That's just it – you're treating me as if I *were* a child! It's not fair - am I not allowed to change my mind about someone? Am I not old enough to choose my friends? Other girls can, back home.'

'You're not back home, my girl, and if you can't take a gentle hint or two, I'll have to be candid: your father and I are not at all happy to see you getting too friendly with young Raven. It's one thing to chat in the saloon over dinner - no-one minds that - but it's something else altogether to go off ashore on your own with him. And if you can't see why, then you are a baby indeed.'

'You didn't mind my walking up Carn Ingli with that Henry Morris last summer. What's the difference? He might have done the most shameful things to me for all you knew.'

'Don't be absurd, Nelli. Henry is a decent young man, well brought up...We know his father and mother.'

'Yes, and I know *him* too! He's an absolute soft.'

224

'H'm - very ladylike language! Anyway, better be a soft than be wild like Raven.'

'Wild? How is he wild?'

'He goes - No, I don't think it's fitting to tell you. Your father knows about him; he can judge best what's the right thing to do.'

Eleanor looked up, and caught sight of John leaning diagonally back to haul the hoist back over the lighter. The sight gave her courage to speak bluntly: 'I don't know why you beat about the bush,' she said. 'I suppose you mean he chases girls in port?'

'Not exactly girls...'

'What then? Elephants?'

'Whatever's got into you today, Nelli? You're just rude and impossible.'

'I expect you mean tarts - girls who are on the game?'

'Wherever did you pick up these disgusting expressions? Very well, then - yes, that is what I meant. Now what do you think of your charming young gentleman? I suppose you'll approve of that?'

'No I don't approve at all, and you know I don't. But it's the kind of thing sailors do, because for so much of the time they're cut off from women. But it isn't just sailors, is it? How would all the thousands of prostitutes back home - in Cardiff and London and Liverpool - how would they make a living if they didn't have plenty of so-called gentlemen as regular customers? It's only your precious gentlemen who can afford to be customers - and they don't have the sailors' excuse of isolation, either.'

Mair controlled her impatience, and made an effort at peace and reasonableness (recognizing too as a woman that there was some justice in what Nelli said); she laid her hand gently on her daughter's sleeve: 'Never mind all that... Let's not squabble. And do pick up your tray-cloth before someone puts a dirty boot on it. Do trust us, Nelli, to have some judgment in the ways of the world, and to love you enough to want to save you from being... from being hurt. The world can be very cruel, and especially to young women who have made... mistakes. You're very young to be serious about any young man; you're not twenty till next October. No, wait a minute before you speak. Listen: there'll be plenty of time when we get back home to find somebody nice, someone we know, someone who'll be kind and faithful. And then there's your teaching; before we left you were very keen on going to the Training College.'

'I don't want to squabble either, Mam, but this is so ridiculous - talking about marrying and this and that! I'm only talking about having a ride now and then with a friend of my own age and choosing. Good Heavens, we've only been together once, for an hour or so! And next time there wouldn't be any accidents.'

Her mother withdrew the peace-making hand and sat back with a loud 'H'm!' Eleanor at once understood and blushed scarlet, but still said defiantly: 'And what does that "H'm" mean?'

'You silly, aggravating little minx, you know what it means: it means there's more accidents than just falling off a horse, and some of them have worse consequences. Can't you see - we live an odd life here among all these men, all of them under your father's command? For his sake as well as your own, you need to be so careful. It would be different if we were in some civilized port like Newcastle, New South Wales, where there are dozens of nice, young Christian people for friends, and nice, well-run, respectable Church clubs where you could meet them. Here there's nowhere ashore where a decent girl could possibly go for the evening - no, don't say another word, Nelli. Your father and I know best, and we're in complete agreement: other than ordinary conversation, we don't want you to have anything to do with anyone aboard this ship, and certainly not that young Raven at any price.'

*   *   *

That young Raven, working his hoist in the strong sunshine at the for'ard hatch, might have appeared to an observer as a strong, smart young mate earning his keep. Heaving hand-over-hand on the guy-rope, he skilfully plumbed the lighter; a nod to the hands at the winch sent the empty sling plummeting down with a whirr of well-oiled blocks. He watched the *cargadores* hook on the new sling, and waved his forefinger round in the air as a signal to the winch-men. He could feel the gear take the strain as the heavy sacks came up, spinning slowly, out of the lighter and above the ship's rail; he slacked away his guy as Grant hauled in, and saw, for the thousandth time, another bundle disappear into 'Figaro's' cavernous womb. The hands rattled up the empty sling, and the whole laborious cycle began again.

Except that, for John, it had never really started, for although apparently present on duty at the hatch, he was a kind of disembodied spirit. Only his trunk and limbs were loading nitrate. So when Grant first called to him, the words meant no more than the creaking of the ropes or the crying of the sea-birds around them.

'Eh?'

'I said "How much more in the lighter?"'

'Another three slings, about.'

'Right, that'll finish this tween-deck. Nip back and see if the brassbounders have finished sweeping the main hold yet.'

John walked aft, shaking his head symbolically to bring it back from its fantasies to the here and now. It was gratifying that when the half-idle brassbounders heard his hail they started guiltily and put their backs into it. They all looked like sweeps now, their mouths and noses covered by grimy cloths against the dry choking coal-dust that danced in the sunbeams. 'Jump about, down there! Nearly finished, Perkins?'

'Nearly, sir. Just going to shovel it up.'

'Aye, aye. Take it to the galley.' It would be handy there for banking up the stove overnight. He went back for'ard. 'Nearly finished,' he said to Grant.

'And the main tween-deck? Have they swept that?'

'Oh no... I don't think so.'

'Think so? Don't you know? Christ, what the hell's the matter with you this morning?' There were winks and grins of furtive delight among the cluster of hands at the winch at this tiff between the afterguard. All fuel for gossip, and you could never have too much of that. John, back at his toil, scarcely noticed the Second's irritation; his mind was too possessed by a strange blend of elation and desolation. A new level of feeling and being had opened to him. He had never, he realized, really met a girl before; had never before been able to treat a girl as an equal, a companion; had never before grasped how marvellous, how captivating, that companionship could be - though by God there was more than companionship to it! There was the magic and excitement of her body, too - no good pretending, for he could feel himself stiffen even at the thought of her! It was like a blinding light on the Damascus road; and he had thought himself so seasoned and experienced about women, had boasted about it to the younger apprentices. In fact, he'd known nothing real - only a few physical facts on the most sordid and animal plane. How could he know more - stuck in an Oxford boys' prep school at nine, off to a boys' boarding school at thirteen, then Conway? He'd known no-one but boys and men, except for formidable middle-aged matrons and closely-guarded skivvies. As for life at home in Oxford, he was never there long enough to get to know anyone well. The only girls there were the daughters of his parents' friends, and they'd all seemed a dull and dowdy lot - respectable, child-like, prudish, toothy; all pretending to be very swell, full of chit-chat about clothes, goings-on in church and college, complaints about tradesmen and servants - interminable drivelling eye-wash!

Now here he was, practically living with the most topping girl - and what good was it? They were barely able to talk, and then only pointless chat at meal-times - just as bad as at home. They'd never be able to touch each other, to caress and fondle, unless they - No! He brought himself up sharply: that idea was too dangerous even to contemplate. And anyway, what did she really think and feel? Did she feel the same about him? Sometimes he thought she did, but it was hard to say for sure...This morning she'd merely made a cool, polite enquiry about his damaged head, just as if she'd been talking to Dai Dome, but last night when her father had been carving the beef and all the others were preoccupied, she'd flashed such a secret smile of friendship, happiness, mischief and complicity, all combined, that his heart had jolted in his breast. The next instant it was gone, and she was saying innocently: 'O no, Dadi, really, that's plenty for me.' Hells bells, she was a goer! What an idiot he'd been in all his judgements about her - like a stupid blinkered donkey, just seeing what he'd expected to see a dull, chapelgoing, sanctimonious goody-goody!

His joy in these new revelations had been a bit dampened by Simon Grant; the two young men often strolled after supper on the poop, enjoying their cigars and an hour of quiet. Grant was, on the surface, as cool, casual and detached as ever, but in the steady trend of his words he was as full of prudence and admonitory advice as Mair to her daughter: 'How's the head standing up to it?' he asked, one evening.

'Fine - throbs a bit, that's all. No worse than a clout from a stays'l block, as I told Eleanor.'

'O, it's "Eleanor" now is it? H'm... You got a nasty knock, but perhaps it was a blessing in disguise.'

'Blessing? How's that, for God's sake?'

'Yes, blessing. With your thick skull you'll soon get over the clout, and it's made Jake change his arrangements. He won't make you go riding with his darling daughter again, and you're well out of that.'

John snorted scornfully: 'Don't think much of his new idea. He should take a look at that groom: most disgusting old lecher in Chile, not to mention being a murderer, so he claims. No woman's safe with him.'

'Don't worry about that, old son. I've met Senora Gomez, and she's a pretty formidable lady, like all these high-toned Spanish *aristos*. I've no doubt she's got one of those little Derringer pistols hidden up her petticoats, and she wouldn't think twice about letting some daylight into a peasant or two if she chose... Tough as nails.'

'Still can't see the point...'

'Well, if you can't, you're a real chump.' Grant halted and detained Raven by a touch on his sleeve. His face briefly glowed a dull red as he drew on his cigar in the cool dark air: 'Listen, old boy, to your old uncle Simon - and *think*, if you can manage that. It's better for *you*, never mind her. She's just a passenger, she'll be gone again soon. You're at the start of your career, and if you're like me it's the only trade you know, so you don't want to scupper y'self before you start. And for a bloke like you, nothing's more dangerous than mixing your pleasure with your business, if you follow me.'

'No, I don't follow you – don't know what you're...' John turned away from him abruptly, and pitched his cigar-butt overboard in a fleeting arch of sparks.

'You do, old son, or you wouldn't be so shirty with me. Come on, you know what I mean all right: you're young and vulnerable and always gawping after women; she's a damned good looker, even if she is old Jake's daughter, and I sometimes think she's got a bit of a gleam in her eye... Well, that's all right on board, because you're kept apart, but it's not safe sculling around ashore on your twosome. That's dynamite! You could finish up on the beach with a bad discharge for character. I saw it happen in the "Devonshire" on the Calcutta run. Second mate started fooling around with the Old Man's missis...'

'Look, I haven't fooled around with anyone! Barely touched her! I spent an hour or so jolting around on a horrible dago screw, and landed on my bonce on a rock. Christ, I didn't seduce her, and take her off to Valparaiso, did I?'

'No, but by God you'd like to - admit it! So would I, for that matter, to be quite candid. The fact that you're so waxy shows you have taken a shine to her. I suppose, despite the ugliness of your mug, it's even possible she might have taken one to you, God help her...Take your uncle's advice – it's well-meant: get yourself that sort of fun from the girls at Gomez' or the Palazzo - you can afford it, now you're a third mate.'

*   *   *

Naturally, John and Eleanor's trip ashore and their return, bandaged and dishevelled respectively, had not gone unremarked in the foc'sle. Any scraps of gossip would do to enliven the dull hours. Isaac Hughes, while professing apathy and disdain for both young people, fed this appetite with tit-bits. In the second dog-watch, after supper on the Monday, he sat on the for'ard hatch (now newly covered and battened over the pyramid of nitrate) and talked to Billy John Ffynnongroes and Jimmy Protheroe. Bosun Mathias and Curly Kellock reclined against the port-side bulwark a few feet away, bosun darning a sock, Curly half-absorbed in a dog-eared Anarchist pamphlet by Kropotkin.

'Don't know why,' Isaac was saying, 'but things do seem different since they come back.'

Billy said: 'Well, damn, they would be. I reckon he had it up her, then she hauled off and bashed him after – she thought better of it, like.'

'Nothing of the sort, boy,' said Jimmy. 'I bet you she fancied it too, and that Raven got so shagged-out, he couldn't stay on his horse.'

'Well,' said Billy, 'one way or another, I bet the dirty young bastard got his leg over her.'

'You know what?' said Curly, lowering his pamphlet and peering over his spectacles. 'You're a pathetic pair, you are, going on about what he did or didn't do, when you know sod-all about it. It's just your own wet dreams you're telling us. You'd like to have had her yerselves, but you wouldn't dare try, so you trot out yer half-cracked yarns. Talk sense: young Raven wouldn't dare neither, and she's brought up strict - so nothing happened, I lay.'

'I don't know, Curly,' said the steward judiciously. 'Something's different - the atmosphere, like. The missis had a long chat with the Old Man in the cabin last night after madam had gone to bed. Of course, I couldn't hear properly - not that I was trying, mind - but they was having words, and getting worked up about something. As for that young hussy, I'm not so sure she's as pure as you make out... I saw the look she gave that Raven over supper... Grinning from ear to ear. Disgusting, I thought. If she were mine, I'd have her across my knee...'

He was interrupted by a crow of laughter from all four men. Curly said kindly: 'And take her what-nots down, I suppose? Isaac, old mate, she's a strong filly – you'd never manage it, and if you did you wouldn't know what to do next, would you?'

*　　*　　*

Life on board a windjammer, however, was like being anchored in the midst of a wide sluggish river after a flood. You were static, but all sorts of objects - large and small, natural and artificial - came floating past, some a cable's length away, some a few yards off, some bumping and scraping down the ship's side, some snagged for a while in the cable or under the bow. All these various things were worth a glance, some were sources of wonder and amazement, but in the end all of them glided past the foc'sle, down the waist, past the cabined poop and the idle rudder, to be lost in the lazy swirls of the current astern.

So it was with the gossip in the 'Figaro'; the young people's Atacama escapade was worth chatting and joking about for a day or two, with its slight spice of mystery and sexual innuendo, but it was not long before it was replaced, for some at least, by news of much greater general moment. Late on Tuesday afternoon Mair, sitting alone in the cabin reading, heard the bump of the gig against the gangway, and knew that Jacob had returned. She knew something was wrong from the heaviness and slowness of his tread on the companionway, and one look at his face confirmed her fears. Instead of his usual cheerful greeting and bearish hug (well flavoured with cognac and Havana tobacco) he gave her the merest of grunts and a peck on the cheek, before slumping heavily into his big leather chair, his face set in lines of morose depression. She rose, went over and crouched before him, laying her hands on his knees: 'Jacob *bach*, whatever is it? What's the matter, *cariad*?'

'Been with the agent - damned dago rascal... He's just told me...' He stopped abruptly. 'Just a minute – where's that steward?'

'He'll be for'ard in the galley, helping the cook with cabin supper. He'll be back to make tea directly; do you want him to...?'

'No, woman, leave it! Don't want that tattling old fishwife anywhere near when I tell you what I've heard today.'

'O Jacob, whatever is it? Tell me quickly.'

'That goddamned Rodriguez has chartered us to Cape Town. He's sold the cargo to some firm down there... Says the UK and Europe market is very slack because of all these damn great Hamburg barques landing nitrate all over the shop.'

'Sold? How can he sell it? We haven't even finished loading it.'

'It can be sold and re-sold half-a-dozen times from now until it's unloaded – that's one of the headaches of this job. Never know where you're going until you get there. Dollars – that's all these owners and agents ever see. That's why they usually send us to Queenstown or Falmouth for orders; nobody knows whereabouts in Europe it's going to finish up when we start out from here. But at least it is generally in Europe, not blasted South Africa.'

'But Jacob, I've heard Cape Town's lovely - a nice climate, not too hot, plenty of nice English and Welsh people. Mrs Capten Lloyd, Dinas, was out there - she liked it very much.'

'Mair *bach*, you don't see the half. Never mind what Cape Town's like, or what Mrs Lloyd thought, it's not Europe, is it?'

'Why should that matter so much?'

'*Duw*, you're slow, gel. It means we don't finish the voyage. No UK port, no big pay-day for the crowd, no long shore leave to go home. By God, they're not going to like it.'

'But it may not be so bad, *cariad*. It's on the way home, more or less. They'll probably give you a cargo to take home.'

'Not they - not a chance. Damn steam-kettles are getting all that South African trade now. You'll see: we'll be chartered straight back out here, or to some stinking hole on the River Plate, and then back here. I know just what the crowd will think of that. Poor dabs, they're already counting the days back to Liverpool or Cardiff. And you know what they're like - overgrown children; there's no reasoning with them. This could put another year on to the length of the voyage, and when they find out, they'll take it out on me and the rest of the afterguard. And this has always been such a happy ship…'

'But can the Owners do that to the poor fellows?'

'Can they not! They can pretty near do what they damn well like. The Crew Agreement says that the ship can go anywhere in the southern hemisphere for up to two years. Well, there's still well over half of that to run; we're all sewn up by that bit of paper.'

'Couldn't you protest? Send Mr Powell a cable?'

'What for, gel? He's within his rights. I'd just find myself out of a ship. No, you know the old foc'sle saying: "Growl you may, but go you must." That's what I've got to do, but *Duw*, they will growl, some of them. Jump ship, I shouldn't wonder, so we'd better keep it a secret for as long as possible. Hope that tattling old woman Hughes doesn't get to know. I'll put the cable and the other papers in the safe, to make sure.'

Unfortunately, Jacob not being the tidiest of men, the sight of a neat, almost clear desk was to Isaac the first sign that something was seriously wrong. As he cleared the tea things later, his mind went to work on this startling development. Capten's desk all tidy, and him as black as thunder... Must be connected... Could be his missis interfering - but then he didn't seem cross with her. He hurried for'ard after washing up, and found Curly deep in the Kropotkin pamphlet, his wire-rimmed spectacles incongruous on his tanned, lined face.

'What do you think, Curly?' Isaac asked, after he'd explained his speculations.

'I dunno - I ain't a mind-reader. Could be a barney with his trouble-and-strife.'

'Trouble and...?'

'Wife,' said Curly patiently. 'It rhymes, see?'

'O, I see. You don't half talk funny, you English... I'll tell you what I think, then,' he went on self-importantly. 'I reckon it's to do with the unloading port... He's found we're chartered to Hamburg or Stettin, or some place miles from home... Anyway, I bet I'll find out – I'm not so bloody dull as he thinks. I knows him and his ways.'

Two days later he cornered Kellock again: 'I think I know for sure now - and it's much worse than I thought... I believe we're chartered for the Cape!'

'What! - South Africa?' Curly whistled solemnly. 'Jesus, there will be some growling if that's right, Isaac. But I never heard of no nitrate going there... What makes you think it's the Cape?'

'Well, like I say, I knows him - sailed with him for years. Now you see, he never went to no college like most of them aft, so he's extra careful about his navigation. Before he goes to a place he'll read and read all about it in the Pilot - you know, them big thick books about...'

'I know what a Pilot is, mate. Well then?'

'Well then, when I looks at his bookshelf - while I'm dusting and tidying in the cabin, see - I finds the South Atlantic Pilot's been moved, I'll swear...'

'Well, we got to go through the South Atlantic to get home.'

'Ah, but' - lowering his voice dramatically, and bursting with self-esteem and self-importance – 'there was a new book-mark at the page on Cape Town!'

'New? How could you tell? Might have been there for donkey's years.'

'No, it was new, Curly. I can tell because it was a bit of paper torn from a page of the "Teifiside Advertiser", and he only got that last week.'

'Stone the crows, Isaac, you're wasted on this hooker, my son. The Guv'ment ought to send you off to Paris or Berlin or Petersburg as a spy to find out what them foreigners is up to. But listen, my old son: this is a bit serious; you ain't really sure yet, and a buzz like that could cause a packet of trouble with some of the lads. So you be sure to keep mum. Poor sods, they'll find out soon enough, and then, by Christ, there'll be some sea-lawyering.'

Isaac's suspicions were confirmed only a day or two later by a snatch of conversation at the supper-table. Grant had casually observed that, by starting a voyage in October, they had at least dodged a whole British winter, whereupon the mate, in unusual good-humour, said: 'Yes, capten, and you should be back at just the right time for all the summer shows,' adding for Grant's benefit: 'The capten's a fine judge of cattle and horses, you see, mister. Got a gift for it, especially in the Welsh breeds - Welsh mountains, Welsh blacks.'

Jacob seemed oddly taken aback and non-committal in his response, and he was rescued by the quick-witted Mair saying smoothly: 'O yes, it is his great delight to be asked to judge a line of ponies... Perhaps he should have been a farmer, not a sailor. And what is your summer pastime on leave, Mr Grant?'

The conversational hiccup, unnoticed by Evans or Grant, was instantly detected by Isaac's quivering antennae. It was certainly not apprehended by the young pair at the bottom of the supper-table, for the very good reason that their own lives had, at that moment, taken another odd lurching step forward. John Raven had always had some difficulty in stowing his long legs and big feet under tables, and now, shifting his feet a little, he accidentally encountered, knocked against, Eleanor's feet. He was about to apologize when a quick, keen, open-eyed glance from her told him not to. Then he felt her foot, neat in soft kid's leather, stay against his, not withdrawing, then giving a gentle, delicious pressure. God, that was no accident, for it was accompanied by a cool glance from her and a tiny tremble of the left eyelid that was a quarter of the way to being a wink.

That poor muffled touch of bodies made the cabin supper a delight for them both. Luckily, neither was expected to converse much - the talk was all between their four seniors. Raven's opinion on professional matters was, naturally, never sought; Mair sometimes, out of sheer good manners, made polite chat about family matters, but on such topics he was keenly aware of how boring he was, for he didn't really know his own family well because of his schooling and his sea-time. Now he and Eleanor were happy to be silent and enjoy these secret touches.

The next night it was the same, except that, at the first contact, she drew her foot sharply away as one might from a stranger, causing John to feel a burst of disappointment - God, she'd just been teasing him, playing a silly malicious game - until a moment later the foot crept back, gently resting on his, pressing and squirming. She did feel as he did, want him closer! It wasn't all his heated fancy! And, realizing the difficulty of his position aboard, she'd been bold enough and generous enough to make the first move.

After that, at night, turning in early after his exhausting day, he would lie awake listening, his door a little ajar. The afterguard's quarters formed a kind of flat, below the poop and above the lazarette - the food store. The centre of the flat was occupied by the mess-room, and aft of that, its rear bulkhead fitted to the broad curve of the ship's stern, was the captain's saloon. On either side, four small rooms opened on to either saloon or passage: the captain's bathroom and cabin, and the first and second mate's quarters to starboard; on the less august port side, Eleanor's cabin, the steward's cabin and pantry, and the third mate's cabin, furthest for'ard. Thus, Eleanor was cut off from him by the most lynx-eyed, crafty, nosy old fox west of Cardiff, and in any case her cabin opened on to the Old Man's saloon. She might as well be a fairy-tale heroine locked up in a castle. Still, at night he could hear her step, sometimes her voice, could hear her door close; then she was lost to him until next suppertime's delicious torture.

Eleanor too used to watch his broad shoulders disappear through the mess-room door after supper, used to catch glimpses during the day of his shirt-sleeved, brown-armed figure in the waist - nearer now that they were filling the main hold; saw him throw his weight repeatedly on the derrick guy-rope. It seemed to her so wrong that a man from a good family, and serving in a skilled profession, should have to labour like a navvy. She couldn't help noticing at supper how his hands were broad, battered, broken-nailed, with coarse rough skin, ingrained with dirt and grease. She remembered how that silly, snobbish old trout of a headmistress used to say: 'And you can always tell a gentleman, gels, by the condition of his hands.' Well, not always! She too, listening for his heavy footstep, his laugh, thought herself more star-crossed than Juliet.

Both, being young healthy animals, took, before they slept, the oldest and simplest way to relieve their bodies and their vivid hopeless fantasies, gasping with as much urgency of release as if it were indeed each other's bodies that they grasped or caressed.

14

Captain Roberts dipped his pen again and continued the log:

Position by P.M. sight: Latitude 25 degrees 18 minutes South, 74 degrees 11 minutes West. Trade wind south-east, light. Ship close-hauled on port tack Course SW by W a half W. Hands employed bending on best suit of sails.

He grunted with some satisfaction as he closed the book She'd run pretty well to be here in such light winds, and it was good to be back at sea, where he could feel he was master again. Those damned Chilean ports! Months wasted getting cargoes out and in again, hanging about waiting for launches, while every launch in the place was clustered round some monstrous great P Line ship from Hamburg. Britannia Rules the Waves? Huh, not these days, *bois bach!* The Dutchies are beating you hollow, girl! Then the secret he was carrying returned like a dull ache in his heart; how he hated secrets, and how he wished Mair and Nelli were back in Newport and not here, where they'd suffer some of the unpleasantness when the secret did get out. He went down the winding stairs to the saloon sighing deeply.

On deck there was no disturbance to the peace, however. The ship was sailing quietly in the light breeze, her yards braced round hard, every stitch of canvas set and drawing, the whole huge mass of ship and sail leaning gently to starboard. The captain had made his regular after-supper visit to the deck; the mate, who felt the fatigue of his years after a day spent changing sails, had decided that with the wind light and steady and only the vast empty Pacific ahead, it was safe to leave young Raven to keep the watch alone for an hour or so; that young man, brimming with pride, now stood in the sacred place on the weather side of the poop, leaning on the teak rail. His only company was Curly Kellock, the helmsman, who stood some yards away, silent and immobile at the wheel right aft; the gentle wind and his own delicate skill as a helmsman meant that the wheel needed scarcely any movement - just a spoke or two now and then. His strong, lined face was lit eerily from below by the dim, whitish light of the compass bowl. Raven strolled back to stand beside him for a moment and ask, just a trifle self-consciously: 'How's her head, Kellock?'

'Same as ever, sir - south by west, a half west. Close as she'll go, I reckon.'

Raven muttered: 'Very good' in his best laconic mate's voice, and went back to the rail. It was a good moment for him, alone in charge of this great ship, trusted with her welfare for the time being, the sea quiet, a dense blackness all round, save for the semicircle of water tinted red by the port sidelight and an occasional faint gleam of phosphorescence from 'Figaro's' stately progress. Nothing ahead but hundreds of miles of emptiness, probably, but then again there could be some barque out there bound north to the Coast; he couldn't relax altogether. The lookout had to sound a bell every half-hour to show he was awake, but he might snooze off between the bells. It was all up to him now, standing there on the Old Man's own bit of deck. He heard the chart-room door open and close quietly, and felt a twist of irritation; Jake checking him - again? He'd been up only half-an-hour ago. So much for trust!

He was astonished a few seconds later to hear a quick light step behind him and Eleanor's voice close in his ear; her figure filling the dark to his right. His heart leapt with joy and excitement, just tinged with alarm; suppose the Old Man came up now? His first words to her arose from that unease: 'Has your father gone to bed?'

'Yes...Poor Dadi, he's not himself these days.' She smiled to herself in the dark: 'And he's not a man-eater, you know.'

'No, but he might...'

'Don't worry; I'll deal with him if he does come up. Anyway, I'm not interfering with your work, am I? After all, if Mr Evans was here I expect you'd talk to him.'

It was John's turn to smile at the absurdity of the comparison, but he just said: 'There's very little work to do; look how calm it all is.'

'Where are all the men - the watch on deck?'

'Them? Well there's the helmsman back there, and the lookout, right up for'ard, and one of the apprentices - they call him the policeman - handy down there if I should need to yell for him. From what I know from my time on the lower deck, all the rest will be draped about, snoozing in odd corners. We let them do that on a quiet night – they've worked all day, after all.'

238

'I know - I saw. They've spent hours taking off one lot of sails and hoisting others in their place. What on earth for?'

'Oh, that's just economy. In the tropics where it's generally calm, we put up a suit of old scruffy sails, so as to save the wear on the good ones. Well, we'll probably be getting some hard blows soon, so your dad decided it was time to fit the number one suit.'

'I see... There's so much work, and not many to do it, either. It's so different from life on a steamship. People ashore don't realize that, when they see sailing ships go by, looking so calm and peaceful.'

They fell silent and stood, each revelling in the other's presence, each anxious for the spell to continue, each sure that it would not do so for long. Eleanor was still astounded at her own temerity; she had crept out of her cabin into the saloon and waited for her parents' voices to cease, then quietly mounted the steep stair to the chartroom, and thence out on to the poop-deck. Now that she was here, she was lost for something to say: what she really felt in her heart certainly could not be said yet, and small talk about the weather or the food seemed too banal. As usual after a silence, they both started to speak at the same instant and both broke off laughing. 'No, you first,' said John.

'Oh, I was just going to say, I'm worried about my father. He seems so depressed and quiet - not like himself at all. I think my mother knows something, but she won't say what.'

'Yes I'm puzzled too. After all, after that day we went riding, the cargo work went well. We filled the two after holds in two weeks. Everyone else was delighted to be leaving that hole of a place.'

'There's something bothering him, something quite bad, I'm sure.'

'No offence to your father, but captains are often like that - very remote, silent, not mixing much with anybody...Perhaps it's just the job and all the worries they have. I often think, by the way, of that day we went riding.'

'Yes, I do too.' She felt she could not risk saying any more on that topic. A sudden little lurch by the ship (it must have been that) caused her to brush gently against him. 'O, sorry, I haven't really got my sea-legs yet.'

The mere mention of those limbs would have brought a surge of unbidden and unsuitable images to Raven's mind if he had allowed it to, so instead he changed the subject to the commonplace: 'You'll need them soon, in a week or two, when we pick up the strong westerlies in latitude fifty or so. Then she'll pitch and roll like the devil. No more nights like this.'

'Isn't she just beautiful now - alive and moving, with all that horrible dust gone? She's like a living creature.'

Even Raven's blunt, practical, philistine mind could see that beauty tonight, now there was someone he loved to share it and (as it were) display it to him, strip away its commonplaceness: right before their eyes that huge tower was dark against the stars, the sails on the mizzen, a dizzy row, six high, tapering up, up, up, and in the gaps between the strips of sail, the long perspective of canvas on main and fore masts, dimly glimpsed; to their right the sharp-pointed sails of the jigger mast, spanker and topsail. He spoke quietly: 'All plain sail – that's all it says in the log. Doesn't do her justice, does it?'

'She's lovely, lovely; much better than that old liner, where somehow you could always smell coal-smoke and oil. I can see why Dadi's so proud of her, even if she is full of that awful acrid dust. I can see now why even Mr Evans gets poetic about ships sometimes.'

'Ah, he remembers the real clippers, sailing to China and Australia - now they were good lookers, and fast too. Mind you,' he said, with a return to the prosaic, 'all that dust will soon be set as hard as concrete in the moist air.' And he added, for he could not dismiss the subject from his mind: 'How was it, going riding with Senora Gomez? Good fun?'

'I wouldn't say that. It was all right. I only went twice, as you know. She's a wonderful horsewoman - much, much better than I am, but she couldn't speak much English - or Welsh, of course - and I know hardly any Spanish, so I found it a bit slow. She was rather haughty and superior, too.'

'And that revolting gaucho specimen?'

'Absolutely terrified of her, I'm glad to say, so he was no trouble. She had a beautiful little pistol in her saddle holster.'

'Yes, Grant said she would have one of those, only…'

'Only what?'

'He didn't think she'd keep it in a holster.'

He thought (too late) that she might be irritated by the silly male joke; but she merely tutted easily and said 'Men!' then turned to him and said: 'I was really sorry, you know, that...'

'I know. I was too; I can't tell you how sorry, in spite of that clout on the head.' Without any thought on his part, as if it had a will of its own, his hand reached out in the dark and found hers, cool and moist. He squeezed lovingly, and would have drawn her closer, had she not gently extricated her hand and whispered: 'No, John, you must-n't. It's too... The helmsman can see us, and be sure to gossip about it.'

'Not he - not old Curly. He's a good chap, though a bit of an anarchist, so they say. But he's not the kind to gossip.'

But the spell was broken: 'Never mind, you're on duty, and I shouldn't be here, I know. I will come again; we'll talk again one night soon.' Then she was gone, and Raven heard the chartroom door open and close quietly. He was in a tumult of joy and frustration: she must like him quite a bit, or she wouldn't have risked that visit - but what was the use? Perhaps he shouldn't have grabbed her hand like that; perhaps that had scared her off. Jake wouldn't approve of him as a suitor - that was certain; Jake knew too much about his capers ashore, going off like an idiot to knocking-shops just to show what a big grown-up man he was. Those horrible scented whores, all white and soft and plump... Anyway, Jake was in a foul mood about everything these days, so if - or more likely, when - he found out, there'd be a hell of a row. Three bells sounded from for'ard, followed by a sleepy cry of 'Aaall's well!' Raven called back: 'Very good' and tried hard to dismiss captains and their beautiful daughters from his mind.

* * *

Miraculously, in the weeks since leaving port, Isaac Hughes had heeded Kellock's words and kept quiet about their destination. Only Jacob and Mair knew the whole truth, Eleanor and the officers nothing. The captain's morose mood was accepted philosophically by all; as John had told Eleanor, that's what captains were like sometimes. Back at Caleta Buena, Jake had allowed all the usual 'homeward bound' ceremonies popular with the West Coast sailors: the youngest appren-tice, Robbins, had duly ridden up on the last hoist of gunny-sacks, vig-orously waving a Red Dragon flag; as night fell, the crowd had hoisted into the rigging four lights fastened to a frame, to represent the South-ern Cross, and that hoisting had been movingly accompanied by the loud and frantic ringing of the ship's bell, a peal joined across the water by the bells of all the other loading ships in honour of the Homeward Bounder.

The sounds had been echoed cheerfully by the dark cliffs

241

around, and even, remotely, by the mighty peaks behind; clouds of sleepy roosting seabirds had risen squawking and screaming in protest. Jake had sent the steward with the traditional bottle of rum for each foc'sle, and each bottle had been rapidly sunk by men bored and exhausted by months of cargo heaving and delays, tired by a day of working at the heavy moorings, but happy at the thought of a voyage in which every day would bring them nearer home.

Next morning, Raven remembered the day in Powell's barque 'Oberon' when he had been the youngest apprentice - such a while ago, it seemed - grinning, waving, doing a silly and dangerous dance on the sacks as he was ceremonially hoisted and lowered three times. Now he was facing his first voyage as an officer, in charge of men stowing the anchor chain as it came, link by link, off the huge windlass, the crowd cheerfully bawling the choruses of 'Y mochyn Du', with Jimmy Protheroe shouting, as the chantey ended, 'Come on, boys, them Liverpool whores is on the tow-rope!' All joined in the deceitful joy of casting off the shackles that had bound them for months to a hot, dusty, laborious routine.

The ship too seemed glad: she stopped her endless inert rolling and wallowing; as the first topsails caught the wind and filled with a lazy snap, she swung her bow to seaward and began, very slowly at first, to gather way; then, as sail after sail, each one a long narrow rectangle - dropped or rose steadily up the mast to the chantey 'Reuben Ranzo', she began to move at her proper gait, lifting gracefully to the swells, leaning away from the wind's pressure, the huge steel hull, three hundred feet long and forty wide, coming alive as the foam-flecked sea began to slide past, as the little anchorage and its patient ships receded and faded into the huge bulk of the land, blue-grey in the early dawn. The breeze stiffened as the ship made an offing, and even Jacob's spirits rose as he set course for the Horn, singing out to the helmsman, 'Full and by, my lad, and no shenanigans!' He had put her close-hauled on the port tack, heading south for the Cape; no windjammer could sail close to the wind, so she would sag further and further offshore on that course, but that was as well, because the Chilean coast, for most of its length just a steep-down wall of mountains, had been fatal many times to ships becalmed close in; no wind to move them, no bottom to be reached by an anchor, and the ceaseless, steady urging of the onshore swells - a horrible end. This course also took them out of the contrary push of the Humboldt Current. No captain minded being set a few degrees west, for once the brisk cool westerlies were picked up she would soon run that off.

To Eleanor and John their night meeting had proved to be sweet poison; it had been a sharp spur to greater desire and closeness, but the chances of that closeness were rare indeed, and thus the torment of their young minds and bodies was only increased. Dai Evans had always been dreadfully - almost morbidly - conscientious; now he had the additional motive of needing to prove himself indispensable; in addition, he had the old man's normal distrust of the young. For these reasons he scarcely left the deck.

With characteristic feminine astuteness, Eleanor took to strolling innocently on the lee side of the poop, well clear of the watch-keeping officers, before turning in, so that she could see if John was alone, and also to establish that practice as her unremarkable custom. Half suspicious (for she remembered her own youthful follies and stratagems) her mother said coolly: 'Don't forget that the officers all have an important job to do on deck; they mustn't be distracted. You and I are only passengers aboard this ship.'

Her father grunted agreement: 'And another thing, my girl: it'll soon be too damn cold and wet up there for you, once we get into the westerlies - catch your death, you will.'

Her mother took up that cue eagerly: 'Yes, and you'll only start your chest trouble again - and you've been so well lately.'

Their daughter replied peaceably: 'All right, Mam, all right. I shan't distract anyone, or catch a cold.' She bowed her head over her sewing, grinding her teeth and concealing her fury at this blizzard of nagging. Better, wasn't it, to keep it all quiet, and not have a big row?

Only once in the three weeks of balmy nights did Eleanor again find Raven alone. This time Evans had gone down with a bad cold and taken to his bed. Again Curly Kellock was at the wheel; again she stood close, their bodies swaying with the ship's gentle motion; again they talked quietly about ordinary things - home, family, and school-days. But without doubt, a great change was happening, and barriers between them were going down for ever; for this time, quite naturally and unselfconsciously, they held hands as they talked under the grateful mantle of the dark, the secret touch cementing the bond between them, as well as stirring their longing for leisured, solitary intimacy.

This tide of feeling was bringing to Raven - at last - an ability to give it expression, so that he frequently astonished himself by his eloquence. When she gently removed her moist hand from his and whispered: 'I must be going now...Dadi is very restless at night - I don't know why,' John sighed deeply, and she asked: 'What's the matter, *cariad?'*

'You know what's the matter - don't you feel the same? I love you coming to talk with me, but we're not alone, and I'm not properly free to be properly with you. I mean, I'm in charge up here - I can't neglect that, so I can't really get my mind off it. I know it's not a bit likely, but there could be another ship out ahead there, and some of them save money by sailing without lights in these waters. If our lookout happened to be dozing, she'd be into us and it'd be my fault; these things do happen. And besides, your father could come up at any time. D'you see what I mean - we're never alone. Luckily old Kellock at the wheel is a quiet, decent sort of cove. But it's not like that other time - ashore - when we were really alone in that desert.'

Despite herself, she could not resist a giggle: 'Yes, and when you were half-conscious, bleeding, and bringing up your breakfast. It was so... *romantic.'*

'Come on, you know what I mean, Nelli - afterwards.'

'Yes, I know, John *bach*, but we must be patient...'

'Patient? I could be that, but it's so hopeless. We'll be a good three months at sea getting home, and then your father and mother will whisk you off to Wales. I don't think they like me very much, so I can't see them asking me down to stay. I'll be stuck in Oxford, where it's all so dull, especially in the long vac, that it'll drive me crazy. Then next voyage you probably won't be here... It's hopeless.'

She answered by taking his hand again, squeezing it hard, and laying her head against his shoulder, saying cryptically: 'I didn't mean patient for ever and ever, John. But John, you will have to promise to be very, very good.'

'Good? I don't follow...'

'You'll see, you'll see... And John?'

'Yes?'

'I *think* - I can't be sure because it's all so new - but I think I love you too.'

With one last tender squeeze of his hand she was gone. A bare ten minutes later - Raven whistled at the closeness of the shave - Jake came on deck again to check the course, the wind, and the set of the sails, before descending heavily to his sleepless bed. He and Mair were both anxious, though not about the same things in the same degree: he was finding sleep harder and harder to come by, though, as he told himself often, he'd weathered much worse problems before - hands deserting in benighted tropical ports, a dismasting five hundred miles east of Fremantle, even pirate attacks in the Gulf of Tonkin in the old days. But those crises had been thrust suddenly upon him without warning or choice. This was different: he and Mair, and nobody else - as he thought - shared secret knowledge which would in time affect the whole crew. Soon everyone would have to be told, for every seaman knew what course he was steering - you couldn't hide that. After Cape Horn was rounded they would want to know why they were still sailing east instead of north.

Already he had, in a sense, deceived them by letting them celebrate at Caleta Buena, as if they were homeward bound; he'd done it for the best of reasons, for, if they'd known the truth, all the young hotheads would have deserted en masse, sacrificing nearly six months of pay - a princely sixteen pounds ten. But - he had to be honest with himself - his real reason had been his reluctance to fill up their vacant berths with a motley rabble of waterfront loafers, hoodoos and bums who'd ruin life aboard, not only for him and the officers, but also for the tidy boys, the ones who stayed. He had been justified, he was sure; nevertheless, he had in effect lied, and that was hard for anyone who feared God as he did. Some might despise his silence at Caleta Buena as mere cowardice; shouldn't he at least have confided in his officers? As if this torment of deciding were not enough, he saw before him a dreary wilderness of months of petty snarling, shouting and wrangling, with all the work done grudgingly, not with a chantey but an oath - and none of it was his fault, that was the unfair part of it.

And on top of that, here was Mair fretting the life out of him about Nelli and young Raven. If only he'd left that cub in the half-deck and managed somehow with the two mates and the bosun. Probably all women's silly fancies: Nelli didn't say much to Raven now, and they'd been alone only that once... Still, Mair said Nelli was altered, was hankering after him, and Mair had always had good sense - none better. Anyway, no point in worrying too much. Keep an eye on them, perhaps; it might be all a false alarm. Once they got to South Africa he'd try to get both the women out of the ship and up-country while she was unloading and loading. He'd have to think of someone out there who'd have them to stay for a bit. Perhaps Nelli would meet some decent steady young chaps there who'd take her mind off that scapegrace brass-bounder. Raven couldn't have her, and that was that; she couldn't have him, and that was that too! Being a father and a captain counted for something still, surely?

Mair saw the matter more subtly; she felt convinced that John Raven was dissolute, unreliable and 'foreign', not only because he was English - she knew and liked many English people -but because he (like Grant) carried all the marks of their upper-class caste - that aloof, polite coldness that she so disliked and distrusted. On the other hand, suppose, through sheer physical closeness, Nelli were indeed to fall deeply in love with him? Suppose (less likely, but not impossible) that he were to forget his public school coldness and fall genuinely in love with her? Then what? How much might that change him? Nelli would be no soft, passive plaything, to be trifled with and put down; there was strength enough in her to transform him totally - make him human, responsive, decent, faithful, loving. Could she herself be sure that she ought to try to defeat him? She felt uneasily that Nelli had already fallen far enough to make an enforced parting from Raven a bitter pill to swallow, and one that might make her hate her parents. And he might not, potentially, be such an unsuitable admirer... And all this on top of all poor Jacob's troubles; why ever had she suggested that they should join him on board? Out of the frying-pan, into the fire!

Thus the ship sailed on southwards with four of her souls in varying torments, and with two others - Curly Kellock and Isaac Hughes - who had at least a whiff of one of the troubles. Isaac's remarkable silence about his theories and deductions was due to Curly's shrewd reminder to him that, if some mutiny over the Cape Town destination started at Caleta Buena, the captain would know beyond all possible doubt who had betrayed him; that had been enough to put the wind up the steward. As for Curly, though he was, ideologically speaking, a convinced revolutionary and hater of the whole system that employed him and his class, he was by nature an excellent seaman, mild, sane, steady, and loyal to any individual officer whom he respected, though, as Grant had found, a firm upholder of his and other seamen's rights and dignity. Like all sensible idealists, he was also a bachelor, so that the length of any voyage did not trouble him; no wilting female or troop of little ones looked for his return. Accidentally, through his presence at the wheel on two occasions, he knew also of the growing bond between Raven and Eleanor, but he had said nothing to anyone of this either. As a passionate reader and thinker in the abstract, he scorned petty tittle-tattle about other people's private lives; as a lover of harmony, he would not be the one to reveal something that might disturb it, even though he had little time for Raven, seeing him as merely the henchman of the bullying Grant.

And so the secrets stayed under hatches as the ship slid through the quiet empty seas towards the Horn. Then there came a day when the steady south-east trade at last faltered and died away, leaving 'Figaro' wallowing in a long swell under a grey sky. Frequent heavy rain-showers and an occasional breath of cool air showed that they had moved to another climate. There was no sign of the ladies on deck, as the mates had given the crowd permission to take time off for *dhobeying* - washing clothes in the plentiful fresh water, and, by long foc'sle tradition, this washing was done in a state of entire nakedness, so that body and apparel could be cleaned and rinsed at the same time. Jacob's discreet hint had raised something of a blush on Nelli's cheeks, and she and her mother had spent a tactful morning below.

Jacob spent the forenoon striding about on the poop, scanning the sky to the west and stopping to peer into the hood of the binnacle at the compass card, once growling at Jimmy Protheroe at the wheel: 'Good God, look at her head, mun! Pointing due east! Can't you...?'

For answer, the man took his hands clean off the wheel and gestured helplessly: 'Wheel's hard-a-port, sir. She won't answer. No way on her, not for the last hour or more.'

Jake glared, rather unjustly, at him, growled again, and strode back to the poop rail. Then, as he grasped the thick teak, he felt a cool draught on his neck; turning, he saw a lowering black cloud dead astern. This was it - a westerly squall coming up, with quite a dose of wind in it too; and the sails were all braced the wrong way, so that the wind might catch them aback - on the wrong side - and do all kinds of damage aloft. Not a moment to lose! Grant was at his shoulder, expecting the next order: 'It's going to blow, mister. Square away, and look lively too!'

The second mate's whistle shrilled, calling the watch of seamen and apprentices from their various tasks about the deck, and Grant himself clattered down to the main deck to lead them rapidly from one mast to another, hauling on the braces to swing each tower of sails round till they were square across the ship. Jacob looked astern again and saw, as he expected, a hard dark line across the western horizon. He went to stand beside the helmsman: 'Here it comes, my lad, and it'll be heavy. Helm amidships; keep her going due east before it till I say, and if you let her broach I'll...' He left the mild threat unfinished and hurried for'ard again to bark to the waiting second: 'In with your royals, mister.'

'Aye, aye, sir. Let go royal sheets! Heave up clewlines and buntlines! Apprentices: aloft and furl them, and get your fingers out, boys!' Soon the three topmost square sails were mere rumpling bags of wind, their bottom corners triced up while, a hundred and eighty feet above the deck, the brassbounders edged out along the yards, their feet on a wire, their chests on the spar, leaning out and down to gather folds of canvas into a tidy roll and bind them securely with the gaskets. 'Hurry up, boys,' called Perkins breathlessly. 'It's going to blow like a bastard in a minute. Old Jake left it a bit late.'

Sure enough, the last boy had barely landed back on deck before, with a kind of swooping roar, the squall hit the ship; the first hard gust filled every sail, snapping acres of limp canvas into clean curves, the chain sheets tightening with a jingle, the huge network of wires groaning at the sudden savage strain. The ship, like a horse rudely spurred, first staggered and faltered, rolled ponderously to port, brought herself back, and gathered speed, the wake whitening, her bow trampling the swells in a white smother of foam, which went swishing and swirling down her sides and spreading on either beam. A yachtsman would have called it a gale, but it was the weather 'Figaro' was designed for - a stiff wind abaft the beam - and she revelled in it. As the cloud overhauled them, there was a glimpse of watery sun, which strengthened as the cloud thinned.

'Bendigedig!' Jacob muttered, and thought: At least the Almighty hasn't let me down about the wind. With any luck we might carry this westerly all the way to South Africa - have a quick passage. But then what? He peered at the compass-bowl again and called to Grant: 'We'll put her on course, mister. Port braces haul!' and to the helmsman: 'Down helm, my lad, but easy does it. Bring her round to due south.' Much happier now that she was running hard, he fetched his sextant from the chart-room; time for a noon sight. Raven appeared, also holding a sextant, and Jacob said, quite affably: 'Come on then, young man, let's see what sort of a sight you can get today. Horizon's nice and clear, but you'll be to be quick, with the sun so patchy. Let's see how far we've got to run to the Horn.'

* * *

When John Raven came off watch the following midnight, he found the ship below decks transformed from the quiet place it had been in the Trades; ever since they left Caleta Buena, the sound of the sea below had been the merest whisper along the steel plates; the ship herself had made now and then only the faintest of groans, as a gust heeled her or a big swell lifted her huge bulk. One could hear easily the ticking of a clock, doors opening, a cough from another cabin, the clink of a spoon as Isaac Hughes stirred sugar and condensed milk into his late night tea. But now, with the westerly blowing half a gale, the ship was joyful, in her element, giving out loud creaks and groans as she constantly dipped, pitched and rolled, the steering-gear grinding as the rudder was moved, the water roaring, slopping and crunching on her sides as it raced past. To a sailor, the sounds were normal and grateful to his ear, a genial hubbub that masked all the little human sounds of the night.

John had parted from the mate on deck with a laconic: 'Goodnight, mister,' and had enjoyed the welcoming snugness of his little cabin after the cold and windy poop-deck; now he decided it was safe to get into his pyjamas - the wind was steady and there wasn't likely to be any crisis demanding all hands during his watch below. Let old Grant and those starboard watch beggars deal with it all now, he thought, stretching luxuriously as he undressed. Sleeping in your clothes was not really sleeping, after all. It had been a long day, what with the watches on top of the work on deck, and he was soon drifting off, his mind approaching the line between connected thought and dream. His thoughts were of Eleanor, last seen briefly at a dreary cabin supper of bully beef hashed with fierce Chilean onions, for already their meagre supplies of shore food were running out; soon they would be back to tinned and salted meat, biscuit and dried peas. As sleep began to overwhelm him, he tried to dismiss thoughts of the girl from his mind; what was the use of torturing himself with her delicious image? Now the decent weather was over, even the fleeting moments of her company on watch would probably cease. Anyway, old Dai Evans was over his cold now, and was always sculling about, in and out of the chart-room. No point in thinking useless thoughts that just kept you randy and awake when you needed sleep... The new fore upper t'gal-

249

lant had got to be swayed aloft tomorrow. That'd keep him and the hands pretty busy for a –

He jolted suddenly awake, for, over the ship's noise, his ear caught a little odd sound - the click of the latch of his own door; the door opened slowly, admitting a long slot of dim light from the small oil lamp in the passage, a slot which widened and was then filled by a figure which entered silently and quickly, and closed the door. He had time to think angrily: What the hell does Grant want, sending someone to bother me already? And why didn't the idiot knock and wait? Then, as he opened his mouth to growl a protest, he felt a hand - a long-fingered, smooth hand - placed on his lips, and a familiar voice whispered: 'Ssh, John! Don't make a row – it's me.'

'Eleanor! What in the *world*...?'

'It's all right! Nothing's the matter. Don't you want me here?'

'Want? Of course I do... but I didn't expect...'

'I never see you these days... I'm sick of being cooped up like a prisoner.'

'But you - here - in my... in the middle of the night! My God, your father... if he finds out...'

'He won't find out - but if you're worried I'll go, of course, and quite understand.'

There was an unmistakeable edge in her voice; she was testing his nerve, and perhaps the strength of his love. Right enough, there'd be the most unholy row, but still...

'No, please do stay, darling.' He sat up in his bunk, found her two arms in the dark, and held them. 'You know I want you so much.' The threat of Jake's wrath had become remote. He released her arms to embrace her, and gave a little gasp to find only the thinnest of silky wraps between her warm body and his hands. He felt her give a small shudder, and asked, whispering close in her ear: 'Are you cold? Would you like to...?'

She giggled and withdrew just a little: 'No, I'm not cold – it's just so nice to feel you holding me, it makes me shiver. As for "Would you like to...?" – if it's what I think you're suggesting, certainly *not!* I want to be with you, but not in your... not like that.' In truth, the warmth of his body and bed was an almost fatal lure, but she struggled to remain sensible. 'Anyway, you must be dreadfully tired, so I mustn't stay long... I've just come to talk, that's all.'

'Of course, dear,' said Raven calmly and reasonably; then in a trice, with the treachery of a lover, he swung himself out of bed to stand inches away from her, drew her firmly back to him and kissed her for the first time – after all those weeks of hunger.

It was a kiss they had both enjoyed in fantasy many times; it was a chaste kiss, of closed lips only, but a long-lasting one, and as Byron observed:

A kiss's strength,
I think it must be measured by its length...

It was also a transfiguring experience for both of them: For Nelli because no gauche suitor at home had held her and kissed her with that strength and passion (and with so few clothes between them, too; Heavens what a difference that made! - his body was so hard!), and for John because, in his few sordid sexual exploits ashore, a kiss had been merely the briefest of necessary preliminaries to a hasty commercial coupling with a woman who had no time to waste if she was to make a living. Now both found this long, gentle contact of mouths, the long swoon of sensual pleasure, the head-to-toe contact of their bodies – all this was a new region of existence, a region full of the most perilous glamour and underlying fears: in Nelli, not only the basic filial fear of being found out, shamed and punished by her parents, but the fear, arising from her strong belief in God, that she was putting her immortal soul in jeopardy, was drifting towards spiritual rocks labelled with the dread and horrible word 'Fornication'. But, for the moment, the urgent demand of her youth was uppermost, and the Ebeneser pulpit a long way off.

From (as it were) a great distance, she heard John give a small moan of pleasure, and slowly realised that one of his hands had strayed disgracefully far down her back till it now cupped and caressed the round of her left buttock, producing in her own body the most delicious melting. Dear God, this wouldn't do, wasn't at all what she'd intended to happen. What on earth had possessed her to take this mad step in the dark? She pushed him firmly away and drew her mouth from his: 'No, John – please. You mustn't be too... You must be good, or I shall have to go. Let's both sit down and just talk - be together nicely without getting too... you know...' Wrenched back from the hectic glissade into bodily abandonment, they sat chastely side by side on his bunk, as on a public park bench, and allowed the riot in their blood to subside.

'There,' she said insincerely, 'that's better, isn't it? To calm down...'

'Oh yes,' he said, even more speciously. 'I was just so - you gave me such a surprise.'

'I've surprised myself too. But don't tell me you've never thought of coming to my cabin? It's so close, after all - only Isaac Hughes and his pantry between us.'

'I've thought of it every night, of course, but...'

'But you didn't dare risk it?'

'No, to be honest, I didn't. Besides, I thought you might be - you know – outraged, and all that.'

'Outraged? What a donkey you are, John Raven! Haven't I shown you plainly enough how I feel? You see, we just don't know each other yet - how could we? That's why I'm here, so that we can.'

'You're wonderful...' He turned and reached in the dark to embrace her again, but she drew away and pushed his arms aside.

'No! You're going to be good - remember? I haven't come here to be your... your... paramour.'

'What a funny word for it... Sounds like something from an old book.'

'Does it? Well, don't laugh, and don't forget, I'm speaking a foreign language now - you do forget that, you English.'

'Foreign?'

'Of course. Welsh is my native tongue. In the family we use it all the time. I really only started with English when I went to an English-speaking school. I had a bad time there at first because my English was so awful.'

'A bad time! What else does anyone ever get in school? Frightful places, I reckon. I was a real dunce at languages and Latin, and all that stuff. Had a job learning enough mathematics to get me into Conway... What are you giggling about now?'

'It seems so funny: we're alone for the first time as - you know - real friends - all right then, as lovers - and here we are, talking about school, of all things!'

'School's a good subject to kill off wicked thoughts - and I can tell you I've got plenty of those.'

'So have I, John, but, seriously now, we've got to control them or we can't meet like this again. I mean, I know I shouldn't be here really; my parents will be furious with me - and with you too, I dare say, if they find out.'

'It was ever so brave of you to chance it. Next time, I'll come to you...'

'You will not, you idiot, not ever! Don't you see why? If Dadi caught you in my cabin, he would say you were attacking me, or at least seducing me, against my will. If they find me here, it's clear that we both want to be together - or that I'm seducing you. I suppose I am, really! Besides, Dadi can give you the sack, or at least de-...de-... What's the word?'

'Demote me.'

'Yes. Well, he can't demote me, because I'm nothing official anyway - only his daughter. It would hurt him, though, and I don't want that... Life is so difficult, isn't it?'

Raven agreed, and they clung together for a while in a comradely, unsensual way. Then he whispered: 'What made you come tonight, and not before?'

'That's easy, you silly. It was too quiet before. I was afraid of waking up that creepy Isaac. Now the sea and the ship are so noisy you can't hear people moving. Besides, he does have a long day, fair play to him, so I expect he sleeps sound. I've left my oil-lamp on, turned down very low, so as to get back into my cabin without crashing into anything and waking him up.'

'But you've got to come through the saloon to get here...'

She sounded practical: 'Well, if Mam or Dadi found me there, I'd say I was on my way to the bathroom. I know it's not romantic, like Romeo and Juliet, but I do have to go there now and then, you know.'

They both laughed very quietly, and, as in the desert, amusement turned to the fiercest sting of desire. This time, the strength of his kiss bore her back and down to lie on his bed, and between kisses she felt both joy and alarm to hear him whisper hoarsely: 'My God, I do love you, Nelli darling.' It was some time before she was able to subdue his passion and her own enough to lift the latch of his door and creep back to her own cold neglected bed, still a virgin, but shaken and dazed by the force of his and her own feelings, and with parts of her body that no man had touched before still tingling from his rough exploring hands.

15

A week later, one forenoon, all the crowd – foc'sle hands, idlers and brassbounders, together with the officers - stood in a semicircle on the sacred planks of the poop-deck, waiting for their captain. They had been brusquely summoned there by Grant, who had the watch, for it was too wet and dangerous for them to assemble in their usual place, below the break of the poop. Instead of sermonizing from above, the captain would have to face them on the level, man to man; what on earth he could have to tell them that required this solemnity was beyond their conjecture, and they muttered their curiosity to each other as they stood there, swaying together with the ship's motion.

Jacob Roberts came out of the chart-room, his face looking as impassive, as granite-like as ever, but his stomach churning with a nervousness he had not felt for years. He cleared his throat and began: 'Well, men, I've mustered you here because I've got to tell you news that you won't like much - no good pretending you will. I didn't when I heard it. I won't beat about the bush: my orders from the company's agent in Caleta Buena are to take this cargo for discharge in Port Elizabeth, near Cape Town.' There was a gasp of surprise from the men, which swiftly turned into a rising growl of discontent and anger; there was also a quick look and mutual nod between Curly Kellock and Isaac Hughes, the latter smirking his smug triumph. Then Jacob held up his hand for silence and went on: 'All right, all right, that'll do. I told you you wouldn't like it - but there's no help for it, and no point in grumbling and whining like a lot of half-baked *crwts;* when you joined this ship, you put yourselves under my orders for a voyage lasting two years at most - if you don't believe me you can see the Crew Agreement that you signed. And remember, I signed it too, so I'm just as much under orders as you are - so are all the officers. All right, we're all fed up, but we just have to take the disappointment like grown men. And look at it this way: back home, jobs and berths are scarce; there's good men hanging round the shipping offices all over the place. This means your job aboard this ship lasts a few months longer, and you know what they say: "Another day, another dollar; the more days, the more dollars." There'll be a decent payday for us all at the end of it... Yes, what is it, Protheroe?' He tried to curb his irritation (he might have known this bloody scrimshanker would be the first to start belly-aching!) and he sought to bring in a light touch. 'You've got your hand up like a little dab in school who's dying for a piddle.'

Nobody laughed or even smiled, and Jimmy Protheroe, brimming with importance as the self-appointed sea-lawyer of the crowd, said: 'You say "a few months longer", capten, but how *many* months? Where do we go after the Cape? Will we have to go back to the West Coast for another nitrate cargo to take home?'

'You weren't born yesterday, mun. You know that I have no idea what the next charter will...'

'Because, look here, capten: they won't send us back out to Chile empty if they can help it, so that'll mean loading another cargo in between, never mind getting another lot of nitrate. They might send us all the way across to Newcastle, New South Wales for a load of coal. Just think how long all that's going to take! The bloody colliers down there are on strike half the time, to start with.' He looked round among his mates for support, and got another mutinous growl out of them which was music to his ears.

Jacob felt an urgent desire to thrust in through the crowd, grab Jimmy's jacket, and hammer his face to pulp, but he strove instead to be diplomatic: 'Listen - like I said before, men, there's nothing in the world I can do about it. We're all under other people's orders. Grow up – isn't it? - and make the best of it. I'll do my best to make things as good as I can for you all. South Africa's not a bad place for a run ashore - not too hot. It'll be near the end of their winter by now. I'll allow all the shore leave I can, and after all (he tried again to lighten their mood), the girls there have got all the same things in the same places as the girls in Liverpool or Cardiff, and if some of the girls are black, well, you know what they say – they're all pink inside.' This time a few men laughed a little, and this encouraged him to go on: 'As well as leave, I'm willing to give advances of pay, and a discharge by consent to any man who thinks he can do better for himself on another ship. What more can I do than that? Now let's all get on with running this ship without a lot of grousing; this has been a happy ship so far, I think, and I appreciate the way you've worked for weeks on end discharging and loading, and since then, changing sails and getting her round the Horn; the steward will be bringing a bottle of rum to each foc'sle at noon to show that appreciation to all of you.' With a sudden flash of inspiration he added: 'Except for you young varmints in the half-deck; I'll see if I can find some mammy's milk for you lot.' The jibe brought a real roar of approval and amusement from the crowd, who, like Isaac, had little time for the brassbounders. The tension relaxed, he was able to end the meeting casually on the right note, nodding to Grant: 'Port watch to dinner if you please, mister, starboard watch return to duties.'

The brief laugh had died, the hands dispersed in silence, and there was no cheer for the gift of the rum; heads down, the men talked in small groups as they trudged for'ard along the raised walkway, clear of the solid water that swilled across the decks.

Watching them go, Jacob's eye was caught by the neat little gig resting on her raised skids above the sliding foam; there was a sudden vision in his mind of warm sun, a white boat, white sails, a blue sea and sky, happy faces, Mair's slender hand on the tiller, and not one worry in the world. What a day that had been - and only a few weeks ago! Now, though it was full daylight, the sky was almost black with cloud, the ship racing at top speed, the course due east, the wind a full gale from the north-west, on her port quarter - her best point of sailing. She was making a good twelve or thirteen knots under lower tops'ls and foresail only, slowly rolling as huge seas built up astern, each wave perhaps half a mile long and fifty feet high, with a curling top of cold white foam. Indeed, the waves were so high that, when in the deep trough between them, the ship sometimes lost the wind altogether and slackened her speed, gathering it again with a jar as the next huge comber lifted her bodily and, for a while, carried her along, surfing on its crest. It had been several days since Jacob had had a decent sight of the sun, but by dead reckoning, Diego Ramirez, the bleak island near the Horn, was abeam fifty miles off to port, while to starboard lay only mile after mile of wild sea and maybe ice.

The weather made normal work on deck or aloft far too dangerous, so all hands were gathered under the foc'sle head or in the sail locker, repairing sails or making new gear for them - rovings to fasten them to the yards and gaskets to furl them. The job gave a chance, usually for yarning and gossiping, now for growling and grumbling. Billy John Ffynnongroes was naturally not the last to sound off: 'What gets me, boys, is the way them bloody owners treat us, and the way that old bastard down aft helps them to do it.'

'How d'you mean, "helps them"?' said Tommy Lewis, a quiet

Milford Haven man. 'He've got to do what they says too, mun.'

'Don't you believe it, boy. He could pull strings if he wanted to, I'll bet, only he wants to crawl to them. Anyway, he could have been honest with us - he could have told us, as soon as he knew. I bet he knew long before we left Calaty Bono.'

'He didn't want all this shenanigans in port, with you and half the buggers slinging their hooks ashore. Can't blame him, really.'

'Well, I blame him, mun.'

'So do I,' put in Jimmy Protheroe. 'It's all right for him, living in his bloody palace back aft there, not like us in our rat-hole for'ard. He's as well off as if he was ashore – he's even got his missis there, if he should fancy a spot of jig-a-jig. It ain't bloody fair.'

'Aye,' said Billy, 'and that precious new English bucko had better not start his capers again, or I'll lay the bastard flat. I won't make no mistake this time; I ain't forgotten that I owe him one, the swine.'

'Me, I'm clearing out at the Cape,' said Jimmy. 'I'm not staying to be cheated like this.'

Lewis shook his head slowly: 'Cutting off yer nose to spite yer face – that's what you're doing. You're as well off here as you'll ever be, all the while you're just a sailor. What captain ever gives a bugger what the crew thinks? Clear out in Cape Town, and you'll just finish up shovelling coal and sweating your guts out in some steam-kettle, more of a bloody slave than ever. They works the arses off the firemen in them steam-kettles.'

In the quiet sail-locker, with a suitably disaffected audience, Curly was finding fertile ground for his more philosophical approach: 'Y'see, mates, this kind of thing is always happening, because the people what own the ships and the mines and the factories - the capitalists and their parasites, the middle-class shareholders – don't give a fish's tit for the working men what toil in them – don't care sometimes whether they live or die. Mind you, it'll all change one day, even if the streets have to run with blood first. There'll come a time - you mark my words - when the people themselves, rich and poor, will be the masters, and own everything - ships, cargoes, the damn lot. All right, there'll still have to be captins, but they'll be employed by the people, by working folk like ourselves, and they won't dare swing their fists and their boots the way some of them do nowadays. Nor yet pay us in pennies and feed us all on garbage, neither.'

Jac-y-Bont, the old sailmaker, gave a smile of kindly scepticism: 'There you go again, Curly boy - castles in the air. Things have always been the same, all my life: there's rich and poor; the rich own the whole bloody lot, and the poor have got to work for them or starve. If you're a sailor before the mast, you do both - you work *and* starve.'

Young Perkins got a laugh from all of them by bursting into song:

> *'Hit's the sime the ole world over,*
> *Hit's the poor what gits the blime,*
> *While the rich man gits the pleasure –*
> *Hain't it all a bleedin' shime?'*

'All right,' said Curly stoically, for he was used to mockery. 'You keep on laughing like that, an' things'll just stay as they are; you'll always be grubbing in the dirt whilst idlers live like lords on their dividends. I dare say young Perkins' dad's got a few of those. But I ain't talking about castles in the air, Jac: we may slog on in the same old way in England – and Wales, of course - but what I'm talking about is starting to happen in other places, especially Russia. Once it's happened there, you'll see it spread, first to Germany, then France, then us. Might not be in my time, but you - young smart-arse Perkins - you'll see it happen. Nothing can stop it, in the long run.'

Nor was the conversation aft less controversial, though it was much less intellectual; when the captain had finished speaking and gone below again, grimly silent, the two senior mates exchanged meaning glances, and Grant said: 'Did you know about this?'

The first mate obviously resented the question, and replied stiffly: 'No, I had no notion of it. What the devil makes you think I had?'

'No reason, mister, but I thought perhaps....'

'You thought perhaps because you're English and a newcomer, we'd talked behind your back, and left you out - is that it?'

'That possibility had occurred to me, yes.'

'H'm. Don't you think, Mr Grant, that maybe we'll have enough trouble with the crowd, without you making up imaginary grudges like that? Don't be so petty, mun!'

'Very well, mister, very well. I apologize, and I assure you I don't need a sermon. As for the crowd, we'll need to be alert for the first sign of trouble, and then jump on it good and hard. Don't you agree, Raven?'

258

John started and coloured, for he hadn't expected to be consulted, but Evans cut in sharply before he could speak: 'Mr Raven is my assistant in my watch, and I will give him all the guidance he needs on discipline. In my judgement, a lot of boots and fists will just make matters far worse. They're not a bad bunch, and they've just had a bad disappointment. Give them time to settle down and accept it.'

'Indeed? Well, in *my* judgement, the minute you start turning a blind eye and going soft, some of the bastards will take advantage of it, and before you know where you are the whole lot'll be out of control. I've seen it happen.'

'Not in this ship you haven't, mister. They're not Yankee hoodlums or Liverpool packet-rats, they're...'

'They're foc'sle hands, who have got to be made to do what they're told, mister. And I may say that I object strongly to this conversation. I have to take orders from my captain, but not from anybody else that I know of. I'm going below for my dinner.'

As he left, Evans looked sternly at Raven and said, exploding into wrath: 'So much for your damned English friend, mister. Bloody jackanapes! He'll bring trouble on all of us – you'll see.'

*　　*　　*

The ship swooped and staggered on her way, running down her easting to the next cape, passing the Horn without ever seeing a sign of it. With such good progress, the hearts of the more sensible hands began to rise; at least she was making short work of getting to South Africa. After that - who knew? It was still possible (they thought) that she might be chartered home from there. However, those who wanted trouble had no difficulty in finding it: the two starboard watch malcontents, Billy John and Jimmy Protheroe, obeyed Grant, for they had, despite their brave words, a healthy respect for his iron will and fists, but they got their kind of petty satisfaction from doing every task, obeying every order, slowly and grudgingly, sailing as close as they dared to the wind of his displeasure. He in turn became harsher and more impatient with the whole watch, hazing them bitterly at the slightest hitch. Yet when real trouble came, it came to Raven, not to him.

One afternoon, feeling that the wind had dropped a little, Grant, who had the watch, had decided to set the three upper topsails, and had called the port watch from their tasks on deck to help. When the sails had been set, Raven, in charge of the mizzen, had noticed that one of the buntlines - the ropes used to gather in the sail when furling - was stretched tight across the belly of the sail, and would chafe it. Without too much thought, he called to the nearest person: 'Robbins - aloft and overhaul that buntline.'

Robbins, the youngest and greenest of the brassbounders, looked aloft without relish; overhauling buntlines was a commonplace job in fair weather - but now? However, future officers are not expected to question orders, so up he went and out on the yard, right out until he was leaning on the spar there, away out over the racing white foam every time she rolled to leeward. He had finished the job, and was about to edge his way back in to the mast, when suddenly the taut sails below him gave a thunderous flap, shaking the yard, the mast, shaking Robbins' whole aerial world with a deadly, sickening force, as if a malicious giant were trying to whip him into eternity. Seized by black fear, the boy had but one instinct - to hang on. He grasped the iron jackstay that ran along the top of the yard with a white-knuckled grip that he would not, could not, release. The horror of falling eighty feet down had soldered him to the shuddering yard.

Had he fallen, his killer would have been the man at the helm, Tydfil Jones from Swansea. Grant had ordered the second helmsman to help with setting the sails, and Jones, an insignificant fellow at the best of times, was not equal to the lone struggle with the jarring, wrenching wheel. Before anyone could help him, he had let the ship start to broach - to swing her head round towards the wind, spilling the wind out of the sails, and causing 'Figaro' to lie right over to port till her decks were a hill and her rail was buried. Raven, clutching the fife-rail to keep himself from sliding down, had the presence of mind to scream aloft: 'Robbins! Hang on, for Christ's sake!' In his terror, the boy had not heard - had not needed to hear - his order; he had got the shakes, and it would need more than an order to shift him now.

Down on the poop both Grant and the captain, feeling the stern's horrible yaw away from the wind, raced to the wheel, and, in sweating panic, hauled the spokes painfully over. 'Come up, come up, God damn you!' Grant sobbed, his chest heaving with his effort. With infinite slowness, as if teasing them, she responded to the rudder, and the stern swung back up into the wind, bringing the seas under her counter again, and the masts back upright. Still grasping the wheel, Jacob said in a low growl, 'Get that second man back on the wheel, you bloody fool mister, and keep him there until I say.'

But their troubles were not over; John Raven looked up from his post at the foot of the mizen, saw poor Robbins still spread across the yard, clinging to the iron jackstay, and also panicked: Christ, he should never have sent the greenest hand aboard up alone in this weather! Now someone would have to go and get him down. Again without thinking, he called abruptly to one of the nearest men coiling ropes at the fife-rail: 'You! Belay that; aloft and get him down!'

Billy John - for it was he – wasn't in the least afraid of the task set; if Jimmy Protheroe had been stuck up there he'd have gone up without an order, but coming from this pup, the order was too much, on top of all the hazing from Grant; besides, he hated Raven for his part in the humiliating *treepas* affair. He went on stolidly coiling the rope, merely snarling over his shoulder: 'Sod you, brassbounder. Go up your fuckin' self!'

Driven now by fury as well as panic, Raven grabbed his arm and hauled him away and round; Billy replied with a wild swinging blow to Raven's cheek, and was following it with a more deliberate right; but he didn't know that Raven had been the best heavyweight in Conway, and he was about to find out. With instinctive skill, Raven ducked under the second blow, and in the next instant landed a terrific right, with all his weight behind it, on Billy's chin - a blow that sent him flying back to crash his head against the mast. Down he went, and lay very still, so still that Raven was half impelled to go to him and check that he was not seriously hurt; but instead he made a dash for the port shrouds, the bottom of the ladder to the upper yards. However, he was too late there: his old rival Perkins was already climbing fast, and called down, forgetting all ideas of hierarchy: 'All right, you bastard, Raven: I'll get the poor little sod.'

For a second or two, Raven stood vacillating; then he decided: Perkins was as strong and competent as he was - he should be able to manage. So he turned to where two seamen were bending over the horizontal form of Billy John, and said curtly: 'You two - take him for'ard and see to him. When you've done that, you - Lewis - get up there and check that he's stopped that buntline properly.'

Perkins, laid across the dizzy upper topsail yard, a good ninety feet up, put an arm round the taut shoulders of young Robbins and said: 'Come on, young Robbie, you're all right now. It's too damn draughty to hang around up here. Let's go down, eh? That bloody swine should never have sent you up here on your own. Let's show him he can't scare you.'

Poor Robbins was weeping, and said through his sobs: 'It wasn't so much Raven; it was the whole lot shaking like that - all of a sudden. Christ, Perky, I thought I was going in the drink then. Now you're here, I'll be all right - but God, I was frightened!'

'Sure you were, old son. I'd have shat myself. But I tell you what: before we go down, we'll climb up a bit further - to the lower t'gallant yard - just to get your nerve back and show that rat down there what you're made of.' If the remarks on Raven were harsh, Perkins' advice to Robbins was sound; he mustn't let a fright like that beat him, or he'd never go aloft again, and that would mean he was finished as a sailor.

In his more judicious way, the captain was equally harsh to Raven; once the emergency was over, he ordered him to the chart-room and faced him grimly: 'Well, young man, you've done well today so far, haven't you? One seaman concussed and off duties for two days at least, and one apprentice within a whisker of being killed. D'you begin to realize what it would have been like for you - and me, never mind him - if that poor little dab had fallen from that yard? He'd have smashed all his brains out on the deck or landed in the water. And you know that, running in this kind of weather, I wouldn't have had the slightest chance of saving him - not a hope in hell. I couldn't even have tried without endangering all the rest of us. I'd have had to leave him there in the wake. Good God, man, if something was wrong aloft, what in the world made you send *him* - the least suitable of all those on deck? And why, in God's name, when you saw that he'd frozen, didn't you instantly go up yourself, instead of picking a quarrel with the daftest, most undisciplined oaf in either foc'sle? Good judgement, Mr Raven, good judgement and common sense are two of the most important qualities for an officer to possess; I don't consider you've shown either of them today, and because of that one of my ship's company very nearly died.'

'I don't wish to make excuses, sir, but it all happened so quickly.'

'It always does, mister, so you have to be quick too.'

'And I didn't send John because I was scared to go myself. I didn't even see which man it was that I was sending... He was grossly insolent to me, and he took a swing at me with no warning at all.'

'He was indeed, grossly insolent to you, and I assure you I

have no time whatever for that stupid *crwt*. I shall fine him heavily, and if he doesn't learn from that I'll disrate him down to ordinary seaman. And of course you had a right to defend yourself, though I may say that you didn't have to knock him into the middle of next week. But you, young man, must learn from this experience too. There's more to being an officer than the stuff they fill your heads with in college. That insolence could and should have been punished later; the important thing was to get that boy down out of danger.'

'Yes, sir. I'm sorry, and I do understand.'

'I sincerely hope you do, for your own sake. Mind, I also accept that you didn't send John because of fear for your own skin. If I thought that I'd put you back in the half-deck this minute. Very well - back on deck with you, and ask Mr Grant to step in here, please.'

When Grant and Raven talked things over later, Grant was reassuring: 'Don't worry any more about it, old son. You'll get plenty of worse bollockings than that in this job. I had one too, if that's any comfort to you, for setting the upper tops'ls too soon, and for taking the extra man off the wheel for a bit. He thinks that's why she nearly broached.'

'D'you think he's right?'

'No I do not; it was the sheer incompetence of that half-wit Jones fellow at the wheel. But I didn't argue, and I hope you didn't either. Look at it this way, old boy: it's done you no harm in the foc'sle. The way you laid out mister bloody nuisance John -wham, bam! - was sheer poetry. I'm only sorry I was so busy at the wheel that I missed seeing it. Jesus! That right hook of yours – I'm jealous!'

'Just a lucky punch - no science about it.'

'Too modest, old boy. Good instinct that was... and good to give it to him on the jaw too; if you'd hit him in the bread-basket his oilskin would have muffled the blow too much - you wouldn't have doubled him up so nicely. As it was, the mizen did you a good turn by laying him out cold. Well done you! You won't find any of them too anxious to start anything with you now. Won't fancy their chances much.'

Raven gave a feeble smile and turned away; he was suffering (as Grant had shrewdly guessed) from the horrors, from a hideously vivid picture of what might have been: a cry from aloft, a small oil-skinned body falling, bouncing off spars and stays to land with a sick thud on the steel deck, or maybe over the side, to become a small black spot in the seething wake, rapidly receding astern and circled by wheeling sea-birds, then disappearing in the huge dreary waste of waters.

Eleanor heard about the affair from her father, and, seeing John's stricken, haunted face at cabin supper, was longing with all her soul to put her arms round him, to take his head on her breast and give him comfort. To sit and eat, to (apparently) ignore his misery, was torture to her. Even Mair was concerned at his drawn face and his silence, but thought it better not to seem to interfere with her husband's discipline. Nor did Eleanor have the chance of another secret cabin meeting with John, for he was on the middle watch - midnight till four - and her parents were up and about and talking until midnight, her father especially more restless than usual. Besides, since her first night visit she had been increasingly worried about the risks she had taken that night, both with her parents and with her own headlong passion - or perhaps, she thought piously, she ought to call it by its proper name: lust. So she had ventured out again at night only twice, though often sorely tempted by the burnt-in memory of those deep-tongued kisses, those hands that had roved all over her body. 'Lead us,' she tried to say to herself, 'not into temptation, but deliver us from evil'. And anyway, as a shrewd flesh-and-blood woman, she did not want to make herself seem a cheap and easy conquest, nor want him to feel that she was pursuing him - throwing herself at his head, as people in Newport used to say when talking of bad girls.

As for the other protagonist, Billy John, there was no chance of feminine comfort for him, but some sympathy from his mate, Jimmy: 'I tell you what, Billy: it's these new young English swine are the trouble - especially that bloody second.'

'You're right, Jim,' said Billy, chewing at his stringy portion of salt beef, and wincing at the pain in his jaw. 'It's just them. If the Old Man had sent me up - or old Dai - I'd have gone like a shot. I wasn't scared, and I don't want no boy landing in the drink. It was just that Raven's way of speaking - like as if I was a lump of shit. An' after all, he was the one who sent the poor little bugger up there.'

'What did the Old Man have to say?' asked Tommy Lewis.

'Not much. Give me a lecture and fined me twenty-five bob, the old bastard. Says he'll put me down to OD if I'm a naughty boy again. Bloody officers! - they stick together, English or Welsh.'

Lewis tried to apply a little mature reason to all this emotion, speaking gently, persuasively, in the soft accent of South Pembrokeshire English: 'You don't suppose, do you, that you was th'only one to get a bollocking yesterday? Th'Old Man had that Raven in the chartroom for half-an-hour after that to-do. I bet a's years were burning when a come out – an' serve un right too, b'y. Listen to me, Billy: you aren't gonna murder all the officers, chuck un ooverboard and run the ship, are you? So best forget the whoole thing.'

'Aye, I'll forget it - when I've got even with that pup.'

'Even? You're even a'ready, b'y. After all, twas you hit un in the eye with the boot that time - though o' course a don't know that aself!'

* * *

'Figaro', as if to atone for the callousness of her owners, sailed as never before: the strong following winds, the stiffness derived from her heavy, stable cargo and the terrific power of her long hull, stout masts and acres of canvas, enabled her to reel off the miles across the South Atlantic. Hour after hour, day and night, the cold harsh winds blew, the 'greybeard' seas of the Roaring Forties overtook her, sliding like huge wedges under her stern, raising her bodily as they drew level with her waist, filling her decks with a thunder of foam, then passing slowly ahead, travelling at twenty-five knots on their voyage round the globe. As the seas drew clear, every wash-port on the main deck spouted a thick gout of water into the seething foam that raced past. In a trough, the officer on watch, looking ahead along her deck, would see little but the steel deckhouses and the lifeboats on their raised skids; in this sea the ship was like a half-tide rock for much of the time. Then, as the wave passed, he would see the ship shake herself free, and little else in the murk but the smooth back of the last giant sea to pass them, or, lifted on a crest, nothing but a grey waste of steadily-marching waves; looking astern in a trough, he would see only the broad white path of the wake leading straight to the foam-toppling crest of the next greybeard, which towered threateningly, as if to swallow them, towered so high and steep that it seemed impossible that the ship would ever rise to it. But windjammer sailors had strong nerves; the two seamen at the wheel sweated in the icy wind to keep her head steady without ever looking behind them - the mate on watch would have yelled a curse at them if they had attempted to do so - and the buoyant stern rose in good time, tilting so high that for a moment or two only sky was visible

265

behind them. Then, as the ship levelled, the white wake again met the eyes, and, leading back into it, the thin dark log-line which led in a rigid clean curve to the spinning brass wheel of the patent log which clocked up her progress - 250, 300, sometimes 330 miles a day. There had been nine thousand miles between her and her destination, but now she was devouring that distance, reeling off a thousand miles every three or four days.

As she left the gloomy Horn behind, and as Jacob sloped her north to the latitude of Cape Town, the weather brightened, and he was able to get good sun-sights. Only once did they sight ice, the deadliest danger of those lonely high latitudes; one cold sunny morning they passed a huge glittering berg, a floating cliff of vividly-glancing ice - white, green and blue in shifting facets, perhaps a hundred feet high and half-a-mile long. Raven, watching the seas smashing with a hideous dull boom into its base, thought with a shudder: Suppose we'd run full tilt into that in the dark! But it was odd, he thought, how he came off watch at night, and immediately stopped worrying about such hazards, totally trusting Grant and Jake between them to keep the ship afloat and on course while he lay warm in his bunk, thinking not a scrap about maritime hazards, but only of Eleanor.

She had come to him only twice since that first incredible encounter, and he understood well enough how she feared the likely shock and anger of her parents and the equally likely danger to him too. So she had to be quite sure they were settled before chancing it; the rough weather and the threat of ice had made her father restless, and on some nights he slept fully dressed on a bunk Isaac had made up for him in the chart-room, right above the saloon. Eleanor, who was astute as well as amorous, did not even contemplate setting out on those nights.

She came two nights after the near-disaster to young Robbins, and was at last able to give John what comfort she could, holding him long and tenderly, sensing that what he needed now was not erotic pleasure but an embrace of motherly, sisterly comfort and reassurance. She was shocked at the depths of his misery, self-disgust and depression: 'Nelli, I nearly killed a boy of seventeen - he might have been your younger brother. Then what would you have thought of me?'

'Cariad, it's no good torturing yourself like this: Robbins is still alive, he's all right - I saw him larking about with the others today as if nothing had happened.'

'That's thanks to Perkins - he got him down, not me. I just sent him up there, alone, in severe weather, and then got too busy bashing one of the hands about, feeling all tough and heroic - like some chap in a cheap novel... How could I have been so stupid? And I've had no-one I can talk to - till now. I've felt really low... awful.'

'I know you have, darling. I could read it in your face - even in the way you've been walking. But what about Grant? You could have talked to him, surely?'

'No, he's too... sort of... hard. He thinks I did well. All he thinks about is keeping on top of the crowd.'

'I know. I've heard Dadi say that, and it worries him. Now listen to me, my boy: I'm here now, and I don't care how long I stay, or how much trouble you pour out to me, but before I go you've got to promise to smile, and start to forget all this. I won't be able to see you smile, but never mind that. What's done is done, as that horrible Lady Macbeth says. Perhaps you were as stupid as you say, but you meant no harm, and you'll never make that mistake again. You can't learn in any profession without making mistakes sometimes – I'm sure my father has made plenty in his time - and you've chosen a dreadfully dangerous profession. Now that I see it at close quarters, I'm appalled at how dangerous it is, almost all the time. You and the hands have to go aloft like monkeys in the dark and in fearful winds; it would be bad enough if you just had to climb up and down, but once you're up there you have to work so hard at such difficult jobs, furling those huge sails when they're thundering and flapping about; you're not even able to hang on properly. It makes my blood run cold just to watch you. I think people ashore would be amazed at how brave you all have to be; if you fall into the sea in bad weather, you'll never be picked up again, and if you land on deck there's no doctor aboard - only Dadi to patch you up again – if you're lucky enough to be still alive.'

'It's always been the same, on any sailing ship; at least nowadays we hardly ever have to reef sails. That was a hard job.'

'It's still too dangerous. I can just see Mr blessed Powell going up there when it's blowing, or letting his own son go... Anyway, never mind about all that now. Just give me a nice respectable kiss to show that you're not downcast any more, and that you like me a little bit.'

'A little bit? God, Nelli, how could I live without you now?'

The kiss began respectably enough, both sitting bolt upright and barely touching on the bunk edge, but became much less so as it went on, till she broke off, sighing and whispering hoarsely: 'No, John, no! We must stop, or I'll... When you touch my breasts like that it drives me wild - and you know it does, you absolute devil!'

'Nelli, I can't help it – they're so lovely and round and soft, with such lovely nipples standing up all stiff...'

She drew away abruptly: 'Mr Raven, you're impossible! You've jolly well got to help it, or I shall stop coming. Someone's got to try to be sensible, or I shall finish up... you know... "in trouble", as they say at home.'

'In the pudding club, as they say in the foc'sle.'

'What a charming expression, Mr Raven, sir! So refined...But at least I think you're feeling better now.'

'Better? I should think I am, thanks to you. You've helped me to see things better - more in proportion, I'm loads better. I still think I was a complete idiot, but I won't make that mistake again'

In the total blackness of the cabin she felt him move closer, felt the warmth of his hand on her thinly-clad thigh, and fought back energetically: 'Yes, well, don't get too much better, that's all. Your hands are dreadful - they get everywhere on me... We ought to try bundling.'

'What on earth is that? Would I like it?'

'Probably not – you're not meant to. It's an old courting custom out in the country, up in the mountain valleys of Wales. The ministers carry on terribly against it in chapel, but I think it still goes on. You see, it's so wild up there, and in the winter it's so dark and cold and wet, that there's nowhere comfortable for a courting couple to go but bed. So their parents let them go to bed together, but to prevent any... you know... hanky - panky in bed they're put in bundles – they're each tied up at the neck in a big cloth bag, so that they can't get too free with their hands or touch each other's... you know...'

She ended lamely, giggling helplessly in the dark, and he whispered: 'I'd have my sheath-knife handy, to cut a few holes in the right places.'

'Yes, being a horrible crude male animal, you would! But I think a nice small pair of scissors would be much easier and safer - no – don't start again, putting your hands in such dreadfully rude places! I'm going, mister mate. You're not mating with me tonight. You go to bye-byes and think about your navigation.' She kissed him primly on the lips and was suddenly gone, as swiftly and silently as a wraith, leaving John achingly erect, and thinking about anything but navigation. But her loving shrewdness, her wit and her fun had lifted the dead black lump of depression from his heart, and his thoughts were of love and healthy lust, not barren remorse.

*   *   *

'Well, mam,' said Eleanor a few days later, speaking so casually that her mother was instantly suspicious, 'it's such a nice morning, I think I'm going to stretch my legs on deck for an hour or so... I'm getting no exercise these days.' She bundled up her sewing and dumped it hastily and untidily beside her on the sofa.

The sun, gaining warmth every day as they headed north-east towards the Cape, shone a delightful bright golden light in at the ports, picking out all the details of the good heavy saloon furniture and panelling, glittering on the polished brass fittings. It was a day to celebrate their release from the endless gloom, rain, wind and spray of the Roaring Forties. Her mother gave a bright, tight, sceptical smile: 'I see... That will be nice. Shall I come too?'

Eleanor blushed deeply, for she felt the sting behind the question: 'Yes, of course - by all means, if you like.'

'H'm! Kind of you to think of inviting me, but perhaps I'll stay and keep your father company.' She nodded ironically towards the table, where Jacob sprawled, heedless of them and everything, over a spread chart. 'You'd like that, wouldn't you, Jacob?'

'What? Oh... yes... Like what? *Duw, Duw,* I don't like the look of this Algoa Bay where we've got to anchor to discharge...Wide open to the south-east, if it should start to blow from there... Like the damned West Coast all over again - no shelter.'

Mair pursed her lips and said coolly to the girl: 'Off you go, then. You can see I've got wonderfully attentive company here. Only wrap up well; the wind is still very cold, even if it is sunny...You still need to be careful about your chest. And wear your stout shoes, because the deck will probably be wet. And don't get in the way of the people working up there.'

As soon as Eleanor was out of earshot, Mair asked Jacob: 'Who is on watch this morning? I expect I can guess.'

'This forenoon? The mate and young Raven, I think. What of it?'

'Jacob, you're enough to try the patience of a saint! Too busy with your wretched charts and pilots to see what's happening to your own daughter! You got us out here; now you don't - or won't - see what's happening to her.'

'Happening? What could happen to her? I can't just leave the ship to run itself, gel; I've got to anchor her safely somewhere in this damn bay. Well, there's patches of shingle all over the place, where the anchor wouldn't hold for five minutes... I've heard people say it's poor holding-ground there...'

'Jacob, I really shall throw something at you in a minute! Come over here for heaven's sake, for five minutes, and listen to me! Haven't you noticed yourself how Nelli's changed? She was so moody and rude and irritable when we left Chile; now she seems so happy and sunny and wrapped up in something. If we were back home, I'd say she was in love with some young man, and seeing him - courting him - regularly.'

'Courting him? What - young Raven? Nonsense - how could she be? Only sees him on deck and in the mess-room at meals, when we're all there. You're just imagining it, woman.'

'Indeed? Well, Jacob Roberts, I'm not one to boast, but I think I know her a great deal better than you do, and I say something is different about her. What about just now, when I said I'd come up with her? She blushed scarlet, but she didn't get in a temper about it. She seems too secretly happy inside to care. You don't think... No, she wouldn't do that, surely?'

'Wouldn't *what*, Mair? Don't talk in riddles.'

'All right, then, I'll put it plainly: wouldn't let him come into her cabin at night - when we're all asleep.'

'*Whaat?* Never mind her - he wouldn't dare do that! He knows bloody well I'd break every bone in his body if he started...'

'Do stop swearing and raging, Jacob, and start thinking sensibly. If I'm right - and I'm sure I am, though I don't understand it – we've got to make up our minds: either we accept that she's a grown woman, and let her do just as she pleases, or we take responsibility for her as a young and inexperienced daughter, and try to keep her apart from this young fellow, at least while we're in port... If only she and I could go away while you're unloading and loading, and stay with someone...'

'H'm, yes, thought of that myself a while back... Don't know anyone in Port Elizabeth, though. Never been there in my life. And by the way, it was you who first suggested you and Nelli coming aboard... in that cable you sent me.'

'Yes, well, never mind about that now. You are so unhelpful, Jacob. We don't have to stay in Port Elizabeth, you donkey. Better if we're some way off. I'm trying to think of someone who might help; I do wish you would too.'

'All right, but I'll tell you this much: it's a damn big place, South Africa. It's not like Wales, you know. Even Cape Town is a good seven hundred miles from where we'll be, and as for places like Johannesburg...'

'Just a moment – I've thought of someone. D'you remember that nice rector in Newport - Mr Gethin Williams? Nelli used to go pony-riding with his daughter - what was her name? - Kathryn, that was it, and his wife Bronwen was nice too. Now, he went out to South Africa to be chaplain and teacher at a women's college somewhere... Now where was it...? They wrote to me from there one Christmas, and I wrote back, so I can half remember the name of the place they went to. It was... something-town... some Christian name...'

'Not much to go on, *bach*. As I was saying, it's a big country.'

'Don't be so... so negative, man. Have you got an atlas in among your blessed charts? Find me that.'

Grumbling at the folly and uselessness of the operation, Jacob went to his desk and dragged out a tattered school atlas he had carried round ever since becoming a third mate. He said ungraciously: 'Here you are, then, for all the good it is.'

After only a brief study of the South Africa map, Mair gave a cry of triumph and amazement: 'Jacob, look! It's like a miracle! Grahamstown is the place; I knew the name as soon as I saw it!'

'Yes, that's all very well, but...'

'Jacob, it's only about seventy miles from Port Elizabeth, and there's a direct railway between the two. As I say, it's like a miracle - as if we were meant to go there.'

'Yes, that's lucky, certainly. But of course, we don't know that they're still there, or that they could have you to stay. After all, it's a bit of a nerve on our part - we didn't know them that well...'

'There you go again, carping and niggling instead of helping. We'll send them a wire as soon as we get in, and then we'll see, won't we? You don't seem to understand: if only we could split them up for a while, she might easily meet some nice, decent young men up there; and as for Raven, I suppose he'll go back to chasing the sort of dreadful women you get in seaports, if what you say about him is true. Perhaps the whole thing will die down. Anyway, we'll have done what we can. Now mind, Jacob, don't say a word to Miss about it, or we'll have tantrums all the way to South Africa. She's sure to raise Cain when she does know, but I suppose I shall have to deal with that when it happens. You grumble about the crowd for'ard, but I sometimes think she's more trouble than the lot of them.'

'I know!' said Jacob. 'Tell her you've both got to leave the ship because the whole place aft is going to be painted - cabins, saloon, mess-room, the whole lot. I've been thinking for some time it does need doing. It'll keep the hands out of mischief as well. That young madam will have to learn to toe the line if she's to stay with us, and learn that we know best, too. As for that English puppy, you leave him to me; I'll keep the beggar busy... Courting my daughter! I'll see him fry in Hell first!'

'Jacob, for pity's sake try to be reasonable and keep calm! After all, he isn't some criminal; he's just a young man who's not suitable as a companion for our daughter, in our opinion. And don't forget, if something wrong is going on, it's possible that it's as much her doing as his. She's not some faultless angel, you know. You're too easily taken in by madam's good looks and innocence. She can be a sly, foxy little minx when she likes.'

'Maybe, maybe. But I know this: at heart she's a good daughter and a decent, honest, clean-living Christian girl, and ten times too good for that puppy!'

16

Captain Roberts, alone in his saloon, stretched back in his padded chair, yawned and belched appreciatively, looking round the sunny, warm, freshly-painted room. *Duw, Duw,* what it was to have Mair and Nelli back looking cheerful, and to have a proper breakfast of proper shore food - fresh bacon, sausage and eggs, with excellent coffee to wash it down! He yawned again, cavernously; grand beyond words too to have Mair back in his bed again after three weeks away up-country, What he'd missed, eh - all those years alone in a bunk! He permitted himself a small smirk of satisfaction; honeymooning like that half the night at your age... you can still do it right enough, boy. No wonder you're still sleepy, mun! Come on, come on, this won't do! There's work to be done and a passage to make. He sighed deeply, reached out for a pen, opened the log, turned to a new page and began in his best scrolly copperplate:

Log of the Barque 'Figaro', towards Rosario, Argentina
April 14th 1896: 37 15 S, 17 26 E. Course West by South. Wind light and variable, mainly SE. From appearance of clouds, I have every hope this is the SE Trade, and trust ship will have smart passage to Rosario. Hands employed in holds securing timber cargo against shifting in possible heavy weather.

He blotted the page and was about to close the book, when a less happy thought occurred to him and he added laconically:

B.J. Davies, AB, fined for insolence to Mr S. Grant, Second Mate.

Drat them, he thought, like squabbling kids, only you couldn't knock their silly heads together.

As he laid the pen down and stretched again in the warm sunshine, Mair came down from her morning walk on the poop, paused by his chair and bent over to kiss his forehead. He chuckled: '*Duw,* it's grand to have you both back. I missed you a lot. Where's Nelli?'

'She's found a sheltery spot in the lee of the chartroom. Davy Jones is putting a chair there for her. She's going to do some work on her French course.'

'Is that young...?'

'No, Jacob, don't worry, he's not on the poop, he's working on deck somewhere. Mr Evans has the watch. And fair play; give her some credit: I've been very pleased with her up at Grahamstown. She seemed quite content there, and she's worked on her French and her chemistry every day without any nagging from me. I thought I would have so much trouble with her, but she was as good as gold. Perhaps that... infatuation ... with Raven is wearing off. Mr and Mrs Williams were so good to us: I had a quiet word with Mrs Williams as soon as we got there, so she understood - she has so much to do with young people all the time. She introduced us to no end of nice educated people, and Nelli seemed very happy and at ease among the students she met - all from very good families, you could tell. She even went walking several mornings with a charming young curate - a Mr Van der Merwe... And there were some lovely sacred concerts, and an excellent performance of "Judas Maccabeus". It all turned out much better than I'd dared to hope.'

Mair smiled with the double satisfaction of seeing her daughter happy, and of being proved to be in the right. She had, she felt, been quite clever to remember the Williamses of Grahamstown. She would have been much less complacent had she been able to see the thick wad of letters from Nelli stowed away at the back of a drawer in John Raven's cabin and a similar cache in Nelli's. Nelli certainly had improved her French and chemistry during those mornings of private study; she had also, with some astuteness and for a small fee, bought the co-operation and complicity of a young black housemaid who, because it was secret and forbidden, found Nelli's amour gleefully exciting, and was willing to fetch stamps and paper, take Nelli's long, passionate effusions to post and bring back John Raven's more halting replies from the Post Restante.

Jacob closed the log-book and shoved it aside, stretching luxuriously once more and knuckling his eyes: 'Well, *bach*, I trust you're right, I do indeed. Damned if I want young Raven for a son in-law, and I don't want poor Nelli made unhappy by him if he's just fooling with her to pass the time... All the same, I'll be honest with you: I'd find it hard to do without him now. Apart from that one incident with Robbins, he's turning out a smart young mate, and the crowd are beginning to respect him. They can see he knows his work and does his share. And besides' - he looked uncomfortable and fidgeted with a ruler: 'I'm getting concerned

274

about poor David Evans - have you noticed? All these so-called colds he keeps getting, and those two bright spots on his cheeks and that shocking cough? I don't like the look of him, Mair, not one bit.'

'You think he's consumptive, is it?'

'I pray to God I may be wrong, but yes, I do think so, and I think he needs to go into a decent hospital for proper treatment. Get him fixed up at Buenos Aires, maybe.'

'I hope so. Poor man, he has worked long and hard and faithfully for very little. But what's that go to do with Nelli?'

Jacob shifted uneasily in his chair: 'Nothing directly, of course. But it means I need young Raven quite badly. He often stands watch on his own already, and there'll be a lot of difficult cargo-work, discharging this timber into lighters. A sling of timber can so easily slip if it's not made up properly - and then, look out! I'd have the devil's own job replacing him at Rosario, I should think, up there in the middle of the jungle. Nothing but steam-kettles go up there.'

Mair walked abruptly away and flung herself into the furthest chair: 'O, quite! I understand. The ship, of course, is so much more important than your daughter's happiness...'

'No *cariad*, it's not. I'm not saying that Raven can do what he likes because he's a good officer, but I am saying that I don't want to discharge him if I can help it. I've got to run this ship - it's what Powell pays me for. I don't even like the young pup much, but he's - Hullo! What's up?'

For the chartroom door above had opened quickly, and Eleanor came down the spiral staircase. Simultaneously, the mate's whistle shrilled above their heads, and there were hasty footsteps on deck, and the sound of rope coils being flung down.

'It's all right,' said Eleanor breathlessly. 'It's a squall coming up astern. Going to pour and blow hard in a minute, Mr Evans said. And he says will you come up on deck? He's taking in the royals and he thinks you may want the upper t'gallants in, too.'

With every sign of relief, Jacob shrugged himself into an oilskin, jammed on his wet weather trilby and pounded up the steps. At last, he thought, an ordinary crisis - the sort I'm used to! And a hefty squall from the south-east - that was often the start of the proper south-east trade - a chance to reel off some miles.

And the trade-wind it was, the squall turning into a stiff, steady breeze on the port quarter that made the ship come alive, pick up her skirts and go, leaving a straight track of white across the empty sea -

empty because they were now hundreds of miles from the customary sailing-ship track, which lay near the South American side of the South Atlantic. Jacob and David Evans stood side by side at the poop rail and savoured the pleasure of speed and progress, though David's mind was, of course, on work: 'Leave the upper t'gallants then, is it, sir?'

'Yes, mister. We'll crack on for the present. Squalls like that are usually strongest at the start.'

'Aye, aye. Perhaps in a day or two we'll have the best sails off her and put the old suit on?'

'No, I think we'll leave them. Don't forget we're heading towards the River Plate; that's just the place for a *pampero*, and you know what a deadly bitch one of those storms can be - calm one minute, blowing like a bastard the next. No, leave the good suit on.'

The mate sighed at this heretical departure from custom: 'Very good, but you know how soon the chafing in quiet weather spoils a good sail.'

'Don't worry, David, I'll take the blame. I've got broad shoulders. And don't forget, things sometimes turn out better than we think they will. We were both afraid that half the crowd would desert at the Cape, and what happened?'

'We didn't lose a man - not even the biggest blow-hards like John Ffynnongroes and Protheroe.'

'No - and d'you know why? Because we had a quick turn-round, and they got plenty of work, money, booze and women – that's all they want out of life, most of them.'

'Yes, sir, and of course, they'd have lost two voyages' pay, not one.' The old man's face cracked into a rare smile: 'They wouldn't want to lose that much money - especially the Cardis.'

Jacob smiled too; the alleged meanness of Cardiganshire people was part of Welsh folklore. 'There you are then, mun. Sufficient unto the day is the evil thereof', as the Book says. Mind, there's things I don't fancy much ahead: this Rosario place is a good four hundred miles up the River Parana from the sea. Going to cost a fortune in towage and pilotage - I hope old Powell realizes that. It was a damned good charter, I know, but the expenses will take the shine off his profit.'

'Plenty of water, sir?'

'No, that's another thing, according to the South America Pilot: they can get ships of twenty-six foot draught up to Rosario, but the river rises and falls a lot, and there's a devil of a lot of shoals. We'll need a decent pilot who's wide awake. What do we draw now, mister?'

'Twenty-one for'ard, twenty-two foot six aft,' said Evans promptly. 'Not as much as when we had the nitrate aboard.'

'Just as well. Don't fancy being stuck on a mud-bank for six months, waiting for the rain to come and the river to rise.' He lowered his gaze from the horizon as a burst of laughter came up from the main-deck, from a group of men working under Raven's supervision.

'Your young assistant seems to have settled down well enough, David?'

'Aye,' said Evans, despite himself. 'Pretty fair.'

'That scrap he had with Billy John - it was all wrong, and should never have happened, but at least it showed the crowd they couldn't monkey with him. Did him no harm in the long run, because it's meant he can relax a bit with them.'

The mate was tight-lipped: 'Maybe, but in my view intelligence and judgement are a lot better than boots and fists. But yes, fair play, he is beginning to find his feet, though of course he has a great deal to learn yet.'

The topic was a touchy one with the old mate, and Jacob said no more.

*   *   *

The young subject of their discussion lay in his bunk that night, quite unable to sleep, though, as he had the middle watch from midnight to four in the morning, he had turned in early after supper, hoping to catch a couple of hours of sound sleep before the hated 'graveyard' watch. He had had a hard day of it with the men on deck, reeving new buntlines and clewlines on the mizen; he had not yet been alone with Nelli since her exile to Grahamstown, but her eyes over the supper table had spoken clearly enough, and said that she loved him as much as ever. He hadn't been able to respond fully to those kind, searching eyes, as he sensed cu-rious looks in his direction from her mother; sitting next to Nelli, Mair could not see her eyes, but she saw his well enough.

There was a piquancy, an enjoyable irony, about chatting coolly and politely with Nelli at table - for now the constant feminine company had broken down his shy taciturnity in public - about the college at Gra-hamstown and its lectures and students and lawns and gardens; about the kind Williams family and their servants; about the scenery, the food, the climate, the pleasant walks, the games of cricket and tennis; about Mrs Williams' skilful playing of Mozart sonatas and so on and so on, while all the time his mind was throwing up tactile images of Nelli's silky skin, her sweet breath, her hair, her lips and tongue, and the cool stroke of her long fingers on his swollen flesh. Sometimes he felt nearly overmastered by a thick sensual triumph, a mad desire to cry aloud that he knew every inch of her hidden body, and she of his. One day, he was determined, they would all have to know, but perhaps not yet. Not till the end of the voyage, Nelli thought. Could he wait that long?

Despite his unsatisfied longing, he began to drift off to sleep, lulled by the slap and wash of the sea; after all, Nelli would know he had the middle watch, so that he would be roused by the watch at a quarter to twelve; although she could be reckless, she certainly wouldn't risk a visit tonight, so early in the night, especially as the ship was so quiet; she always waited till the dead small hours. Tomorrow night Grant would have the middle watch; perhaps then she'd... His mind began to run out of gear, bolting together silly, incongruous ideas. Suppose one night she were in his bunk with him when the apprentice on watch came to wake him? Why was Nelli wearing a captain's blue serge uniform? Why, above all, was some damned brassbounder actually in his bed, shaking him gently and whispering 'John, John'? Christ, it wasn't a brassbounder, it was Nelli herself, in his bed, whispering and shaking his shoulder! And she certainly wasn't wearing navy-blue serge, but a thin silky nightdress! And, best of all, it wasn't a dream either; she was real and warm and leaning over him to kiss his cheek, her breast resting on his naked chest.

He just had time to gasp 'Nelli!' and she to say, 'Johnny, I couldn't wait any longer – it's been so long...' before they plunged into a delicious maelstrom of furious kissing, tonguing and fondling, clinging wildly, strenuously, like wrestlers bent on hurting each other. Then, as his gentle fingers began insistently and lovingly to penetrate the warm moistness of her body, she sighed deeply, moved apart a little, and reluctantly drew his hand away. 'No, *cariad,* not yet, please. We must wait... must be sure.'

'Nelli, I am sure –I've never been more sure of anything. I want you to be with me - you know - always. I'm not very good with words, am I? But I know I want to marry you. Please, please say you will have me.'

She gave him another gentle kiss and whispered: 'John, of course I will... Of course. I've been hoping that you'd... that you were sure too. We women are not supposed to make the first move, even when we'd like to.'

'O Nelli, these last weeks - when you were away - I thought they'd never end. That's what made me sure, not just this - you know, our bodies and what we do when we're together. That's wonderful, but it's *you* I want, not just your lovely body. God, I did miss you so.'

'I felt the same. Those people up at Grahamstown were as kind as they could have been; and I think Mam had had a word with Mrs Williams on the quiet, because everybody treated me - you know – "specially" - as if I'd had some awful illness and had to recuperate. It would have been funny if I hadn't felt so lost without you; it was only the letters that kept me looking reasonably happy. But it was so dull there after the ship. Off went the Reverend every morning at a quarter to nine, and after that all we women sat about useless or thought of pointless things to do until he came home again at half-past-five. On board here there's always something happening: the ship and the sea and the clouds are so beautiful... so... stirring, and there's always men about doing useful work. And there's you too, even if I only glimpse you now and then down on deck. And - can you keep a secret? - sometimes, in good weather when Dadi's not about, Simon Grant lets me take the wheel.'

'Does he, though?' Raven felt a small sting of jealousy, that Grant should have established an intimacy with her, secret from her parents - and, more to the point - from him. He had a vision of Grant very close to her at the wheel, guiding her hands on the spokes, his body touching hers as the ship rolled and pitched, while some bloody AB looked on, grinning.

'Yes,' said Nelli, running on tactlessly. 'I know all about meeting the swing, and not chasing the lubber line and giving her weather helm in a squall and watching the luff of the mizen upper t'gallant...'

'H'm!' said Raven, 'how kind of Mr Grant! I'd like to see what'd happen if your dad caught him at that game. There'd be hell to pay.'

Nelli squirmed nearer in the bed and giggled: 'Well, *Duw, Duw!* I do believe our young third mate is jealous of our handsome second mate, and if he is, he's a stupid old bear, because I never visit Mr Grant's cabin like this in my nightie in the middle of the night. And anyway, you could have let me steer too, but you were too frightened of old Dai and Dadi. Now come on, mister: if you don't kiss me and stop being a grumpy old bore, I shall tickle your ribs and make you squawk loud enough for Isaac Hughes to hear - and then what?'

They exchanged a long passionate kiss in silence; then Raven hugged her close and whispered: 'You're a bit mad, you know, Nelli - not like most of the girls I've met before. But God, I do love you.'

'Darling, I know, and I do too. If I'm a bit mad, it's because girls are so tied down and forced to be respectable at home; you don't know what it's like. Nobody coops boys up like that. And let's be serious: when we're married, if you're still a sailor, we shall have to be apart a lot. D'you see what I mean? We shall have to trust each other or be miserable – there's no half-way. Now, one more kiss and I must go, before some wretched little brass-bounder comes to wake you up. But I'll tell you what you can do for me, one night when Dai's not on watch with you: you can lend me a pair of your trousers and I'll try climbing the mizen shrouds. It looks such fun and quite easy, but I'm not trying it in skirt and petticoats.' She laughed as she opened the door to go, and he called 'Ssh, Nelli' in an anxious whisper.

*   *   *

Mair lay on her back in the double bunk, quite unable even to feel sleepy; it must be that delicious fresh coffee Isaac had given them after supper - too strong by half. It hadn't stopped Jacob, mind; he was snoring soundly. Well, poor man, he had to be awake and alert at any time when they wanted him on deck. Better not disturb him with her tossing and turning; the saloon would still be warm enough...

She crept out of bed and out of the cabin, taking her pillow and some blankets, and made herself cosy on the long curved settee that stretched right across the after-end of the saloon. Here, plumb above the rudder, soothed by the gentle swooping motion of the ship, she began after a while to drift off, when the sound of a door opening snapped her awake. Odd - the door to the port passage must be ajar... only Hughes and young Raven lived along there... Must be one of them going out to the lavatory... it couldn't be change of watches yet, surely? Then - for now she was wide-awake - she caught the sound of a quiet laugh, whispers and a 'Ssh!' - and the laugh was that of a woman!

She jerked bolt upright on the settee in time to see the passage door open, and a tall figure in white come swiftly into the saloon, close the passage door silently, and make for the first of the port-side cabins, *Iesu Mawr!* it was Nelli, and coming from *his* cabin, and practically naked, except for that silly, wispy silk thing she'd bought at Grahamstown.

The wicked little minx – that's why she'd wanted to buy such wanton frippery! Mair had thought it odd at the time; how dull she'd been not to realize!

All this flashed through her head as she sprang from bed and grasped Nelli's arm, feeling her convulsive start, hearing the horrified gasp of '*O Duw*, - Mam!' Even in her blinding fury, Mair had the presence of mind to be quiet; no point in letting that wretched Isaac Hughes hear their shame. She flung her daughter into a chair and hissed: 'Stay there while I light the lamp.' By its light she at once took in Eleanor's ruffled hair, flushed face and crumpled nightgown. Her fury burst out, quiet but uncontrolled: 'You dirty, wicked, deceitful little bitch! How could you? How *could* you go to that young rake's bed with hardly a stitch on - like a whore! God forgive me that I should use such language to my own daughter, and God forgive you for what you've been doing in there, too!'

Eleanor had recovered some of her composure, and said sullenly: 'Doing? We haven't been doing anything - just talking...'

'How dare you, girl! Isn't it enough to have turned yourself into a cheap harlot - a tart - without insulting my intelligence as well with lies? Just *talking!* Look at you - your hair, your face, your nightdress - all creased where he's been hauling at it, no doubt... You sicken me, you do.'

Her bitterness drove away Eleanor's shock and fear, and awoke a wild anger in her, though - somewhat farcically - she too had to hiss in fierce whispers, for fear of Isaac hearing: 'Don't you call me those filthy names! I'm not a whore! I've been to John's cabin because I truly love him, and thanks to you and Dadi I can't meet him openly anywhere else. You've known for weeks that I like him, but you're just full of stupid prejudice against him.' Spurred into reckless malice, she ended: 'Did you think I'd been right round the foc'sle, going to bed with the whole crowd? You couldn't treat me any worse if I had!'

'You're too disgusting and wicked for me to speak to, and I'm not waking your poor father at this time of night. It's not his way, but by God I wouldn't blame him if he took his belt to your back, you strumpet! Now get back to your cabin, and don't you dare come out of it! Your father and I will speak to you in the morning.'

'You can speak as much as you like, and beat me too for that matter, but John Raven wants us to be engaged, and so do I, and you can't stop me, so there! I don't give a damn what you do!' A second later her cabin door shut with more of a bang than it should, and the tired steward woke and drowsed for a minute, thinking: Why can't that blessed girl be quiet when she goes out to make water?

The blessed girl was sobbing too quietly for him to hear, for she had never before quarrelled seriously with the parents she loved so much. Soon Isaac's other neighbour was woken by a quiet messenger and went on watch with the lightest heart in the South Atlantic.

*　*　*

Jacob was puzzled when, awaking next morning at seven, he found no Mair in the bed, but a cold, empty space. He found her sitting in the saloon, a ladies' magazine unopened in her lap, her face tear-stained, her eyes puffy from weeping.

'Mair, *bach!* - What the devil...?'

'You'd better sit down, Jacob, and try and keep calm. I'm trying to, but it's hard. Something quite dreadful has happened - has been happening - and I've been such a pitiful fool not to have seen it.'

'What on...?'

'Be quiet and I'll tell you, Jacob: last night, about eleven, I caught our precious Eleanor going back to bed after being in *his* cabin...'

'*Whaat?* - Raven's?'

'Of course -- who else?'

Jacob leapt up: 'By Christ above, I'll break every bone in his body - and then I'll chuck him in the foc'sle! The half-deck's too good for him!'

'For God's sake, man, sit down and be quiet! That Isaac Hughes will be about soon, getting breakfast; d'you want him to know what sort of daughter we've got?'

'The cub! The little bastard! Touching our Nelli! I'd like to...'

'Jacob, you don't seem to have been listening to me: *she* was coming from *his* cabin - not the other way about - so how can you blame just him? He couldn't have forced her in there, could he?'

'No, but... but I'll wager he's got round her with lies, with his posh, wheedling English tongue...'

'At the moment I've got no reason to believe that; he wants to marry her, so she says, and she is equally determined to marry him. And I must remind you that she went willingly to his cabin - and not for the first time, I'll be bound. She's been fooling us for weeks with her innocent airs, I'm certain. I've had all night to think about it; I think we ought to use our reason, and I think we ought to start with our own daughter, not by handing out punishments to others who may not deserve them.'

'H'm... maybe, but back he goes to the foc'sle, all the same.'

'Jacob, I must beg you not to be so hasty. *Think* first: if you impose any sort of punishment or demotion on Raven, you will have to say why - and then everybody - Mr Powell, the other mates, the whole crew - will at once know or guess what's happened, and from my experience of sailors, what the foc'sle crowd imagine will be much worse than what has actually happened. Eleanor's name will be dragged through the mud, and we shall appear fools. I can't believe that's what you want. As I said, I've had all night to think and brood, and already I feel thoroughly ashamed of myself. I was so furious when I found her coming from his cabin that I used the most dreadful, unforgivable language to her –that's partly why I've been crying. Now, let's both get dressed while I tell you what happened, and then I'll fetch her and we'll have it out with her.'

If Mair and Jacob had hoped for a trembling, submissive penitent to appear before them, they were to be disappointed. Eleanor was red-faced with weeping, and only just managing not to break down again, but her head was up, her shoulders back, and her eyes wide with courage and reckless defiance. Mair found herself absurdly nervous and trembling, as if she were the one on trial. Eleanor seated herself facing them, her look a mixture of shame, fear and determination.

Like a bull at a gate, her father glared at her as if she were a mutinous AB, and growled: 'What's this I hear from your mam? A captain's daughter behaving like a trollop, going into that ne'er-do-well's cabin in your nightclothes? A damned disgrace to us - and how d'you think that's going to finish up, eh? D'you think I want some little bastard of Raven's squalling round my saloon, and that young swine laughing up his sleeve and clearing out at the first chance? Because that's what'll happen, sure as fate. You're a silly booby - you don't know the world as we do. Girls who make themselves cheap get left holding the baby.'

Eleanor flushed deeper, but with anger, not shame: 'Why do you and Mam pour out all this horrible abuse at me and John Raven without even asking me what I have to say? Good God, a thief in the dock gets that chance!'

Her father was stung by her pluck: 'Because it'll all be a pack of lies, I'll be bound. You've fooled everybody aft with your goody-goody airs for months, so why should we believe you now?'

But Mair was calmer now, and as ever, more reasonable than

her husband: 'No, Jacob, we should hear her side. And let us all remember we are a Christian family, sinners all, who follow Jesus and His example. It's not for us to shut out mercy and forgiveness; nor must you, Eleanor, tell us any more untruths, or do any more pretending. And you must accept, too, that all we do and say is out of love and concern for you.'

Eleanor was silent for a moment, clenching her hands on the arms of the chair, striving for calm and reason. She was determined not to lose Raven, but - now she had seen the abyss yawning - was appalled at the idea of some final and violent rift with her parents. Surely it need not come to that? 'Mam, Dadi, I'm truly sorry to have deceived you. I didn't want to; I wouldn't have done if you'd let me continue being a friend and companion with John Raven; but you wouldn't. You seemed to hate him so much. And the man I heard you abuse was nothing like the man I've got to know - though you'll remember, Dadi, that at the start - back in Chile - I was the unwilling one. You forced him on me as an escort ashore.'

Mair protested: 'But you didn't tell us any of this at the time, Eleanor. If you had...'

'If I had we'd just have had another row. You were so prejudiced about him - you still are. But I'll bet you, Dadi, that he didn't go chasing off to brothels while you were at Port Elizabeth?'

'How do I know, gel? I didn't go ashore with him. Ask that Grant fellow... But for you to go to his cabin - to his *bed* - in the middle of the night: d'you call that decent behaviour for a God-fearing young woman?'

'No, I don't, and I'm not proud of it - but I was desperate. How else, where else, was I to meet him? I wouldn't let him come to my cabin because I knew what you'd say if he were found there: that he'd forced his way in and was trying to rape me...'

'Faugh!' Mair exploded with disgust. 'Rape! This is nice talk from a young unmarried girl!'

'Mam, I'm just calling a spade a spade. What has being married or not got to do with it? What's the point of wrapping things up? And Dadi, while I'm being candid: you need not fear having a little bastard in your saloon. John and I haven't... we didn't... I'm still a virgin.' Her inner voice added privately, and perhaps more honestly: But, by Heaven, only just!

Her father was not mollified, but mumbled grudgingly: 'H'm, if

284

that's true, I suppose I must thank God for that one small mercy.'

Eleanor flushed angrily: 'I'm as much a Christian as you are. I don't believe John and I should make love until we are married - I think it would spoil everything. If he and I could be quite openly lovers - an engaged couple – we'd both be prepared to wait. We're not stupid and we're not just lustful animals. We know we're very young to get married. John hasn't got his mate's ticket yet, and I'm not trained for any occupation.' Impulsively, she sprang out of her chair, went to her father and took both of his hands in hers: 'Dadi, please don't hate John Raven! Let me be engaged to him quite openly, and with your blessing, and I swear to both of you I will never go to his cabin again, or meet him anywhere secretly... I *swear* I won't.'

Her father, so much a man of impulse, began to melt, and to return the clasp of her hands, but Mair broke in coolly and (despite her previous piety) not very truthfully: 'Well, your father and I have talked this over, and have decided that you and I will leave the ship at Rosario, and go back home.' Jacob gave a small start of surprise, and she went on rapidly: 'I'll find a cottage to rent somewhere in Newport, and you'll be able to go to a college to study teaching, and ... I mean, this situation here is simply impossible for all of us.'

Eleanor drew back and shot her father a keen glance, which made him shift in his chair and look uneasy. 'I see. I am being thrown off the ship. Well, Mam, it will make no difference to John and me, whatever you may hope. We love each other enough to wait till the end of this voyage - for years if necessary.'

Mair got up with an air of finality: 'I can hear Hughes in his pantry getting breakfast ready. I don't want him to hear anything.'

'Just before we go,' said Eleanor doggedly, looking very directly at her mother: 'Don't I remember hearing - several times - a touching story about a certain Mair Bowen, daughter of a prosperous farmer near St Dogmael's, who fell in love with a young bosun from a wool clipper whom she'd met at a fair? And didn't her parents try tooth and nail to stop her seeing him, because to them he was just a bosun - an unreliable sailor with a girl in every port?'

'That was a quite different affair,' said Mair swiftly. 'My parents were hopelessly narrow-minded and unreasonable - at first, anyway.'

'Quite different,' said her father with dignity. 'You don't know how lucky you are, to be able to discuss things with us. And anyway, your mother didn't get up to your sort of tricks - traipsing about undressed in the middle of the night.' Quite unbidden, the inner voice said to him: What about that night in July, when you'd been lent the trap to go to a concert, and instead you took her to the dunes at Traeth Mawr? Don't you remember the moonlight on her lovely white breasts, and the way she...? He got up abruptly from his chair: 'Anyway, you're trying to change the subject. We're not talking about the past. Your mam and I will talk all this over and decide what's to be done, and you will do what we say. As for that young pup Raven, I shall be seeing him after breakfast, and giving him a piece of my mind about decency and loyalty to his captain.' He winced as, from the other side of the bulkhead, came the sound of a repeated racking cough from the mate, entering the mess-room for his breakfast. *Duw*, life was unfair: there was poor David Evans dying on his feet, and there was that young English cub, fit and strapping, pawing Nelli's body in his bed - and damn it, it seemed only five minutes ago she was a little chubby tot with a jammy face, climbing on his knee. Now by God, quite the grown-up young lady, ready to lay down the law...

'You must understand, Mam and Dadi,' said Eleanor, also rising from her chair, 'that I'm not a child any more; I won't be ordered about any more. The very last thing in the world that I want is to quarrel with you, but I do know that I want to marry John Raven, that I'm determined to do so, and rather than abandon him, I'll go to Cardiff or London and find a job in an office - or scrub floors as a skivvy, for that matter - until we can be married.'

'Not a child any more!' said Mair scornfully. 'No, God knows you have shown us *that* well enough!'

Before anyone could reply, there was a polite tap on the door to the mess-room and Isaac Hughes appeared: 'Good morning capten, ma'am, miss. Breakfast is ready.' His little bright eyes darted from one family member to another; he noted the division - the girl against the old ones - and their stiff, flushed faces, and his agile mind began to click away. Well, *Duw*, they weren't like this last night; what's happened in the night to start this how-d'ye-do? Quite serious, by the look of it, and been going on some time, too. There was that bang in the night... Perhaps that had something to do with it? A door shutting... What if this little baggage here had been... No, she wouldn't, surely? What - with that young *Sais?* Well, nothing to stop her, was there? And he was only just along the passage, the other side of the pantry. Nobody would hear her... It was plain enough she'd done something in the night to get them all worked up. Hell, what devils women were: so pretty, so dainty, so inno-

286

cent, so respectable. Butter wouldn't melt in their mouths... And all the time they were just asking for it, really - dying for some sweaty, hairy ape of a man to shove it up them, as the lads for'ard would say! Well, drop dead, that'd be a blow to missis high-and-mighty Roberts - and serve her bloody right too! Wait till the crowd hear about this! Now he thought about it, there'd been other nights, on the way from the West Coast, when he'd thought he heard someone moving about in the dead of night, but then had thought he'd dreamt it. Damn, you could never tell, could you?

*   *   *

It was not until five o'clock in the afternoon, half-way through the first dog-watch, that Grant was able to speak with Raven. He had seen him summoned to the Old Man's cabin, had noted that he was in there a good forty minutes, and had come out looking ready to jump straight over the side. What was up with the poor young devil? But what with the watches and the endless work on deck and aloft, and old Evans being there all the time, coughing away, he'd had no chance of a private word.

Now Raven was on the poop alone, the ship was rolling steadily west, curtseying to the big following swells, her masts drawing great arcs across the blue, cloud-scattered sky. Hull down on the starboard quarter was a smallish Dutch barque which had crossed astern of them an hour ago and exchanged signals. Grant leaned his back on the poop rail alongside Raven and exhaled blue cigar-smoke, which drifted only slowly for'ard: 'There she goes, back to Rotterdam with a load of rice from Bangkok. Wish we were doing the same... Didn't know I was signing aboard a tramp ship, bound for some awful hole in the pampas, and then God knows where.'

Beyond a low 'H'm', Raven made no reply. Grant turned to look at him, at his intensely preoccupied, strained features, and said sympathetically: 'As for you, old boy, you look like the original Flying Dutchman, bound for hell. And you've been so cheerful lately, too. Come on, tell your Uncle Simon: - what's up?'

'Oh, nothing you can change. I've been a bloody lecherous scoundrel, according to some people, that's all, and I don't know what's going to happen.'

'Ah - I should guess this is to do with the beautiful Eleanor - am I right?'

'Right first time.' Raven stopped, and seemed as if he would say no more, but relapse into his morose silence. Then he glanced round at the helmsman, moved closer to Grant, and spoke in a low, desperate voice: 'Grant, I'm in such a bloody jam. Nelli - Eleanor - and I want to get engaged to be married, but Jake and his missis are in an absolute fury about it...'

'Engaged?'

'Yes – what's so odd about that? Christ, thousands of people do that every day.'

'Yes, yes - no offence, old man... But you've only been with her that once, with the horses - months ago! When did you...?'

Raven looked round again, almost furtively, to check that the helmsman was well out of earshot: 'We've met lots of times since then...'

'But how? Where could you...?'

'You'll keep this to yourself, won't you? You'll swear? She... she's been coming to my cabin at night.'

Grant's cool, detached expression changed to one of utter, wide-eyed astonishment: 'Good God alive!' he exploded, then checked himself and spoke more quietly: 'I can't believe it! She just - turned up in your caboosh?'

'Yes - what of it? Am I such a ghastly, revolting specimen as all that?' said Raven huffily.

'No, it's not that – it's just... phew! She's a dark horse, all right. She seems so... so dutiful and virtuous and... respectable. I didn't think she'd have the pluck...'

Again Raven was edgy: 'She *is* respectable, man. Don't talk about her as if she was some sort of cheap...'

'Good God, no, of course not. Listen, Raven: I'm on your side - and hers. If you want to tell me your troubles, that's fine. But don't keep biting my head off all the time. I haven't done anything wrong, have I?'

'No, I'm sorry, you're right. I'm a bad-tempered idiot. Well, you can guess the rest: last night her mother caught her going back to her cabin, and now, of course, the Old Man's in a fury...'

'Whew! I should think he damn well would be. "How scaped I killing when I cross'd you so?"'

'Eh - what?'

'Nothing - just Shakespeare. It's all in there.'

'Yes? Well, he's in a fury with me - imposing myself on a young inexperienced girl, breaking the terms of my indentures - legally, I'm still an apprentice, you see...'

'Breaking what terms?'

'Oh, you know - the bit about "serving the Master and Owners faithfully" and all that.'

'Can't see you're guilty there; the indentures don't say anything about masters' daughters, and I reckon you've made a top-hole third mate for such a younker - and from the way poor old Evans is going, it's a good job you have... Still, I can see you're in a bit of a fix. I don't like to say I told you so, but I did, y'know, right at the start.'

'I know, but that can't be helped now. I didn't plan any of this. When she came to me the first time, it was just a bolt from the blue. We - Nelli and I - shan't let them stop us. And after all, Jake keeps on as if it was just me - as if she was helpless. You know she's not that.'

'All the same, young Raven, was it wise...?'

'Wise! Come now, Grant - own up: if you were my age and a girl like Eleanor, whom you'd already fallen for a bit, came to your cabin in the dead of night - are you saying you'd be wise, and tell her to clear off?'

'I'm not the marrying sort, old son, so it's not a fair question. Play the field - that's my style; no-one is going to tie yours truly down. But no; if I were the sentimental kind like you I don't suppose I'd be any wiser... So what's going to happen now? He hasn't given you the bullet, has he?'

'No - that's the odd thing. I've had an hour of preaching, lecturing and the father-and-mother of a bollocking, but nothing said about the job - except to say that if he caught us together again on the sly I'd get the chuck at Rosario.'

'I think I can guess his reason: you've become indispensable, old man. Old Jake's a captain as well as a father, and he doesn't want to be stuck up the Parana, miles from nowhere, with only one mate fit for duty. If it'd been left to mama you'd have got the bullet right enough, if it could have been done discreetly. After all, if he were to put you back in the half-deck now, the whole crowd would know about it, and she wouldn't want that. What's happening about you and your inamorata - did he say?'

'Didn't say much; just that he and his missis would talk it all over. In the meantime - nothing doing.'

'You'll keep to that, won't you? I think it's for the best, for the time being.'

'Yes, but only for the time being - till the end of this voyage. After that, if they're still against me, I'm leaving his command and Powell's ships. Then I'll be free of him, and she'll come with me, I know.' To Grant's surprise, and faint embarrassment, Raven moved closer and gripped his forearm: 'She's so wonderful, Simon. I'm like a... I'm a different person now. Nothing's going to stop me - nothing and no-one.'

Grant, his ironic coolness broken down for the moment, reached a friendly arm round John's shoulder and gave a squeeze: 'And good luck to you, say I. I think you're balmy, but never mind. And as for "different person", I should jolly well say you are: I wondered back there in the Cape why you traipsed round the town as chaste as a castrated missionary, not even looking at all the professional ladies. Now I know why! Listen, old man: I'm sure it'll all turn out right in the end. Jack shall have his Jill, but he may have to be patient. They won't be against you for ever - they think too much of their daughter for that. Just hold your horses and be discreet for a bit. My guess is that you've got some nice and fairly hectic little cabin episodes to look back on, eh?'

Raven coloured and grinned foolishly: 'Yes, fairly hectic. Can't really believe they happened now. Oh Grant, you've no idea how...'

But Grant stepped back and held up his hands in a gesture of arrest: 'No, old boy! No lover's effusions, I beg you. I'm a born, dyed-in-the-wool bachelor - I couldn't stand them. And look at that mizen lower tops'l lee brace - hanging in a bight! What sort of watch-keeper are you, for God's sake? Get a couple of hands to take a pull on it, before your future father-in-law sees it and starts growling. "Now silken dalliance in the wardrobe lies", old son. Try and get your mind on the job, I should.'

17

By God, Jacob Roberts thought, as he lowered himself with a sigh into his roomy chair, they could do with Trinity House on this God-forsaken river, to put a few buoys and lights, so that you could navigate properly. He opened the log, but found his hands and bare forearms too sweaty from the sultry, windless autumn heat. He went to wash, grumbling: What the hell must it be like up this damned Parana in the summer? Rather be off Cape Horn, where at least there's some fresh air. Then he sat and began to write:

Log of Barque Figaro towards Rosario, Argentina
May 3rd: Continuing up-river tow by tug "Santa Rosa". Weather calm and extreamely warm. Progress slow because of current and weak engine-power of tug. Earnestly recommend that in future a different vessel should be engaged. Expect to sight Rosario today after extreamly tedious tow from Buenos Aires, following a smart passage from the Cape. Hands employed removing hatch-covers ready for unloading.

He read the entry through, and felt that, though formal and polite enough, it conveyed his resentment adequately: you try your best to make a smart passage, because you know that's what old Powell demands; the Almighty, to be fair, does His best too with a good steady trade wind, and then you arrive at Buenos Aires to find the agent has booked you the smokiest, most stinking, underpowered tug in the place - wood burning, so she had to keep stopping to take on fuel, and that meant anchoring the ship and heaving up against the current every time. No wonder the crowd were so moody, poor dabs. He swore viciously under his breath as he saw that he had spelt one of these damned English words differently the second time he used it. What a stupid bloody language! Not only clumsy and ugly - the words fitting together any old how - but also impossible to spell: once you could say a Welsh word, you knew how to spell it, but in *Saesneg*, almost every word could be spelt fifteen different ways. He felt a sudden burning resentment that a Welsh ship wasn't allowed to keep a Welsh log - just because old Powell had been sent to some toffee-nosed English school, and so had the leather-arsed chair-polishers in the Board of Trade.

The hell with it - who cared about English spelling? He slammed the book shut and got up to go on deck. Better see what that lazy idle article of a pilot was doing. No buoys, no leading marks, no dredged channel since Buenos Aires, only a few feet of water under the keel half the time – *Iesu Mawr*, no wonder captains took to drink some-times! Even before they'd got into the river, David Evans had worried him by croaking away like a raven about how dangerous the mouth of the Plate was.

'Listen, capten,' he'd said, 'for God's sake don't approach the land in darkness. Remember poor Capten Hughes Brynsiencyn, of the "Isabella" - back in the fifties? He didn't know about the strong south-easterly set there, and so he ran her up on an unmarked reef on a calm night, and every man-jack of them drowned but one. Poor old Hughes – he'd mortgaged every brick of property he and his family owned to buy that barque, and his first voyage in her ended like that! So stand off until daylight, sir, when you get near the longitude, or we might all feed the fishes.'

Jacob went on deck, but found no relief from the stifling fug of the cabin, nor anything cheerful for the eye to rest on; nothing but a vast, coffee-coloured river, edged by flat, featureless banks, with here and there a wretched farm and its little grove of clustering poplars, dull black stalks against the whitish haze of the sky. The ship's course wound sinu-ously between numberless marshy islands, and several times a day float-ing islands of fallen trees, bushes and swamp vegetation, fifty feet or more across, slipped slowly past in the current. Heavy summer rain fal-ling on the vast Gran Chaco swamps, six hundred miles upstream, had washed them out into the river, and the pilot, grinning, had warned him back at Buenos Aires: 'You keep clear of the *canalotes*, capitan; they full of swamp snakes, and they pretty nasty bastards, hey! They climb up your cable, give you one bite - and pouf! Finish!'

Jacob snapped his telescope open, and focused on the tug's bridge; there he was, that goddamned young jackass of a pilot, lolling on a high stool, sucking his mate tea from a gourd, cigar-smoke rising in the still, warm air. Call that a proper look-out? The swine would have them hard aground before he was finished, that was certain. Jacob looked down on to the main deck, where the hands were silently, grudgingly, working under Grant's direction; poor David Evans was now lying in his cabin, the mate in name only. The ship's life seemed suspended in a long, warm, brooding trance: no wind, no waves, no motion, never a shout or a whistle or a snatch of song from the crowd, who slunk about, naked to the waist, their heads and shoulders sunk in morose boredom. Trouble there any minute, like as not... And then, on top of that, all this to-do with Mair as well!

As for Raven's life with Nelli, that too was suspended; there had been no more prohibitions, but no relaxation either, simply an uneasy truce. Sometimes in the dog watches they met and talked on the poop, but there were no nocturnal visits, no more foolish, headstrong, wonderful ventures into the forbidden country of each other's bodies. Eleanor had been made tense, unhappy and restrained by the cold hostility between her parents, for which she blamed herself, and Raven could now scarcely believe that this cool, polite, remote girl, who stood always just beyond his reach, had many times been in his arms, nearly naked and between his sheets, lovingly stroking every inch of his body. Now, when he covertly held her hand, he felt no responsive warmth. They too, it seemed, were inexorably drifting apart in this dead brown stream. One still evening, as they stood alone on the poop in the warm, clinging dark, Raven drew her to him and gently turned her towards him to kiss her, for it was nearly time for them to part; her arms did not embrace him, but hung lifeless, and her lips did not part in welcome, but seemed numb and lifeless too. Raven felt his own passion go cold at this rejection, this humiliation, and felt instead a surge of irritable anger: 'Oh, very sorry. I see I'm being a nuisance. I'll go back to my cabin.'

'No, John, don't go like that.' She detained him, holding his hand and resting her head on his shoulder. 'Please don't be angry with me –it's not fair. I do still love you, and like to be with you - but everything is different now. I can't feel the same - not after the things that have been said to me. You've no idea how horrible it was when my mother found me that night. They made me feel cheap and dirty, and made our whole affair seem cheap and dirty too.'

'But we know it wasn't cheap or dirty. Perhaps we went a bit far, but we were really in love - we still are, aren't we?'

'Yes, we are... well, I think so. I want to be, but I've given my promise not to meet you secretly any more, and anyway - you must try to understand, and not be cold or angry or feel I'm rejecting you - I don't feel I'd want to come to you at night now, even if we were alone on this ship for a month. I can't explain it any better than that. You'll have to give me time. I feel we have to start all over again, somehow. If you can't, or don't want to, if you want to finish it all and find some girl ashore, I shall understand, and there'll be no hard feelings from me.'

'How could you think that? D'you think I only wanted you for a quick feel in bed? Now you're making it seem cheap. No, don't draw away like that; I'm not quarrelling with you. I'm just trying to tell you that I'll wait as long as you like, all the while I know you still want me.' He shook her shoulders gently and smiled in the dark. 'And I don't give a tuppenny damn for all the girls ashore, Miss Roberts.'

This time, as they parted, there was some strength, some tender warmth, in her goodnight kiss.

*   *   *

The bitterness between Jacob and Mair went back to the morning when, under topsails only, 'Figaro' glided through the anchorage off Buenos Aires, flying the signal for a pilot. Mair, who had taken Jacob's glass and was scanning the docks, suddenly called eagerly to him; 'There's a PSNC liner alongside, Jacob, with steam up. I recognize the funnel! She may be leaving for England soon. If you were to get ashore and book us a passage, Nelli and I could be packed in a few hours, and be on our way home, where I'd have some peace of mind.'

Completely absorbed in conning his ship, Jacob said, over his shoulder: 'Can't do that, *cariad*, I'm afraid. (Luff her a little, mun, or you'll be athwart that tramp!) That's our tug over there if I'm not much mistaken, getting his anchor. He'll be alongside in a minute; I made our number to the signal station down at Ensenada, so they should be expecting us.'

'Never mind all that; it wouldn't take long for you to go ashore and at least ask…'

Jacob flushed with anger and embarrassment at her raised voice; he didn't want the helmsman and that fellow Grant to hear all their business, especially when he knew there would be trouble. He opened the chart-room door and said brusquely: 'Don't stand on deck shouting at me; come in here, and for pity's sake listen to some sense. Can't you see that if I'm to go traipsing off ashore it means I've got to anchor the ship, lower the gig, and tell the tug and the pilot to twiddle their thumbs for half a day? Well, dammit, I've got to start paying them the moment they come alongside; and from what I know, it'd take you and Nelli hours on end to pack up all the hundreds of fal-lals you brought with you. We'd lose a whole day! And besides, you've no idea which way that liner is bound; she may be off round to Valparaiso for all you know. I can't waste all those dollars on a wild goose chase; you'll have to wait till we get properly docked at Rosario. Then you could both come back down here on the train.'

Mair's tone was icy, cutting: 'I see. And your daughter's happiness and reputation, I suppose, count for nothing compared with tugs and pilots? I'm ashamed of you, Jacob, and you should be ashamed too.'

'I keep telling you, woman: I've got my job to do - a ship to run. If I don't do it well, we'll all be in the workhouse, and then I suppose you'll be happy!'

'That Captain Morris of the "Magellan" - practically a stranger - he had a job to do too, but he put himself out for us more than you will.'

The comparison with a more successful man had a bitter flavour - he flavour of treachery - to Jacob, and he shouted: 'Morris had a fancy liner of fifty thousand horsepower under him! He could easily make up the time - he said so himself. You know nothing, and care nothing, about my problems. Bloody Capten Morris indeed! Why the hell didn't you marry that popinjay if you fancy him so much?'

Mair went swiftly to the door: 'You're too unkind and unreasonable and ridiculous for words, and I won't speak to you a moment longer. And I can tell you I won't forget this easily, either, Jacob Roberts... Being treated like a piece of troublesome garbage!' The chart-room door slammed behind her, and Jacob brought his huge fist down on the table with a blow that nearly splintered it to pieces.

Despite Jacob's attempts at privacy, the helmsman - Watcyn Williams from Llangranog - had heard enough to be able to supplement the gossip about Raven and Eleanor that had gone on among the crowd ever since Mair's nocturnal discovery. Isaac Hughes' graphic account of that night had been endlessly discussed, ornamented and augmented during the dog-watch hours of leisure at the for'ard hatch; what the third mate and Eleanor might have, could have, should have done together was exhaustively and colourfully speculated upon by that group of sex-starved males, many of whom took some pleasure in detailing exactly what they themselves would have done had they been John Raven, for they did not trust him to have their sexual prowess and expertise. However, they were notably silent about it all in the third mate's presence; his swift and brutal flattening of Billy John had not been forgotten.

'See, boys,' Isaac commented didactically, 'the old girl's desperate to get that young trollop home - though it's too late, mind. She's damaged goods now, for sure. The missis made me and Davey drag out one of her trunks yesterday, so she could start packing. Well, damn good riddance to them both, say I; they've been nothing but trouble to me from the first. But she'll have to wait till we get berthed at Rosario now.'

'So our young mister have got a few more chances of dipping his wick, then?' said Lewis, grinning with vicarious lechery.

'O no,' said Isaac, with some satisfaction; 'they've scared him off. I reckon the Old Man threatened to beach him if he tried to get at her again. Quite right too: I've never seen capers like this aft in all my time at sea. Damned disgusting!'

'Ah,' said the AB tolerantly, 'it's different for you, Isaac boy. You don't fancy being up her, the way most of us does.'

*　　*　　*

Another reach of the vast river opened up, and Jacob gave a deep grunt of satisfaction as he made out through his glass the cluster of anchored steamers and, along the shore, a line of wharves below a steep clay bluff; the bluff in turn was crowned with a frieze of high grain elevators, warehouses and factories. He whistled softly in surprise, and said to Grant: 'A bigger place than I thought, mister... Must ship out a lot of grain, by the look of it... Shouldn't be hard to pick up a cargo here. They're going to put us alongside one of the wharves; I expect the tug will let go the tow in a minute, and make fast to our starboard side, so as to manoeuvre us better. Take a few hands and stand by for that, if you please.' To himself he added: Thanks be to God that we got here without going aground, and let's pray there's a homeward-bound steamer for Nelli and Mair, so that I can get on with my job in peace, without a lot of bloody arguments about what I should or shouldn't be doing... Bad enough having to please old Powell...

By noon 'Figaro' had been cleared by the port doctor, and was snugly berthed at a riverside wharf, under big steam cranes. Jacob had been visited by a dapper French harbour official, anxious to begin unloading the South African timber. 'I should be glad, m'sieur, if we could begin this afternoon. We were expecting you two days ago, and we are held up in our harbour works without this timber.'

'H'm - blame the tug for that, not me, mister. Couldn't pull a bloody wheelbarrow, that thing.'

The Frenchman grimaced with impatient incomprehension: 'Why a steamship could not have been chartered I do not know. However, will you now order your men to swing the yards, so that the cranes may plumb the hatches? In the meantime, you and I will go to the harbour office to complete the formalities.'

Collecting the papers below, Jacob grumbled to himself: God damn these ports and officials. Swing the yards! Come ashore this minute! Good God, it's one o'clock and I haven't had my bloody dinner yet. Too bloody slow on the west coast, and too damned quick here!

Much later that afternoon, after a lengthy visit to Powell's agent - a visit which entailed the prolonged consumption of French brandy and Cuban cigars in the best traditions of 'ship's business', Jacob returned to his ship with an uneasy mixture of good and bad news (it would all have been good if it hadn't been for the women), and, over tea in the cabin, he made the tactical error of telling Mair the good news first: 'Decent agent here, Mair; young Italian fellow. Whole place seems to be run by foreigners. You can see we'll be discharged in no time here, and he's fixed up two excellent further charters for us: bully beef in cases for Melbourne, then coal from Newcastle, New South Wales for Valparaiso. After that it'll be sure to be nitrate home from somewhere on the coast. Just hope it isn't some one-eyed hole like Caleta Buena.' He rattled on uneasily, aware of Mair's grim silence. 'Two good down-wind voyages at excellent freight rates... I've been worried that it'd be a trip in ballast round the Horn - nothing but worry and not a penny earned either. As long as the crowd doesn't start...'

'And *our* passage home?' Mair's tone was cold, stony.

Jacob fidgeted with his high collar and sweated: 'Ah, there's a problem there; I wired the PSNC agent in Buenos Aires, but I'm afraid there isn't a boat home now for two months.'

Mair snorted in bitter disgust: 'Two months! What did I tell you? Now we're stuck in this pest-hole... Eleanor and I can't go and stay in Buenos Aires until the ship leaves, because we're paupers, and a hotel bill for two months, of course, would put us in the workhouse.'

'It would cost a fair bit, wouldn't it? There should have been a sailing next week,' said Jacob, trying vainly for a truce, 'but the "Mercator" blew some of her boiler-tubes off Talcahuano and...'

'What the devil do I care about boiler-tubes? I tell you, Jacob: I'm sick to death of all this - of you and Eleanor. She slumps about with a long face, treating me as if I were a murderer because I've stopped her little game with that Raven fellow, and you're too taken up with your own affairs and that man Powell's affairs to give a rap for either of us - so why should I bother any more? I'm tired of struggling and arguing with the pair of you. You can both go to the devil, for all I care. If she's so set on throwing away her... her decency - well, I can't stop her, not here nor back home. I'm quite disgusted with the change in her. Even if I took her home, she might start setting her cap at someone else I know from Fishguard. I can't lock her up. And wherever we are, I can get no help from you with family problems.'

She flung herself into a chair, picked up her sewing and stabbed the needle viciously, audibly, into the fabric. Jacob sat too, uneasy and confused, at his desk, shuffling things aimlessly on its shiny top. 'Aw, come on now, gel: no point in us falling out when it can't be helped... Perhaps when we go down-river again...'

'Jacob, I can see what's happening, though I know you think I'm a halfwit: this isn't a slow place like Caleta Buena; you'll have your cargo for Melbourne weeks before the steamer's due. Eleanor and I can't live on the pavement in Buenos Aires until then, and we can't afford a hotel, because I was foolish enough to spend all my money on our passage out to Chile; so I wash my hands of the whole thing. I've learnt my lesson, that's all: a wife aboard a ship is just a useless encumbrance - just a puppet. What she wants - needs - is of no importance, compared with ship's business. I should have known how it'd be.'

She expected Jacob to fly into a rage, but he was still benign from the agent's brandy, and sued for peace: 'Don't talk so bitter, *bach*. You know I think more of you than of twenty Powells. Think of the lovely times we've had since you came. And it may all turn out better than we think now; those young folk have learnt a lesson, I believe. There'll be no more nonsense from them. And we should have a quick passage to Australia; there'll be plenty of decent liners home from there...'

'Jacob, I've no wish to keep quarrelling with you, but I have nothing more to say on this subject. And neither have you.' She thrust her needle through the crisp linen, and her mouth closed so firmly that her lips disappeared into a thin tight crease in the flesh.

*   *   *

With coffee and brandy before him, Simon Grant sat alone, replete and content, at a waterfront cafe table and let the blue smoke of an excellent cigar trickle slowly out through his lips. That was more like it, by God! A damned hard day at the cargo, getting out the last of the sweet-smelling sawn timber, then a fresh-water bath, an excellent beefsteak and several glasses of Chilean red wine - and now... what? He paid attention to his body, and felt a gentle pricking of lust. Whew, it had been a long time since he'd had a good woman. On the other hand, wasn't he a bit too tired, too sleepy, too full, too drunk, to want it? Jesus, she'd have to have fire in her drawers to keep him awake and on the job tonight! Some really corking, tip-top, high-toned, half-caste bint, all black curls, creamy breasts and long, smooth, coffee-brown thighs... But God, he was tired... Leave it tonight, maybe?

As the fumes of the liquor began to mount into his brain, the thought of spending money on a woman led to a long, muddled calculation of the past and future months of the voyage, multiplied by his monthly pay; it'd be a tidy sum by the time they saw Falmouth again. And all this time as a second mate: would that count against him when he tried for a berth one day as a master? In practice, he was the mate now, with poor old Dai Evans in such a state, but still, on his record he would...

Then, in a second, he was savagely jolted into wakefulness and sobriety by a hoarse cry and the sight of a man - Billy John Ffynnon-groes - blundering in through the door from the street. He saw other men from 'Figaro' behind Billy; it looked as if Billy had shaken off their re-straining hands, and now thrust himself, eyes blazing, towards his hated enemy.

'O, mister bastard bucko!' Billy said thickly, grinning. 'There's lucky I seen you as I was passin', eh? We got things to settle, isn't it, go-ing back to Calaty Bono? On'y this time you got no bloody skipper to hide behind, nor no brassbounder to help you; this time I got the jump on you, boy, and by Christ you'll know it!' Without another word he lurched across to Grant's table, reached out, snatched up the wine-bottle and smashed its bottom off on the table's edge, sending the remaining wine spraying to the floor, and converting the bottle into a hideous rough dagger.

Grant leapt to his feet, and felt the wall against his back. Trapped! But at least no-one else could get behind him. For all his case-hardened toughness, he felt a sickening lurch of fear, a feeling that all his bowels had turned to water. As he would with a wild animal, he forced himself to remain still, and to fix his opponent with a steady stare; out of the corner of his eye he glimpsed a young waiter dashing into the street and eeling his way through the gaping sailors. Off to fetch the police? Maybe, but he himself might be dead meat by the time they got here. For the present, he'd have to fend for himself, and do it bloody well, too. Spin it out, slow it down! John hadn't seen the waiter leave, he was sure. As for the men, they were drunk and vacillating; they wouldn't help Billy, but they wouldn't try to stop him either.

'Listen, my friend,' he said, as steadily and calmly as he could, 'listen and have some sense, for Christ's sake! You've done nothing yet but break a bottle. I can see you're pissed as a skunk, so it doesn't matter what you've said. Now just about turn and get back to the ship - or wherever you like. I haven't seen you or heard you - so far.'

'No, but I've seen you, by Christ, bucko, and you're gonna be sorry I did. You're not bullshitting yourself out of trouble now.'

'Bullshit nothing, my friend.' While he talked for time, Grant watched Billy's hand on the bottle, keyed up to duck, dodge or strike. 'Bloody well think, for a change! You carve me up with the bottle - all right, you'd enjoy that - but then what? The dagoes will shove you in the calaboose here - and have you any idea what that will be like? And then you'll be slung back aboard when the ship sails - in irons, like enough - while she just about goes round the world, and then a bad discharge, damn-all pay, and more time in jug for mutiny. That's what you want, is it?'

'Shut it, you bloody crawling weasel, you! I don't give a fuck about all that, not if I can get even with you. It'll be worth it, boy!' On the last word he moved, sensing, even though drunk, that if he didn't make a move, his revenge would fizzle out in words. Like lightning, and at full stretch, he lunged with the bottle at Grant's chest, and though Grant went flat back against the wall, the glass dagger-points slashed his jacket and scratched his chest. Only the solid table saved him from a bad wound.

Billy grinned: 'Felt that, did you, Mister Grant, sir? Don't worry, mun, that's nothing to what you will get!' Billy feinted to the right, then made to come round to the left of the table.

Grant sweated in silence: Christ, the madman might be drunk, but he was quick on his feet. He cursed the fact that he had no stick, no weapon himself - nothing. Sooner or later he'd have to grapple with him, get that bottle off him - and that'd be a bloody business at the best.

Where the hell were those dago coppers? No time to think about them - Billy was moving again, dodging cat-like to and fro, shifting his horrible weapon from hand to hand like a practised gaucho knife-fighter. This can't go on much longer, Grant thought; he'll get me sooner or later. Must get out of this trap somehow. Then he remembered the one thing left on the table - his full glass of brandy. In a single movement and without taking his eye off John, he snatched up the glass and flung the strong spirit into the sailor's eyes, temporarily blinding him, and hurled himself round the table to get himself into the clear. But Billy was a skilled veteran of many a bloody bar-room brawl, and though blinded and in pain, stuck out his left foot and sent Grant crashing to the floor. With the quickness of desperate fear, Grant got to his knees, and was just able to reach up and grab Billy's left wrist and stop the descent of the deadly bottle. Using all his stocky strength, Grant got back on his feet, and sobbing for breath, the two men fought for control of the bottle, blundering and crashing about among the tables, crunching glasses and plates under their feet, watched by a shocked and cautious audience of respectable Argentinian diners.

Then, through the sweat and blood (for the bottle had glanced twice across his forehead), Grant saw blue caps and silver badges by the door and gasped out: 'The police are here! Now give it up, you crazy idiot, give it up! Don't make it worse for yourself!'

For answer, Billy John spat point-blank in his face and growled: 'O no, you crooked bastard, you can't catch me out with that trick...'

But the words were hardly out before Billy felt another strong hand on his collar; brimful by now of a mad, berserk fury, and quite undeterred by the mounting odds, he gave the bottle hand a brutal jerk and simultaneously brought his knee sharply up into the second mate's groin. As Grant doubled up in agony, Billy, to get rid of his new tormentor, swung himself full round to his right, his dreadful glass dagger burying its points in the cheek of the first policeman.

But there were two other policemen there, no strangers to combat with drunken foreign seamen, and they, unlike Grant, certainly did not lack weapons; they drew their long night-sticks and rained blows on Billy's head and shoulders, while Grant, staggering to his feet, took Billy's legs from under him with a huge sidelong kick to his right knee. Red rage made the policemen merciless; while their unlucky comrade moaned and held his cheek, blood welling through his fingers, they beat and kicked the seaman unconscious, beat him until even Grant, mustering up some passable Spanish, cried: 'Enough, *senors*, enough, I beg you! He will do no more tonight. I will take him back to the ship!'

They left off their bastinado, and in silence hauled Billy up between them like a lifeless sack. He moaned quietly, his face a red mask and blood dribbling from the corners of his mouth. They set off towards the street-corner, where a two-horse van awaited them, the seaman's feet dragging useless along the pavement; one of them - a sergeant - called to Grant as they went: 'One of your own rotten apples, hey? He's ours now. By Christ and his holy mother, we'll give him something to remember us by when we get him to the jail. We give him to you before you sail; you take him and give him to the sharks, maybe.'

'Believe it or not, sir,' said Grant later to his captain, 'I found myself feeling sorry for the idiot, even though he'd been trying to carve me up. But there was nothing I could do. He'd committed an assault ashore and hurt one of their own fellows pretty badly; they'd got him and they wouldn't let him go.'

Even in his striped flannel pyjamas, Jacob was a figure of severe dignity: 'This is why, mister, I don't like feuds - personal feuds - starting up between officers and hands. They always result in this sort of how-d'ye-do. Not your fault this time, of course: that boy was always wild and stupid. I only signed him on because his uncle's a friend of mine and begged me to take him as a favour. He thought the discipline on board ship might do him good.' He sighed heavily: 'Never do people favours when you get to be a captain, Grant. You always live to regret it.' He seemed to sink into the world of his own troubles, and said, as if in soliloquy: 'So often you try so hard for months to do the right thing, and just end up being treated as if you were a monster.' He shook his head to bring himself back to the present, and said: 'I'll go and see the police and the Vice-consul tomorrow, but it'll do no good - not if he's injured one of their men. They'll get their own back on the crazy fool... Do you need any help, mister - bandaging, and so on?'

'No sir, thank you. He got me with his knee down here, where it hurts, but I'll recover, I dare say. The rest is just a few clean scratches.'

'Very well, then. I'm sorry you've been attacked, mister, but I think you may learn something from it: that it's never wise to make ship's discipline a personal matter.' His eyes fixed Grant with a steady look of quiet reproach, which made the younger man shift uneasily. Then he rose and stretched: 'I'm going back to bed now. Come and see me after breakfast tomorrow. It's about the mate: I've had a wire to say they've a bed for him now at the Yankee hospital in Buenos Aires. Poor fellow: I pray I may be wrong, but I doubt he'll live to set foot in Wales again - not this side of the Judgement Day, anyway.'

That man has changed, thought Grant, as he hobbled stiffly to his cabin. He's quiet, sad, tired, somehow. When I first knew him he'd have been in a towering rage with me, the police and Billy John. Now, he seems to have given up, lost that Welsh fire. A shame ....

* * *

Morning brought to Jacob perhaps the keenest pangs of sorrow in all his sea-time; a ship cannot but come to resemble a family, however large and however discordant at times, for in a sailing-ship people of all races and kinds are thrust together in a partnership against Nature, against its wiles, its cruelty and its callous indifference to Man. The afterguard especially forms a tight group, which may cohere for a very long time; Jacob and David Evans could recollect voyages together which stretched over years, over tens of thousands of miles. Each knew the other better than he did his own brother; each knew he would never see the other again, and thus each strove to lie comfortingly about David Evans' future; Jacob lied, being unable to express his utter grief, and the mate because, dour and taciturn as he was, he could sense the force of that suppressed emotion, and did not want to unleash it. Jacob saw too in the old man's sickness and weakness the shadow of his own approaching old age.

The two men stood in the warm sunshine at the top of the poop ladder; the cab which was to take David to the station stood alongside the gangway, its old bay horse hanging his head, twitching his ears and swishing his tail against the pestering flies. Jacob laid a hand on the old man's bony shoulder, and was shamed and embarrassed to feel his eyes pricking with tears: 'Time, David, I suppose? You've made your farewells with Mair and Eleanor, I daresay? They'll be more than sorry to see you go, and so shall I.'

'Aye, sir, and they've been very kind, more than kind. Mrs Roberts has even made me a cake - a *teisen lap* - to have for my tea in the hospital... Very kind...'

'Well, no doubt you'll not be long in that place before they ship you home in a liner, eh, David? All night in a cosy bunk, no more buntlines or ratlines or pulley-hauley or night watches! Just sitting back in a deck-chair with the steward bringing you a glass of something tasty now and then, eh? That's the style, mun!'

The old man's face broke in a weak smile: 'Yes, I shall enjoy a snug passage home at Mr Powell's expense. He owes me that, I think. And once I'm back in Aberaeron and I've got over this stupid cough of mine, I'll be looking round for a cosy billet somewhere as harbourmaster - some nice small quiet place like Aberystwyth or Cardigan, or Burry Port, say, where there's not too much to do.'

'That's the ticket! And Mair and I will be glad to come and look you up, and yarn over old times, whenever I've got shore leave.' The easy lies flowed, like the jokes of men under a gallows, as they descended to the main deck, and thence to the quay. Jacob said: 'I could come to the station if you like, to see you off?'

'Good heavens, sir, I wouldn't put you to that trouble, just as long as Davey Jones peggy can come to help me with my dunnage. You've got your ship's business to attend to. Goodbye Mr Grant, Mr Raven. I trust you'll have a good passage to Australia, and so on.' Spontaneously, as if they had rehearsed it, both the young mates gave a smart, solemn salute that expressed better than words their sympathy and respect for a stricken comrade, and then shook his hand in silence.

Jacob, now unashamed of his flowing tears, shook his hand too, and said: 'Goodbye, old friend, for now. May God send you a swift recovery; we shall all pray for you, for you've been my best support for many a year, and in many a storm.'

Too overcome for more words, the mate also saluted, then turned about and boarded the cab in silence.

*   *   *

For the two mates and foc'sle hands, life at Rosario was a gruelling test of stamina. If Caleta Buena had been a place of tropical lassitude, tedium and leisurely bungling, here they were at the mercy of fiercely energetic enterprises, run by expatriate Europeans on the make, and for the crowd the result was no better. They were slaves to the steam cranes, which never tired, which swung and bowed over the open holds like huge, long-necked, insatiable birds of prey, pecking out sling after sling of timber. When the last of it had been whisked into the air one forenoon, only three days after the old mate's departure, the men, and officers too, wellnigh collapsed where they stood on the main deck, sprawled against bulkheads, crouched on hatch-coamings, roosting one above the other on companionway steps. The muscles of their backs, arms and shoulders ached from the constant lifting of heavy planks; in a few days, between them, they'd manhandled three thousands tons of wood.

Grant, now officially the mate, rose and stretched wearily, looked about and commented:

'The many men so beautiful, And they all dead did lie...'

To Raven's blank stare he retorted: 'Coleridge, you benighted philistine, you,' and got to his feet. 'I'll go and see what the doctor can do for us.' He put his head in at the door of the galley, where Wellington Jones sweated over the stove, simmering a beef stew - this time with real shore beef and fresh onions and carrots - on the coal stove. Tactfully, Grant did not enter, for the galley was Jones' kingdom. He asked politely: 'Any chance of some coffee for the crowd, Mr Jones? The poor buggers are all in - flat out.'

'I'm awful busy, mister, but - okay, I get some for them in a minute. You find that no-good peggy an' send him here to lend a hand, Mister Grant, sir.' When, ten minutes later, Davey toured the main deck with mugs of coffee, even the unpopular Grant rose just a little in the crowd's esteem, though none admitted it. At least the bastard had seemed human for a change. The coffee was fresh too, and actually smelt and tasted like coffee. Grant had taken only two gulps from his mug, however, when AB Lewis, looking towards the gangway, called out: 'Mister Grant, the cap'n's coming aboard.' Turning, Simon saw the Old Man already on the poop-deck and striding towards the ladder in some agitation. Now what, he wondered; the old boy was like a wet hen in this place; back on the Coast he'd been happy to disappear every day for hours; that was better, really. The row with his missis was at the bottom of it, no doubt, and young Raven's affair with his daughter was at the bottom of *that*. Life was simpler when you kept women and ships well apart - no question!

Jacob clattered down to the main-deck, and made his haste and his choler obvious to all: 'Good God, mister, what's this? Middle of the forenoon, and all hands loafing about guzzling like goddam bums! By Christ, it won't do, mister!'

'They've been working very hard, sir, for days, keeping up with...'

'Iesu Mawr, mun, they're paid to work, and so are you two.

Stow that damned coffee and get ready for the tug. Look - that one out in the stream by there; she's waiting to take us down-stream to Fraser's.'

'Fraser's?'

'Yes, Fraser's - the Yankee beef-packers. You've heard of them, surely?' The hands were now all on their feet, scalding their mouths with gulps of the delicious coffee, disgusted with their lot and their captain, and with only the slight satisfaction of hearing the bucko getting his balls chewed off in front of them. 'We've got to be down there by noon, mister, or lose our turn for loading; there's half-a-dozen steamers anchored off, waiting. And I'm paying dues for every minute the ship's alongside here, so look lively, the lot of you, and get your fingers out of your backsides!'

Grant clamped his jaw in silent fury, the big muscles bulging visibly, but he spoke coolly and held on to his coffee: 'Aye aye, sir. Two minutes to finish your coffee, lads, then it's out warps fore and aft, starboard side. Bosun to the helm, if you please.' The captain stood, scowling at this near-defiance of his orders, then marched off into the poop, slamming the passage-door behind him.

As the barque - high, empty, slab-sided - slid easily down-river, the men on deck had the chance to take in their surroundings - the wide brown river speckled with ocean tramp ships, river-steamers, barges and little low islands, the clay bluffs to their right crammed with warehouses, silos and factories, each with its wharf below, each wharf lined with ocean-going steam vessels. As they rounded a headland a jumble of big, gloomy, grey, square concrete buildings dominated by a huge chimney came in view, and the captain of the tug waved in extravagant gestures to show Grant that this was their destination. 'Stand by with your warps port side, lads,' said Grant. 'Davey, tell the doctor the hands will be ready for dinner when we've made fast alongside.'

As they came closer, the tug swinging them round to approach upstream, the warm autumn breeze brought to them the heavy smell of cooking beef - appetizing at first, but then cloying, sickening, especially as blended with it was the underlying reek of dung from the acres of cattle-pens behind the factory. The place was quiet but for the dreary lowing and bellowing from the great penned herds of cattle and the whistle of locos as they hauled and marshalled the endless lines of box-cars which had brought the beasts from the wide green pampas to their hot, crowded, well-organized deaths in this outpost of American industry.

Late in the dog-watches that day, when the floors of the holds already had low stacks of cases, the weary hands sat and loafed about the

decks in the gathering dark to have a last smoke and a yarn before turning in early. This was often the time for a lively 'fore-bitter' - a cheerful
leisure-time chantey - but the men were too tired and dispirited for that.
Reuben Mathias bosun knocked out his pipe on the rail and stretched
luxuriously: 'By damn, worth having a pipe, isn't it, to shut out the stink
of this place. Put you off your grub, does it, Curly?'

'Hell, no, mate. I've ate so much garbage called beef and pork in
me time, a bit of real meat cooking won't hurt.'

'Funny, though, ain't it?' said Lewis. 'Here we are, fed on the
cheapest old salt junk Powell can get his hands on, and we'll be sitting on
top of thousands of tons of real good bully-beef - the sort they eat back
aft.'

'P'raps we might get a taste too,' said Jimmy Protheroe darkly.
'I knows my way round this ship, I do.'

'That big mouth of yours,' said Reuben, 'will land you up in
Swansea jail one day, you'll see. As for eating junk and carrying good
beef, young Lewis, you ask Curly about that. He'll give you one of his
blinking sermons on it.'

Curly shook his head: 'No need for a sermon, Reub. Any working chap can look round and see for hisself how unfair the system is. You
and me - we're like a poor old carthorse, what's fed on chaff and rubbish; he's hauling a load of oats, but he never gets a chance to taste them
hisself.'

'Bully beef is nothing,' put in another man, somewhat missing
the conversation's political drift. 'When I was on the Australia run in the
Blackwall Line we used to carry all manner of stuff for the *crachach*:
whisky, champagne, crates of women's dresses and fancy underwear -
even some carriages one trip, lashed to the stanchions in the tween-
decks. And we had the horses to go with them. I liked that trip because,
me being used to the Welsh cobs back home, the mate told me off to look
after the nags. That was better than laying aloft on a tops'l yard, I can tell
you, boys.'

Curly grunted: 'H'm: and I lay you them horses fed better than
you did, Ianto?'

'*Duw,* I never thought of that - I s'pose they did, really. There
was some first-class hay and rolled oats aboard, and even some bags of
carrots for a treat... and some flaked maize, to keep up their
condition, like.'

'There you are y'see, mates,' said Curly, warming to his sermon after all, as Ianto had provided the perfect text. 'Them horses cost their owners money, so they'd got to be fed proper. Now with us, nobody gives a fart about our condition, because if we croak today there's always more hands on the dockside t'morrer looking for a berth, and if they can't find enough white chavvies they can fill up the foc'sle with lascars and blackies, who they can get even cheaper than us.'

Jimmy Protheroe was bored already: 'Old Curly do go on, don't he, boys? Drip, drip, drip.'

'I'm only tellin' you what you should be able to see for yourself, y' silly sod. What it amounts to is this: you can't call a foc'sle hand a beast of burden, because he ain't so well fed or cared for as that. And he never will be until he learns to combine against the fat bastards who...'

'Never mind about all that guff,' said Jimmy impatiently. 'Never mind about things you can't do nothing about! What about my mate Billy? Stuck away in the calaboose with dago cops kicking the shit out of him, for all we know. They were treating him rough enough when they nabbed him that night. Why don't you do something about him?'

'Talk sense, my son, for once in your life. It's too late to help him now. Them that was with him that night - and you was one, wasn't you? - should have stopped him before he started on Grant; but you was all too pissed or too stupid or too yeller to do it. So don't blame me - I wasn't there.'

Jimmy spat on the deck in bitter disgust and frustration: 'You English - you...'

'Never mind about "English"!' said Curly, stung out of his usual detachment. 'A bloody fool is a bloody fool wherever he comes from and whatever lingo he speaks. And if you'd only *listen,* and use your loaf, you'd see that my ideas are about all men - and women too - all over the world. And as for Billy, p'raps you don't remember the night you two silly tools come aboard with the *treepas* and wanted to fight the mates? Me and the doctor and some others saved both of you from a damn good kicking that night - so you can shut yer gob.'

'So can you, bloody English windbag! Never mind all your speeches: stand by your mates is what I say. We all ought to go on strike to make the Old Man go ashore and get Billy out of the calaboose.'

'Nah there's a *wonderful* idea, boys!' said Curly satirically. 'We'll all go on strike, and then Jake can do us for mutiny, and we'll all end up alongside of Billy doin' time. That'll really help him! No, my son, anyone who's a real friend of Billy's will tell him to use his head a bit bet-

308

ter in future, instead of asking for trouble the whole time, and picking dirty fights with blokes he couldn't face in a fair fight.'

'Yes,' said Reuben, 'and doing it in front of fifty people, so that whatever happened - even if he'd won the fight – he'd have been sure to be nicked by the dagoes. You can't help a chap as stupid as that, Jimmy my boy.'

However, when, at the end of a week of crippling drudgery, the hold was full, and the police van delivered Billy back to the ship, none of the crowd could help feeling strong pity for him. His face was cut and bruised, one eye was blacked, and he dragged one leg as he shuffled up the gangway; his body and clothes were filthy and, strangest of all to those who knew him, his indomitable, unreasonable spirit seemed broken. He was silent, except for a persistent dry cough, and answered all questions in monosyllables.

Curly was the first to sympathize: 'Christ, Reub, they must be a bad lot up at the jail. Look at the state of the poor bugger! How you feeling now, my son?'

'Got a cough... I'm all right.'

'I reckon you should see a doctor, boy,' said Lewis. 'You ain't looking too clever, are you?'

Billy just shook his head: 'Lea' me alone. Gonna get my head down.'

Curly said kindly: 'Yea, you do that, mate. Only you did ought to have a good wash first, and ditch all that clobber you're wearing. Jails is bad places for sickness.'

'I'll wash later. My bloody head's splitting, mun. An' these clothes are the only shore clothes I got; you ain't ditching them.'

'Listen, my son: we'll all have a whip-round and sort you out some fresh gear, or c'lect a few dollars for you to get some more. You shouldn't keep these.'

But Billy just shook his head miserably, and Curly was too full of pity to argue further, and just at that moment the mate's whistle shrilled, and Grant bellowed: 'Bosun, single up the warps! Tug's coming alongside. Get the towlines out, for'ard and aft!' He came closer to the group of men by the foc'sle door, and looked at them suspiciously: 'And where's that precious specimen of a jailbird? He can bloody well turn-to as well. He's done nothing all week.'

He made to go into the foc'sle after Billy, but he found Curly blocking his way and staring stonily into his face. Sails and the bosun moved silently to stand beside Curly in support. Curly spoke quietly: 'The man you're looking for is unfit for work, sir. He's been beaten up real bad, he doesn't look as if he's been able to wash or sleep for a week, and he's got a cough and a bad headache.' With withering scorn he added: 'If you wanted your own back, isn't that enough for you?'

There was a supporting murmur from all the other hands around, which made Grant waver, and he merely said petulantly: 'That lip of yours will get you done for mutiny one day, my friend, and then not even your god Karl Marx will be able to help you.'

'Maybe, sir, but in the meantime we all think Billy John needs to see a shore doctor - *now*.'

'Oh, a medical expert now, are you, Kellock, as well as a bloody sea-lawyer?' said Grant, his face red as his anger mounted. But he noted too the increasing murmurs of support for Curly, and knew that this was no time for a show-down with him. 'Very well, the captain will see him once we're under way. In the meantime, get those bloody warps out, and pronto!'

Curly drew breath to protest, but his friend the bosun, scenting danger to him, elbowed him in the ribs as he shouted: 'Port watch, out warps; starboard watch, single up to head-rope and stern-rope! Jump to it, boys! We're off to see them Aussie gals!'

18

Getting the anchor next morning was a slow, gruelling slog for a tired crew; the swift brown river slid silently past, causing a ripple at the bow. The bar-taut anchor-cable led out ahead, quivering, and the hands, trudging sullenly round and round the capstan, were being obliged to haul the ship's huge bulk upstream against the current. Link by link the chain ground up the hawsepipe; the rhythm of the pawls was agonisingly slow, so slow that, after watching for a few moments, Grant nodded to Raven and both mates added their weight to the bars.

Their help didn't stop the growling: 'This is the last fuckin' workhouse of a windjammer I'll ever ship aboard,' said one man. 'I'm going in steam after this.' Some of the older men like Johanssen thought wistfully of a vanished age twenty years back, when ships were smaller and crews were larger, and included a fiddler; then the capstan went clicking cheerfully round to the tune of 'Rio Grande' or 'Bound for Vallipariso'. 'Too much verk, und de verk too bloddy hard,' mumbled the big Swede, nevertheless plodding and shoving his best.

Jimmy Protheroe was, of course, not slow to comment: 'We've got the tow-rope fast; why the hell don't the Old Man tell the tug to give us a pluck ahead an' take the weight off this bastard cable?'

Grant was himself entertaining much the same thought but could not appear to sympathize: 'Stow that grousing and shove, men! We've nearly finished with this damned creek.'

As the anchor at last broke out of the river mud, the barque fell rapidly astern, and the towing hawser, which had been floating loosely, suddenly took the full weight and sprang taut, the brown river water being wrung from its whole length. Grant snorted scornfully to Raven: 'Look at that for seamanship! It's a wonder he didn't part the hawser, and that's worth a packet. Don't like being towed by idiots.'

The tug took them round in a wide circle and headed for the sea, and now, with the current behind them, the ship fairly flew downstream, the factories and silos of Rosario soon slipping out of sight astern. 'Stow the capstan bars, lads,' Grant said, 'and cheer up; for God's sake. At this rate we'll be off Buenos Aires this time tomorrow.'

'Aye,' said AB Jones morosely, 'an' off to bloody Melbourne, instead of going home.'

After the captain's homily about discipline and the uneasy standoff with Curly, Grant was forcing himself to be more conciliatory than was his wont. At work under his orders, the men shouldn't have been talking at all, but gritting his teeth, he said diplomatically: 'Never mind, boys: the more days, the more dollars, eh? We'll not cat the anchor, bosun, in case we have to let go in a hurry; wouldn't be surprising, with this dago half-wit towing us. Rig the pump, and let's give the old girl a good wash-down - get rid of all the shore filth. Put the boys to squaring the yards, and let's make her look like a ship again, instead of a dockside shit-house.'

'Figaro' became absorbed in the traffic of the busy river: high, crowded, decrepit river-steamers from Asuncion, hundreds of miles up-stream in Paraguay, slowly overtook them, their paddles pounding a watery drumbeat; sea-going tramps bound up-river laboured past with big rolls of dirty foam at their bows, their engines giving out a deep thunder, their funnels pouring black smoke. They overtook long tows of barges, deep-laden with pine logs and quebracho wood, and sinister swamp islands that drifted, slowly spinning, downstream; and all the while South America slipped silently away on either beam. 'An' I tells you, boys,' said Lewis, 'if I never sees this place again, it'll be too bliddy soon.'

'Goo on,' said Curly. 'You had some sport up Rosario there. Dipped your wick a few times, I'll be bound.'

'Ah, the senoritas was all right, but twas hot beyond, boy, and by damn, I'd like to think that now we was headed for Cardiff and them nice Bute Street tarts, and a few pints of proper beer!' And then, in stark contrast to these delights, the image of the battered, silent Billy John came into his mind, and he called across the deck: 'Jimmy, how's your mate Billy t'day?'

Jimmy shook his head morosely: 'Still bloody rough, boy. Can't eat, won't talk - just lies there coughing, as if he's given up, like. But they don't care, them bastards aft.'

However, as if to belie his complaint, the captain himself appeared, making his unaccustomed way for'ard, attended by the bosun, as the senior member of the lower deck. In the dark, cramped foc'sle they bent over the still figure on the bunk, and Jacob asked: 'How are you feeling today, John? Any better?'

Billy slowly shook his head, his eyes still closed, wincing as he moved: 'No, sir. My head aches all the time - and my leg, where that sergeant kept on kicking me... Can't stop coughing, neither.'

'D'you feel hungry? I'll get the doctor to knock you up some broth - with proper shore beef and onions, I mean.'

The only answer was a further burst of harsh, dry coughing. The two men went out into the fresher air, and Jacob said: 'Still in poor shape, bosun. I dare say he'll soon pull round, but I think, to be on the safe side, we'd better put him on his own, in case he's got something infectious. We'll put him in one of the spare cabins aft - the for'ard one, port side...'

'Mr Raven's?'

'Yes. I'll get the second to shift to Mr Evans' old cabin, starboard side for'ard.' He added cryptically: 'That'd be better anyway – it's where the second mate has always berthed in this ship,' thinking, with grim satisfaction: That'll stop your gallop, young puppy - get you away from my Nelli.'

The bosun looked uneasy: 'With all respect, capten, I think - and so do most of the crowd - that, in case it's something serious he's caught in that jail, you ought to put him ashore to a proper hospital and doctors in Buenos Aires. It'll be your last chance for a long time.'

Jacob's feeling of petty triumph was replaced by the more familiar one of irritation: '*Bobl annwyl,* mun, I can't hold up the whole ship and cargo for one drunken worthless scrimshanker with a bit of a headache! I'd have to pay through the nose at the hospital, and then waste days and pay harbour dues while I try to find another hand to take his place. You can't pickup real sailors here like you can on the west coast - it's all steamers here. I'll do my best for the useless *crwt;* I'll put him in a cabin and get the steward to look after him. I'll give him fever mixture and a headache dram from the medicine chest. I'll even see what Mrs Roberts thinks – she's had nurse's training, you know. More than that he can't expect. All this trouble is his own damn fault, and I've got to get *on,* mun - you must see that.'

Mathias shook his head doubtfully: 'All the same, capten, you said yourself...'

'No, bosun, that's my last word. The fellow's young and strong as a horse; a drop of my jollop will soon put him right. I'll put all of this in the official log, so I'll carry the can for it. Why should a decent man like you worry about the bloody fool?'

Later, in the cabin, Jacob had much the same conversation with his wife, though he was more diplomatic with her, and, as she had not seen the patient, was able to put a more optimistic gloss on his condition. Their relationship had been an uneasy one lately, since his preoccupation with the ship had lost Mair and Eleanor their passage home, but Mair had grudgingly resigned herself to 'playing second fiddle to that man Powell', as she put it, and the last thing Jacob wanted was a fresh quarrel to sour his days and chill his nights in bed.

'He'll be right in a few days, *cariad,* you'll see. I'll put Isaac Hughes to look after him, and I'll dose him good and proper out of the medicine chest. These young fellows soon get better at sea, away from the drink and the women.'

'And those brutes at the jail... By the way, have you taken off him all the clothes he wore there, and burnt them? That's a precaution you should take, I remember, in case there's infection in them. And his bedding too, of course.'

'Well, no... I mean, he's like a lot of them up for'ard: feckless and broke all the time. Got nothing but what he stands up in.'

'But you could fix him up from the slop-chest - you've got all he'd need in there.'

'Oh, aye, I could fix him up, but who's to pay for the gear? I've paid good money for that stuff - *our* money. I'm not giving hand-outs to men who attack my officers, and if I give it to him and dock it from his pay, then, come pay-day, he'll make such a damned to-do about it in front of everybody in the Shipping Office. He'll say I did it for my own profit. A damned sea-lawyer like Billy John can make a lot of trouble. Like enough he'll go yapping and whining to some trade union nuisance too; he'll have forgotten all about the state he's in now, and all I've done for him. I've seen it before, many times. When he asks for some new gear, I'll sell him some.'

'And what does Reuben Mathias bosun think of it? Does he perhaps think John should be put ashore at Buenos Aires?'

'Well yes, he did say something about that. But he soon realized why that was impossible.'

'Inconvenient, Jacob, to you and your blessed Mr Powell - not impossible. Billy John Ffynnongroes is in the same boat as myself and Eleanor - he's an inconvenience.'

'Mair, for God's sake let's not begin to quarrel about that again! I'm not free, gel, to do just as I please with the ship - go here and there with her like a hackney-cab. I'll tell you what: give me a few days dosing him from the Medical Guide in the usual way; if he isn't right after that, I'll take you to see him – I'll be grateful for your opinion. But, you mark my words, I'll bet you ten dollars he'll be up and about, working and grousing again by that time. I'm shifting Raven, by-the-by, to Mr Evans' old cabin. He'll be out of harm's way there, if you see what I mean. John can go where Raven was till he's better.'

And by the time that happens, his captain's mind was thinking, we'll be out of this horrible shallow Parana and into the River Plate itself. We must be doing eight knots or so, with this current behind us, and there's a breeze from astern. By God, to be rid of the tug and into some sea-room, with a fair wind to run her out into proper deep water! After all, there was nearly two hundred miles to go down from Buenos Aires before you could say you were clear of the land; with a head wind that could mean days and days of beating about in shoal water. No, he wasn't going to waste a decent slant of wind - not for a drunken sojer who'd practically tried to murder an officer! I'm a God-fearing Christian as well as a captain, he thought, but not as Christian as *that!* Let the stupid hoodlum take his chance!

The same steady westerly was blowing when, just after dawn next morning, the lights of Buenos Aires appeared on the starboard bow, and dimly Jacob could see on either side the huge expanse of the Plate. He could even, to his intense delight, feel the ship come alive, and lift and fall a little under his feet as they encountered the gentle estuary swells. He thumped his fist on the poop rail and growled to the mate at his shoulder: 'Both watches aloft, mister, and cast off the gaskets. Let the sails hang in their gear till we've cast off the tug.'

The mate leant over the rail, to where the hands were at early morning muster below them: 'Make sail, boys! Up with your upper tops'l and t'gallant yards! Don't sheet home yet, bosun.'

The hands and apprentices, tolerably cheerful now they scented the open sea, dispersed for'ard to half-an-hour of strenuous work. The brassbounders, once away from the old man's awesome presence, clambered like monkeys up the shrouds, whooping wildly, to the dizzy tops of the t'gallant masts, where they shuffled out along the foot-ropes of the royal yards, a hundred and eighty feet up, to loose the light upper sails. The men, led by the bosun and Raven, tailed on to the halyards to haul the heavy lower yards aloft, timing their heaves with rhythmic cries. Soon the formerly bare forest of masts and yards was clad with long strips of fluttering canvas, each sail still looped up to the yard above. By now, the port itself was abeam, and the tug was threading its way through anchored steamers. A long blast from her siren signalled that she was about to cast off the towrope, and Jacob called: 'Set lower tops'ls, mister, the minute she lets go.' It was vital to get some sail on her and have some steerage-way, so that when the tug cast off, the barque wouldn't drift helplessly in the current among the anchored ships.

'Stand by tow-rope!' The bosun and three hands ran up to the foc'sle head; the tug hooted twice, stopped her engines, and as the warp slackened, released it from the massive towing-hook. As it splashed into the water, to be hauled back aboard, Grant bawled: 'Tops'l sheets!' Blocks squealed and chains rattled as, with urgent heaves, the lower corners of the sails were hove down taut; the three long strips of canvas filled with a snap and, free of encumbrance at last, 'Figaro' began to gather her own momentum and to glide murmuring through the smooth water of the Plate.

'Starboard helm, Kellock!' cried Jacob over his shoulder. 'You'll be into the tug in a minute, mun. He's too *twp* (stupid) to get out from under our bow. Midships now. See the buoy ahead? Steady on that, and leave it to starboard.' He smacked his hands in satisfaction as he felt the breeze cool and steady on the back of his neck. On either beam big anchored steamers slid past, to be swallowed in the morning haze astern. Dead ahead, the sun rose over wide clear water. He was tempted in his euphoria to cram every stitch of sail on her, but no, he must show himself a prudent captain, and pick his way slowly, carefully, through this tangle of shipping and buoys and shoals. It looked a big river, but the water was spread thin, and he must stick to the dredged channel. He turned to the helmsman again: 'How's she answering, Kellock?'

'She's answering, sir, but sluggish-like.'

'We'll wake her up a bit. Mister Grant! Upper tops'ls and lower t'gallants, if you please!' Grant's whistle shrilled again, the chain sheets jingled in their blocks, and soon each mast had three taut sails pulling the ship seawards, and, crossing to the rail, Jacob could see the water beginning to swirl, to pirouette, to break in tiny ripples along her side. Her huge steel hull began to curtsey as she met the low incoming swells. 'Come a few points to starboard... Well! That'll do. See the next buoy now? Steady on that.'

The city, the harbour and the anchored steamers were astern now; no more officials with bits of important paper, agents with bills and charter-parties to sign, no more swindling chandlers or grousing policemen, no more worries about deserters or stowaways, no more drunks falling aboard and asking to be dosed with the clap mixture! And best of all, a damn good slant of wind to take the barque clear out of it! A minor irritation struck him: where was that idle steward with his morning tea? Should have been up with it half-an-hour ago. Then he remembered with a slight start of guilt: Billy John! He'd forgotten all about him. Last night he'd been transferred to Raven's cabin, and this morning Hughes was no doubt fussing over him like a wet hen.

'Your tea, capten,' said a voice at his elbow, and there was Isaac with his usual greasy smile of discontent. 'Very sorry to be a little late, capten, only I can't do everything at once - especially when I've had extra work landed on me - though I do try.'

'John any better this morning?' asked Jacob brusquely, ignoring the steward's whine.

'Much the same, sir - the drunken, murdering lunatic. *Duw!* There's some bad lots up at Ffynnongroes, and no mistake. Anyway, capten, your tea and everything will be on time tomorrow; I've put Davey Jones peggy in charge of that ruffian, so that I can get on with my proper work. *Chwarae teg,* now, sir, I didn't sign aboard as a nurse, did I?'

'I didn't tell you to hand him over to the peggy,' said Jacob sharply. 'That *crwt* is too dull, mun, as well as too young, for that job.'

'It's only to keep an eye on the man - help him when he wants to pass water or - you know - move his bowels. Not that he seems to want to do either of them much. Davey can tell me if anything's wrong. Otherwise, I don't know when you'll eat or what you'll eat.'

His shrewd blackmail forced Jacob to drop his bluster; his nature was too sensual to contemplate late and wretched meals. 'Very well then, but I hold you responsible, mind,' he said, with a feeble attempt at dignity. 'By the by: if John doesn't get any better in a few days, Mrs Roberts will be coming to see him - she was a nurse once, you know, and she nursed her mother through a bad dose of pleurisy once. I'd like her opinion. So have things ship-shape down there, for God's sake.'

The steward left in silence, rolling his eyes up in saintly martyrdom, foreseeing more criticism from his old foe. Grant moved to his captain's side and gestured towards the last of the anchored steamers, whose towering, rust-streaked hull was now sliding backwards past the taffrail: 'We're clear of the anchorage now, sir. All plain sail?'

Roberts roused himself in some relief from his gloomy thoughts on troublesome stewards, mysterious illnesses and difficult wives: 'Aye, why not? Let's leave that damned pest-hole behind us. All plain sail, mister. Set sea watches and stream the patent log. Let's get this bully-beef to Melbourne, for I can tell you this is a decent charter - the best I've seen for years, and it should be down-wind all the way.'

* * *

Davey Jones peggy gulped with apprehension as he turned the knob of the cabin door. Of all the jobs he'd had on board, this was easily the worst. It had even been better when that Raven had been in here; he was a pretty hard case, liable to give you a bollocking or a thick ear for nothing, but that was better than looking after a bloke as sick and nasty as Billy John Ffynnongroes. It wasn't fair, the way everyone always dumped all the rotten jobs on the peggy, because no-one else could be bothered with them. Three days now, he'd been doing the job on top of all his other work. Capten only looked in for two minutes once a day and shoved a lot of medicine down Billy's gob, and that didn't seem to be doing him any good; Isaac, the old fairy, never came near the place at all... Not bloody fair...

The boy tried to be kind, to cheer Billy up, but the stale stink of the sickbed, the dreary lifelessness of the man in the bunk, and most of all, the fear of the unknown illness that gripped him - all these made Davey afraid. 'Hallo, Bill,' he said nervously. 'Feelin' any better?'

Billy, his shifty, handsome face pallid against his black hair, and tight-drawn to resemble the face of a fox, stared silently up at the deckhead.

'We're well out to sea now, Billy. Did have the south-east trade for a bit, but now it's gone flat calm and all cloudy-like. I expect you can tell we've lost the wind...'

'My bloody head... Get me some water, boy.'

'Yes, I brought some, look... D'you want anything to eat, Billy?'

'Don't want nothing but a bit of peace. Just want to be rid of this bloody headache. My eyes hurt, an' all.'

'Want to go to the head - have a piss or anything? You ain't done nothing for days, mun.'

'Don't want nothing, I keep telling you, you stupid *crwt*... Except I'm too damn hot. Get this shirt off me, for Chris' sake. I'm all itchy under it!' Wincing and groaning with the effort, the sick man sat up in the bunk and Davey hauled off the thick, damp flannel shirt, nauseated by the sour smell of sweat. Then the boy started back, quite unable to conceal his fear and horror: the man's whole trunk and arms were covered by a fierce red rash of spots, as if a fine spray of blood had been shot at him. Hearing the lad's gasp of shock, Billy opened his eyes, to show that they too were suffused with dark blood.

'O Jesus, mun - look at you! You're... like... covered with blood! I better go an'...' Without another word Davey dropped the shirt and bolted out of the door and along the passage to the main deck, where he vomited long and painfully into the scupper. He rose to his feet, pale, cold and sweating, to hear the second mate's harsh voice above him: 'Hey, peggy! You disgusting little skunk! Get yourself a bloody bucket and a broom and clear that up. Why the hell didn't you do it down the head?'

Before he could obey, Davey felt a brotherly arm round his shoulder, and Tom Lewis, the Milford AB, spoke kindly, quietly, to him in his slow, South Pembrokeshire Flemish accent: 'Never mind about him. What's up, Davey boy? Not sea-sick, surely?'

'No mun – it's Billy John... He's all over terrible spots, an' his eyes are... like... bloody... Aw Christ, mun, he give me such a shock when I took his shirt off.'

Raven called again sharply from the poop rail: 'Lewis! Stow that gabbing! You're supposed to be washing down decks. Let that mucky young idiot clear up his own mess.'

Lewis felt a strong spurt of anger, but checked himself; he had learned a lot from Curly Kellock about dealing with unreasonable officers: 'Aye aye, sir, but there's something the cap'n should be told, and this poor dab is all upset and frightened. A's very young to be lookin' after a man who's real bad.'

Raven hesitated; this quiet, respectful independence was hard to master, harder than downright insolence: 'Very well then... I'll see the captain's told. Now back to work, the pair of you. Get that filth cleared up, Jones.'

Lewis did not budge from the foot of the ladder: 'Aye, sir, but begging your pardon, I thinks the cap'n should be told at once. I mean, it must have been something serious to make the poor lad spew like that. A's not a namby-pamby, is a?' Seeing Raven about to cut him short with a harsh dismissal, he put one foot on the poop ladder, as if to mount. Two other seamen stood behind him listening curiously and showing a symbolic solidarity with a cause they knew nothing about: 'Don't you see what I means, Mister Raven? Billy could a caught somethin' real bad in that jail – somethin' we might all catch off of him - you too, sir. It's too serious, sir, to be left to a poor little *crwt* like Davey here, now isn't it? You got to see that.'

Again Raven dithered, caught between doubt and exasperation; good God, this bloody AB was telling him what to do, and needed jumping on hard, Grant would say. All the same, what he said might be...

Suddenly matters were taken abruptly out of his hands anyway, for the captain's voice broke in from behind him: 'Mister Raven, will you kindly tell me what the devil is going on here? Half the hands standing about idle while you chat with two of them, and in the meantime I see there's been a serious worsening of the weather, which you have failed to report to me! Hell's bells, man, look at that damn great mass of cloud astern! Didn't you think that was worth mentioning to me? If that's not a *pampero* brewing up, I'm a Dutchman.'

As if to complete Raven's humiliation, Lewis now claimed the captain's attention before he had a chance to apologize or explain: 'Cap'n sir!' the AB called from the bottom of the ladder. 'I begs your pardon, but Davey here says Billy John is real bad this morning - all over terrible spots. I think a've caught somethin' in that dago jail back there. You saw what a looked like when a came out - all dirty, like.'

'Yes yes, very well, Lewis, very well. I'll do my best for him when I've got a chance, but not now. Look at that lot astern, mun! That's a *pampero*. Have you ever been through one of those? No? Well, I can tell you this: if I don't get on with my proper job this minute, the whole lot of us will be feeding the fishes soon. One hoodlum with a bit of a rash will have to wait.' Then, without a pause for breath, he yelled: 'Mister Raven, all hands on deck to take in sail!'

Raven sent two brassbounders sprinting off, one to hammer on the port foc'sle door, the other to rouse Grant and the idlers. In a few seconds the formerly humdrum scene on the main-deck was transformed to one of purposeful chaos and noise, as men came rushing out of doors, dragging on oilskins. Mair and Eleanor, coming out of the cabin companion for a quiet early-morning stroll, were amazed at the hubbub, and the former went straight to her husband at the poop rail: 'Jacob, what on earth...?'

'Got a bad *pampero* coming up astern. Got to get the sail off her. And as if I hadn't got enough troubles, I've had one of the hands yapping at me about John - the sick AB.'

'What's the matter with him now?' she asked, instantly concerned and attentive.

'Don't know – haven't had a chance to see him yet. Something about a lot of spots - a rash. May be nothing. Ah, Mister Grant: we're in for a *pampero,* I believe - a real dusting. Snug her down to lower tops'ls, and for God's sake get the crowd to hurry – we've not got long, and that's our best suit of sails up there - worth hundreds. This blow will rip them to shreds.'

Mair said: 'Jacob, this is really serious, and this time you really must do something, and not keep putting it off. A rash! If he's got a temperature as well it means he's got a really bad jail fever - typhus, I think they call it. Why didn't I think of that before? We'll have to...'

'Not now, *cariad,*' said Jacob curtly. 'I've no time for anything now but saving the ship. You'd better both get below.'

'O no, Dadi!' said Eleanor, young enough still to have romantic, Byronic notions about wild weather and deep seas. 'I love to watch a storm.'

'Not this sort you won't. A *pampero* – you get them round the mouth of the Plate this time of year - hits you like a hammer, and then God help you. Now away you go, and tell Isaac to secure everything down below – don't want to find all the cabin china smashed.' Mair opened her mouth to speak in protest, but her daughter, seeing the tension - even fear - in her father's face, tugged at her sleeve, and they left in silence.

If Jacob had had a moment to spare from his own worries, he might have been disturbed at the look on his daughter's face, and in her eyes, a look that had been gathering for weeks. She had, after all, been wrenched with some violence from the burst of life and joy which her passion for John Raven had brought, and then trapped in the cabin, unable to avoid the pressure of her parents' reproachful disapproval, or the ensuing coldness and dreary bickering between them over the lost passage home. It was hardly surprising that she had, so it seemed, aged ten years in a few weeks; she had lost the rosy freshness that had so devastated the ship's young men; her face had acquired instead a dogged, stoic stolidity, shut in upon itself. Her mouth, which had, in that far-off Chilean sunshine, seemed so ready always to break into a smile, was now set and straight, with small downward lines of determination at its corners.

Despite her father's orders, she halted near the companion and looked about: 'O mam,' she said softly, 'how awful it is! I've never seen cloud so black and heavy. It's as if the sea and the sky have died, except for this horrible long swell. And the air's so heavy - have you noticed? - that all the sounds of our feet and our voices have gone dead and muffled. I'm sure we're in for a fearful storm; even Dadi looked afraid, and I've never seen that before. All we have to do is go below out of it - but those poor men up there! Heaven help them if the storm comes before they've finished furling the sails! O, why does God make their lives so dangerous, as well as so wretched?'

Her mother snorted brusquely: 'H'm! Don't blame God; blame Henry Powell and his like! The hands suffer because they're poor men, and poor men always have to do the jobs and eat the food that no-one else wants. Just thank God you're not born to be one of them, and don't forget: it's a short trip down to the gutter to join them. Young people who fall out with their families, who are only trying to love and help them, and go flouncing off on their own - they're the ones who finish up there, often enough. Come along, let's get below. We can't help them furl the sails, can we?'

'I wish I could. I wish I had the skill and the nerve to be up there with them. I'd do anything, rather than be a useless lump of flesh being carted round the world like a piece of cargo. It would be all right if we were happy like we were at first, back at Caleta Buena.'

Her mother grimaced: 'Happiness! That's something that comes and goes when it will, and there's little enough of it about. No use chasing it, or looking for it in ways that God has forbidden, my girl when - O Heaven help us - look at that!'

She pointed directly astern; there, right across the western horizon, was a line of livid, almost phosphorescent, white, and in the dead silence came the sound of a muttering, like voices speaking in anger in a distant, cavernous hall. 'I've seen one of these storms before, when I was with your father on the Australian run. That's the first squall of wind coming.'

Her daughter gasped and put her hand to her mouth in fear, then swung round and looked up at the peopled rigging, and especially at the yard of the mizen course, where Raven was leading the men in fastening the huge stiff sail with rope gaskets. 'Yes,' said Mair, 'he's up there too, isn't he? Well, he'll have to take his chance with the rest, and hang on, won't he? It's a pity he didn't keep a better lookout, and obey your father's orders, two hours back. Then we'd all have been ready for it.'

Eleanor flushed deeply; tears started in her eyes. To hide them from the men working near them, brailing the spanker, she ducked into the companion and clattered rapidly down the steps. Mair suddenly knew she had been cold, cruel and malicious, and went after her, calling: 'Nell, I'm sorry; I didn't mean to be so unkind. It's just that we seem to have one trouble after another. Don't worry, *cariad,* he'll come down safely with all the rest of them. And he's very young - he can't be the perfect officer yet. I know I was a horrible old witch; but I'm so worried about that sick man, and your father won't do a thing about him. Well, if he won't, someone else will have to. Come on, we'll have some tea before it gets any rougher.'

For Apprentice Ieuan Davies, the sound of tinkling china and spoons in a comfortable cabin was a world away. Lying across the main royal yard, he was struggling urgently to undo one of the gaskets securing the sail; most of the men had now left the rigging, and he had been on the point of leaving the yard - with great relief - when Grant's bellow, thinned by the oppressive air to a flat, faint cry, had come up: 'Davies! That last gasket on the starboard end! It's too slack, you useless sojer! We'll lose the sail. Make it fast properly, and be bloody quick about it!'

The boy wrenched, all fingers and thumbs, at the tight clove-hitch fastening the gasket to the iron jackstay on top of the yard; he'd only just made the knot, and it was tight. His haste made him clumsy, and because of it he neglected to put his arm through one of the beckets, the loops of rope which gave a modicum of safety to men standing on a wire and working a hundred and eighty feet up. At last the knot was loose; he undid the turns and put them back, hauling each one tighter, tucking in each fold of sail, for the mate's wrath was not a thing to be taken lightly. He made the last turn, and had got to the point in the job where even now, after months of working aloft, he still felt nervous - the point where you had to let go of the solid jackstay and duck down below the yard, holding on to the sail only, to pass the rope underneath. Nearly finished now, thank Christ!

Then suddenly, another bellow, louder, more urgent, than the last: 'Davies! Leave it! Hang on, boy!' For, sooner than he expected, Grant had felt the breath of the coming tempest, and knew the first hammer-blow was upon them. Mentally, clutched by a deadly cold fear, he cursed the boy for his slowness; everybody else was on deck now. His dread and anxiety disguised itself as petulance: let the halfwit hang on till the wind eased a bit; the royal sail would have to take its chance. By God, though, the fool would have to hang on hard; the ship, devoid of steerage-way in the flat calm, had wallowed round broadside-on to the coming storm, despite the helm being hard-up. The wind wouldn't, as it usually did, press the boy's body against the solid yard, but blast him sideways.

All this passed through his mind in an instant, and in that instant he knew that his shout was too late; the idiot was down on the foot-rope, passing the gasket under!

The cold blast, when it hit them, was like the end of the world; Ianto was reaching up for the jackstay with his right hand, his left clutching a fold of sail. The fearsome wind struck his ballooning oilskin, tore his hand from its grasp, and hurled him sideways, clear of all the rigging and clear of the ship's side, for 'Figaro' too reeled heavily to starboard at the wind's impact. He gave a high scream: 'O Jesus!' as he felt his body weightless, falling in an arc; then, mercifully, he was knocked senseless by the brutal icy blow of the water. He was not aware, a few moments later, of coming back to the surface; he saw no shadow and heard no noise of huge wings when the questing albatross came down on him, and he felt no pain when it struck his bare head with its cruel hooked beak. He didn't see the ship - his home and only refuge - start away from him like a spurred horse as the sails filled. He did not see, neither did any of his shipmates, when the white, tormented sea finally closed over him.

The deck of the ship, as she reeled and staggered on her way, was full of horror-struck men shouting; the captain, his soul torn with pity for the boy, still had to be a captain and observe the correct forms. He yelled 'Bosun!', and as the old man ran aft, called to him: 'Bosun, I want you to witness that I can do nothing to save the man overboard. I cannot in this storm turn the ship round without imperilling all of us, neither could any boat hope to live in this sea.'

Reuben Mathias stood for a moment grasping the mizen fife-rail to steady himself, listening to the hellish scream of the gale in the wires above him, watching the white wake as the ship tore off before it; he shook his head slowly: 'No, capten, nothing... May God rest his soul, poor lad.'

'Aye, indeed. My prayer is the same, Reuben. Later on, I shall have to ask you to sign the entry in the official log.' Then he called to the senior apprentice, trying to conceal the tremble in his voice: 'Perkins, when you go below, it'll be your job to get Davies's gear together to send to his people.'

Among all the hubbub of the storm, he remembered a quiet winter afternoon in Cardiff Dock, the ship lying lifeless under the coal chutes, and a solemn, soberly-dressed couple from St Davids taking tea with him in the cabin and saying: 'Well, capten, since the boy's so set on going to sea, we're glad indeed to be able to find him a berth in a Welsh ship with a Welsh capten and crew... O, very glad. We know we can trust you to look after him; boys can be so foolish, isn't it?' He thought bitterly: A wonderful job I've made of looking after him! And he thought too of his earlier gleeful words to Grant: It'll be down-wind all the way... My God, it was down-wind today, right enough! He shook his head to clear it, and found that he was gripping the poop-rail as if to save his life, and that his eyes were pricking with tears; the mate was at his elbow, and, mastering all emotion, Jacob said: 'Square the yards, mister. Let her run before it. Course south-east by east.'

Grant repeated mechanically: 'Aye, aye, sir. South-east by east.' He too was stunned by grief and guilt, and after a pause said quietly: 'I should have called the poor chap down sooner, sir. What the hell does a few shillings'-worth of canvas matter, after all?'

But Jacob would yield none of his own guilt to others: 'I'm capten,' he said harshly. 'I take the blame for everything. You shouldn't have sent him back perhaps, and young Raven should have let me know about the weather, and perhaps young Davies himself should have had an arm through a becket. But you all failed to do the right things, and now he's dead, and I'm his capten. I'm responsible.' He cleared his throat, and with an effort dragged himself back to the present: 'We can't bring him back, mister. Send the starboard watch below now, if you please. They'd better get some rest if they can.'

Far astern now, a lifebuoy, which someone had found time to throw over for Ianto, drifted useless in the rising seas, proclaiming its origin: 'Figaro, Cardiff'.

*   *   *

The pampero had come suddenly with its fatal blast, but did not leave them until it had tossed, shaken and tormented them for two days. All that time Jacob Roberts' stocky figure was fixed, solid and immoveable, rock-like, at the weather end of the poop rail, through showers of spray, heavy driving rain and pelting hailstorms. The great marching seas, soon built up by the storm, slowly overtook 'Figaro', towered over her poop, then slid along the waist, their high crests tumbling thunderously over both bulwarks, so that for much of the time, Jacob could see nothing of his ship but three black islands - the half-deck, the midship house and the foc'sle - forging stubbornly ahead through the angry white waste. Behind him the best of the ship's helmsmen - two at a time -sweated and wrestled with the big wheel, desperate to prevent the stern from being slewed round by the battering of the huge combers, to leave the ship wallowing helpless in a trough, waiting to have her hatches pounded in by the next sea.

Even the misery of the boy's death had for a time been superseded in Jacob's mind by his present worry: should he perhaps have hove her to when the storm started, and let her ride it out in relative comfort and safety, taking the seas diagonally on the bow? A terrible waste, of course, of a favourable slant of wind, but a damn sight safer than this headlong helter-skelter, the ship going nearly as fast as the waves. Too late to change his mind anyway; he'd never get her round into the wind now. He glanced aloft for the thousandth time at the sails, the three lower tops'ls of Number One canvas, thick as boards, and forged by the wind into iron curves, darkened by the drenching rain. How long could they stand the strain of the wind? What would happen if they didn't? Every now and then the steward brought him sandwiches and coffee, which he ate and drank without tasting; now and then Hughes brought a bucket too, so that Jacob could relieve his bladder without leaving his post.

Late in the evening of the second day, Grant appeared at his shoulder, and bawled in his ear: 'I think it's easing off a little; the seas are not quite so high now, and there's a bit less wind. You should go below, sir. You've been here too long. I'll take her now - for the night, I mean, not just the first watch. I won't leave young Raven with her. You must be all in; get some sleep, sir. I swear I'll let you know if it worsens, or if anything carries away. The tops'ls are standing up to it so far. Away you go now, sir!'

The Old Man pondered, looked around briefly, and said: 'Very well, then. I'm obliged to you, mister.' Then he shuffled wearily to the chartroom, pausing only to bark gruffly at the helmsmen: 'South-east by east, mind, and no shenanikens. Watch her if she starts to broach.'

Mumbling, dazed by fatigue, he dragged open the chartroom door and stepped over the high coaming.

'Poor old bugger,' said Lewis, his eyes glued on the compass in the binnacle. 'Out on his feet, he is.'

As Jacob came down the spiral stair into the cabin, Mair started
to her feet, all her grievances against him lost in her pity. She rapidly
took in his utter weariness, his stiff movements, the water still streaming
from his oilskins: 'O Jacob *bach!* You've been too long up there, *cariad*,
far too long!'

She stood helping him off with his heavy coats and handing
them to Eleanor, all three of them swaying and lurching, for, as always
when running before the wind, the ship was rolling heavily, forty degrees and more each way, and here, right in the stern, they felt the giddy
lift and fall of her pitching. 'Tst, tst,' she said, as if to a little boy, 'your
socks and trousers are wringing wet.'

Jacob slumped heavily into an easy chair, not just exhausted,
but low in spirits too. 'I had to stay, gel... Had to... One soul is enough to
lose, isn't it?'

'Yes - poor, poor boy. Always so pleasant and decent... I know
how you feel, Jacob, but you mustn't keep blaming yourself for his death.
It was a terrible accident, but the kind that will always happen when
men have to work aloft in bad weather.'

Eleanor seemed to have some cheering news, and said, aside to
her mother: 'Shall we tell him...?' but was stopped by Mair putting a finger to her lips.

'Not now, Nelli. Nothing now.' Then, aloud to Jacob: 'I kept
back some soup at supper-time; will you have some before you turn in?'
He made no answer; she put a bowl of Jones' best pea soup on a small
table and drew it in front of him. She and Eleanor sat across from him,
watching some colour and life return to his stiff features as the thick hot
liquid went down. The warmth of the cabin and the comfort of the chair,
however, overwhelmed him before he could finish, and Mair rose: 'Nelli,
help me get him to bed. He's too exhausted even to finish his soup, poor
man. The boy's death has upset him cruelly too.' For her shrewd insight
told her that Jacob's long stay on deck had been dictated not only by
duty, but also by a desire to avoid the thoughts, the guilt and remorse
that bodily rest might bring.

When Jacob struggled awake, late the next morning, it was to
find a beam of sunlight shifting, chasing, over his cabin bulkhead. He
could feel that there was still a big following swell, but the ship's motion
was easier, and he guessed that she was being steadied by having more
sail spread. Sure enough, he found as he came out on deck that the wind

was no more than what deep-sea sailors satirically called 'a yachtsman's gale', and that the mate had spread more of her wings to it - the upper tops'ls, the huge fore-course and many of the staysails. Grant saluted him with a smile and made a comprehensive gesture towards the sea, the sky and the sails: 'Good morning, sir. No need to ask if you slept well, I dare say? It started fining down about dawn, so I took the liberty of giving her some more canvas. Didn't like to disturb you, as you were so fagged-out last night. D'you think perhaps she might stand up to the t'gallants and the other two courses?'

'Aye aye, mister. Let's crack on. Give it a try.' He couldn't really like Grant, or feel close to him, as he had to David Evans, but by God the fellow was like a rock for reliability, and a seaman through and through. Pity about his temper and his way with the hands...

Eleanor came to join them, well wrapped against the chill wind, which had whipped some colour into her cheeks. By Jove, Grant thought, that girl really is a looker, whatever she wears! Nice to see her looking more cheerful, too. No wonder young Raven was... She smiled dazzlingly at him: 'Good morning, Mr Grant. How lovely to see the sun again! Dadi, Mam wants you to come down for some breakfast now.'

'Good! *Duw, Duw,* I could eat a horse.'

'And we've got some good news for you, too - when you've eaten a good breakfast, Mam says.'

Jacob smiled, looking happier than for many a day at the return of family affection, and joked with the mate: 'Never mind what the Crew Agreement says, mister: you can see who's the real master of this ship!'

After his leisurely breakfast, Jacob permitted himself the luxury of a good Cuban cigar and said: 'Very well then, what's this mysterious good news I've been promised?'

Mair smiled: 'It's about William John Ffynnongroes: I think he's going to get better quite quickly now. His temperature has dropped, his rash is fading, and he's beginning to eat and enjoy his food. He's even eating the foc'sle food.'

'O, and how do you come to know so much about the fellow? Has Isaac Hughes told you, or the peggy?'

Mair moved nearer and took his hand, her manner winning and defensive against a possible storm: 'Now Jacob, you're not to get upset or cross about this, but no. While the storm has been on I've been nursing him myself. I could see you couldn't possibly spare the time, and I also knew something had to be done without any more delay. After reading your Medical Guide I'm fairly sure the man has jail fever - typhus, and in some cases that can even be fatal, the book says. When I went into that cabin, I found out how hopeless Isaac and the peggy were as nurses; I've told you before what that man Hughes is like, and as for the boy, well, he's far too young and stupid. As well as the man's body and hair, all the bed-clothes and bedding were filthy, so out of the port-hole they went...'

'Good God, you didn't have a port open in that storm, did you? You could have flooded the whole ship, woman.'

'I'm not quite as *twp* as you think me, Jacob; I had the sense to wait for a good roll to starboard. Anyway, out they went, with all the bugs, fleas, lice and dirt that he'd picked up in that dreadful jail. Then I washed him in carbolic soap from head to foot, and Hughes found me a spare mattress and sheets and blankets from the cabin store, and some clothes from the slop-chest - grumbling all the time, of course, about what you'd say. I knew you'd approve of what I was doing - in the end. John seemed to me to start getting better straight away.'

Jacob felt a vague resentment at having things taken out of his hands in this way, and at having been so convincingly proved to be in the wrong, but he stifled the feeling as unworthy of him. After all, if it put paid to the whole schemozzle about John... 'Yes,' he said. 'You've done well, Mair, and I'm grateful to you, though I don't like to think of you having to deal with such matters -washing seamen's bodies, and so on.' That rankled - that she should have to wash the naked body of the most worthless man on board. Then he thought: I pride myself on being a Christian who believes that his Saviour, when on earth, was not ashamed to wash the feet of his disciples, so my resentment is unworthy. Still, a holy disciple was not the same as that damned skate Billy John. Despite his attempt at piety, it still rankled, as if the rascal had somehow deliberately insulted her by exposing himself to her. Then he dismissed that thought too, as even more unreasonable, and merely said: 'I shall put it all in the official log, and old Powell can damn well pay you for your nursing duties when we - Good God, what the devil's going on out there?' For, from the passage-way on the other side of the door, there came the sound of a loud yell of anger from Isaac Hughes, followed by the heavy thud of something falling to the deck - then dead silence.

Jacob stormed out of the door, to find the steward, his eyes wide with fear, standing over the fallen body of Davey Jones peggy: 'It's the boy, capten! I found him leaning against the bulkhead, doing nothing. I thought he was just loafing, but when I shouted and pushed him he just

329

fell down flat, like you see him. Didn't say nothing, just fell flat on the deck! He'd been saying he felt tired, but I never took no notice - well, you know what boys are...'

Mair spoke from over her husband's shoulder: 'Well, now you can see, Isaac Hughes, what you've done to the poor scrap: thanks to your leaving all the dirty work to him, he's caught the fever too, and I can tell you now, we shan't leave *him* to your tender mercies. Get that fellow John back to the foc'sle, and then come back and help me get this lad to bed in his place. And this time I'll take charge of him from the start.'

Jacob merely stood irresolute, feeling less of a captain than he had ever done before.

19

Six days later, Jacob and his family sat at the breakfast table on a fine South Atlantic morning, the strong pool of brightness from the sky-light shifting in a steady circle over floor and white-clothed table. The keen north-westerly still blew, and the bogey-stove burned to make the saloon cosy. 'Figaro' was still revelling in the quartering gale, reeling off nearly three hundred miles a day. Jacob's contentment at their progress, at the good breakfast, and perhaps most of all at their restored harmony, was clouded slightly when Mair folded her napkin neatly and made to rise.

'Don't go yet, *cariad,*' he said genially. 'Let's have some more coffee. Nelli, call that miserable scrimshanker of a steward, will you? I've checked the set of the sails, and those young fellows can manage up there for a bit.'

'No, Jacob, no more, thank you. It's time for me to go and see young Davey. There's no holiday for nurses.'

'How is the poor little *crwt* now? I forgot to ask last night.'

'As expected, Jacob - very poorly. It's a horrible disease. He's got no rash yet, but that will come. He's got the same dreadful headache that John had, and his tongue's all furred and stiff, like a piece of wood. I could cry sometimes, when I look at him... all these thousands of miles from home.'

'As to that, gel, look at it this way: he's got a better berth, and a better nurse too, than he would have if he was home at Ty'r Yet, among that rag-tag lot up there.'

Eleanor put her cup down: 'I'll come with you today, mam. It's time I helped a bit; you can show me what to do, and we'll take turns.'

Mair's reply was instant; 'No, *bach,* you keep away, That old Medical Guide is pretty vague about how the typhus is passed on. They don't think it's contagious; they think it's passed on by infected lice, and by the dust from dirty bedding and clothes, but they're not really sure, so there's no point in running risks.'

'But mam, all the dirty bedding and clothes have gone, and both the patients have been scrubbed all over with carbolic. There can't be any more danger, surely?'

'No,' said Jacob genially, smacking his huge hands together, 'thank God all that's gone now - like a bad dream.'

There was a pause; then Mair spoke in a tone which was somehow chilling to the others: 'You two haven't thought it out, have you? Who washed those men, and who threw out their clothes and bedding? You see? The danger's not over yet; the disease takes time to show itself. I've been thinking,' Jacob, 'that, to be on the safe side, neither you nor Nelli nor anyone else ought to visit Davey. Nelli, perhaps this morning you'd help me make up a bed in the saloon; I don't think I'd better sleep with you, Jacob, for at least a week.'

Jacob joked uneasily: 'Aw, come on now, *cariad!* With the nights still cold, I need you there.'

Mair shook her head, and Eleanor, sensing the grim warning behind her mother's words, changed the subject hastily: 'Yes, why is it so cold here, dadi? We're not very far south, after all.'

'No, but there's no land down here, see? Nothing to get warmed up by the sun. And the sea's cold, with all the icebergs drifting north from Antarctica. The wind and the sea can sweep right round the globe with nothing to stop them, and you just get one westerly gale after another. Good for big ships like ours, that can stand it, and sail full tilt before it. "Running the easting down" they used to call it in the old clipper-ship days.'

'I suppose,' said Mair, 'that with germs about it's better for the weather to be cold. Still, if I'm to be stuck down below nursing most of the time, it would be nice to have some warm sunshine, and take a nice turn on deck instead of having to dodge these tremendous waves, and getting frozen to the marrow by these gales you seem to like so much. Sometimes I feel quite lifeless and listless for lack of fresh air.'

Jacob smiled, his mind on the voyage again: 'Don't worry, gel, I won't take her far south - not like one tight-fisted old Cardi skipper I sailed with once, who kept her heading south into the cold until he'd sold all the oilskins and thick jerseys from his slop-chest! Fine sunny weather's all very well, but it doesn't push ships along. Hard following gales – that's what this ship's designed for; she's not some namby-pamby yacht.'

At supper that night, Grant reported Billy John fully fit again, and Jacob beamed: 'What did I tell you, Mair? These fellows are tough as old boots. You see - I was right not to go a yard out of my way for that hoodlum.'

Grant asked politely:

'And how's your other patient, Mrs Roberts?'

'Very low and lifeless, poor boy, with a shocking headache.'

'Aye!' Jacob said heartily, 'but you'll see, he'll soon be right as rain too.'

'I don't know, Jacob,' she said, with a shake of the head. 'He's not naturally strong like William John. You know how pitifully poor his family is. Haven't got two ha'pennies to rub together - half-starved, most of the time. Those Johns are a lot more prosperous; they should be, they're so mean and grasping.'

Grant broke in: 'Talking of that, I'm sure that our friend Billy is fully recovered and back to normal, captain. I hear he's been complaining in the foc'sle about the destruction of his clothes; he's going to demand compensation for them, and refuse to pay for the new stuff you gave him from the slop-chest.'

Jacob snorted in disgust: 'There you are! There's gratitude, isn't it? What did I tell you? I knew he'd make trouble, once he was better.'

'Let that man Powell pay for all the new clothes,' said Mair. 'He can well afford it from the profit you're making for him.'

Sensing the slight friction between them, Grant adroitly changed the subject: 'The westerly breeze is keeping up well, sir. A decent run yesterday, I expect?'

'Good enough, yes. Two hundred and eighty. By the by, tell young Raven I'm expecting to sight Gough Island to port quite soon. It'd be as well to check the longitude; and anyway, with this sea running, you can't even get a decent horizon for the sextant, for the latitude. I'm just going by dead reckoning and the patent log; can't altogether trust that, can we? But we both reckon we're on forty-thirty South, so we'll go quite close.'

'Dadi,' said Eleanor, 'that sounds dangerous. What if we're so close that we hit it in the night? I bet there's no light on it.'

'No, but in this weather the lookout would have to be blind and deaf, or dead drunk, or asleep. You wait till you hear and see the surf - sounds like thunder miles off.'

'Well, if I were captain I'd keep well away.'

The men smiled at each other indulgently, and Grant said: 'Your father needs to check our longitude, Miss Roberts. The latitude is pretty easy: you see us every day at noon taking sights and checking with each other. Even Cabot and Drake and those old fellows could do that. But getting the longitude is a lot harder; as well as needing a first-rate sextant reading of the sun or a star, and being able to do a long calculation, you also depend on your chronometer giving you exactly the right time.'

Jacob broke in indignantly: 'Yes, and if our blessed owner wasn't so mean, we'd have two of those. As it is, we need to check by seeing the land now and then. But don't worry, *cariad*, we won't run into it. Cigar, mister?'

Eleanor got up abruptly: 'If you're going to smoke, I shall take a turn on deck. I can't stand the horrible smell.'

Jacob made a small private grimace at Mair, who shrugged imperceptibly. They both saw all the signs of a revival of the affair between Raven and their daughter, but when it took the form of utterly respectable chats in public they felt they could do nothing, short of forcibly shutting her up below decks, or following her like spies. Nelli had seemed truly repentant for her past disgraceful conduct, and they too regretted the bitterness of their reactions and words. Anyway, Raven's cabin and bed were now well out of her way, for'ard on the starboard side. To get there, she'd have to walk right past her father's cabin door, and she surely wouldn't have the nerve to do *that?*

What a pity, though, that she still liked the fellow! They'd hoped the interruption and their anger would have killed off her fancy. But there, Mair thought shrewdly, after all, he was the only young man about. Perhaps it would still be all right if Nelli didn't compromise herself any more; the voyage wouldn't last for ever, and there were lots of more suitable young men at home, and once she was there, it would be Raven who would be out of sight, out of mind.

*   *   *

From where he stood, doing his trick at the wheel during the first watch that evening, Johanssen, AB could, in the starlit darkness, see only one patch of black at the poop rail where the second mate and the Old Man's girl stood so close together. By Yimminy, it would be good to have her beside you, cuddling up, warming you! Then he grinned at himself in the dark and shook his head. She wouldn't like a big, rough, grizzled old Swedish bear. He'd do better to think of his own stout, bustling, capable Gretta, back home outside their cabin on the lake shore, stumping through the snow with hay for the beasts, and deftly splitting pine logs for the big stove. Then his practised hands felt through the spokes the pressure on the rudder increase as the wind gusted, and saw the compass needle begin to slide as the huge ship strove to come up into the wind. He hove down hard on the wheel and watched the needle come slowly back to south east-by-east. Never mind about the girl, even if she was a real strongbody! Keep bloddy ship on course!

Eleanor had felt Raven stiffen and. draw away, and she said, 'What's the matter, John?'

'He let her yaw to port; didn't you feel the wind shift?'

'No - how would I?'

'You feel it on the back of your neck. Helmsmen - even good ones - are like that at night. Their minds wander; old Johanssen was thinking about the senoritas back in Rosario, I dare say.'

'Nonsense. I expect he's a respectable married man with a nice proper wife back in Sweden.'

'Yes, maybe, but...'

She put her arm through his and drew him closer: 'But nothing, Mister Second Mate Raven, sir. If - *if*, mind you - I should ever be foolish enough to marry a sailor, I should expect him to behave himself wherever he was - Chile or Brazil or Australia. After all, he wouldn't want me to be setting my cap at all the young men in Swansea or Cardiff or Liverpool, would he? Haven't you got a saying in English: "Sauce for the goose is sauce for the gander"?'

He turned to where her face glimmered pale: 'Whatever makes you think I'd misbehave in any port - if I were married, that is? O Nelli, it's so good to see you so much happier. I'm so glad to have you back, even if we can't... you know...'

She tightened her arm: 'I'm glad too to be with you again. If we have to be respectable now, perhaps that's all to the good. I did behave very shockingly before, now I think about it - so did you, of course; quite dreadfully, really, though it seemed so wonderful and right and so heavenly at the time. And I'm glad Mam and Dadi have stopped quarrelling with me and with each other. In a way, this typhus business has done good: it's made them realize what really matters, and stopped them from going over past grievances. But I do hope poor Davey will get better; he's such a sweet little lad, and so obliging always.'

'H'm! I wish him well, of course, but he could be a cheeky young swine to the apprentices - except to his chum Ianto.'

She moved away slightly at the mention of the dead boy's name: 'Poor, poor Ieuan! It seems so cruel that such young fellows have to do such a dangerous job - going aloft in storms.'

'We all have to do it. And it isn't only the young who suffer, nor just aloft. One of the old mates got smashed up on deck just before you came, otherwise I wouldn't be here now, perhaps. The job's got to be done.'

'Not if all ships were steamships.'

'I suppose they will be some day, but not for a very long time yet. This ship, for instance, is brand new off the Clyde. The owners will want to get at least twenty years' work out of her. Anyway, even if I decided to change to steam, I'd still have to serve some time in sail to get my mate's and master's tickets.'

'That's silly! You men and your ridiculous rules...'

'No, I think it's right. How could you learn any real seamanship in a steam-kettle, where you can stand in a nice warm wheelhouse, point the ship the way you want to go, and just turn a tap and shovel some more coal to get more speed? Besides, just look at the ship tonight! Who'd want that stink of smoke and grease when the wind will drive her like this - faster than any damned engine?'

Above and below them, 'Figaro' was revelling in her ideal wind - a steady gale on her port quarter; the huge dark shadow of her sails swayed across the pin-prick lights of the stars; the long overtaking seas bore up stern and bow in turn in a steady see-saw rhythm; her speed and massive bulk made her give out a deep thunder, and white foam spread for acres around and behind her. When Eleanor leaned over the side she could hear the sharp hiss of her speed through the water; now and then, as the ship rolled heavily, the crest of a sea flopped in over the bulwarks to swill about on the main deck.

'Yes,' she said, 'I can see she's lovely, more beautiful than any machine, but isn't she going too fast to be safe?'

'No: she'll stand it. Your dad is a good man for cracking on, even if...' He stopped from belated tact.

She giggled: 'Even if he's quite old, you were going to say? Well, if he weren't, I'd still be in baby clothes. Would you like that?'

'No, I much prefer you as you are - and even better out of any clothes at all.'

'Really, *Mister Raven!*' But she gave the same soft laugh as had devastated him before. Then the amorous nonsense was cut short by a cry from the lookout: 'Light dead ahead!' and Raven started guiltily.

'I must concentrate, Miss Roberts, ma'am.' He took the telescope and scanned the horizon ahead till he found a dot of light that came and went. 'Got it! It's the stern-light of a ship on the same course as ours. Want to look?'

She took the glass: 'Yes, I see a very faint light. But it keeps disappearing.'

'That's because her stern-light, like ours, is mounted on the rail, so that every now and then it's hidden by the big seas. I'll have to get the Old... um... your father - up here.'

He leant over the poop-rail and was calling for the messenger when he heard the chartroom door open and shut, and felt Eleanor move abruptly away from him to the lee side. It was the captain, and he spoke first to Eleanor in Welsh: 'You'd better go below and look after your mother. She's gone to bed with a nasty headache. Came on suddenly after supper. She's not quite herself.' Then he spoke irritably to Raven in English: 'You were calling the messenger; what's the matter, then, mister?'

'Ship dead ahead, sir. We're coming up on her quite fast.'

'H'm. We shall see quite a lot, now we're on the track for the Australia and East Indies shipping. If she's that slow she might be a whaler dodging along.' He took a long look through the glass: 'Very good, bear away a point until we're past her. Taken a bearing of her light, have you? No? What do they teach you cubs? How the devil can you pass her safely if you don't know what course she's on? Good God, she might be steering right across our bows for all you know. I expect my officers to have their wits about them when they're on duty, and not to be chatting with - with passengers. You let the helmsman yaw her right up to windward just now - I could feel it down below.'

Eleanor went rapidly aft, at first merely annoyed with her father's interruption of a totally innocent chat. That was just an excuse to be awkward and interfering! Then a sudden chill struck like a spear in her heart: a headache! That was the first thing both Billy John and Davey had complained of! What if...? Mam had been the one to handle John's bedding and clothes; she had washed him head to foot, and done the same for Davey. She had taken more risk than anyone except Davey. That's what she'd been hinting at this morning... But then again, she had done a lot of reading down below in all the rough weather, and she often got headaches after reading. She probably needed spectacles, but wouldn't go and buy any. She always said she didn't want to look a frump and a blue-stocking. Perhaps it was just that...

But she found her mother pale, and lying on the sofa in the saloon, very listless and with a slight cough that made her wince with pain. She cut her daughter's enquiries short, speaking in a voice which betrayed the pain she was in: 'You see how it is, Nell. I thought it would end up like this. Get me a draught of the fever medicine from the chest, there's a good girl. I shall stay in here till I'm better. I can understand now why Davey fell down. I've no energy, and it's hard even to think. But listen, *cariad:* now all the dirty clothes and bedding have gone, I think it's safe for you to nurse me - but *only* you. It looks as if I've got that wretched fever; you'd better read the bit in the Medical Guide about typhus - it won't take you long because they don't seem to know much about it. Now mind, I don't want your father near me. The Guide can't say for sure how it spreads, so keep him away. I feel bad enough having you near me - I couldn't bear it if you were to catch it.'

'I won't, mam; I'll be very careful. And of course I'll look after poor Davey as well. I'm so tired of hanging about idle; it'll be good to do something useful. In fact, I'll go and see Davey now, unless you want anything.'

"No, only a drink of water... But it will be so awful for you looking after him - you know, when he wants to... But before long he'll be able to get up, and he can use our bathroom, and one of the apprentices can take him.'

'Mam,' said Eleanor tenderly, putting the flat of her hand on her mother's forehead, 'don't you worry about any of that. Thousands of women all over the world nurse other people for a living, as you yourself did; so why shouldn't I, for a few days? What's so special about me? It's better not to spread the risk.' She saw a tear beginning to trickle down Mair's cheek, and said gently: 'What's the matter now, mam? What are you thinking?'

Her mother wept openly, murmuring between her sobs: 'It's just that you're such a kind, good-hearted girl, and your father and I have been so cruel and horrible to you for weeks about John Raven. Listen, if anything should happen to me you must please yourself; never mind about what's been said in the past - marry him if that's what your heart truly wants.' She gave a weak smile through her tears: 'Isn't it funny – I've just remembered a line from an English play we acted years and years ago in school. It went: "Marry him directly, Julia; you'll find he mends surprisingly". How strange, that that should come back to me now!'

Defying all medical prudence, Eleanor bent and kissed her

mother; then, to hide her own tears, she bustled about, tidying the saloon, saying over her shoulder: '"If anything should happen"... What
nonsense! You'll be up and about in no time, like that awful Billy John.
You must settle down now and go to sleep. I'm just going to look in on
Davey; but thank you for what you said about John. I think I do love
him - but perhaps I'm too young to be sure. I only know that I feel quite
differently about him than about any other man I've met. Perhaps he's
been wrong and foolish in the past, but he's not as bad as you were
thinking. And anyway, I just can't help how I feel.' Her mother said
nothing, but gave a weak wry smile that could have been encouragement
or resignation.

It was an odd feeling for Eleanor to go back to the same cabin
where she'd writhed secretly, passionately and deliciously in John Raven's muscular arms, only this time to go quite publicly, and to find on
that same bed a poor puny lad lying sweating, staring up at the deck-
head, his eyes, his whole body totally lifeless. 'Hello, Davey *bach,*' she
said briskly but kindly. 'I'm going to be looking after you now.' There
was no reaction from the boy. 'I'll help you to sit up; I want to get that
shirt off you for a moment, to see if you've got any rash yet.'

She gave a smothered gasp of shock and revulsion as she saw
the livid pink rash on the boy's scrawny trunk; so he had got to that
stage! I only wish, she thought, that the Medical Guide could suggest
some *cure* for the fever sufferers. I don't believe that blessed fever mixture does any more than dope the patient into sleep. Still, while the boy
was sitting up, she gave him two tablespoonsful in a glass, then gently
lowered him back onto the pillow.

Davey shook his head and frowned, obviously making a huge
effort to think: 'Where's the missis, then? Not ill? She hasn't caught this
plague like me and Billy? *Duw,* I'd be real sorry if she had.'

She lied to comfort him: 'No, she's just tired and lying down.
And Billy is fit and working again, by the way, so we'll soon have you up
and about. Go to sleep now, *dyna bachgen da.* ' She blushed, and was
furious with herself for her silly prudishness: 'Unless you want to - you
know - pass water, or anything, first.'

'No miss,' he whispered, oblivious of her blush. 'Never seem to
want...' He tailed off in sleep or stupor; the effort to talk was too much
for his poisoned blood. Eleanor looked down at him in love and pity, and
felt shame when she realized that it was her mother's illness that was
really worrying her, not his, though in all his pain and misery, he had

shown concern for Mam. She slipped the thermometer into his mouth and waited, watching him slide into sleep, the small head on the pillow, lank black hair plastered down in strands by his sweat; his features thin, pale, pinched like a small child's, fragile as an eggshell, the thin dark down on his upper lip. She thought of his mother, thousands of miles away on that wretched little cluster of fields among rocks and scrubby trees on the mountain slopes of Carn Ingli; no doubt this little scrap was dear to her; she must try as hard for him as his mother would. She took out the glass tube and turned it to read the scale: Heavens! A hundred and one - no wonder he was so sweaty! The fever was really burning him up; she'd give him a nice warm wash in fresh water tomorrow. Apart from that, and praying for him, she could only wait for his body to over-come the horrible infection, or - God forbid - succumb to it. Billy was bet-ter - that was something, but Davey and Mam still had the dreadful course to run, and she must sit by, helpless.

For days Eleanor kept below, reading and re-reading the vague and technical phrases of the Medical Guide on 'Fevers, tropical and sub-tropical', and getting little guidance or reassurance from them. She con-scientiously dosed, tended and watched her two patients, sleeping little and only fitfully herself. Her mother showed little change, and was clasped by a dreadful lethargy; coughing seemed the only activity she was capable of; as for Davey, his temperature rose another degree, and then steadied. According to the Guide, when that started to fall on the twelfth day of the sickness, recovery would be in sight - unless, as the book said chillingly, laconically, coma and death followed.

Meanwhile her world, the ship, plunged and raced on its course across the South Atlantic day and night. Down below, the roar of the waves and of her speed was muffled, but Eleanor could hear, at every long slow roll, deep groans and small creaks like the ticking of a clock as her plates and rivets, her massive ribs and stringers took the huge strains of her motion. In the saloon, the quiet click of falling coals in the stove, the shuffling rattle of the steering-chains and the metallic grinding of the rudder in its bearings punctuated the long, dead, endless hours between meals. Jacob came and went on his business; when he took a spell below he spent long hours silent in his chair, speaking only to ask after Mair. When, on the fifth day, the pink rash duly appeared on Mair's body, he went to rummage in the chart-room and brought down an armful of charts, over which he pored with his parallel rule and dividers.

Davey's rash was now at its worst - horribly thick and bloody.

Eleanor surprised even herself with her ability to bathe and wash the lad's crusted skin without flinching or nausea. It just had to be done by someone, and she was inevitably that someone. All the same, it was a great relief each morning to take a quick turn on deck in the cold fresh wind and to chat briefly to the watch-keeper about something other than disease. I could never, she thought, be a doctor or a nurse, spending my whole life doing this.

One morning she came out of the chartroom to find John at the binnacle, busy taking bearings, and Grant training his glass on a high rocky island to port. After all the days and days of rolling ship and restless marching seas, it was somehow strange but comforting to see some dry land which did not move.

Grant lowered his glass and smiled at her: 'Good morning, Miss Roberts. You look tired; how are your patients?'

She shook her head: 'Both suffering in their own ways. Little Davey is delirious, talking to his mother and calling "Meg, Meg!" - some sheepdog of theirs, I expect. My mother's rash gets redder and more unpleasant every day. They both have the cough and the headache. The worst of it is, I feel so helpless and useless, just watching them; I can't do anything to help them, or cure them.' Her voice broke, and there were tears in her eyes.

Even Grant, the hard-case bucko, was moved to go to her side, put his hand gently on her arm and say: 'I should say, Miss Roberts, that you've shown yourself the exact reverse of helpless and useless. What would their plight be without you? It's possible, from what I've heard, that even qualified doctors in hospitals could do little better. I too feel some guilt, as one of the ultimate causes of all this trouble. But then I never sought to make William John my enemy, and I did my utmost not to fight with him. Had it been possible, I would have taken to my heels, but he had me trapped. So don't be hard on yourself.'

Eleanor said, with a naive air of discovery: 'You're very kind, Mr Grant, but I've done little for them, and I've had much time to sit and brood and think bad thoughts: for instance, why does God allow such suffering to be inflicted on complete innocents like these? What could be His purpose? Where is His Justice?'

Grant shook his head: 'There you have me, I'm afraid. I also fear that if I were to answer you candidly I might shock you. In the mean time, your father, as you see, is getting a check on his longitude, and that in turn will enable him to check his chronometer. That's Gough Island

341

over there - one of the Tristan da Cunha group. Barren-looking spot; care to see it?'

She took the glass and steadied it on the jigger shrouds; her father had run the ship close, only two miles off, and the glass showed a tower of bare rock, clouds of sea-birds and a fringe of brilliant white surf round the base. As the huge, world-circling seas were driven by the gale against the island's shore, foam and spray exploded, climbing a hundred feet and more up the cliff, then subsiding. Beneath the steady roar of 'Figaro's' headlong progress she could hear the dull, double-bass thudding of the sea's enormous blows. She handed back the glass: 'It's an awesome sight... terrible. Imagine if we were swept on to those rocks!'

Grant nodded: 'At least it would be a quick end for us - five minutes at the most before she went to pieces.'

'I thought I'd seen heavy seas back home in Newport, when the wind goes into the north-west, but I've seen nothing like that. Well, I suppose I must go below again.' She paused, as if unwilling to leave: 'But tell me: why would I be so shocked by your answer about God's purpose and justice?' She gave a little smile: 'I am a grown woman, after all.'

'Very well then, I will give you my considered opinion - but you must remember that I give it unwillingly. Well then: God does not protect the world's innocents from harm for the simple reason that He does not exist, except as a comforting notion in people's minds.'

Grant had been right; she was shocked. She put her hand to her mouth: 'But that's a dreadful, appalling idea, Mr Grant! If that were true, then all the holy scriptures would be nonsense, and all the generations of good Christian men and women deluded fools And worse still, there'd only be this troubled world - nothing beyond but a cold grave. I couldn't bear to contemplate life on those terms.'

Grant pointed astern to where an albatross soared effortlessly on his great four-foot wings: 'And what about him? A beautiful creature, with wonderful powers of flight and navigation, faithful for life, so they say, to his mate, and devoted to his young: has he an immortal soul and a place in heaven to look forward to? What of the squid that he preys on, or the crab, the weevil, the limpet? Have they? I think you'd say not; well, if not for them and that magnificent bird, then why for a faulty specimen like me?'

She stood silent at the rail, staring unseeing at the blue ocean, the white-crested seas and the small black island. Grant again patted her arm: 'I'm sorry; I see I have upset you. Forget what I said. No doubt it all springs from my invincible ignorance. What does any of us really know?'

'No, why should you apologize? I did ask, and you answered me honestly, I'm just taking in what a big world it is, and how much peoples' minds vary. I was brought up in a very small town at the far end of Wales, and educated in a slightly larger one twenty miles off. In those places, things seemed so tidy, so certain - settled for good. The very idea of an educated man saying, "There is no God" - well, it could not be contemplated.' She smiled, feeling something of a liking at last for this aloof Englishman. 'But my question about God was just a passing feeling, arising from weariness and sorrow and anxiety. I'm sure in my heart that you are wrong.'

He took off his cap and swept it sideways as he bowed in an eighteenth century gesture of gentlemanly acceptance: 'On the whole, I hope you are right, though I personally cannot hope to qualify for any great reward if there is a Hereafter - Yes, Hughes, what is it?'

'Beg pardon, miss, sir: I thought I'd better tell you, miss, that I can hear your mother's voice coming from the saloon. Quite loud, it was, but I couldn't make head nor tail of what she was saying...'

He broke off as Eleanor dashed into the chartroom and down the spiral stairs into the saloon. 'O, I didn't mean to put her into a fright, Mr Grant. It may be nothing much...' But then his natural cringing *schadenfreude* broke through and he said, shaking his head wisely: 'I know that Billy John got better, but then he never raved like Davey and Mrs Roberts do. And then, he was young and strong, but Davey's not strong and she's - begging your pardon, sir - no spring chicken, is she? I don't know, I'm sure... But it would have been be better if that fellow John had never come back, or if the capten had put him ashore when he started to be sick... much better.'

Grant looked at him coldly, disdainfully: 'Well, when you're captain of a ship, Hughes, you'll be able to make that kind of decision. Until you are, I suggest you stick to your pots and pans.'

'Yes, sir,' said the steward, seething with cowardly hatred. 'I know my opinion is of no consequence to anybody.' He slunk below again, muttering inaudibly, and feeling, on the subject of Grant, a strong sympathy with the despised Billy John: to shove a broken bottle right into that English toff's mug – *Iesu Mawr!* - that would be good!

Eleanor stood, helpless and irresolute, in the saloon by her mother's makeshift bed; the sick woman tossed and turned, coughing painfully, and between bouts of coughing uttered incomprehensible scraps of speech in a feeble voice. Isaac must have been (as usual) listening industriously to hear it in the passage. She heard her father's heavy step on the stair and was glad to share the burden with him.

'What did that fellow want just then?'

'He came up to tell me he'd heard Mam's voice - that she might be calling for something. But she's still asleep, as you see, and delirious - talking bits of nonsense about you and me and some blue table-cloth - the one at home, I suppose. She says it wants ironing...'

'Delirious, eh? How about her temperature? Still high?'

'Yes, just over a hundred-and-one this morning - a little more than last night. She looks even hotter now.'

'What about the rash? Odd that it never comes on the face.'

'Still very red and starting to bleed a little, like the others. Look.' She drew Mair's arm from under the sheet and pulled up the sleeve to show a mass of angry spots weeping blood.

'Good God alive! She looks worse than John or Davey.'

'Much the same as Davey. His temperature dropped a fraction this morning, by the way... Could be a good sign.'

Her father didn't hear her; he was staring at his wife's hideous arm unseeing, some other thoughts whirling in his mind. He spoke in a shaking voice to the unconscious form: '*O cariad,* what you're suffering is all my fault. I could have put you ashore at Buenos Aires, and you'd both be out of all this. But I was too stupid to see the need, and too mean as well. I balked at a few days' hotel bill, and now I'd give two years' – ten years' - pay to see you safe ashore.'

Eleanor plucked at his sleeve: 'Don't, Dadi! Don't go torturing yourself like this. You weren't to know - none of us knew - what was wrong with that awful man John.'

He seemed not even to hear her: 'God forgive me for this - though He knows I don't deserve any forgiveness.' Then he focused back on Eleanor: 'Well, my girl, we can't go on like this. I can't do anything about my folly back at the Plate, but I can do something now, and by God I will.'

Without another word he clattered up the steps into the chart-room, and she heard the door bang as he went out on deck. She sighed and went to the bed: 'Come on then, mam *bach,* we'll have your nightie off and bathe those horrible spots. Dear Jesus, if only I could make you better! I'd give anything for that.'

20

On deck, Jacob called brusquely to Grant: 'Man the braces, mister, I'm altering course.'

Grant was a little surprised by the urgency of his manner, but not by the order: 'A point or two south, I take it, sir, now that you've had a good sighting of land?'

'No, I'm bringing her round to north-east-by-east.'

Grant gaped in amazement, and Jacob added testily: 'I'm heading for Cape Town, mister. My wife – and Davey too - are worse today. I've got to get them seen by a doctor; this has gone on long enough. We can be there in six days at this speed, and anyway, once we get into the steamer track we may well come across a liner carrying a proper doctor. Get both watches on deck, mister.'

Grant did not make the automatic reply of 'Aye aye, sir'; he did not question the decision about heading for the Cape, but his sailor's mind was grappling with the immediate problems arising from it. 'Captain, I assume that before we come right round to north-east–by-east you will shorten sail?'

'Shorten it be damned! This is an emergency. I want to get there quickly, mun, not hang about here. Now get the men on those braces; she'll stand it!'

'She certainly will not! With all due respect, sir, you are acting wrongly. If you bring that wind and sea on the beam with this press of sail, you'll drive her right under, or get her knocked flat, or else have half the masts and rigging down on our heads.'

Roberts was scarlet with fury: 'Christ Almighty, mister, are you asking to be logged and disrated down to AB? I gave you an order, and I'm waiting.'

But Grant too was thoroughly roused, and certain he was right. When the wind came abeam, the pressure on the sails would more than double, and her increased speed would plough her into the huge seas, not over them. She might even be forced right over to starboard; the cargo had been well stowed and secured (he'd seen to that) but a heavy list might cause all those thousands of cases of bully-beef to shift - and then, good-night! 'I've signed that I'll obey all your lawful orders, sir, but that doesn't include suicide and mass-murder. Come on, man, you're a seaman - one of the best I've come across. I'm desperately sorry your wife's so ill, but you're letting your personal feelings for her ruin your judgement as...'

'By Christ then, I'll bloody show you whether I'm capten or not!' Beside himself with rage, Jacob aimed a huge wild blow at Grant's head. Grant easily ducked under the swing and caught Roberts' arm; for a while the two men, encumbered by their thick, stiff oilskins, wrestled to and fro, while the men at the wheel nearly forgot to steer in their astonishment. Grant sensed that if he could only hold the captain long enough, the hysterical fury arising from his grief and worry would subside, and he could be reasoned with.

His breath labouring from the effort of holding a man as strong as Roberts, Grant spoke quietly, soothingly: 'Come now, captain: deep down, you know I'm right – don't you? Don't you? You know she'd never stand this spread of canvas reaching, don't you? Don't you?' For answer, Jacob wrenched himself free and fell against the poop rail, staring for'ard, his mind frantically racing, tortured by grief, guilt and fear. He felt Grant's arm across his shoulders, and the mate spoke quietly in his ear: 'Go below, man, and see to your wife. We'll get her to a doctor at the Cape, if that's your will, but leave the ship to me for the time being. You've too much on your mind. You know I'm no fool with a ship – that's why you signed me on. Raven and I will get her there at top speed. Go below now, captain, and be with your wife; she'll pull through, I'm sure. North-east-by-east you said, I think?'

Roberts stared ahead, silent and trembling, crushed under the burden of a fresh, even worse, shame. On a sudden whim - in a panic - he had nearly thrown away his beautiful new ship and every soul aboard her. It had taken a better man, with more guts, to resist his criminal folly; intuitively, he knew how hard it must have been for Grant, after a lifetime of obeying orders, to defy him. But he could not attend to that now; Mair was below, perhaps dying, and through his fault. Now he must stay with her. He said only: 'Yes, north-east-by-east,' and went below, leaving the helmsmen still goggling in amazement.

Grant meanwhile snapped back into a professional stance and manner, as if nothing untoward had happened; he yelled 'Messenger!' and when the duty apprentice appeared, said curtly: 'Call Mr Raven. All hands on deck, and get the bosun aft.' When Mathias arrived, he too was astonished when Grant said: 'Bosun, we're altering course to port. Got to get a lot of this sail off her.'

'Altering course? Where to and what for?'

'Captain's orders. We're not here to argue about them. He's going to the Cape to get the fever patients to a doctor.'

'But good God, sir, that's....'

'As I've just said, it's not for us to argue, bosun. Those are his orders. We'll start by getting the courses off her. You take the foremast, I'll take the mizen, and Mr Raven will be here in a jiffy to take charge of the main. Make the crowd jump about now, and they'll need to put a damn good stow on the sails too. It'll blow like the very devil when she luffs across the wind. After the courses, the royals and t'gallants. Then I think she'll stand it. Leave the staysails for the present.' The bosun shook his head in silence and went forward.

Furling the courses, the huge lowest sails on each mast, was exhausting work in that wind, for each sail, when the sheets were slackened, and the clewlines and buntlines hove up, became a vast, unruly, flogging balloon of the thickest canvas, that had to be fought into submission, while the ship's sickening rolls stood each yard on end at times, and nearly dipped the yardarms into the sea. Slowly, fold by fold, the sails were gathered in, the men and boys standing only on the wire footropes, grimly hanging on with bloody, broken-nailed fingers to what had been painfully won whenever a squall threatened to mock their efforts. When the last gaskets on the courses had been secured, and the boys went up to the tops of the dizzily-swaying masts to furl the upper sails, Perkins yelled to them: 'Remember poor old Ianto, boys! For Christ's sake hang on, whatever you do!'

It was a good hour before the sails were furled and the tired men and lads back on deck; then Grant sang out: 'Starboard braces, bosun! Brace her round to reach on the port tack.' Bringing the brace-falls to the deck capstans, the men swivelled each huge tower of sail round till it slanted obliquely across the ship, and Reuben called up: 'Ready, Mr Grant!'

The mate turned round and stared aft, where the ship's stern rose and fell: rose so that only the grey clouds could be seen, fell to show a world of white-crested, foam-streaked rollers, each forty feet high and more, steadily overtaking them. He looked and waited patiently till he saw a succession of smaller waves approaching; then he walked back to where Lewis and Jones stood at the wheel and called: 'Now, boys! Ease down the helm... Well... Now meet the swing... Well done. Now steady her on north-east-by-east, and God help you if you let her gripe!' Now that, even with reduced sail, she was pressed hard over to starboard, there was that danger - that she might gripe, or shoot up into the wind, causing the sails and the masts to shake dangerously, and losing way, so that she could not be steered. And if she then came up so far that the wind blew on the front of the sails, that might bring the masts down in half a minute or less.

He stood for a long time, Raven at his side, getting the feel of the ship on the new course. 'By God, John, it's about as much as she can stand, even with that canvas off her. She's burying the lee bulwark half the time. But Holy Moses! She's not half moving – eighteen knots at least, wouldn't you say?'

'Best I've ever seen her go - as long as everything holds. Won't be long getting to the Cape at this rate. Good thing too. With her mother so ill, poor Eleanor looks so worried and tired all the time.'

Grant's mind was still on the ship: 'When you take over the watch you'll have to watch the helmsmen like a hawk - and don't let them look sideways at what's coming, either.' The tremendous power of her massive long hull and big spread of sail were driving her pell-mell in line with the crests of the huge seas, so that each one lifted and dropped her forty feet as it passed. It wouldn't do for the men at the wheel to look too hard at the next monster wave as it hung above them on the port beam! Never mind, he thought: crack on, old girl, and get us to land. With all his heart (and there was a heart under the stiff blue serge) he wished for Mair to be seen and made well again by a proper doctor. A real lady, AI at Lloyd's, if ever he'd met one; she'd done so much for the fever sufferers, and she was so much part of the Old Man's soul that God only knew what state he'd be in if anything happened to her.

Then he heard Raven mutter in his ear: 'We've got visitors - a deputation, by the look of it.' He gestured towards the figures of the bo-sun and Curly Kellock mounting the poop ladder, and exchanging asides as they did so.

Grant felt - with some justice - that his day had been difficult enough already, and asked in some irritation: 'Well, bosun - what's this then?'

'We need to see the capten, sir, on an important matter.'

'You must know, man, that he's frantic with worry about his wife. Perhaps I can help?'

'No sir, you can't. I've known Jacob Roberts many a year now - a lot longer than you have, and I need to see him on a crew's welfare matter. It's our right.'

'I see. So what's Kellock here for? Has he put you up to this?'

'Able Seaman Kellock is here because he's the senior foc'sle hand. And I don't need him nor nobody else to tell me what should be done aboard this ship.'

'Very well then. Raven, keep an eye open for me here for a moment. And watch the steering, mind.' He clattered below, and found Jacob slumped in an easy chair, his face half-buried in his hand, which supported his brow, the picture of desolation and despair. 'Sorry to disturb you, captain, but Mathias and Kellock are up top, asking to see you. I've tried to get rid of them, but I couldn't without a shindy.'

'No, don't try to get rid of them. I think I know what they want. We've got our customs in this ship. Tell them to wait in the chartroom; I'll be up directly.'

Grant could not himself divine the bosun's purpose, and later, standing outside the chartroom and hearing the raised voices inside, he wished that he could hear properly, for something serious was being said in there - that was certain. He spoke quietly to Raven, so that the men at the wheel would not hear: 'I think I may have done the wrong thing, you know - but I don't know their confounded Welsh customs. Perhaps I should have sent them packing. You've no idea the state the Old Man's in about his wife – she's quite a bit worse, apparently. I expect they've gone in to chivvy him about something they don't like - the change of course, I suppose - making the voyage longer and so forth. Still, they're both decent quiet chaps on the whole -except that Kellock is a damned sea-lawyer of the first water - a proper maritime Citizen Tom Paine.'

'Tom Paine? Who the devil is he?'

'*Was* he, you mean. Never mind - too late to start educating you now. You can go back below again if you like until eight bells.'

Raven seemed not to hear him: 'I feel sorry for Eleanor too, you know. All this is an awful strain and worry for her... All that responsibility... For her father too now, I suppose. Remember her when she first came aboard in Chile? She doesn't look much like that now, does she, and that was only a few months ago. I think he should have sent them home from Buenos Aires - though I wouldn't have liked it at the time.'

'If he'd known all this would happen, I'm sure he would have packed them off, and Billy John too, into hospital. But it's easy to be wise after the event. It's damned difficult for a skipper when his wife and family live aboard – I've seen it before. He gets torn between his missis on the one hand and his job on the other; I've just experienced a pretty remarkable example of it up here, but never mind about that. In the highly-unlikely event of my plunging into the maelstrom of matrimony, you can bet your bottom dollar I'd leave my beloved spouse at home.'

* * *

'Now then, Jacob Roberts,' the bosun was saying: 'I've sailed under you more years than anyone, except poor old David Evans mate, and never a hard word between us that I can remember. Well, now I'm talking to you man to man - not bosun and capten, like out there. And I'm telling you straight, man to man, that you've been wrong, badly wrong, in what you've done. And Kellock here thinks the same as I do.'

'*Diawl!* (The devil!) mun, don't you think I've got enough troubles down below there, without all this? What the hell's the matter with you?'

'It's not just me, I'm speaking for all the foremast crowd, and I'll soon tell you what's the matter: it's this altering course for the Cape, to get your wife to hospital...'

'And the peggy, don't forget.'

Curly broke in gently, reproachfully: 'You didn't alter course for him, did you, sir, when he caught it, a week back? You got to see our side of it. The men don't wish no harm to Mrs Roberts; – we're more grateful than I can say for the way she looked after Billy and Davey.' His natural eloquence and fire began to kindle. 'But can't you see: all of us – foc'sle crowd, idlers, brassbounders and officers – we're all human beings what have got a right to be looked after properly, equally-like, when we're ill? What you've done now is to put the people on board into diff'rent classes, y'see, and to say some is worth looking after well and some not so well. That's what's wrong.'

The captain stood swaying with the motion, his back against the chart table, in what they felt was an ominous silence. Into that silence, Reuben Mathias spoke diplomatic words: 'We know ships aren't hospitals, sir, and captens aren't doctors; and we know you've always dosed the hands and set their limbs the best you could; but this time...' he gulped nervously as the inevitable words approached – 'this time the illness is too serious for you to treat, and you've been wrong all along –

ever since we left the Plate without putting Billy ashore to the hospital. I mean, you got to treat us all the same when it's a really bad fever like this one. God Almighty, sir, we might all catch it! Someone could die... And we did warn you at the time, remember.'

He halted lamely, and awaited the impending storm of fury from his volcanic captain; he had never before confronted him with such blunt words – couldn't have done it now without good old Curly there to back him. But instead of a storm there was more silence, during which Jacob Roberts slumped wearily into his chair. When at last he spoke, not looking at them, but down at the deck, it was with a low, bleak voice they hardly recognized: 'You fellows for'ard must be blind as bats. Can't you see, or guess, that I've been thinking all those same things myself? D'you think I'm proud of what's happened? D'you think I *wanted* to have a ship where people are struck down and God alone knows when it will finish, or how many will be struck? You know damn well that I shall have to give an account of all this to the Owners' (he waved brusquely to his official log on the table) 'and, what's more, some day, to the Almighty Himself? D'you think that makes me happy? I'm called the master, but I'm just another man like you, really. I acted every time for the best, as I saw it, but it seems I was wrong every time. Isn't everyone wrong sometimes?'

Curly and the bosun looked at each other, each one scrunching his cap in embarrassment; they'd been prepared to stand up to vitriolic abuse, but this quiet surrender had floored them. Jacob's eye came back from its stare into vacancy, and saw them for what they were - a deputation from the foc'sle to him, their master under God. This wouldn't do, by Heaven! Something of his habit of command came back and he cleared his throat abruptly: 'Very well, then: I will enter your protest in the log, and you can sign the entry. Cape Town it is, and then I shall act entirely as the doctors recommend - about the whole crew, I mean, as well as the present sufferers. Those who want it can have shore leave and an advance of pay. Does that satisfy you? Of course, if I meet a liner with a doctor aboard I shan't put in at the Cape. Can't say fairer than that, can I?'

The men mumbled their awkward assent, and Roberts was back in the saddle: 'Bosun, as we're reaching in a gale of wind like this, any sail that gets loosened by the wind will flog to pieces in no time, and that's our best suit up there. I want you to check personally every damned gasket aloft. Get young Perkins to help you – he's the best of that bunch. Canvas costs good money.'

Duw, Duw, thought Mathias as he shuffled out, he may have spoke like a human for a bit, but he's back now to being a capten! He said to Curly as they walked for'ard: 'Well, he listened to us, Curly, but it didn't get us very far, did it?'

'Nah, but you can't kick a man when he's down like he was. Look at it this way, Reub: we've made the old chap think a bit. P'raps if this was to happen again he'd look after his crowd a bit better. Nothing big changes quickly, mate. Most captins don't give a fart for their hands; maybe this one will from now on. And then again, one or two of the young ones may have got themselves a bit more backbone through seeing us stand up to him – tidy, like, not shouting and yelling. That's summat, me old son. One day, working chaps all over the world'll be properly looked after when they're ill - but it'll take a long time. Softly, softly catchee monkey, ain' it?'

*   *   *

Five-to-four in the morning, and John Raven sagged wearily against the weather end of the poop rail, staring into the empty blackness ahead; near at hand the foam of 'Figaro's' progress cast a milky white glow which outlined the port main-deck bulwark, and further for'ard, at the break of the foc'sle, the strong red glow of the port navigation light picked out nearby breaking crests and coloured them pink. The ship still reached, leaning to starboard, across the big swells, but all the time now the fierce westerly was slowly slackening.

Mair still lay fevered and delirious below, and the Old Man, quite frantic with worry about her, had been for hours scurrying between her bedside and the poop. John could see that he was frustrated by two impotent desires: to make the barque go faster, or to contact a liner whose doctor might be able to perform some miracle of healing. He had spent the whole middle watch popping up to check that no ship's light was in sight, and that the absolute maximum spread of sail was being set. The lower t'gallant sails had been set at nightfall, causing the barque to bury her lee rail most of the time; the crests of high seas reared over the raised port bulwark and raced in a solid torrent down the sloping deck to where the white water boiled in the lee scuppers.

At two o'clock the Old Man had appeared again and gone to the weather rail to snuff and test the wind. Then he had growled at John:

'Wind's fallen a bit lighter. We'll try her with the upper t'gallants. I'll look out here while you roust out all those scrimshankers and set the uppers. Lively, now – don't want to hang about!'

With only one watch of seamen, setting the three t'gallants had been a long job, and John had had to join in on the high, swaying yards, casting off the gaskets to unloose a wild, flogging monster of canvas which had viciously shaken the yard they were perched on until the men below could get the sheets to the capstan and haul them taut. All the time the certainty was forming in John's mind that the new sails would press her too much, that they would soon have to come in again. The Old Man's worries were upsetting his professional skill, as they had the other day, Simon had said.

At about three, the hurtling, staggering ship had, despite the desperate sweating efforts of the helmsmen, griped sharply up to windward until she hit a wave the size of a house, travelling at twenty-five knots. That had brutally knocked her back on course, but not without shaking every mast and yard and every plate and rivet in her stout hull. Seconds later the Old Man had burst out of the chartroom, bawling: 'Why didn't you tell me it was freshening, again, you bloody fool? Get those blasted uppers off her, and look sharp too. You useless bastards at the wheel: steer the course, can't you?'

The wind hadn't freshened, and the helmsmen were doing their best with an over-pressed ship, but neither John nor they said anything. The Old Man had been wrong, and the wind and sea had proved it mercilessly. No point in arguing with the poor old sod. So it was back aloft and furl the upper t'gallants, and now, twenty minutes after getting back on deck, John was utterly exhausted, and had to fight to keep awake and vigilant.

At the first stroke of eight bells a calm crisp voice spoke at his elbow: 'For this relief much thanks, I dare say?' Whatever Simon Grant's failings might be, he had the great virtue of punctuality.

'Phew, I should think so! The Old Man's been like a cat on hot bricks: - set the uppers, furl the uppers! I'm a wreck now.'

'At least you can get your head down now, old boy. I've had little peace in my bunk with your great starboard watch oafs trampling and bawling outside my cabin. Can't you train them to furl sail quietly?'

John felt his stiff cold face bend in a grin: 'You know what they say in the Navy: "It serves yer right, you shouldn't have joined."' Then, more officially, he added: 'Course the same, north-east-by-east; keep a good lookout for liners; tell the captain as soon as the wind falls lighter. But take it from me: she's got more sail up than she can handle already.'

Twenty minutes later, John was drifting off into a sleep of exhaustion, his chilly sheets gradually warming to his body, his rational thoughts beginning to turn surreal and absurd with the approach of oblivion. He was alone, balanced across a horribly thin and flexible yard, trying to furl a huge black sail, but every time he made a gasket fast the rope fell apart, and the sail flapped at his ears and hair. Then he was no longer alone; a beautiful woman, naked to the waist, dark hair flying, was beside him on the footrope, putting a warm cheek against his. Then, with a gasp, he was struggling out of sleep to feel a real warm soft cheek against his, and a hand ruffling his hair. A well-known voice was whispering, 'John, John, wake up.'

'What the - ? Christ Almi-! Nelli!' His tone was of astonishment rather than of delight; it had been so long since those delicious nights, before all the trouble, that he had given up wishing and hoping for her to come.

'Ssh, ssh, John - and don't blaspheme so! It's me. I had to see you - be with you.'

'But your father! I thought you...'

'Dadi's fast asleep. He's gone to his cabin quite exhausted, poor man; and you must be the same, so I won't stay long. I mustn't leave Mam for more than a moment, either - she might need me.'

'But still, your father would...'

'Don't worry, John. Things have changed a lot since that first awful time I was caught. I don't think he's got time to worry about you and me any more, and as for Mam...' Her voice was on the edge of tears.

He sat up and embraced her as she sat forlornly on the bunk in her nightdress and dressing-gown. 'Darling Nelli,' he said, 'you understand, don't you? I don't care what happens to me; it's you I worry about; I've thought so much - and dreamed so much - about you, ever since that first time in the desert with the horses.'

'Dear John, I've thought a lot about you too, until lately; but now it's different. Things are so bad, my mother's so ill that I can't think of anything else but her. I haven't come here to...'

'No, I understand. How could you?'

'It's just that I've spent so many hours watching, bringing bedpans, wiping sweat and bloody sores, listening to her suffering. So many hours alone, or with a totally silent father... I had to talk to someone or go mad in that saloon. I can't talk to Dadi, he's too wrapped up in his misery and guilt. I know I promised them I wouldn't come to you again, but none of that seems to matter any more. I just *had* to come...' She broke into silent, desolate sobbing, her body shaking in his arms. He felt his own tears running down his cheeks.

'Darling, darling, don't cry. Your mother's going to be better soon, I'm sure. Why, your father himself told us yesterday that Davey has passed his crisis, and is starting to eat a little. It's a horrible disease, but people do recover from it.'

'Yes, Davey's better, and I'm glad of it, but my mother is worse than either of the men - I know she is, John: sicker, more delirious, a higher temperature - a hundred and two today. John, I'm terrified that she's going to die.'

'Ssh, Nelli... She'll be all right, you'll see. Any day now we're likely to sight a liner with a doctor...'

'I don't think even a doctor could make any difference now. I've read all there is to read about typhus; it can be deadly... deadly. And I can do nothing of any use. It's so utterly cruel, cruel and unjust, when I think how she helped the others, I'm beginning to think Simon Grant was right about God.'

'Simon...? God...?'

'Never mind - it was something he said the other day. I'm selfish, I suppose, to burden you with all this when you're so tired, but I've been so frightened and so lonely for days and days. Who else can I talk to?' She twitched the blankets back and swung herself into the bed. 'John, hold me tight for a while, and kiss me so that I feel alive again, I've been feeling like a kind of ghost - a drudging piece of nothingness.'

Raven kissed her, gently and chastely at first, out of tact and concern; he amazed himself by his own delicacy. The old John Raven, brassbounder and cad, would not have been so restrained if a beautiful girl had suddenly got into his bed, but now he sensed that her need was emotional, not physical. He embraced her and soothed her, ignoring his own inevitable arousal, and refraining from attempting to arouse her too. But the soft warmth of his bed and the relief at finding comfort in her desolation were, to her young passionate flesh, treacherous agents, and despite all her grief, worry and preoccupation - or perhaps because of them? - she found herself pressing against his hard body and opening her mouth in a kiss of passion, not comradeship. Grief on the one hand, and sympathy on the other, slid unconsciously into mutual desire. He gave a kind of gasp, a groan, at her demand, and it was as if a floodgate had opened and all their frozen, pent-up longing was released.

Some time later - neither knew how long - she came to herself enough to realize that they were on the point of taking the final bodily step. Her nightdress and dressing-gown had gone - onto the deck presumably - together with his pyjamas. After all that intimate fondling of each other it would be natural for her to take him into her body (though Heavens, that thing she had been stroking was so big it made her a little afraid!), but something in her rebelled against that, and it was not piety or Christian chastity, but love of John Raven. She whispered warmly: 'Darling, darling John, I should so love to have you inside me, but not now. When we make love properly, I want it to be free and peaceful, with time for each other. I don't want to be listening for my father, or for a cry from my mother. Do you understand? Can you bear it, love, if we stop now and I go? I'm so sorry to have aroused you so much and then cried off, but it just doesn't feel right now, and I've stayed much too long already. O Heavens, what a wretched worthless thing I am, to be tormenting you and at the same time neglecting my mother! But I did so need you, and even if I should feel ashamed I don't really. One more kiss, then I must go.'

* * *

The next day the westerly swell moderated and the wind fell lighter - to no more than a fresh breeze, and to Jacob's dismay it veered to the north-east - a dead header for the Cape. Sail after sail was unfurled and the yards braced sharply round until she was, by nightfall, slipping along close-hauled on the port tack under all plain sail.

Jacob could scarcely eat a morsel, but spent the day pacing the poop and staring into the distance for ships; he was a haggard wreck of his normal self, his features sunk, even his clothes hanging loose as his corpulent body shrank. He wished with all his soul to see just one of those formerly despised passenger steamers; he wished too, for the first time in his life, that he had a powerful steam engine below his decks which could spring into life and send 'Figaro' surging straight for the Cape. These huge new windjammers were not much use on the wind, though superb in a following gale; in between his tortured thoughts about Mair, he found himself thinking of a neat, slim Porthmadog schooner he had served in as an AB before he met Mair - the 'Eliza and Jane'.

In a wind like this, with her sharp lines, she'd have picked up her skirts and sliced to windward, instead of plodding and sagging away like this hooker.

When Eleanor came on deck, pale and with dark hollow eyes, she shook her head when her father asked: 'Any better, *cariad?*'

'No dadi, no better. It's as if she's in a furnace. She was up to a hundred and three this morning. *A hundred and three!* How can her poor body stand it? It's dropped a little tonight, but...' She shook her head again, unable to speak her real thoughts. Her father clasped her hand and they stood silently together by the rail; the normally cheerful AB Lewis at the wheel felt the sting of tears as he watched them, lonely and isolated by their grief from the commonplace bustle of the ship's working day.

Clinging to the merest shred of hope, Jacob said: 'Dropped a bit, is it? That could be a good sign.'

She looked at him directly, without comfort: 'No, Dadi, that's not always a good sign. You've read the Guide: it's just a sign that she's reaching the final stage - the crisis; and you know that that stage can end either way. There's no sign that she's any more conscious, or that she feels better. When she sits up and notices things, or talks, or asks for food or drink - then we can start to be hopeful. In the meantime we can do nothing but pray with all our heart and soul. I must go back to her now.'

'Have a bite of supper first, *cariad.* You look all in.'

'No, I've no appetite. Ask the steward to bring me some coffee and biscuits. I mustn't neglect her again.'

'Again? You've been devotion itself for days and nights on end - to little Davey too.'

She shook her head vehemently: 'No - I left her the other night. God forgive me, I felt I had to get away for an hour or two.'

Jacob put a heavy arm across her shoulders and said: 'Don't reproach yourself, *bach* - I understand.'

No, she thought, Dadi, you do *not* understand - fortunately.

At dawn the next day Jacob was harshly awakened from his troubled sleep by a hammering on his cabin door and the voice of Robbins the apprentice calling: 'Beg pardon, sir. Message from Mr Grant: large steamship in sight, coming up fast astern.'

'Very good. Tell Mr Grant to hoist our number flags and the code flags for "Request medical assistance". I'll be up directly.'

Hauling on clothes, he made for the upper deck, and emerged

into a fine calm dawn, still buttoning his jacket. 'Signal?' he said abruptly, and Grant gestured to the end of the gaff, where the hoist of flags already fluttered. 'Good, but in case she can't read it, get a distress rocket out of the locker and stand by to fire it if she doesn't alter course in a minute. As she's steering now, she'll pass well astern of us.'

'Heave-to, I take it, sir?' said Grant. 'Back the main-yards to stop her?'

'Yes of course, mister. Heave her to.' Jacob was irritated with himself that he had not thought of that obvious need; mustn't forget his seamanship again, whatever happened! The mate's whistle shrilled and all hands, alive to the new situation and its possibilities, sprang to the mainmast braces, and swung that whole tower of sail across the ship, so that its sails, aback to the wind, cancelled out the drive of the other sails, and the barque lay wallowing without headway.

They must have been keeping a good look-out on the liner's bridge, for at once Grant and Jacob saw her turn end-on, heading straight for them, the wave at her bow increasing as her skipper rang down for full speed. Eleanor, in her silent vigil in the saloon, had heard the commotion on deck and guessed what it meant. She flew out of the chart-room, to find her father's face beaming at her: 'Look, Nelli, a ship at last - and a big one too. Sure to have a doctor. And she's seen our signal.' He called over his shoulder to Grant: 'Who is she, mister? Can you make out her number-flags?'

'Yes, sir: MKQY - Raven, get the code-book quick. Look her up, will you?'

Raven flicked the pages: 'Here we are, sir: the "Wabash", registered in New York; Ocean Steamship Company.'

'A Yankee, eh? Better still! They've always got every mortal thing aboard. Thank God she came in time.'

Jacob and Grant watched through their glasses as the big, black, red-funnelled ship came to a halt a hundred yards away to windward and turned, rolling heavily in the swell, to make a shelter for the boat she was lowering. Presently the boat, smartly rowed, came climbing and bobbing over the heaving ocean towards them, and Grant called: 'Bosun! Rig the boarding ladder port side.'

In the silence of waiting, Jacob was disturbed to hear, not joy but a sob of agony from his daughter: 'There, *bach*, don't cry, just as we've got some proper help at last. Now your Mam will be safe, you'll see.'

'No, Dadi!' - and she flung herself against him - 'It's too late, too late, I know it is!'

'Don't say that! We mustn't give up hope. You see already that God has answered our prayers.'

Her voice went hard: 'Oh, has he indeed? You haven't seen her this morning. Dadi; she's dying, I'm certain. Her temperature is down to ninety-eight...'

'Down! That's good, surely?'

'No, it isn't good! You keep saying that, but it isn't necessarily good. Dadi, I can't wake her or get any response - not like it was with the men. She lies there as if she's dead already, except that she's just breathing. I've taken her pulse, and it's nearly gone.'

Jacob put an arm round her, and a wet and grizzled cheek next to hers: 'Never say die, gel. Look, here's the doctor.'

Two young officers, immaculate in blue, one carrying a black Gladstone bag, had scrambled over the port bulwark and were now ascending to the poop. The first - he with the bag - a fresh-faced, intelligent-looking man with hair the colour of corn, saluted Jacob smartly and introduced himself: 'I'm Doctor James O'Brien, sir, graduate of Harvard Medical School. How may I help you?'

'It's my wife, doctor - very ill. Typhus fever, we believe. Two of the crew have had it and recovered, but she seems very poorly.'

'Where have you called, captain?'

'The last call was the Plate River - Rosario. One of my scallywags got clapped in jail and caught it.'

The young man nodded: 'That certainly is a plague-spot, though not the worst. Let me see the lady right away.'

'Of course. My daughter Eleanor, who's been nursing her, will take you down. And thank you with all my heart for coming.'

'You're entirely welcome, captain. It's the least we can do for our fellow-seafarers. Now then, miss.'

Eleanor asked in some surprise: 'Dadi, are you not coming too?'

Though he had spent so much time at his wife's bedside, Jacob felt he could not face the immediate intimacy of a medical examination, and said gruffly: 'No, I'll be here when the doctor wants to speak to me.'

Eleanor stood back in the saloon as the doctor went to work; she stepped forward only to help him remove her mother's nightdress to reveal the disfigured trunk and limbs; she felt, as she had so often, the pain of her pity at the ruin of a body so youthful and handsome. Over his shoulder, O'Brien asked: 'How old is your mother? Fifty-six... H'm... She is the first typhus sufferer I have attended, though of course I'm familiar with the medical and research work on the disease.' He continued his quiet, methodical examination, gravely listening with bowed head as he applied his stethoscope to chest and back, lifting the passive eyelids, opening the mouth to see her tongue, studying the rash minutely. At length he motioned Eleanor to help him replace the nightdress and stood awhile in silent thought, his back towards her.

Finally, as if summoning strength to do it, he turned round, bit his lip for a moment, then resolutely faced her with his blue eyes and youthful good looks: 'Well, miss, I'm sure you and your father are right in your diagnosis; your mother shows all the classic symptoms of typhus at an advanced stage. You say two men of your crew have had it and recovered?'

'One has completely recovered, and the other - a young cabin-boy - seems better every day.'

'The crewman was young too, I guess?'

'Twenty-three or four, I think,' said Eleanor, and waited in agonized suspense for what seemed hours while O'Brien stood silent and abstracted in thought. For God's sake *say* something, she thought. Don't stand there like a tailor's dummy!

He lifted his head, and once more fixed those bright, blue, direct eyes on her; but, to her surprise, before he spoke he reached out and took her hand: 'Eleanor, sometimes it's hard to be a doctor. You try as hard as you can, you learn as much as you can, but sometimes... well, sometimes the enemy is too strong...'

'My mother is dying, isn't she? That's what you are trying to tell me?'

He was grateful for her help in saying the unsayable: 'With deep regret - yes. Typhus, despite all our research, is still a deadly disease, for which there is no medical remedy. Some recover, some - about ten per cent of cases - do not. We do not even know for sure how it spreads; youth seems to give the best chance of recovery, but it is not known why. In your mother's case, it grieves me to say, I can see little chance of recovery. The fever has damaged both heart and brain too much...'

She clutched his hand in desperation: 'Suppose you took her back to your ship, where you could tend her properly? I would come too, to help.'

He still looked at her with that calm, old man's gravity: 'I would do that most happily, and I'm certain my captain would agree, but it would be of no use, miss. We should simply upset and disturb her for nothing. I could do no more than you are doing. We just do not have any drugs or procedures which could help her. I can see she has been admirably cared for here; I could do no better on board the "Wabash". I'm more sorry than I can say.'

'There must be *something* you could do! There *must* be!'

'No, miss. Only Almighty God can now save your mother. We must believe in His power to achieve miracles, but we poor sinning mortals have our limits.'

'How long, then? Days…? Weeks…?'

He licked his lips nervously: 'Hours, Eleanor, not days or weeks. Her heart is barely holding its own. We can only pray and throw ourselves on God's infinite mercy.'

'His mercy?' said Eleanor bitterly. 'As you can see, she's had enough of *that* already.'

The young man winced at the blasphemy, but asked calmly, officially: 'How many days is it since your mother showed the first symptoms?'

'Twelve, I should say. What of it?'

'As a doctor, I must consider everyone involved. I take it there are no more recent cases? No…? Then I can at least offer you the comfort that your epidemic is over - there should be no more victims. I realize that there is indeed little comfort for you and your father in that, but I must do my duty to all. Ah, captain…' he broke off as Jacob came down the spiral stair, unable to wait any longer on deck.

Jacob spoke as he descended: 'You've been a long time down below here, doctor. I need to know…' He stopped as he took in the faces of Eleanor and O'Brien; their expressions instantly answered all his questions: 'What? No hope at all?'

The American shook his head slowly and sadly: 'No, sir. The finest hospital in the States could not save her. I cannot say how sorry I am. She is not conscious, and therefore will feel no pain or fear, but only a miracle from the mercy of God could restore her now.'

Jacob sank into an easy chair, grief and frailty robbing him of all power of action: 'O *Iesu Grist!* Mair…dead…'

'Not dead, sir, but beyond any science or cure I can command.'

'Dead - and worth more than the lot of us… She gave herself for those sick men… Why, in God's name?'

O'Brien stood over him and tried gently, kindly, to answer his cry of agony: 'I understand the bitterness of your feeling of loss, but who are we to comprehend or question the will of God? Perhaps in His great purposes there is a reason why some of the best are gathered early to His kingdom.'

Eleanor had regained some of her composure; she felt that in a moment she would be angry at the young man's pious and kindly banalities, and that that would be unfair. She knelt by her father and took his hands: 'Doctor O'Brien, we are most grateful for your visit, which has at least made us know the truth. I am sure you mean to be kind, but now I think my father and I would most of all like to be left alone with her.'

He gave a slight, silent bow, and with some relief went up to the poop, deeply touched by their grief, and disappointed that he had not, like some modern knight of medicine, been able to come to the rescue. Being a very moral young man, he then dismissed that thought as a product of mere personal vanity. He found his companion, the liner's fourth officer, chatting with Grant and Raven; they too divined the news from his expression, and Grant shook his head: 'No go, eh? A damned crying shame... The Old Man's going to take it badly.' Raven said nothing, but felt a keen personal pang of sorrow and a deeper vicarious pain when he thought of Eleanor's grief. He leant against the rail, staring out to leeward at the empty sea, while Grant, mindful of maritime etiquette, escorted the two officers to the ladder and saluted as they went over the side: 'Very many thanks, gentlemen - and perhaps you would convey those thanks to your captain too? This is a sad moment, I can tell you, for all of us.'

'No hope for the missis, then?' said Reuben Mathias, as the doctor's boat pulled away. 'There's a lot on board will be sorry beyond about that. She was a good woman all her life, and she's died from her own goodness. That's often the way of it.'

'You're right there, bosun... Now then, I think we must allow the captain to see things to the end without disturbance, don't you? So get both watches to the braces, will you? I'm going to put the ship back on course for the Bass Strait and Melbourne. I think that's what he'd want now.'

'Damn, I'm sorry Curly and I spoke to him like we did a few days back.'

'You weren't to know, man. None of us knows what his actions will lead to in the end; if we did we'd be a bit more careful.'

Mathias understood that the mate was reproaching himself, and replied with respect: 'That's true enough, sir, true enough... Right, square away, is it?'

Jacob was so wedded to his ship that even down below, and transfixed by grief, he knew from her altered motion that the course had been changed, and why; he murmured to Eleanor: 'He's put her back on course for Australia, but if you want it I'll carry on to the Cape and get you a passage home from there, out of all this?'

'No Dadi, indeed! I can't replace her, but I think you need me to finish the voyage with you.'

'There may be months of it yet, *cariad*. We'll get chartered to take coal to the West Coast for sure, and then nitrate home.'

'I don't care,' she said passionately, 'even if it were years. I need you, and I think you need me, don't you?'

She was still at his feet, exactly as when the doctor had left them; he bent forward to fold her in his heavy arms, and they sat watching the still, ash-pale figure on the couch, while the ship, now easily, slowly, pitching to the slight following swell, headed back for the world of cold gales to run her easting down. The 'Wabash' had hoisted her boat, and, with a long mournful blast on her siren, re-started her engines and swung back onto her former course. An hour later, she was no more than a distant faint smudge of smoke on the port bow.

21

'**D**amn your eyes, Johanssen,' said Jacob with amiable severity, 'steer properly, can't you? Keep in the tug's wake, mun, or you'll run us ashore.' Turning his back, he wiped his eyes deftly, furtively.

'Sorry, cap'n. It voss all de noise, und de boats so close abeam.'

If the Swede, normally the best helmsman in the ship, had been distracted from his task, it was no wonder. As 'Figaro' wound her way slowly down the Hunter River away from the coaling berths at Newcastle, New South Wales, she was surrounded by a dozen launches and little steamboats, all packed with friendly Australians, many of Welsh descent, who liked, on a fine Sunday evening, to escort departing windjammers down the channel to the sea. Though the Newcastle coal-loading equipment was modern and efficient, 'Figaro' had been in port a long time - a month or so - partly because there was such a crowd of ships of every nation waiting to be loaded (the thick bristle of their masts and spars could still be seen over a low grassy spit of land astern), and partly because the English and Welsh miners who had brought their skills to this corner of the new country had also brought their stubborn independence - a trait that often caused them to go on strike. Almost all the sailing-ships which came to Australia left with a coal cargo for the coal-less West Coast of South America, and a miners' strike was, from their captains' point of view, the major hazard of this friendly port.

As for the crews, especially the brassbounders, the more strikes the better, for the hospitable Aussies opened their clubs, their chapels and their homes to the men of the tall ships. While in other ports only whores and the owners of sleazy bars gave them a sordid and expensive welcome, here in Newcastle sailors – and especially the crews of Welsh ships - encountered the rare pleasure of friendship and civilized entertainment. 'Figaro's' boys had enjoyed boating on the river with cheerful, decent girls, with whom they had held hearty picnics on the river's green shores; the crowd had found themselves guests of miners' clubs, families and chapel congregations. Small wonder then that, as the ship towed slowly towards the sea, the men and boys leaned on the rail waving grateful farewells, and that many a tear was, like Jacob's, secretly wiped away. Several of the boats contained parties from choirs, and their melodies sounded sweet and poignant, drifting across the water in the still evening air – 'Will ye no Come Back Again?', *'Calon Lan'* and, of course, 'Auld Lang Syne'. Even hardened sinners and cynics like Billy John and Jimmy Protheroe felt the pull of sincere brotherly and sisterly love, and joined heartily in the cheers that came from the ship as, one by one, the launches slowed, turned, and headed back for home. 'By damn,' said Billy, 'they're a decent tidy lot here, boys! Why couldn't it be the same in London and Liverpool and Frisco?'

'That's easy, me old son,' said Curly Kellock, who leant close by. 'It's because this place is a proper democracy run by ordinary working chaps and women, not by a lot of cold-hearted money-making snobs, like in England, or by a bunch of crooks, like it is in the States. Back home, the only people who take an interest in poor old Jack is a lot of bloody villains who are after his little bit of money. This place is what it should be like all over.'

Grant and Raven, up there on the poop with their captain, felt very different reactions to this emotional departure: to the mate it was a great relief to be heading for the open sea and a long voyage to Valparaiso. Back there in Melbourne and Newcastle there'd been a distinct lowering of standards of work and discipline; all the work of discharging and loading had been done by shore dockers and stevedores, a cheery, matey lot, but far too egalitarian for his taste. He remembered, with irritation, being greeted each morning by the foreman: 'What cheer, me ole blue!' With a coal cargo to be loaded, there had been little point in cleaning or painting the ship, and so some days he had had to rack his brains to find work for all the hands aloft. Idleness, he knew, led to the worst kind of rot, and there was always the danger of hands deserting, tempted by the well-paid jobs and handsome girls of New South Wales. He'd heard tales of ships, back in the days of the gold-rush, stuck in Australian ports totally devoid of hands, and that prospect had forced him to be tactful and considerate to the crowd, even when it had pained his soul to be so. But - he had to admit it - the good thing about this Welsh ship (despite its clannishness and confounded incomprehensible lingo) was the cement, as it were, that bound its crew to each other and to the ship. Like a family, they could have shocking rows, but like a family, they stuck together - not like most English ships' crews, where you had a crowd of dog's-bodies from all over the world, with loyalty to no-one. To be slipping out to sea with a full and sober crew - that was good. And so it would be to be able to get the beggars jumping about a bit; the ship looked like a coal-heaver's privy at the moment.

As for young Raven, all his thoughts were retrospective and pleasurable, and totally disconnected from the ship. He had also been kept busy in the dreary confusion of cargo-work and supervising the men at the endless task of checking and repairing the complex system of ropes, wires, blocks and canvas aloft. But now he remembered only a magical Sunday when, at last, he and Eleanor had been able to spend a day together at liberty. Feeling somewhat guilty of the severity of his opposition to Eleanor's attachment to Raven, Jacob had given the expedition his grudging permission. Taking the train, the young couple had travelled inland to the little town of Maitland, and from there they had walked in the green foothills of Mount Barrington, revelling in the warm sun, the peace, and the space in which to stretch their legs. Remembering his Chilean embarrassment over his shore-rig, John had bought himself a cool linen suit, while Eleanor wore a simple loose flowered dress which, pressed now and then by the breeze, gave subtle hints of her body's shape within it. The tense, haggard look, brought on by the strain and grief of her mother's final weeks, was beginning to give way to her natural, sun-tanned beauty.

Underneath some shady trees, by a small stream, they stopped to eat sandwiches that Eleanor had made from proper shore bread and real ham. As they ate, they laughed and joked and teased like young children, but afterwards, as they lay together between two rocks, smelling the woody scent of the ferns their bodies had crushed, they became open to, aware of, a deep sad irony about their intimacy: they were together and alone only because her mother was dead and her father numbed by grief. Eleanor was thus too sad, too preoccupied by her own keen sense of loss, to be the free, wild lover that she had been in those nights in John's cabin. They and their love had, as it were, come of age - a very mixed blessing.

Now, though they embraced, kissed and fondled, their kisses and touches were graver, more restrained. She felt John's fingers beginning to unbutton her dress, and laid her own hand on his: 'No, John, please don't - not today. One day... yes. Don't be angry... I can't feel about you as I used to - not yet.' She sat up and clasped her knees: 'I can hardly believe how wild and bad I was then – how I threw away all those years of careful upbringing and moral teaching. It's only a few months ago, and yet it seems an age. Everything's changed so much. I was a wicked trollop and you' - she gave him an affectionate smile -'you were no better, my lad. Then they caught me and more or less locked me up. Even before that, I thought I'd go mad from boredom and frustration when I was cooped up in Grahamstown, and could only pour out my soul in those long, silly letters, which I'm sure you found very tedious. Now it's all so different; I don't think my poor father will make us stay apart any more.'

She let him draw her down to where he lay in the ferns, and he whispered: 'Darling Nelli, I understand, and I feel almost as much grief as he does over your mother's death.' Then she kissed him long and slow and gently, and lay beside him, their faces very close, their hands clasped, and she said softly: 'Yes, I think you understand, don't you? We've got time now. After all the troubles we've been through, I'm still in love with you, I think - but I'm such a beginner, such a duffer (isn't that your English word for it?) - about these things, that I'm not sure.'

'Well, I'm sure, Nelli. I want you like anything - but it's not just a feeling in my body. I want *all* of you; I love being with you and talking to you. But you're so intelligent and I'm such a booby about most things - it must be dull for you.'

'Does it look as if I think you dull? Would I be lying in the grass with you if I did? You're not a booby, you're just a bit like... like a horse that's always worn blinkers. School and college and the half-deck and ships and sails and sextants – they're not the whole world, you know. But we'll enjoy learning about the world together. As I said, we've got all our lives to do it in, if that's what we want. Those times when I came to you at night, we were... desperate... as if we wanted to do everything in five minutes - a bit like birds snatching at crumbs before some cat catches them.'

'In fear, you mean?'

'Yes, and in my case, in guilt too. I knew it was wrong. I truly believe that love-making belongs in marriage - that that is what God demands of us - though it's very hard sometimes to refrain.'

He moved closer, propping himself above her, and kissed her long and deeply, before lying back and saying with a sigh: 'Phew! I suppose I can refrain too. But you're so beautiful and... and.... desirable, it's going to be hard. I suppose I believe that too, really - that you ought to wait till you're married. It's funny, my old man's a parson, but I've never thought much about religion and God and all that sort of thing. It was just... just *there* in our family, and I went to church and got bored as a kind of family duty - to support my dad. I don't think religion ever made much difference to what I did. And then, of course, I got into some bad habits at sea.'

She drew up his hand, which was stroking her thinly-clad thigh, and said firmly: 'That, Mister Raven, is painfully obvious, and I don't know why I'm so foolish as to be here alone with you, lying in the grass in the middle of a wood and trusting you.' But she belied her words by placing his hand on her breast, and pressing it there.

He chuckled: 'Oh, you can trust me, old girl. Only *just*, though. I'll behave myself until I can get you to church...'

'Or chapel.'

'Yes, or chapel, I don't mind which. But after that, look out!' The easy, happy laugh between them ended in a long kiss, while the sun shone, and odd, unfamiliar birds sang in the trees above them.

*   *   *

As 'Figaro' followed the tug, Jacob stood back by the helmsman, listening to the sweet voices coming over the quiet water, tears coursing freely down his cheeks. As so often, the kindness and affection of others had touched him, had pierced whatever stoicism he had managed to keep up. The sentimental, nostalgic tunes had a magic power of their own to affect the soul, but in Jacob's case they were a sharp, urgent reminder of that calm day in the Southern Ocean when he had bade his last farewell to Mair; when he had seen her coffin (made by the sail-maker, old Jac-y-Bont, and weighted with some iron bars) slide out from under the covering ensign and slip down the tilted plank into the sluggish sea. He remembered that morning so clearly, though many weeks had elapsed since then: the grey sky and the grey heaving sea; the gently-leaning ship hove-to, her main-yards backed, the loose buntlines slatting idly on the canvas; all the creaks and groans from her gear as the ship rose and fell on the long swells; the unaccustomed quiet and stillness as all hands abandoned their tasks and assembled in the waist, even the helm being left to twitch aimlessly to and fro; he even remembered the oddness of standing bare-headed on deck with a book in his hand - the English Book of Common Prayer, for he had felt that, after the hymns and prayers in Welsh, the very last words about her should be in a tongue which all could understand.

The day before the burial, Grant had overcome his confirmed

atheism enough to offer to conduct the service for him, to save Jacob that last terrible strain, but he had refused gravely, saying: 'No, Mister Grant, that would not be fitting; when there is no priest or minister aboard, the master must officiate. It will be an ordeal, but God will give me the strength to go through with it. I have failed her in life; shall I fail her in death too? But I thank you all the same.'

Jacob had indeed gained from somewhere the necessary calm to read the prayers and lead the hymns, to bear the aching beauty of the music rising from the men there between the high masts - the sad, graceful triple-time melody of *Blaenwern,* and, the dark, rolling, slow-march music of *Aberystwyth,* the voice of Jimmy Protheroe rising above the others in a sweet high tenor, all the voices blending in a deep, solemn male harmony that spoke even to the aloof unbeliever, Grant.

Then, as the last notes of the hymn died away, the final, worst moment of Jacob's personal Gethsemane came when, into the ensuing silence, he had to read those words of terrible finality: 'Forasmuch as it hath pleased Almighty God of his great mercy to take unto himself the soul of our dear sister here departed, we therefore commit her body to the deep, to be turned into corruption, looking for the resurrection of the body when the Sea shall give up her dead, and the life of the world to come, through our Lord Jesus Christ...'

At 'commit her body' Grant had given a discreet nod to Reuben and Jac, who had raised the inboard ends of the planks to send the rough coffin sliding, to fall with a sullen splash into the lifeless sea. Jacob had closed the book firmly, cleared his throat, and said: 'I thank you all for your prayers and your sympathy. I'm sending the steward for'ard with a bottle of rum for each foc'sle, so that you can all drink to her memory. As long as she had strength, she did all she could for all of us, and like our dear Lord himself, she paid for it with her own life. Very good, mister: square the main-yards, hands back to duties.' Then, with Eleanor on his arm, pale and weeping desolately, he had gone back below.

His first task there was to open the log and add to the day's entry:

I have this day conducted the funeral at sea of my dear wife Mair, deceased of typhus fever. She now lies buried in 38 degrees, 34 minutes south, 17 degrees, 20 minutes east.

He lifted his pen and mused for a while, then, with a kind of defiance, added, in most un-log-like language:

*All hands now fit or recovering. Like our blessed Redeemer, she gave
her life for them.*

Then, seeing that a tear had blotted some of his elegant script, he closed
the book and fell forward, resting his arms and head on the desk, and at
last gave way freely to his grief, his whole body racked with weeping.

Eleanor, coming back from her cabin after changing out of her
funeral clothes, found him there, and knelt beside him to take him in her
arms: 'Dadi, Dadi, don't grieve so! Look, I'm crying too, and perhaps it's
best for us both to do that now. But remember, she died without pain, as
far as we can tell, and remember above all that she's gone to a far better
place than this, where you'll find her again one day, when your own time
comes. She's with our Saviour now; what greater happiness could she
have than that?'

Her father checked his racking sobs and turned to hold her tight
in silence for a while. Then he said in a low voice: 'You're a good girl,
Nelli, and you mean well. But what chance have I got of seeing her
again? What judgment will such a miserable sinner as I get at the last? I
murdered her with my folly, murdered the best woman - the best person - that I've ever met, and it's no thanks to me that half the crew didn't
perish too from my wicked neglect. So what reward can I hope for
among the blessed above?'

'You must stop torturing yourself like this! Perhaps some of the
things you decided were wrong, but you intended no harm to anyone at
the time. If you made mistakes - well, who doesn't? Mr Grant does, for
all his cleverness. He kept poor Ianto up on the yard when the *pampero*
struck. John Raven nearly caused the death of young Robbins. Perhaps
Mam herself did when she decided to join you aboard. And you know
only too well how badly I have behaved, grieving and shocking you and
Mam. But that's because we're all human beings, fools and sinners, and
it's in our nature to err, to be bad, selfish, stupid and lustful. But we worship a kind and loving God: surely we can trust Him to judge our lives
mercifully, not harshly? Your life's work, your care of ships and men,
your great love of Mam over so many years - those are what will count
with God, believe me.'

'From my heart I wish I could, *cariad,* I wish I could. But I feel
low, worthless, not fit to command a ship, and even more, not worthy of
the love of souls like you and your mother.'

'Dadi *bach,* you mustn't destroy yourself like this. What's done
is done; we must grieve and repent for it, but then life must go on.' She

rose to her feet, dried her eyes, and went to the medicine-chest: 'You need rest, lots of rest. Then, when you wake, things will seem different. Mr Grant will manage the ship for you while you're resting. Here, drink this; I've put just a few drops of laudanum in it. That will help you to go off peacefully. And when you do wake and begin thinking of Mam again, you must think of the happy times you've spent together. Don't keep going over and over the past.'

'You're not in my shoes, gel; you don't know how hard that is. Whatever you or anyone may say, I feel the guilt, feel it every moment, in here.' He clapped his hand to his breast.

Eleanor took the hand and kissed it: 'Dadi, you're judging yourself more harshly than God will judge you at the last. In His eyes, a wicked act is one that is done with a wicked intent. You have never intended any harm to anyone. You might have been thoughtless sometimes, and perhaps too preoccupied with the ship and Mr Powell's business - but there, I'm not twenty yet! Who am I to sit in judgement on you or anyone?'

'By God, Nelli, you're a good girl and a proper Christian too. I don't deserve such treatment.'

'Hush! I'm going to put you to bed now. But remember always what I said: we know for certain that this life isn't all there is; looked at from Heaven, all our deeds, good and bad, must seem no more than the pitiful struggling and scurrying of ants in an ant-heap. Now lie there and rest, and at suppertime I'll tell the steward to dig something tasty out of the lazarette for you. Sleep well now. I'll see Mr Grant and explain.'

She saw that the strong drug was beginning to do its merciful work; her father's eyelids drooped and finally closed; his face lost its tension in sleep. She released his hand and left the cabin quietly. After washing away the signs of her tears, she went on deck. Somehow, her father's prostration had made her feel strong - strong enough to be captain herself, had she the nautical skill. Grant, busy in the chartroom with parallel ruler and dividers, felt the impact of this authority, this confidence; she was no longer a pretty female passenger, but a woman with the power to command respect. 'My father is resting, Mr Grant,' she said. 'I've given him a strong draught to make him sleep. I think that's what he needs most. I've told him you and Mr Raven will manage until he is... is well enough to take charge again.'

'I quite understand, Eleanor. Yes, we'll get her to Melbourne, though as there's only the two of us now, I shall have to promote the bosun to acting third mate, to stand some day watches, while John and I get some rest.'

'I leave that to you, Mr Grant. I'm sure you know best. How long will it take to get to Melbourne?'

'It's another several thousand miles. That would take at least six weeks in this wretched calm yachting weather, but I'm going to take her south into the Roaring Forties, and if they roar sufficiently, we'll do it in under a month.'

She gave a weak smile: 'Oh dear, you are as bad as my father - never really happy until you're in a cold following gale, with the decks full of water and everyone hanging on to lifelines!'

'Indeed, miss. The dread hand of Commerce, I fear; the fewer days on the trip, the less the Owner has to stump up for pay and provisions - if you can call them that. Were I the captain of a P and 0 liner, I would steam you peacefully through halcyon seas, but a ship like this needs a howling gale on the quarter and the decks awash all the time.' He dropped his bantering tone and said quietly: 'If there is anything - anything at all - that I or John can do to help you, you know you have only to say.'

'That's very kind, Simon - may I call you that now? - but for the moment I'd be grateful if you would just take the weight of running the ship off his shoulders. He needs a thorough rest and some care from me, and the chance to recover his strength and his confidence. He's feeling very low at present.'

'I'm sure he is; and may I say, it is a thousand mercies that you are here to comfort and console him. Otherwise - it would take a very long time. But don't forget, you must look after yourself as well.' His eyes twinkled at her: 'I am sure my young colleague, our Second Mate, would agree with that.'

She blushed at the reference to John, smiled and pressed his hand for a moment: 'You are very kind, Simon; I'm sure you and John will understand if for the next few weeks I spend my time with my father, even if that seems unsociable of me.'

*   *   *

For the next few days the ship ran on under all plain sail in quiet warm sunshine, heading south-east; but then, one morning, an arc of heavy grey cloud appeared astern, and Grant commented to Raven: 'Here it comes, my old son. Welcome back to the Roaring Forties. Get your oilskins out again; we're about to get a good cold blast up our rear end, and get a few knots out of this hooker. I think we'll get the boys up there to furl the royals while it's calm, to be on the safe side. It'll be a relief to be sailing again instead of lolling about in catspaws.'

After a few hours of grey calm and fickle wind, noon brought the expected chill westerly storm, which appeared first in the guise of random squalls of wind accompanied by light showers. Grant looked at the clouds and up at the huge expanse of sail, and blew his whistle to summon the hands. The port watch, on duty since eight, were expecting any moment to be going below for their salt pork hash and a smoke, and were not pleased at Grant's words: 'Bosun, tell the doctor to keep the port watch's dinner warm. Both watches aloft and furl t'gallants. We'll get the crojik in too. It's going to blow soon, so look lively, boys!' The crojik (properly, the cross-jack) was the course, or lowest sail, on the mizen mast, and in blowy weather was not popular with the watch-keeping officers, for it produced a strong cold down-draught just where they stood on the poop.

Only a few weeks ago, such an order from the mate, just at din-ner-time, would have produced a near-mutiny. Even now, there was plenty of growling and scowling. Billy John, as usual, was the loudest of the growlers, but even he had changed - matured - and at least he worked as he growled. Between heaves at the sail, he grumbled to Tydfil Jones, flat across the yard beside him: 'Just like that bloody *Sais* (English) bucko, this is: picking on us just at dinner-time! He does it on purpose, he does.'

'Well, you know what they say: Growl you may, but go you must, Billy. Besides, he's missing his dinner too, mun.'

At two, when the port watch were at last eating their salt junk, they felt the ship list and stagger as the first strong gust struck her; they felt her surge forward, and through the iron plates, only a foot from their heads, they could hear the roar of her bow-wave. Lewis looked up from demolishing the hash: "Ah, yere we goes, b'ys. Them Aussie gals've got hold of the tow-rope.'

Billy still growled impotently: 'Now that lot aft'll be happy, and we'll be wet through and bloody frozen half the time. An' when we do get to Melbourne and unload, they'll only send us up to Newcastle for coal, and then off to some miserable poxy hole in Chile for more nitrate. Weeks and months, it'll take, before we're homeward bound.'

'Stow it, Bill,' said Curly; through a choking mouthful of food:

'You're spoiling me dinner, you are, wiv yer moaning; spoils me diges-
tion, it does. If you don't like Chile, and you wants to be warm, git
yerself a berth as a fireman in a steam-kettle on the Red Sea run. That'll
fry the arse off of yer nicely, that will.'

Rolling and pitching, her decks streaming with solid water,
'Figaro' thundered before the gales, through the dreary grey wastes of
the Southern Ocean on her Great Circle course for Australia, then
through the scattered islands and treacherous winds of the Bass Strait
until, running into calm and sunshine at last, she approached Port Phillip
Bay, with Melbourne at its head. All this time, Captain Roberts was a
passenger, a silent stranger to his officers, coming on deck rarely on better days, and then greeting them only with a nod, spending hours
hunched over the taffrail, staring out at the great, grey, white-bearded
combers, with Eleanor silent at his side. She and her father took their
meals in the cabin, and even to John she became remote, taciturn, preoccupied, answering queries about her father politely but briefly: 'He is
recovering slowly, thank you, but still very shocked.'

Then, one fine morning, when the barque lay hove-to off Gee-
long, waiting for a tug and pilot to take them up the narrow bay, suddenly everything changed. The chartroom door opened briskly and Jacob
stepped out onto the poop-deck in immaculate uniform, his hair cut and
beard trimmed, his manner alert and brusque, as of old. To the startled
mates he smiled, and returned their salutes: 'Good morning, gentlemen!
Signalled for a tug, mister? And pilot? Good. I'm obliged to you, mister,
for your care of my ship these last weeks, but now I'm fit again for the
fray. That looks like our tug coming now. I know what these Aussie tug-
boat skippers are like - damned robbers. I won't pay him more than
twenty-five dollars, mind - not a penny more.'

* * *

'Loose upper and lower tops'ls, mister,' said Jacob. 'The tug will be letting go soon. Let the sails hang in their gear for the present.' The mate's
sharp whistle stirred the men at the rail from their happy torpor; the last
of the Newcastle launches had turned for home, and was now only a
speck against the land. All those lucky land-folk were returning to good
suppers and good beds; the shore itself, twinkling now with pricks of
light, was beginning to disappear into the twilight, leaving the barque to
shape a course into the dark, somewhat east of south, so as to clear the

South Island of New Zealand and the treacherous Snares Rocks, a hundred miles south, then to take a long sweeping arc down into the Forties again, to pick up the strong winds which would drive the ship and her three thousand tons of coal to Valparaiso. Not the last lap of the voyage, her men were thinking, but at least the next-to-last; so as they clambered aloft to cast off the gaskets and release the sails, they were cheerful enough. This would be a simple and shortish trip, with good strong winds astern, clear across the Pacific.

Twenty minutes later, the tug hooted twice and the men on the foc'sle head could hear the splash as her end of the towing-hawser was let go. John Raven, in charge for'ard, said cheerfully: 'Don't bother with the capstan, boys! We can haul it in faster ourselves', and he lent his own weight to the men's concerted heaves. 'Huh,' said Lewis *sotto voce*, 'Tis a wonder he've a got the strength, after his capers with the Old Man's gal!'

Further aft, the quiet of the night was disturbed by the cries and snatches of chantey as sheets were hauled down and the upper tops'l yards were hoisted. By the time the tug's stern-light had disappeared, 'Figaro' was slipping along under tops'ls before a gentle north-westerly breeze. For the moment, however, there was no respite for her crew, for Jacob called to Grant: 'All plain sail, mister! Stream the log.' Men and boys vanished aloft into the mild darkness, and sail after sail filled with a quiet rumple and jingle of chain sheets. The great ship became a living thing again, not just a long steel box full of coal, and she began to sway and to nod rhythmically into a slight swell. Trailing astern on its rope, the brass screw of the patent log began to turn and the dial on the rail began to click off the miles to South America.

The men, chatting quietly, gathered outside the galley to collect mugs of cocoa from the tireless Wellington Jones; the thick, sweet nightcap went down well, for supper had been taken early tonight. Cabin supper, on the other hand, had been postponed; while John Raven walked the poop-deck on watch, Jacob, Eleanor and Grant sat down in the lamplight while Isaac Hughes and Davey - now plump and fit - bustled to and fro. All was as it should be, except for the keenly-felt absence of Mair. Eleanor was still sad and quiet, but Jacob, in his hard-won determination to go on, showed, on the surface at least, a forced geniality. 'You'll take a beer with your supper, Grant, won't you? It's Aussie stuff, but not bad, though it's not like what they make in Llanelli. Davey, get a couple of bottles from the lazarette - only two, mind. Quite a decent slant of wind up there, eh? Get us clear of the land by morning.'

'Indeed, sir. No great navigational problems here - not like leaving London and clawing your way down-Channel in fog and head-wind. Just get ourselves clear of the South Island, and pick up a good westerly. Well then, your very good health, captain, and yours too, Eleanor. *Iechyd da*, I think you say? Mmm... a very reasonable bitter. Someone must have brought some good hops out here, as well as the barley.'

'It'll do till we get to Valparaiso; there's plenty of excellent German lager there, as you know. Seems odd, doesn't it, to be setting out for the West Coast from here instead of from home - not having to punch to windward round the Horn to get there.'

'Almost like cheating, sir, and very pleasant too... Do I take it you haven't been this way before?'

'No, never. Been to Melbourne many a time, but in those days we always went home east-about, round Good Hope.'

'Yes - that was before Maury's day, of course.'

'Maury?'

'Yes, sir - you know: Lieutenant Maury , the American hydrographer back in the sixties. He changed everyone's ideas about passage-making.'

'Not mine, mister. I know all about him, but I don't need any damn Yankee to tell me how to navigate. They always think they know everything, those Yankees.'

Grant looked surprised: 'D'you mean we haven't got his "Sailing Directions" on board? I thought everybody had that now. When I found there wasn't a copy in the chart-room, I assumed you had it in your cabin.'

'If we've got one I haven't come across it yet. *Bobl annwyl,* if it cost another five shillings, old Powell wouldn't buy it, not he!'

'I see... Yet it's a book that's highly thought of these days. It's not just Maury's theories, it's based on hundreds of ships' captains' reports, made over several years. It's because of Maury that ships homeward-bound for Europe from Australia go round the Horn now instead of round Good Hope. Maury showed that...'

Jacob cut in, with an edge of irritation; navigation was entirely the province of the master, and he could not tolerate any questioning of his methods: 'As I've told you, I know all about Maury, mister! But I wonder how many windjammers he captained in his career. On our last trip from home we were a good two months out of sight of land, and I still raised Caleta Buena right on the end of the bowsprit. Besides, I'm surprised at you, having the nerve to lecture me, and to bore my daughter here to death with all this dreary sea-chat.'

Eleanor, who had indeed been totally detached from the conversation, lost in her own thoughts, started and flushed deeply. Grant, though a little nettled, and dissatisfied with Jacob's attitude, inclined his head towards her politely: 'Indeed, captain; I stand rebuked. I am, as you suggest, forgetting my manners... I take it, Eleanor, that you have found New South Wales, as its name implies, a real home-from-home, and a place to remember with pleasure?' The bland question was not without its touch of banter, for Grant had seen John Raven after his Sunday ashore with her, and had noticed his new happiness, his underlying serenity, and guessed what it meant.

She had now, however, acquired sufficient poise not to lapse into gauche confusion, and smiled equally politely: 'Yes, Mr Grant, I made many new friends, and it was pleasant to find, all these thousands of miles from Wales, people who could converse in the language of Heaven.'

Grant smiled too, appreciating that she had replied to his gentle teasing with a mildly-barbed comment on his monoglot Englishness. 'I stand rebuked again, ma'am, this time for my ignorance. I see that, if I am to serve in Welsh vessels, I must acquire the linguistic skill necessary. But I shall then, alas, be able to understand what some of my friends for'ard are saying about me, and that may not be a pleasant experience.' He rose from his place: 'You'll excuse me, won't you, captain, Eleanor? I've got the graveyard watch tonight, so I'll try to get a little shut-eye before midnight.'

When he had gone, Jacob called for the steward to bring their coffee, and mused over it: 'Not such a bad fellow, this Grant, is he? Didn't take to him much at first. Smart enough officer, but I used to get the feeling that he was always watching me... criticizing. Even now you heard him telling me we haven't got the right navigation books on board.' He fetched a deep sigh: 'I don't know... perhaps he's right... perhaps I am getting too old for this job. It's not like it was when David Evans and Leyshon were the mates; they could be cantankerous old devils, but somehow we were all of a kind – like brothers; we understood each other better... knew our places. And when I was a mate myself the sea was a better life too: smaller ships, bigger crews, passengers, good cargoes of tea and wool and rice - not just coal and that damned nitrate, and not just sailing from a Welsh coal-tip to that God-forsaken West Coast...

endless waiting for cargo, blistering hot, dry as a bone, nothing ashore but a few sheds.'

Eleanor went to him and put an arm round him: 'Dadi, I know why you're feeling down: our first meal at sea in the mess-room here without Mam. But your life's got to go on; you're master of one of the finest British sailing ships afloat – don't forget that - and you got here by your own efforts, not like Grant and John, who had rich fathers to pay their way through college. You should feel very proud. This other feeling - of missing Mam - will maybe never go away for either of us, but it will fade in time.'

'Maybe, maybe... But every day I feel more and more sure that this will be my last trip. You can't have any idea how lonely my life is at sea generally, and how long the voyages seem. Somehow it was different when I could think of you and Mam living there at Ty Coch, waiting for me, keeping a place for me. Now it's all gone - or going. We've lost her and Ty Coch, and I can't expect you to spend years traipsing round the world in a wind-jammer with me, and anyway you have your own life to lead. I'm not blind, you know; I can see the way things are going: you will soon be gone too. Mind, I don't blame you one bit – don't think that. He's turned out better than I thought he would, too. He's a keen young officer, a hard worker, and handles the crowd well enough; he should go far in his trade. I could wish that you'd fallen for a decent Welsh boy, more like us and with a good shore job - but there, you're the one that'll have to live with him. I just pray to God he will prove genuine - a proper loving husband for you - one you can rely on. There's far too many of the other sort about these days.'

'I *know* he will be, Dadi. I know we started in quite the wrong way, but that was more my sin than his. Now' - she hugged her father and giggled – 'we are so respectable, it's as if we were sitting among the deacons in the front pew at Ebeneser, Newport, on a Sunday morning.'

He relaxed too and chuckled: 'That, my girl, I doubt very much, if you are anything like your mother and I were when we were courting. But now: if I should give up the sea, and find myself a place with a bit of land, or maybe get a harbour-master's job somewhere, you and Raven would come and stay with your old dad sometimes, wouldn't you? And bring the little ones too, for me to see?'

She blushed again, but laughed easily: 'Dadi, I'm surprised at you! Little ones, indeed! We're not even engaged yet - not officially.'

*　　*　　*

Grant stood next to John at the break of the poop and looked for'ard through the thick fog to where, by the half-deck door, the brass-bounders were larking and shoving like puppies; further away, on the for'ard hatch, the crowd were enjoying their dog-watch freedom; Tydfil Jones was squeezing melancholy tunes out of his old concertina, Curly and the bosun were deep in talk and clouds of tobacco-smoke, and others sat, mending or washing clothes. Now and then chill drops of water, condensed on the sails from the fog, dripped on their heads. The gentle westerly breeze swirled the thick mist between the masts, and every two minutes the mechanical foghorn, cranked by the lookout on the foc'sle head, sent out mournful tinny bleats into the nothingness ahead. The ship slipped slowly south-eastwards to the sound of groans from her shrouds as they took the strain of the huge masts leaning first this way, then that in the heavy ocean swell. The grey water slid noiselessly, without a trace of foam, past her long sides. The ship was so quiet that the music, the hum of chat, the boys' cries, came clearly to the two officers aft.

Grant pointed at the youngsters: 'There – don't you sometimes feel it would be good to be like that again - not a care in the world? And here we are; we've come south for a decent wind, and instead we're groping along at about three knots through this goddamned fog; can't even see the jibboom from here, never mind what might be ahead.'

'But we know what there is ahead: thousands of miles of bloody ocean.'

'Yes, and maybe ships coming the other way, and maybe islands.'

'Not many of those round here, surely?'

'No, you nincompoop, but you don't need many, do you, to settle your hash? One will do that nicely. I wouldn't mind the fog so much if I thought the Old Man really knew where we are, but he can't by now, not after a solid week of thick cloud, and not a glimpse of sun or star.'

'You're worrying too much. I've known him longer than you have. He may not have been to any college, but he doesn't get lost – you'll see.'

'I'm not so sure. After all the nitrate trips he's done, he may know the way to Chile and back with his eyes closed, but these are waters he doesn't know - he told me so himself. And after a week of nothing but dead reckoning anyone could be lost. There's no black magic about navigation: you get a fix and you know where you are, or you don't get one, and you don't know – that's all. And we're going so slowly in these light airs that if there is a set - a current - one way or another, he could be miles from where he thinks he is. And the trouble is that, like all captains, he keeps it all to himself, he doesn't discuss his problem with me or you, and he doesn't show me his log or our track on the chart.'

'Good God, no, he'd never dream of doing that!'

'No, and when I asked him politely the other day about our position, he nearly bit my head off. He said there was a two-hundred-mile gap between the Snares to the north and the Auckland Islands to the south, and he hoped he might be relied upon to find *that* and get through it. Really sarky, he was. And I'll tell you something else that worries me: you remember from college about Maury's book "Sailing Directions", don't you - the American book? An absolute bible for anyone taking a big ship round the world? Well, because of his stupid prejudice against Yankees and the Owner's meanness, we haven't even got a copy on board! It's mad - like wandering in the dark when you could have a lantern. And I'll bet he's using some old Admiralty Pilot that's donkey's years out of date.'

'He's had a bad time lately, Simon. We mustn't criticize him too much. And look - out there to starboard! The fog's beginning to break up.' He pointed to where, off the starboard bow, the wet rags of fog had parted, to reveal a lane of grey heaving sea stretching to the south between the almost solid-looking walls of vapour.

'Thank God for that! Perhaps we may soon be able to see where we're going; then all we shall need is a glimpse of the sun, to tell us where the hell we are, for I'm damn sure the Old Man doesn't know within fifty miles. Of course, the worst of it is, he may think he knows, from the compass and the patent log, but, as I said, if there's a strong set, north or south, he'd be miles out.'

'Well, you can criticize him all you like, but he seems to me a damn good navigator, whatever his faults, and careful too.'

Grant gave a snort of good-natured scepticism: 'Maybe. Perhaps, because of the beautiful Eleanor, you're already thinking of him as a close relation, not as your skipper. But I'm entitled to criticize if he's risking my neck. All joking apart, he worries me a lot, John; I get the feeling that he's fed up to the back teeth with his job - he told me this would be his last voyage - and he just wants to get it over with and retire ashore. Now that's a dangerous attitude for a ship's master to have, because he's like a little god - he decides everything with no discussion. It's like a batsman in cricket: it's so easy to get out on the last ball before lunch, because you're thinking of lunch, and not of the bowling. He may want to finish, but he hasn't finished yet.'

'All right - what would you do, then, if he's so damned wrong?'

'In this fog? Heave-to until we can see a bit further, or until I got a decent sun-sight. Just the latitude would do. Mind you, even he must be a bit worried, or he wouldn't have told us to double up the lookouts.'

'There you are then; as I say, he's careful.'

'Is he, though? Then tell me - why isn't he up here now? Most skippers I've sailed under would never leave the deck in this sort of visibility - not even the last old swine that I had such a row with - the one who used to collect – *O my Christ! Did you hear that?*

All the time, as they had been talking, the foghorn had been sending its doleful blasts into the void ahead. This time, Grant's practised ear, unconsciously alert, had caught, in the intervening silence, the sound of a faint muffled echo! There was something - something large - ahead and to starboard. In an instant, the quiet scene was chaos: Grant screamed: 'Hard down the helm! Hard down!' Then he gave a shrill blast on his whistle to bring the idle hands scrambling to their feet: 'Let go port braces! Let em rip! Starboard braces, boys, and quick too, for God's sake! Bosun, close-haul her on port tack! Apprentices, set all the staysails! Messenger, get the captain.' Then, more quietly, he spoke to the ship under his feet: 'Now then, come round, come round, you great lumbering steel bastard, if you want to see Cardiff again.'

With so little way on, the ship swung with torturing slowness; Grant watched the compass card slowly pivot round, and felt the thin cold breeze on his left cheek. Every sail, now end-on to the wind, flapped ponderously, jingling its chain sheets, and the ship, all its motive power gone, began to wallow helplessly in the steep swells. John Raven ran aft and single-handed, began to haul in the slack sheet of the spanker. Down in the waist, the boys heaved desperately on staysail halyards.

Jacob burst out of the chartroom door, hauling on a coat and yelling: 'In God's name, mister, what are you at?' and at the same precise moment there was a hoarse, panicky cry from the lookout for'ard: 'Land to starboard - close! And breakers too!'

The fog was thinning and shredding fast now. While the men on the main-deck, under the bosun's orders, heaved and chanted at the braces, Grant and his captain stared out to starboard. All along the beam, flat across what had been their course, was a high dark wall of basalt rock; low-hanging vapour hid its top, but they could see clearly enough at its base the thick fringe of white where the massive ocean swells smashed themselves to pieces. Between the cries of the men, they could hear the dull, sullen roar of the breakers, now and then punctuated by a deep, doom-laden boom like that of a cannon, as some great mound of water drove into a cave in the cliff. As each swell exploded on the basalt, it sent a wall of spray high up the cliff, to stream down again in thin fingers of white.

Utterly shaken, Jacob clung to the poop-rail, his face yellowish, sweating: '*O Iesu Grist!* One of the Auckland Islands - must be - right in our track! Christ, mister, we should be fifty miles north of here! I thought I'd allowed plenty of sea-room...'

Grant looked at him stonily: 'Nevertheless, we're here!' He turned his back on his captain, and called to the helmsman: 'Full and by, Lewis, and don't pinch her, for God's sake. Keep the way on her. Is she answering now?'

'Aye, sir, slow-like. But she's a-pickin' up, now the sails is braced in and drawing.'

Grant and the captain watched as the sails filled, the ship began to move, and the high, horrible black wall began to slide past, not four hundred yards away to leeward. Jacob, his teeth chattering from chill and shock, said quietly: 'In the dark, or with a gale astern, we'd have run full tilt into that... We'd all have been dead mutton. God has been good to us, very good - and you've done well too, mister, fair play to you.'

Grant's reply was icy, cruel, cutting: 'Yes, I should say that, of the two of us, and on the whole, I've done rather better than your precious God.'

22

Jacob had, it seemed, aged ten years since leaving the chart-room. He clung to the stout mahogany rail as if it could save him from all perils, and shook his head slowly: 'Duw, Duw, I can't begin to understand it, can't understand it at all. I read the Australia Pilot, and it did say there was thought to be a southerly set, so I allowed a good forty miles. But this must be Enderby Island, the one at the north end of the Auckland Group.'

Grant was cold, curt; in two minutes their relationship had been reversed: 'Never mind "must be"; I think we've had enough of that style of navigation. Let's try and find out what it *is*. Why the devil didn't you heave her to in that fog? You knew the distance run from the log, and you knew there was a southerly set, so you should have seen the danger. Well, too late now to argue about that. You've got a chart with the Aucklands on it, I suppose?' He strode off to the chart-room, Jacob following almost humbly in his wake.

'O yes, mister. But it's just a sketch-map in the corner of the New Zealand South chart. It's only a few sealers who ever come here, so they say in the Pilot.'

Grant had the door open, and was raising his foot over the coaming, when another hoarse yell came from for'ard: 'Land ahead! On the port bow!' Grant dashed to the rail to see, through the swirls of thinning fog, another patch of high cliff, ahead and to port. He felt a stab, a clutch, of panic right at his heart, but forced himself to keep silent, and fought for calm and sanity, He had scarcely mastered his fear when the lookout cried again: 'Rocks! Dead ahead!'

Raven, at the poop rail, saw them too - small black islets over which the swells exploded lazily, thunderously. He called out coolly: 'It's all right, sir - just a small skerry.'

'I see it,' said Simon, and called to the helmsman: 'Keep away a point to clear it.' He turned to where Jacob stood, dumb and irresolute, and said grimly: 'If this is a bay we're heading into, then you've lost your ship. She'll never tack in this light air, and there's no room to wear her round. I'll bet my last bottom dollar that it's too deep to anchor, so all we can do is to go on - and may that God of yours forgive you for landing us in this hole.'

Raven called again, calm and rock-like in the crisis: 'Sir, that land to port: it's just a small island, about a mile across. I can see all of it now.'

'Very good. I'm going to look at the chart, John. Keep her full and by, once we're clear of the skerry. Don't let him pinch her, for God's sake. I don't know yet what we're sailing into.' At his elbow, Jacob was feeling the sting of Grant's contemptuous harshness, and beginning to recollect his position and dignity: 'I'd better remind you, mister, that I'm the master of this ship, not you. I'll decide what we do or don't do, and I've a mind to order you out of the chartroom this minute.'

It was as if Grant scarcely heard him: 'No time for all that now. Make a fuss about it when we get home - *if* we get home. Saving our skins and the ship comes first. Where's this chart? H'm, not much of a sketch-map, but it's all we've got to go on.' He spoke and reasoned to himself only, ignoring the old man who bent trembling over the chart-table at his side.

'Now then: what we've got down the starboard side must be the west coast of the main Auckland Island - vertical cliffs four to five hundred feet high. Then the island to port must be Disappointment Island, and the rocks ahead must be the Sugar-loaf Rocks - there's nothing else off the west coast.' Then he said aloud to Jacob: 'Well, at least we know now where we are; but then a rat in a trap knows where he is too, and much good it does him!'

Jacob spoke in a firmer voice: 'I still don't like your manner, mister, and you'd better damn well remember who you are and change it, before I log you for insubordination. I'll keep her on the wind until she's weathered that North-west Cape of the main island, and take her another twenty miles north, to be quite sure. Then there's nothing between us and Valparaiso; and once we're there, you and I are going to part company, be sure of that'

Again Grant, taken up with his own grim thoughts, hardly heard him: 'If only it would blow a bit, to get some way on her. And I'll bet there are some bad tidal currents in this sound. Let me see the Pilot; does that have something about these God-forsaken islands?'

'I expect so,' said Jacob with feeble dignity. 'I didn't take much notice of that, because I didn't expect to be here.'

'No, by Christ,' said Grant with terrible scorn. 'None of us expected that, but here we are all the same.' He read silently, his lips moving as if in prayer. 'Yes, here we are - just to make it perfect: "Strong tidal eddies during spring tides reported by HMS 'Daedalus' in 1854". Good God! Forty years ago, and this is the best guide you've got! Couldn't your Owners have found something by Captain Cook? Well, there's been no moon, so it's spring tides all right... "Climate cool and wet, with almost constant strong westerly winds." I wish to God we had some of those now, and she'd weather that cape. "Main island rich in fur seals, elephant seals and sea-lions... Extensive low scrub forest... Cattle introduced in 1873, and now run wild...Huge population of sea-birds." Oh, how splendid! When we're all ashore as castaways we can have steak and fried eggs for breakfast every day.'

'If that's your idea of humour, mister,' said Jacob bitterly, 'I find it quite unsuitable and disgusting.'

'Indeed, sir? Well, I find it unsuitable and disgusting to be in deadly peril of our lives, when we should be a hundred miles north of here, running free for Val- Ah, good evening, miss.' Suddenly he was aware that Eleanor had come quietly up the spiral stair from the saloon, and was close behind them.

She at once sensed that something was terribly wrong, that something had changed profoundly. 'Dadi,' she said in English, 'what on earth...?' Then, out of the starboard porthole of the chart-room she caught sight of the high black cliffs, still scarcely a mile away. '*O, bobl annwyl!* What in Heaven is that - so close?'

Grant spoke first, cutting in before her dazed father could speak, and answering with cold irony: 'Oh, allow me to introduce you to the beautiful Auckland Island to starboard, and to the lesser joys of Disappointment Island on the port hand.' She glanced briefly at the dark shapes, and turned to where her father stood at the chart table, his face averted, his body drooped in helplessness, shame and humiliation - a humiliation which was twenty times worse because his beloved daughter was there to witness it. Grant had not yet got his rage and secret fear under control: 'Your father has decided to make this a scenic cruise of the South Pacific, and this is some of the awesome and impressive scenery he is presenting for your admiration - good enough for Baedeker's Guide, don't you think?'

Eleanor flushed with anger as she grasped the full meaning of what she saw and heard; her eyes blazed back at him with a fierce filial loyalty: 'I'll tell you what I think: I think that, for a man who sets up to be so cultured and so gentlemanly, your sneering and jeering are shameful - beneath contempt! Are you so perfect yourself that you never made a mistake? Ask Ieuan Davies about your precious judgement - if you can find him! I'm sure my father is more capable than you of navigating this ship out of whatever danger there may be…'

Grant had been deeply stung by the reference to the dead brass-bounder, and replied with equal fury: *'May be?* Oh, my dear young lady, whatever makes you think we're in danger? We damn nearly ran full tilt into a five-hundred-foot cliff, and now we're caught in currents we don't know about, with a failing wind, night coming on, and a lee shore less than a mile away! Go on - just ask your father, in Welsh if you prefer, how he got us here and how he's going to get us out again. Then perhaps you can explain it to me. I should be so delighted to hear.'

She went to her father's side and spoke quietly, swiftly, in Welsh to him: 'What's happened? Why are we so close to those dreadful cliffs?'

He shook his head, mumbling in his wretchedness: 'There was a strong current to the south. I didn't know about it like I should - I didn't have the right books. It's never happened to me before. As he says, we could all have died, and things still look bad.'

'Don't give up, for God's sake! You can get her out of this safely, can't you?'

'O yes, she's a good ship. She'll weather the cape ahead and get north, out into the clear, if only the wind will keep up…. But *Duw,* I'm so tired and sick to death of all this. If I went by the book I'd have had Grant demoted and locked in his cabin by now for what he's said, and the way he's said it. But what's the use? He was right and I was wrong, isn't it? Anyway, all we can do now is to keep her going to windward, and pray to God that she'll go clear.'

'But you must show him you're still capten!'

'Must I? How? This business, on top of everything else, has finished me; all the crowd must know what's happened by now. How am I fit to be their capten?'

Grant understood not a word of their talk, but, watching them, grasped everything, and his better nature began to feel shame at his harsh cruelty. Good God, who was he to judge like that? If he were master, could he be so sure that he wouldn't make horrible mistakes too? The Old Man had years of being a good skipper behind him, and he'd had had the most diabolical luck; nine times out of ten they'd have seen the islands in time and easily avoided them. Nine times out of ten they'd have had a good breeze, so that the set wouldn't have taken them so far out of their course. The sea was a cruel profession for fallible humans; it could punish trifling errors with merciless severity; it wasn't like adding up columns of figures in a cosy bank. He put his repentance into the shape of a formal bow, and said: 'Captain, I owe you an apology for my insubordinate manner. Those cliffs gave me an attack of panic.'

Jacob still stood hunched over the chart table, as if unable to reply; Eleanor coolly resolved the awkwardness: 'It seems to me you have upset him grievously, Mr Grant. Perhaps it would now be better if you were to attend to things on deck; no doubt there is much to do there, and we shall not save ourselves by quarrelling.'

'Very good, miss. And as I say, I'm sorry.'

Raven looked at him enquiringly when he returned to the poop rail, and Grant shook his head: 'Poor old devil, he's in quite a state. Well, wouldn't you be if you were him? He can see the danger he's landed us in, but somehow I can't see him being able to get us out of it. I think his nerve's quite gone. It's up to you and me and the bosun, I'm afraid.' He leaned over the rail and called: 'Bosun, come up, will you?'

Reuben's brown leathery face was drawn with anxiety, and Grant said quietly: 'Well, what do you make of it? Think she'll go clear? You must know her better than I do.'

The bosun did not answer, but looked about the poop: 'Where's the Old Man? Why isn't he in charge at a time like this?'

'He's in the chart-room with his daughter. In a bad way, I'm afraid. On top of all his other troubles, this has knocked the stuffing out of him.'

'I thought he was back to his old self... I've been with him many a year, and he's always found his way about. But *Iesu Mawr!* he must have been miles out of his reckoning this time this time.'

'Forty or fifty, I should think... Anyway, he seems to have left it to me - to us, bosun, and I think that's best. I don't want to have to argue and fight with him. Once we're out of this I dare say he'll recover.'

The bosun stroked his long bony chin and cast a sailor's all-round glance at the grim cliffs to leeward, the set of the limp sails and the sea and sky to windward. 'Getting out of this... That might not be too easy. If we could see the cape we've got to weather it would help a bit - for you'll never tack her, will you, in this wind? And there's no room to wear her.'

'No, we can't get her round either way. And the tides are bad here too, so the book says.'

'Maybe, but likely enough the currents will run up and down the coast, and not set you in. It's not the tides I'd be so worried about.'

'No? What, then?'

'Why, the swells of course, mister. As long as the wind blows they don't matter - you can steer up into them, but if this bit of wind should drop altogether - then look out, Mister Grant.'

Raven said: 'I fancy it is a bit lighter than it was; there's very little way on her.'

'Aye,' said Mathias, 'and you know how it is at home: in fine weather like this the wind often drops right away at sunset.'

Grant was irritated with them: 'You're like two damned croaking ravens, the pair of you! D'you think perhaps we haven't got enough problems, so you'd better think me up some more?'

The bosun shrugged: 'You asked me what I thought, Mister Grant, so now I'm telling you. I'm remembering a time like this off the Chile coast near Taltal. I was in the "Criccieth Castle", Capten Gwynfor Lewis. We got becalmed only a few miles from the port and he let her get too close in under the cliffs. Flat calm, it was... Well, the swells kept pushing, pushing at her broadside, until we were nearly in among the surf. He'd have lost her if a tug hadn't turned up, looking for us. We'd been reported as being close in by one of the big German barques. Just luck saved her, that's all.'

As if to provide a stark epilogue to his story, there came a cry from Lewis at the wheel: 'Mister Grant, sir! She won't answer the helm! Her head's paying right off to starboard, and I've a-got the wheel hard down.'

The bosun raised his eyebrows and whistled: 'By God, sir, there'll be no tug this time... Try and anchor her?'

'You can try the depth with the deep-sea lead, but I guarantee you'll find no bottom. These damned islands stick straight up from the sea-bed.'

The great ship wallowed helplessly in the beam swell, rolling her masts like pendulums, the sails slatting uselessly against the masts, tortured groans coming from the network of wire shrouds and backstays. After twenty minutes' work with the lead, the bosun mounted to the poop again: 'You was right, Mister Grant. No bottom at two hundred fathoms. So now what you going to do?'

Grant stood silent for a while. The fog had cleared now, but darkness had fallen. The black mass of the cliffs stretched across the lee bow as the ship swung lifelessly in the current, no more under command than a piece of driftwood. Not a breath of air stirred; the smoke from the galley funnel rose straight up between the masts; Wellington Jones was cooking a salt-beef hash for supper, for his gruelling work went on regardless of the crises on deck. In the stillness the officers could hear the clash of his pots and pans and his high-pitched calls to the recalcitrant Davey. When the mate spoke his voice was calm, despite the dreadful implications of his words: 'The boats, bosun. Before the men go to supper, get the boats righted and swung out ready for lowering.'

'The *boats!* Jesus, it hasn't come to that yet, has it?'

'We can't be sure, can we? Better be safe than sorry. It looks as if the wind has packed up for the night; where shall we have drifted to by dawn? You don't know, and neither do I.'

Raven spoke up, urgently: 'That's it - the boats! Put me and most of the hands in two of the boats and we'll try towing her.'

Grant paid him scant heed: 'A thousand tons of hull and three thousand of coal, and you're going to shift that with a dozen men thrashing at the water with bits of wood! Talk sense, for Christ's sake!'

Reuben came to the young mate's support: 'It might be worth a try, mister - better than doing nothing. I've heard of ships being towed by their boats.'

'That was in the old days, when ships were small and crews were a lot bigger... Still, as you say, there's nothing else. I suppose you might be able to haul her round to take the swells on the bow. That might make a difference. Very well, bosun: get the two quarter-boats ready for lowering, and pick the strongest hands for the pulling. Let them have their supper first – they're going to earn it.' He lowered his voice and spoke quietly to Raven: 'Bosun's right. You can feel it, can't you? Every time a swell passes under her she gets shifted another foot towards the cliffs... Like a long Chinese torture, this will be.'

The deck was quiet once both watches of the hands and the apprentices had gone below for supper; quiet enough for the dull booming of the surf to assert itself, to become a hypnotic, obsessive sound that filled their heads and dominated their minds, making it hard for them to think connectedly. 'By God,' said Grant, 'I've been becalmed often enough, and I've been too near the shore a few times, but never the two together: All the while there's a wind you can try *something;* this is driving me mad - to be standing about so helpless, with that damned surf pounding at my skull.'

Raven's practical, unimaginative nature was useful now; he was able to focus better on the immediate task in hand: 'She's swung so far round to point at the cliffs, I think it would be better to try and haul her by the stern. Otherwise - Oh, Nelli!' She was standing at his side, the sound of her approach muffled by the surf's roar.

Whatever she may have been feeling, she was very calm and matter-of-fact: 'I take it we're in considerable danger, Mr Grant?'

Grant spoke formally: 'Indeed, miss – in very great danger. As you see, there is no wind, and we have established that it is too deep to anchor. In short, I am completely helpless. I saved a ship once by running her ashore in a gale when my captain was absent. Now…!' he spread his hands expressively. 'How is your father, by the by?'

'Resting... He's not yet able to take charge... This has broken him. Yet I'm sure it would not have done if he had not lost my mother. That has so changed him... Destroyed him…' She was very near tears, and was grateful to feel Raven's arm round her in the darkness.

'Will you tell him that Mr Raven and most of the hands will be taking the two big quarter-boats to try to keep the ship off? I needn't tell you that that is a very long shot indeed. In the meantime, I shall be using the other hands to furl sails. As for yourself, I should like you to prepare yourself and your father for abandoning ship. You will both need oil-skins and plenty of warm clothing; the usual weather here is perfectly dreadful, apparently. May I suggest that you raid the slop-chest and kit yourself out in seaman's gear? That would be better in more ways than one.' His over-active mind was already foreseeing the chance of danger in a long, idle stay ashore, with one attractive girl among a score of young and perhaps ill-disciplined men. Rough, ill-cut seaman's gear might help a bit to disguise her sex and its dangerous fascination, for it wouldn't be possible there, as on board, to keep her remote, apart from them. On an afterthought, he added: 'I'll just dive below and have a quick word with your father myself.'

Grant, however, was not being totally truthful, for a few moments later he came into the mess-room where John Raven was having a makeshift supper before taking to his boat. Speaking quietly so that the steward would not hear, Grant said: 'Here, John, take this revolver and this box of cartridges. I got them from the Old Man's cupboard - he was too upset to notice what I was doing, poor old devil. Know how to use one of these, I take it? Good. With this crowd, I don't for a moment think you'll need it, but we can't tell how bad things may get ashore, especially if we're stuck there for a long time, so it's better to be on the safe side. If and when we all abandon ship, I'm putting the Old Man and Eleanor in your boat for you to look after – you'd want that, wouldn't you? Don't let the men see you've got a gun, and for God's sake don't use it unless you absolutely have to. Don't forget, anything you do on some God-forsaken pile of wet rocks out here might have to be justified in front of some fat, comfortable old landlubbers in wigs and silk at home. Well, I'm going to get the crowd together after supper for a few words.'

Ten minutes later the crowd, some wiping their mouths after their greasy hash, stood swaying with the ship's motion in a silent, uneasy half-circle aft, while Grant leant above them on the poop rail. He spoke, raising his voice above the dull roar of the surf, and gesturing for'ard, to where the land showed as a towering mass, blacker than the night sky, the breaking surf showing along its bottom edge, fearfully close now, as a long line of faint moving whiteness. He spoke in an almost brotherly way, as if rank had lost its importance in the face of such deadly danger: 'Well, lads, you're all sailors. You can see the plight we're in. If any of you fancy praying, now's the time to do it, because – I'll be honest with you – I've no ideas left that might save the ship. As you know, we've tried the lead, and it's far too deep here to anchor or lay out a kedge anchor. As you see, it's gone flat calm, so we can't steer or move the ship in the normal way. As I see it, the only chances we've got are that the tide might shove us clear, or that we might get a slant of wind at dawn from north, east, or south; but you know as well as I do that if it does pipe up, it's likely to be from the west, and in that case, she's so close in now that we'd never get way on her before she hit the shore. The only thing we can think of is to lower the two quarter-boats and put about half of you in them to try and tow her off, or at least keep her off, until she drifts clear, or the wind saves her. I don't have to tell you chaps that you'll have to pull like the very devil to shift her an inch, but I know you'll try. Mr Raven will take charge of the boats, and some of you precious brassbounders can bloody well try and remember what I taught you about rowing back at Caleta Buena.' The jibe brought a chuckle and some relief of tension among the hands, for brassbounders were traditional butts of foc'sle humour. Then Grant went on: 'I'm going to say something to you that I've never said to any crew in my life before, and it's this: if any of you have any other ideas we could try, tell me now.'

There was a long silence, as each man foraged in his mind of despair for a useful answer. Then Jimmy Protheroe, complainer to the last, said in an injured whine: 'The bloody Owners ought to have been made to fit these ships with engines, isn't it? Then we'd get her clear.'

The preposterous inanity of his words brought a loud groan of impatient contempt from all. Grant merely said: 'Very useful observation, Protheroe. I'll tell them that when we get back to Cardiff. Anyone else?'

Curly Kellock spoke up: 'Well, sir, by the way she's pointin' now, if she does hit the shore, it looks like it'll be with her bow, right? Well, if she does, in this swell it might be a bit okkard to lower and load the boats, so what say we do like we used to in the Andrew - the Navy - and rig a lower boom, only not from the side but over the stern? The spanker boom would do – a few of us could soon shift it. Then you got summat to secure your boats to without them getting smashed to bits; anythink you wanner put in is lowered over the counter, and same with the people. How about that, then, mister?'

Grant reflected a moment on his old opponent's idea, and then smiled: 'Thank God there's someone with some sense aboard. Yes, Kellock, later on, if it comes to that, a boom over the stern might be an excellent idea. I'll bear it in mind. Very well then, boys, we're going to do our damnedest to save her, eh? Bosun will pick two boats' crews, and I shall want the rest to furl the sails; they're doing no good, and if an onshore wind should pick up they'd just push her ashore all the faster. Now then, it's no time for despair; if the very worst comes to the worst, it'll be easy enough in this weather to row or sail the boats round to the east side of this island, where there's several sheltered inlets to allow us to get ashore safely. And according to what I've read, there's a New Zealand Government shelter and food-store - for we're not the first ship to finish up here - and a steamer drops in once a month to check for castaways. There's wood for fuel and plenty of seals to knock on the head and eat.' He looked beyond the hands to where the burly figure of Wellington Jones stood, wiping his hands on his apron; he called genially: 'You could cook a seal, doctor, couldn't you? Or a petrel's egg?'

'I c'n cook any damn t'ing, mistah, so long as he dead and keep still.'

There was another laugh, and even the cool and sardonic Grant felt a rush of affection for these men, who knew that they had been led into appalling danger and the loss of all their poor possessions, not by the stress of weather, but by their captain's carelessness, and were yet not bitter nor despairing nor mutinous. However, he knew there was something else that had to be said, and that now was the time: 'Right then, lads: we may save her, and we may not. If we don't, we shall be living together on a deserted island, possibly for a long time, in a bad climate, and maybe with problems that we can't foresee at the moment, so I'll say this to you now: wherever we are, and whatever happens, you are still a crew, and - for the time being - I am your commander. That means that you will have to go on obeying my orders and those of my officers - Mr Raven and Bosun Mathias - exactly as you would on board. And if anyone doesn't, the consequences will be just the same; I'm going to have discipline, boys, *at all costs,* and don't you forget it. You may not love me very much, but I think you know me well enough to know that I always mean what I say.' He found that he had been leaning forward over the poop rail in a threatening posture. Now he straightened up and smiled again. 'Very good then, bosun; let's give it a try. Away lifeboats' crews, and good luck, everyone! I want two hands up here with some light warps to stand by to pay them out over the counter to the boats.' He turned to where John stood, looking pale but determined: 'Good luck to you too, old chum. Look, it may well be that I shall want the boats back in a hurry if this doesn't work, and she looks like hitting the cliff. Two long blasts on my whistle mean: "Come back PDQ, for God's sake". I'll take up friend Kellock's suggestion, so when you come back you can moor to his lower boom. We'll rig a rope ladder and two mooring-pendants on it. Right? Good luck then, old son, and make the buggers bend those oars!'

Twenty minutes later the long ash oars were indeed being bent, as the two six-man crews laboured at their task, stretching the warps in taut curves, struggling to bury the oars securely in the steeply-heaving water, the boats rising and falling as the swells passed under them. John looked back at the barque's high overhanging stern, looking with a desperate hope for any sign that they were gaining, that they were getting her huge bulk under way astern, but still the boats were rooted to the spot for all their efforts, with no sign that 'Figaro' was coming back towards them. Ten minutes went by, the only sounds the splash of the oar-blades biting the water together, the groan of the rowlocks as they took the strain, the gasping and panting of the sweating oarsmen. John called: 'Easy oars a tick! Lewis, take a spell at the tiller while I pull; then you can relieve one of the others. Right, boys? Let's shift the old bitch, eh? Give way *together!*'

But now that he was at the oars he knew for certain that their efforts were useless; the water, when he dug his oar into it, seemed solid as a rock, for the boat was not moving an inch, and the ship, from his angle, looked so close to the surf along the cliffs that her jibboom must surely be nearly poking the rocks. The night was dark, but he was sure that a high peak of the cliff to his right was farther away now; the tide was taking them steadily north. No harm in that, but in the meantime the ship and her boats were being relentlessly pushed - steadily, mercilessly pushed - by the smooth sullen swells towards their grave. The barque's rising and falling stern-light looked to be almost a part of the dull white gleam of the breakers. Another ten minutes went by, and the toiling men were at the point of exhaustion, when, to no-one's surprise, they heard the summons, two blasts of the mate's whistle, cutting through the dull roar of the sea. Raven gave up his oar, took the tiller and cast off the useless warp; it was a nice piece of hemp, and worth a few pounds, but whether it would ever be hauled in or not didn't matter now.

When, following his crew, he came back to the barque's poop-deck, edging his way cautiously along Curly's lower-boom, he found a scene of uproar and confusion. The other hands were still busy furling sail aloft, but Grant was quite unable to supervise them, for he was involved in a furious argument with his captain. The Old Man had come on deck coatless, his loose white shirt-sleeves flapping as he gesticulated wildly, a demonic figure of strife and confusion. Not content with yelling at his mate, Jacob was grabbing the arm of any seaman within reach; he was screaming hysterical abuse at Grant and impossible orders to the hands: 'Anchor, you bloody fool, anchor! I should never have left you in charge. You're not fit to run a bumboat, by Christ! You're going to lose me my ship. Here, you - Johanssen! Up for'ard! Man the cat-davit. Swing out the starboard anchor ready for letting go!' The seaman stopped and gaped, torn between conflicting loyalties.

Grant strove to pacify Jacob, to keep some semblance of order and purpose. 'It's no good, sir. We've tried with the lead, and got no bottom at two hundred fathoms. These cliffs go straight down for miles. Besides, she's too close now; even if an anchor held, she'd swing round to hit the cliffs if the wind was onshore - you can see that! But she's still got a chance. If you'll just go below...'

'I'll bloody show you what I'll do, you no-good English swine! Here, Johanssen, get two more men and take this so-called officer below and lock him in his cabin. He's no use to me up here.'

Again the big Swede stood and gaped, wide-eyed, quite disabled by the officers' conflict; Grant yelled above the surf's loud ceaseless roar: 'It's all right, man. The captain's not himself. Get on with brailing up the spanker, then lower your jigger tops'l.'

The captain sprang at the sailor and shook him like a rat: 'I'm giving you an order, mun! Don't listen to that lunatic, or you'll find yourself in irons too!'

Raven appeared from aft, and Grant called: 'John, thank God you're here! Look, I want you to...'

But Jacob also saw him and grabbed at his arm: 'Here, brass-bounder! If you want your mate's ticket you'd better listen to me! Help me collar this mutinous bastard and get him below. By Jesus, Grant, I'll see you do time for this when we get back!'

With a flash of inspiration Grant said: 'Very good, captain, I'll go with Mr Raven.' They moved off, as if to go down the poop ladder, but as soon as they were out of earshot in the all-embracing surf-roar he stopped and said: 'Quick, go below and get Eleanor, for God's sake. I can't get anything done, can't even think straight, with him yelling at me all the time and the sea bellowing too. She might be able to get him below.'

Raven darted back and into the chart-room; he was about to descend the stair to the saloon when Eleanor appeared, incongruously dressed in blue jersey and trousers, a seaman's cap jammed on her curls, a brand-new stiff yellow oilskin coat encasing her like armour. 'Oh Nelli, I'm glad you're ready. It looks as if we shall have to abandon ship. Please help us by getting your father below. He keeps ordering impossible things and Simon can't get anything done. You're the only one who might be able to calm him.'

She looked up at him, wide-eyed and for a moment irresolute, for taking sides against her father seemed like treachery, whatever the rights and wrongs of the dispute. Then she nodded: 'I'll do what I can. Poor man, he's at his wits' end - or beyond that. He loves this ship so much; I remember how proud he was when he was given the command. He just can't bear the thought of her being lost. But I can see how it is - you have to prepare for that. I'll see what I can do.'

'Do try, Nelli. I swear to you that we're right, and that what he wants to do is completely impossible.'

'All right, John, I'll believe you. But you can see he's desperate, quite beside himself with grief and guilt.' She went out on deck, strode for'ard to her father's side and clasped his arm: 'Come, Dadi, I'll help you get the ship's papers together, just in case. We must save them, and only you can do that.'

He looked round at her and stared incredulously, his hair standing up dishevelled: 'Iesu Grist, girl, what the devil are you up to, togged up like a dog's dinner? Everybody's stark staring mad! I've got a mutiny going on up here, you know. That English bastard...'

She pulled at his arm: 'No, Dadi, it's not a mutiny; they're just doing what they have to. Just in case we do have to abandon ship, come below and sort out which papers you'll need to take with you. They'll just have to manage up here without you.'

Reluctantly, step by step, grumbling deeply as he went, Jacob allowed himself to be led down below, and Grant was able to turn his mind to what should be done: 'Phew, well done our Nelli! Right, John, all told we've got twenty-eight people to save, so we could do with one more boat; take three hands, get the for'ard starboard lifeboat in the water and then haul her aft to the boom. Leave two hands in the boat; we've got cases of bully and biscuit to lower, and they can stow them away.'

The big lifeboats were well for'ard, just aft of the foremast; as John and his men ran for'ard, the ship's danger became hideously apparent. Things had looked bad enough from the poop; now that he was two hundred feet nearer, the sight and sound of the surf were truly appalling: the glow of the leaping, swilling foam dimly lit the scene - the barque's bow, the black shaft of her bowsprit, the gleam, like shiny coal, of the wet cliff rocks; only yards away now, the big swells were dashing themselves against the black cliffs, springing up them half the height of the masts, falling back in hissing streams. The sight and the din were so horrific that they had to be ignored, or sick fear would disable every muscle. Yet still the ship kept her bow steadily pointing at the rock-wall, and still she was whole, unscratched, not a rope-yarn parted. John saw his men sharing his terror, staring mesmerized, unmanned by the din and the dreadful closeness of the cliffs, so he yelled at them angrily: 'Come on, you bloody fools! What's the good of gawping? Swig up on that after boat fall and let's get her off the skids, or I'll put my boot up your miserable arses!'

That was better! A raging, threatening mate was a familiar evil - better than looking at acres of angry foam and breaking swells thundering against the rock, rebounding in chaos and heaping themselves again for another leap. In ten minutes the boat was in the water, heaving, rising and falling fifteen feet, and two of the men, captured now by the routine of work and obedience, had gone hand-over-hand down the lifelines into her. Raven and Jones hauled the boat right aft, and it was some relief to be back on the poop, seventy yards farther away from the watery hell of the cliff-face. John halted right aft by the wheel, sweating hard from towing the heavy boat; Grant approached in the dim light: 'Well done, old man. We'll get it loaded now. The boats are all tossing about together, knocking the paint and lumps of wood out of each other. Remember old Dai Evans and his paintwork? He'd cry to see them – but it doesn't matter now, though.'

'You should go and take a look up for'ard, Simon. She's damn nearly hitting the cliff-face - the jibboom must be only a few yards away now. It's horrible, I can tell you. You can hardly think straight for the noise. It's time to go, I reckon.'

Grant could not face yet the utter finality of that step: 'No, I was always taught that while the ship's afloat and not holed it's safer to be aboard than in a boat. She might be set offshore by the tide; we might even get a slant of wind we could use. We'll hold on for a bit yet.'

John picked up a crate, and was making a rope sling for it when he felt a cool draught on his hot face: the breath of air gave him not relief but a sickening lurch of fear; the light gust was from the west, from astern - an onshore wind. It was the finish now, surely? 'Simon, did you feel that - that puff of wind? Due west! And look at that.' He pointed to the west, to where an arc of cloud was rising, beginning to shut out the feeble stars. For a bet that was the start of the next westerly storm, and here they were, pinned to the cliff by tide and swells. 'Better leave her now, surely?' he said, as quietly as he could, suppressing the yell of panic that his fear wanted to utter.

'Not yet, old son. Keep your nerve. She's not touched yet; what we felt then might be just a random gust. If we got a steady breeze from either beam we could soon set some staysails and use it. Anyway, it'll be dawn soon; a bit of daylight would make everything easier - Jesus, what's the matter with *them?*' Two men were still at work aloft on the foremast, putting a rough stow on the sails; from both of them, high-pitched against the dull roar of the waves, came screams of utter terror. Grant said: 'Quick, old chap, get for'ard and see what's up. Those are good hands - they wouldn't be in a funk for nothing. I daren't go, in case the Old Man comes up again spreading chaos here. Quick, now!'

Raven didn't even contemplate demurring, yet he found his feet would scarcely bear him along the deck towards the white hell for'ard.

He forced himself to run along the starboard side, and when he was half-way up the main-deck he heard the footsteps of a man dashing aft on the port side, yelling some incomprehensible gibberish – 'She's goin' in! She's goin' in!' As he reached the foremast shrouds he saw a black shape above him, and heard the other man land heavily on deck. In the gloom he saw him make to run aft too; he seized his arm roughly and forced him to halt: 'Rees, is it? What in hell's the matter with you, man? You haven't finished, I can see two sails still...'

The man tugged savagely to free himself, totally clutched by panic: 'Bugger the sails, and you too, brassbounder! The whole bloody lot will be on deck in a minute, and us with it! She's goin' into a bloody great cave - right in! Look for yourself if you don't believe me!'

23

John Raven looked, stared, ahead and up as the AB, released, raced off aft shouting. God, the fool had really lost his nerve - was imagining things, surely? A *cave?* That was too weird, wasn't it? He grasped one of the huge bottle-screws at the foot of the shrouds, to steady himself in the violent motion of the backwash, and to reassure himself by holding something real and solid. A cave? No, Rees must be off his chump! What cave was big enough to hold a three-thousand-ton four-poster with a forty-foot beam and masts a hundred and eighty feet high? Mad! But as he stood there, rooted, his scoffing confidence oozed away.

The dawn was spreading a dull grey light over the ship, but on either hand the cliffs were still coal-black, and now as he looked ahead and forward he found himself staring into an utter blackness, blacker than the darkest night; and as he listened to the maddening, mind-numbing surf-roar he began to hear, as a dull bass counterpoint, a muffled echoing boom, as of waves bursting deep, deep, within some huge cathedral. Yet still it seemed a sick fantasy; ships sometimes hit coasts and outlying rocks or grounded on shoals; they didn't slide neatly into caves big enough to hold them! It was clean against everything he'd been taught or told about, everything he'd ever encountered.

But still… here was the breaking surf right alongside, lit by the cold eerie glow of the starboard light, and yet so far the jibboom - thirty feet or more in front of the ship's bow, which in turn was a good fifty feet ahead of where he was standing - still hadn't touched anything. So dead ahead there must be nothing - a giant hole in the high cliffs. The sailor he thought mad had been right: by some horrible freak of wind and tide, 'Figaro' was being relentlessly, tidily, shoved into a cave, or rather, a tomb, for, short of a powerful steam tug appearing in the next five minutes, nothing would ever get her out again. And yet still she was afloat and undamaged, not smashed or ripped apart by the awesome power of the swell and the cruel rocks alongside; no, not so much as grazed either side! Rooted to the spot by the appalling noise, the blackness, the horror of it all, he stood for a while clutching the cold solid metal of the bottle-screw, dumbfounded, with the brooding image in his mind of a huge cavernous mouth sucking them in as a prey - like a lizard with a fly - an enormous black throat into which the sea's waves marched ceaselessly, to annihilate themselves distantly, thunderously, at its far-distant end; a hideous trap that had waited, century after century, for its random victim. Then his practical, officer's brain clicked into life again; mustn't dwell on the horrors - there were lives to be saved, including his own. He ran aft to the foot of the main-mast, where the bosun and two men were steadily, quietly working at the buntlines and clew-lines, helping the men aloft to furl the sails, as coolly as if the ship were being peacefully towed into Cardiff Docks.

'Bosun, belay all that! Get all the men down off the masts quick! Doesn't matter about the sails now - she's a goner anyway. We're drifting into a damn great cave! No - don't argue: tell Mr Grant what's happening. I'm going for'ard again.' Later he could never explain, even to himself, the mad quixotic impulse that took him back to the bows, for there was nothing useful that he or anyone else could do there now. He just felt he must see for himself the progress of the most bizarre shipwreck in history, though the danger was appalling and the surf-noise too loud to bear. But there was not time enough for him to reach his old station by the foremast shrouds before he sensed, rather than heard, the first contact with the land.

It was like a powerful brake bringing a slow train to a dead juddering halt. He felt that something aloft had suddenly stopped the slide into the cave; the roof was obviously not high enough to clear the masts. The fore t'gallant stay! That must have been driven against the top arch of the cave entrance; the whole bulk of the ship, all her slow momentum, all her windage, all the pressure of the swells, was being held by the bight of one thinnish wire stay. Within seconds the ship gave another forward lurch as a mound of sea passed under her; there was an explosive bang as the wire parted under the impossible strain, followed by a loud splitting of timber as the fore t'gallant mast - the top third of the foremast - fell like a cut tree aft and down. Raven, standing transfixed by his fear, could make out the grotesque sight of the truck - the ball at the top of the mast - swinging just above the deck, the t'gallant mast hanging upside-down, its heel still held aloft by its gear. The heavy royal and upper t'gallant yards, huge bundles of half-furled canvas and countless fathoms of rope, landed on the deck with an ugly jar. Christ, if that had happened to come down to starboard he would now be dead or hopelessly trapped in that nightmare tangle!

Then, louder than the surf, he began to hear another noise from above his head - a high grinding, grating noise that came and went with the swells; what was happening was so utterly weird, so wildly freakish, that none of his seaman's training or experience was of any use to tell him what it might be. The ship rose heavily again: there it was again, that horrible grinding from something - but in God's name *what?*

An instant later, as if to give a cruelly prompt answer to his bewildered question, something the size of a wardrobe hurtled down past his face - he felt the wind of it - landed on the Number One hatch, smashed through its stout wooden beams and finished up on the coal beneath, leaving an ugly gaping black hole instead of a neatly-battened hatch-cover. Jesus! That was a damned great rock! The strong steel stump of the fore topmast must be jabbing at the cave's roof, starting to prise out great lumps of loose stone! Good God, was there no end to the shocks? It was like being one of Nelson's men under the French cannon-fire, waiting for the ball that would destroy you. And another danger occurred to him: the steel lower masts were so strong under compression - the downward thrust - that sooner or later the heel of the lower mast, resting on the keel, might be shoved clean through the ship's bottom, or at least open up her seams. It was all unheard-of, mad, but it was happening! While he pondered this helplessly, a smaller rock whizzed down, struck the port lifeboat, and at once converted it into useless matchwood.

Blind panic sent his feet pounding aft, and he could hear the men from the mainmast running aft too; but then, as he passed the midship deck-house, something stopped him in his tracks despite his fear: there was a lamp burning in the galley! He burst in at the door, and there was Wellington Jones busily engaged - with an air of utter normality - in stoking his stove fire and tending a pair of huge kettles. 'Good God, man,' Raven yelled, 'what the devil are you doing here?'

The cook looked round, his eyes gleaming indignantly: 'What you chargin' in here for, brassbounder? You botherin' me in me own galley! No damn mate got a right to do that.'

'No, all right, but...'

'Don' you t'ink de boys need a decent sup of cocoa after all that boat-pulling?' Jones, like many ships' cooks, believed that the ship was a device for carrying his galley across the oceans, and that the galley was sacred territory, exempt from all the ship's emergencies. They were not his concern.

'Yes, but listen, man! The ship's drifting into a huge cave and nothing can stop her. The fore t'gallant mast's already come down - you must have heard it - and a rock the size of that stove has smashed in the for'ard hatch. The main t'gallant will go in a minute, and then something - mast or rock or both - could squash this place flat with you in it!'

Jones looked at him with calm resentment, as if Raven had placed some tiresome, pettifogging restraint on his routine: 'All right, sailor-boy, don't wet your trousers. I come aft in a minute when de cocoa ready... On'y no bugger gives me orders in me own galley. You shove off an' save your college-boy's hide.'

There was a deep rumble from for'ard as a whole shower of smaller rocks landed on the foredeck. The cook looked up, the whites of his eyes gleaming. 'You see?' said Raven. 'In a minute the mainmast will go - right above your head. You're crazy to stay here.'

There was another juddering halt as the mainmast stay met the roof arch; at once the t'gallant mast split and fell, for the loss of the mast ahead of it had reduced its support. Inside the galley both men started as, with a fearful clang, the wreckage - mast, yards, blocks, cordage - landed on the flat steel roof above them, denting it so that flakes of paint fell gently from the deck-head above them. 'There - see what I mean?' said Raven vehemently. 'That was nothing! You wait till the first bloody great rock lands on you! Come on, man, for Heaven's sake!'

Jones had not interrupted his work at the stove, and said coolly: 'All right, mistah mate, suh. De cocoa ready now. I bring de jugs, you bring dat tray of mugs. I even put mugs for you and de bucko. We go down aft and give you and de boys a drink. What you waitin' for?' They had reached the break of the poop, and were about to mount the ladder when, with a sudden hollow clang, much magnified by the cave's claustrophobic echoes, a great rock, prised out by the stump of the main topmast, landed on the port side of the deckhouse, abruptly crumpling the house from a tidy rectangle to a triangle. Jones looked calmly up at Raven, above him on the ladder, and said: 'You see, dere was just nice time to get de cocoa made.'

The poop seemed brightly lit, after the intense gloom of the cave, by lamps hung on the taffrail, and by the lights of the chartroom. Grant and the bosun had all hands scurrying to and fro, bringing jerseys, serge trousers and oilskins up from the slop-chest, and lowering cases of bully beef and biscuit and casks of water into the lifeboats, which now rose and fell sharply under 'Figaro's' counter as the chilly west wind strengthened. Two hands in each boat were kept busy fending off from the hull and from each other; if any of these boats got smashed, there was no replacement now.

Grant called: 'All right, men, take five minutes off to drink your cocoa. God knows when you'll get another hot drink. That reminds me: doctor, if we got a fire going ashore we could heat water in those tin jugs, couldn't we? Let's have them in the boats then. John, bosun, we'll go into the chart-room where we can hear each other without bawling. That surf is driving me stark staring mad.' They entered to find Eleanor standing over her father, murmuring comforting words to him as he sat, hunched, motionless, at the chart-table, head in hands, over a neat pile of ship's books and papers.

Raven spoke quietly, urgently to Grant: 'We've got to leave her *now*, Simon, before all the masts go! Perhaps you can't tell from here, but she's not just losing the t'gallant masts and yards; the tops of the fore- and main-topmasts are poking and gouging great lumps of rock from the cave roof. Everything for'ard is a shambles - Number One hold smashed open, port lifeboat in bits, mid-ship house flattened. You've never seen anything so awful in your life. It's not safe now for anyone to go for'ard of the mizen.'

Grant was only half attending: 'We've taken soundings aft; she's in five fathoms of water - plenty to float her. Uncanny! She's docked herself in this damned cave better than you could do it with tugs and hawsers - hasn't so much as touched the sides - amazing!'

'What good is that?' said John angrily. 'You've got to face up to it, Simon - she's gone. There seems to be no end to this cave, and if we wait any longer and the wind freshens, we might have a job getting clear of her in the boats. And the masts are hitting the roof so hard they might be pushed out through her bottom. Leave her now, Simon!'

The captain raised his head slowly, like an old wounded lion returning to life, and suddenly growled: 'I don't know what you two up-starts are arguing about. I am this ship's master under God, and I alone will decide when to abandon her. And I'm reminding you that in any event I must be the last - the very last - to leave her.'

Eleanor clasped his shoulders from behind and said anxiously: 'Don't you think, Dadi, that as you're not well, Mr Grant could…'

He shook her off irritably and said with cold harshness: 'Don't you "Dadi" me! I'm still captain of this bloody ship, and I don't need a damn nursemaid and passenger telling me what to do!' Eleanor turned away, hurt and weeping; she found herself in John's arms and heard him trying to comfort her with soothing whispers.

Grant said, diplomatically, as if the captain had indeed ordered abandoning ship: 'Aye, aye, sir, I'll get the hands to…' He stopped, staring and pale, as the ship's slow wallowing drift was halted with a shudder, with a dull shock which they felt like a blow to the body, a blow which the ship seemed to feel in her very bones, in her being, as a final death-stroke.

Jacob spoke first, clearly and soberly, in a voice free of anger, strife or fear: 'O, my God Almighty, now she's finished for sure. She's hit a spike of rock – she's stuck on it. Can't you feel her grinding against it - that terrible shaking? I've felt it once before, in a Portmadoc schooner on the Labrador coast - you never forget it.' He turned to Grant, a competent master again: 'What soundings have you got here, mister?'

'Five fathoms, sir.'

'H'm, quite deep enough to drown the lot of us... In this swell, she'll have a hole ten feet long in no time. Very well, mister, abandon ship it is. The boats are provisioned? Got their oars, masts and lugsails? Good. Get the men and yourselves down into them, mister - you too, Nelli.'

Grant turned to John and Reuben, calm himself now that the die was cast: 'Bosun, Mr Raven: take these sketch maps Miss Roberts has traced for me from the chart. Don't lose them or get them wet, for God's sake, in case we should get separated. You see that inlet on the north-east corner of the main island called Port Ross? I'm going to make for the western shore of that - it should be sheltered enough water there to beach the boats, and it's only about twenty miles off. Once you're in your boats, row straight out for half-a-mile to give yourself sea-room to rig up your mast and lugsail. Then stay there - just jill about until we're all gathered, and then keep close astern of me – it's not a regatta race, remember. Luckily it's a fair wind for the inlet, but it may be roughish going. Sure to be some tide-rips round the end of the island in the sound between the main island and those two little off-lying ones. Re-member: *keep together!* It'll be daylight by the time we start.'

He paused, as if his attention had been distracted, and looked slowly round the neat, warmly-lit chartroom, with its beautifully-made gleaming mahogany panelling, polished only two days ago by three brassbounders under his stern direction: 'But by God it's a shame, though; a brand-new ship from the best yard on the Clyde, and here she is, being pushed into a dark hell-hole, and we can't do a thing to save her…. A damn crying shame…'

Eleanor, her eyes flashing with fury, plucked hard at his sleeve and gestured towards her father. He had sunk back, head in hands again, and tears were trickling between his strong brown fingers. She hissed: 'You damn fool! Can't you see how you're upsetting him again? What's done is done; ships are lost every week. He's never lost one in his life before, all the time he's been captain. Now you're just making things worse, you idiot!'

'Very well, Miss Roberts; I will say no more on the subject.' Grant came to himself again, as if by an effort. John divined the cause of his reluctance to leave: Grant was ambitious; ever since the Old Man's collapse (as you might call it) he had had a burning desire to finish the voyage, to bring 'Figaro' back to Wales with himself as her commander. That would have given him a much better chance of a command of his own before long. Now all that was gone - indeed, the ship was being lost while arguably under his own command, a bitter blow. To be fair, his love of the ship was probably genuine too; no-one got to feel the very bones and soul of a ship like her mate.

'Now then, Bosun,' said Grant, 'split the crowd up between the boats - share out the ABs and the boys and the idlers. Leave room in Mr Raven's boat - the inboard quarter-boat - for the captain and Miss Roberts. You take the other quarter-boat and I'll take the lifeboat.'

'Aye, aye,' said Mathias, but paused before he left: *'Duw,* you can feel the old girl's done for, can't you? The bow's hardly rising at all now. She's filling up, I'll wager, but I can't go for'ard to sound the well without getting a rock on my head. This poop'll be under water soon. Come on, capten *bach,* let's get you and your girl into the boat.'

'Don't talk like a jackass, Mathias! I've just said: I don't go till every other man-jack has gone. My daughter will go with you.'

'No, dadi, I won't move until you do.'

Grant spoke with an edge of panic in his voice: 'Nonsense, miss! I'm in charge - I mean, the captain has put me in charge of loading the boats. If you don't go this minute, I shall order two men to carry you. I don't think you'd like that, would you?'

Her face flushed with sudden rage; she looked down at her father, but, lost in his own grim thoughts, he gave her no support, waving his hand silently in dismissal. Tears streaming down her face, she embraced him briefly, perfunctorily, then strode angrily out on deck, was helped up onto the boom aft, and gingerly edged her way out to the ladder, holding the steadying-line which Curly had rigged. At the top of the ladder she knelt, felt cautiously with her foot for the top rung, and went down, swinging, to the heaving boats.

'This boat, miss,' called Tydfil Jones. 'Let go the ladder now – I've got you.' As she dropped, her oilskin coat crackling when he caught her awkwardly in his arms, a memory flashed into her mind of a hot Chilean afternoon, a beautiful white liner in the sunshine, a smart boat's crew of boys in white, and her mother and herself jumping decorously from 'Magellan's' ladder, to be clasped by young Perkins. Only a few months ago, yet it seemed like another world, where there had been happiness, family love and a new adventure for her! Now it was all gone, all cold, all dead: her mother horribly killed by fever, her father a mere walking shell of himself, a lovely ship - her home - gone to her end in a dark, clamorous, murderous, watery hell, and all of them destitute of everything but what they wore, and facing an unknown fate on a cold, wet, stormy island at the end of the earth. Thank God she had met John, and that he was still loving, still with her – otherwise the whole world would be indeed dark and bare of all hope.

Now that she was outside the ship, she too was appalled and numbed by the terrible roar of the surf - noise which was doubled and re-echoed from all round and above by the huge vault in which 'Figaro' was now entombed. Every now and then she could hear a rumble from for'ard as another shower of rock pounded and ruined the trapped barque. She could see that, while the ship's stern still rose and fell, it was with an ominous sluggishness, and the water rose much further under her counter than before. She sat down and clutched the bench she sat on, for the boat was bobbing and bouncing crazily in the back-wash from the cliffs. Presently, there were urgent voices above her head as a solid line of men came edging out along the boom and down into the boats. Her boat filled with men, the ABs taking to the rowing-thwarts and two of the boys, Smith and Robbins, and old Jac-y-Bont the sail-maker joining her in the stern-sheets. She watched anxiously for John, and was relieved to see him come nimbly down the ladder and drop into the stern.

There was a keen west wind blowing now, and a nasty chop on the sea, on top of the swells and the backwash. The boats tossed, snubbed savagely at their painters, clashing together sometimes in spite of their crews' efforts. Raven sensed the fear, the dangerous tension among his crew; as for himself, his first fear up by the foremast had been so appalling that, once that had gone, he felt strong, able to face the horrors; but the men had known only the relative safety of the poop, and now their fear was threatening to master them, to drive them into the chaos of panic. Time to assert himself, get them busy at something: 'Smith, Perkins: ship the rudder and the tiller. The rest of you, don't sit there like goddam useless sojers! Unlash the oars and ship your rowlocks ready. In the bow there, fend off the lifeboat, can't you? Jones, Johanssen, unlash the mast and yard and sort out that halyard! You can see it's just a bunch of buggers, all twisted up. What the hell's the matter with all of you?' Better for them to be grumbling at his bad temper and impatience than to be going to pieces with funk!

The other boats filled with men, cast off and laboured away under oars into the teeth of the brisk wind, their bows jerking up and crunching down in the short, steep head seas. As his boat pulled away, Grant yelled: 'Cast off as soon as the captain's aboard – it's getting bad here!' Soon, in the grey, sullen morning light, the boats were white specks up to windward across a foam-streaked sea. Craning his neck to look back over his shoulder, Raven watched the inboard end of the lower boom, expecting any moment to see the Old Man's bulky figure heaving itself up over the poop rail... Nothing.... Only the hideous roar of the hungry surf, the smash of the waves against the doomed barque's counter, the gold letters 'Figaro, Cardiff' glinting dimly in the gloomy light, the sudden vicious jerks of the painter as the steep seas snatched dangerously at the boat's bow.

Five minutes passed, and still no captain. A well-known voice was raised from the midship thwart: 'My Christ,' said Billy John Ffynnongroes, 'where is he, then? Hasn't he landed us in enough trouble already? We'll all be drowned like bloody puppies in a minute.'

Raven felt his unbearable tension turn to red rage (though he had been thinking much the same): 'Shut up, John, unless you want your teeth knocked down your throat!' Billy John lapsed into mumbled curses.

At last Jacob Roberts' voice hailed John from the poop: 'Mister, come up here and take this, and for God's sake don't drop it – it's got all the ship's papers in it. Look sharp now!'

John climbed up, shuffled inboard, and took from him a small leather suitcase. 'Got it, sir. I'll just nip down with it, and come back to give you a hand if you like. It's getting a bit ugly in the boat.' That was the nearest he dared go to telling his captain to hurry up!

Jacob glared at him angrily: 'Give me a hand? What d'you think I am, you bloody pup - some damned cripple of a landlubber? Wait while I go and check...' the rest of his words were swallowed in the surf-roar; his head and shoulders disappeared as he turned to walk for'ard. John stood irresolute on the round boom, anxious what might happen to his captain, worried about having to face the difficulties of command in front of Eleanor, in such an impossible crisis. Besides, he was only too inclined to share the sailors' desperate urge to be away - free of the dying ship and the murderous waves, some of which had breaking crests now. He thought enviously of the other boats, with their safe offing beyond the breakers, and their masts and shrouds no doubt rigged by now. He looked down at the pale oval of Eleanor's upturned face, taut with fear and worry. Then he knelt on the boom, felt for the ladder and swayed down into the boat, handing the suitcase to her.

As he did so, she reached out and clung to his arm: 'John, for the love of Christ, go back and make him come *now!* I'm so afraid - for myself and you and these poor men, but especially for him. Wherever is he? I can hear the rocks crashing down all the time. Do go and bring him to me.'

'All right, I'll try - but you know what he's like. Now then, Johanssen: I'm going back up to fetch the captain, and I'm putting you in charge of the boat. Take the tiller off, and if anyone starts moaning and grousing again give him a good belt round the head with it. Jones, you come with me."

The seaman nodded, pale and tight-mouthed. Raven had his hand on the ladder when, above the overwhelming sea-noise, they heard a tremendous crash and heard (they thought) something that might have been a sudden short cry. Looking at the ship's stern (the rest was invisible now within the cave's dark, rock-fringed maw) they could see, on the starboard quarter, a length of shattered spar and a net of cordage hanging over the ship's side, the broken mast grating on the rocks at the cavern entrance. 'O God!' said Raven, 'that's the mizen gone! She must have gone on sliding in. Quick, Jones, up on the poop!'

The boom was perilously close to the sea's surface now; a leap from the dancing boat and a few rungs upward brought them back onto the poop, to see a scene of desolate chaos and destruction. All that wonderful, intricate web and framework of steel and wood and wire and hemp was gone; only the jigger mast now stood. They could hear that the sullen swells were now breaking and swilling clean across the main-deck. They both dashed to the pile of wreckage that had been the mizen; Raven whistled: 'Hell's bells! The topmast came down as well this time!

Jones, you go and look for the captain in the chartroom and the saloon. I'll look here.'

But in truth there was no need to look; as soon as Jones had gone Raven saw Jacob's grey head projecting from under the wreckage. He lay in his own special place, at the break of the poop; where he had always stood when the barque was on the port tack. The massive lower t'gallant yard lay clean across his body, which was covered too by a raffle of back-stays, braces and halyards. Only the upper chest and the face were clear. He lay on his back, his eyes wide, staring. A small rock, dislodged, landed full on the other end of the fallen yard, and Raven heard the Old Man give a deep groan of agony at the cruel jar; the heavy spar must have crushed his body terribly. Jacob did not speak, and seemed oblivious of his presence; Raven was about to yell for Jones when the man appeared at his elbow: 'No sign of him... O *Iesu Mawr*, capten *bach!* What can we do for the poor soul, sir?'

'Nothing, I think.' Raven had been trying to summon up practical ways by which two men might raise the big steel tube from their captain's broken body, and knew the struggle would be pointless: 'It's too late, I'm sure, even if we had all the hands here. He's crushed to bits - must be. He's strong, I know, but no-one's body could stand all that falling on it.'

Then Raven gave a start, for he heard his captain's voice, as if it were from the dead. His tone was quiet and firm: 'Is that you, Raven? I told you all to abandon ship, so what are you doing here? Get in your boat, man, and cast off. You've not got long before she takes you down with her.'

'Captain, we're not leaving you. I can get six more men up here in a jiffy; we can rig a handy-billy to the jigger shrouds, and have you out of that in two shakes. I'll...'

'You'll do what I say, boy. I'm not a fool. I know I'm finished. I'm not in much pain now, but I can't move or feel anything below my waist. I'm done for all right. Listen, boy: I can't look after my Nelli any more, can I? Now I want you to look after her - not to get drowned uselessly in this miserable hole that I put you all in.'

'But sir, let me...'

'No, listen, I say, because I feel I haven't got much longer. You're not a bad young fellow, even if you are a *Sais;* I've been no friend of yours sometimes, I know, but that's all in the past now. What I ask now is this: you will look after her, won't you? And be faithful to her?

For my sake and her dear mother's sake, God rest her?'

Raven, his eyes pricking and streaming in the cold wind, answered with more passion and gravity than he knew he possessed: 'Before God sir, I will, for the rest of my life. I swear it, and I swear I will never again be the womanizing idiot I was once. But let us try rigging that tackle, sir. Don't give up yet, please.'

'It's no go, boy. I know when I'm done for. Besides, what is there for me any more? What have I got to live for? In my cursed folly I've thrown away my wife, my ship, my livelihood and now my life. Even if you got me out without us all drowning I'd be nothing but a pitiful cripple, a wretched burden for my girl to tend, perhaps for years and years. I won't end like that - not after what I've been.' His voice died away in a gasp of pain, and then came back more strongly: 'I'm giving you my last order, mister: into the boat with both of you, and get away while you can. Jones, I give you a good discharge; Raven, tell Mr Grant that. Now go. I'm feeling very tired, very heavy. While I can still think, I want to talk to my Maker - I shall be with him soon, I trust. Away you go, mister, and good luck to you.' He closed his eyes and began to pray aloud in his own tongue, his voice strong at first, swiftly weakening until the prayer tailed off and ended with a gasp of *'Iesu!'* Then silence and stillness amidst the surrounding din.

Raven heard Tydfil Jones whisper, close to his ear: 'He's gone, sir. I reckon that's what he wanted - to die with the ship. I knows him well, see. That's what he came back for, really. And look – he's died where he always used to stand, isn't it?'

As they both knelt, silent in unconscious reverence beside their captain, the sea suddenly and ruthlessly recalled them to reality; the crest of a wave-topped swell came seething, slopping, sliding across the poop-deck, swilling carelessly over the captain's head, soaking the long grey hair, brutally washing it like weed across his face. Raven sprang to his feet: 'Come on, man, or we'll be dead too. Nothing we can do for him. He was a good skipper, even if he didn't like me very much.'

'No, don't think that, sir. Fathers are always like that when you're courting their daughters - happened to me too, years back. No, he was one of the best... I been with him a good while now - Good God, look, sir! The boom's only just above the tops of the waves. Poor old hooker's nearly gone too.'

* * *

Half an hour later the little flotilla of boats was reaching along with a stiff breeze on the port beam, making for the North-west Cape of Auckland Island. The line of savage black basalt cliffs slid slowly by. The day was gloomy, rags of cloud racing across the sky from the west, each boat periodically lost to view as it dipped into the trough of the huge swells - the same swells that, in a monstrous cave a few miles back, were remorselessly knocking to pieces the barque 'Figaro', and spreading her cargo of bright Newcastle coal across its sunken floor.

There had been some bad moments as they left her; the boat repeatedly crashing against the boom, for the spar had sunk so low; Eleanor so wildly distracted with grief that Raven had had to wrench her back from climbing the ladder again, while at the same time he screamed to his terrified crew: 'Cut the painter! Fend her off, for Christ's sake! Give way *together!* Come on, boys! Keep the stroke! *There!* ..... *There!*.... *There!* .... That's the way! Well done, lads!'

While he yelled, one hand was on the tiller, the other arm clamped like iron round the distraught girl, who sobbed inconsolably: 'I never said goodbye properly... We parted so hastily, so coldly, so angrily .... I never told him how much I loved him!'

'Ssh, ssh, darling... He knows that – he always knew it. I believe he's watching you now, and he knows you love him. He told me, back there, just before he went, that he wants you to stay alive - to stay alive and be happy again with me.. one day.'

Now, all her shyness, all his gauche self-consciousness lost in grief, they sat huddled in the stern-sheets, Eleanor still weeping ceaselessly, uncontrollably, John Raven weeping too, but still steering expertly, instinctively, between the breaking seas in the wake of Simon Grant's boat. The men now sat up to windward to balance the pressure of the taut, strained lugsail, all hunched in their oilskins in the cold slashing wind, each one busy with his own sombre thoughts. Twenty yards astern, the bosun's boat foamed along, rising, falling, pitching and rolling in the steep cross-seas.

All nine souls in Raven's boat - the four hardened stalwarts of the sea, the two young brassbounders, the old man who stitched sails and the twined couple in the stern - all were silent as the heeling boat sped north to the island inlet, and to whatever awaited them there. But for the girl's sobs, all were silent, for it was no time for words.